THE SIXTH PRECEPT

LARRY IVKOVICH

THE SIXTH PRECEPT

LARRY IVKOVICH

The Sixth Precept

Melbourne, Australia
IFWG Publishing International
ifwgpublishing.com
ISBN: 978-1-925148-50-3

Acknowledgements

Thanks to all my friends and family who have supported my writing endeavors through the years and to IFWG Publishing for believing in my work. A special thanks to the Pittsburgh Southwrites (past and present members) - John Branch, Barb Carlson, Ann Cecil, Steve and Jamie Chew, Chetan Chothani, Judy Freidl, Lynn Hawker, Randy Hoffman, Henry Tjernlund - for all their help and encouragement. You guys are the best! And a very special thanks with love to my wife, Martha Swiss, for patiently allowing me to dimension-hop, shape-shift, explore new planets, fight dragons and demons and otherwise let my imagination run wild for the last twenty-three years. Couldn't have made it this far without you, babe!

Dedicated to the memory of Ann Cecil.

CONTENTS

Part One 1

Part Two 53

Part Three.. 129

Part Four 155

Part Five 279

Epilogue... 425

PART ONE

Past/Present

PROLOGUE

Ise, Japan—1910, C.E.

The bullet struck the old man's shoulder. Piercing his suit jacket, the deadly projectile skimmed off the thin layer of protective mesh he wore underneath his clothes and ricocheted away like an errant beam of light.

Spun completely around by the force of the shot, the old man fell hard against the wall at the back end of the alley. He lay stunned and gasping for breath as he blinked in surprise. *No*, he thought, struggling to get up from his knees, his hat falling to the pavement, his shoulder throbbing. *I must get away. I must get the Sacred Artifact to the girl!*

Despite the openness of the marketplace at midday, despite the throngs of people all around him, the old man had been discovered and followed. He reasoned the alleyway might afford some cover, might enable him to lose those who followed him. He had committed the layout of the city to memory; he knew exactly where to go. But it had not been enough.

He tried to lever himself up with his ebony walking stick, gripping the sculpted ivory handle tightly. But despite the training he had gone through, despite the years of conditioning, both mental and physical, his weakened muscles failed him— now at the penultimate moment of his life.

The bruised and burning pain in his shoulder caused him to cry out and lean against the cool brick of the building. Frantically he felt for the artifact, nestled in his inside jacket pocket. Yes, it was still there, at least a reproduction of it was. Others of his sect were also searching the country with their own facsimiles. The one he sought as She-Who-Comes-Before may, in truth, not be the one.

It was only luck and risky prediction that had brought him to Ise. He must, at least, hide the artifact he carried somewhere. His attackers must not find it, copy or not, or all would be lost!

But, as two figures marched purposefully towards him, he knew he was too late. Here in the back streets of this sacred city, amid the closeness and dirty confines of this alleyway so near to the Ise Jingu, the Shrine of Amaterasu, he would meet his ignoble end.

And all for nothing! He would never attain the goal of the *Shuugouteki*! He would never get the artifact to the girl, even though she was one of many who might be the *Yomitsu*'s forerunner and ancestor. He had failed!

No, he thought grimly. *By the Yomitsu, not yet!* It was in an alley the legends said the Spirit Winds took Ko the Little to safety—through the Void to a future time. Perhaps this deserted street would afford him his own salvation as well.

Two men walked confidently toward him, agents of the *Totou*, he knew beyond any doubt. Who else would hunt him down so brazenly and in broad daylight? No mere thieves or cutthroats were these two. They had the power of that malignant cabal behind them—they had discovered him and his purpose and were poised to stop both.

"An old man!" one laughed, eyeing him disdainfully.

"A black African, as well," snorted the other. "The *Shuugouteki* must be desperate to drag the bottom of the pits for one such as he."

THE SIXTH PRECEPT

Both were arrogant young Japanese, trim and lean with hard features and glittering eyes, and dressed, like himself, in western business suits—wool jackets over vests sporting chained pocket watches; derby hats perched atop shaven heads. The *Totou* and his own group had changed with the times; both had always kept in touch with new developments, new styles, devices and inventions. It was how they had blended in and survived all these centuries.

Perhaps one such invention could save him now. He must complete his mission! The warlord Omori must not defeat Ko the Little at the Pavilion of Black Dragons on that day so long past! The Yomitsu must send Ko back through the Void from a future time to her own past to prevent victory by the followers of the Left Hand Path! The Sacred Artifact in the hands of She-Who-Comes-Before would set those wheels in motion. If the old man could delay these two…

"You can have all of my money," he said in perfect Japanese, feigning ignorance. "Please. Just leave this unworthy one alone." As he spoke, he shifted his body subtly, maneuvering his walking stick to a forty-five degree angle—its gold-encased foot on the pavement and the handle pointed straight at his two attackers.

"We want the artifact," one said, holding a gun with one black-gloved hand and pointing it at the old man's head. "And the identity of the girl. Don't play games with us, old one!"

Young fools, the old man thought, more sure of himself now. Had these two just followed him, kept their presence hidden, they could have captured both objects of their hunt. They had just needed to wait. The over-confidence and deadly enthusiasm of youth would be their undoing. If so, their masters would not be pleased that the identity and location of the Yomitsu's possible forerunner had not been identified.

He thanked the Yomitsu they hadn't sent a shadow-tracker in their stead. The *Totou* must think one old man not worthy of that unholy creature's time. "I...I don't know what you mean," he said, running his right hand slowly up to the handle of his walking stick.

The second agent walked to his comrade's side, a sneer creasing his face. They both stood in front of him now, only a couple of feet away, well within range. "Talk, old one!" the agent barked. "In the name of the Eminent Lord, who is the girl? Where is she? Tell us now and your death will be quick!"

As if in answer, the old man's gnarled, black finger found the firing stud on the underside of the walking stick's handle. "The Eminent Lord?" he said, uttering that cursed name with disgust. "I think not!"

He pressed the stud, closed his eyes and turned away.

There was a popping sound as the handle exploded. Shards of the glass-lined interior blew up and out like a cloud of stinging bees.

The young agents reacted quickly, covering their faces and ducking as they stumbled backwards. But not quickly enough. Several of the glass and ivory splinters had found their mark, piercing the skin on the agents' unprotected foreheads and jaws.

The two men dropped their guns, tearing at their collars as they struggled for breath. The fast-acting poison coating the glass, a derivative from a certain puffer fish found off the coastal waters of Japan, and more powerful than curare, instantly closed the *Totou* agents' lungs and throats and began to stop the beating of their hearts.

Faces purpling and swelling, the two men fell to their knees, convulsing, their eyes bulging. They hit the pavement, jerked a few more times and then lay still.

THE SIXTH PRECEPT

The old man let out a long, ragged breath, turning away from the horrible sight. At the entrance of the alleyway, business went on as usual in Ise. No one passing looked towards him; no one had seen or heard what had happened.

Gingerly, he picked out a couple of small glass splinters that had backfired and pricked his own flesh. He flicked them to the ground, a shudder running through him. A momentary dizziness passed and he relaxed. The poisons he and his fellow *Shuugouteki* members had taken in small doses every day for years would give him the immunity he needed. At least long enough to accomplish his task.

He struggled to his feet, his victory empowering him, and forced himself to rise despite the sharp pain shooting through his right wrist. *Broken,* he thought with a grimace. *By the recoil of the shot. They had warned me that might happen, especially for one with bones as old and brittle as mine. But…* He looked at the two bloated corpses, a rueful smile crinkling his leathered face. *This old black African, wounded and broken, is still alive.*

Leaning on his damaged walking stick with his left hand, he shuffled down a side alley and then into another intersecting street. The Ise Jingu complex was not far. *I must find the girl,* he thought, short of breath. *I sense no one else following me now but these two may have others with them. I must be quick!*

He had served the *Shuugouteki* all of his life. Their mission, conditioned in him since birth, had become his—they must stop the *Totou* from changing history. And the *Shuugouteki* could do it, if their members adhered to their own intricate plan and all of its complex parts as they had done over the last three centuries.

Three centuries, he thought in wonder. *And finally, we could be close.*

He walked briskly now, his group's lifelong purpose giving him strength. *I pray she is the one, that she is the forerunner. Perhaps I will be granted the knowledge to know if that is so before I finally pass through the Veil to the Other Side.*

CHAPTER 1

Odawara, Japan—1520, C.E.

Yoshima Mitsu walked through the muddy streets of the Gettoo, her young charge, Shioko, respectfully lagging several paces behind. Mitsu stared straight ahead, trying not to let the trash, filth and smell of the slum district's open sewers distract her from her purpose. Here, in the poorest section of Odawara, it wasn't unusual to encounter travelers, but a *shirabyoshi* and her attendant might attract some attention. Even in disguise—dressed in a *monpe*, a traditional field worker's uniform of sashed, cotton trousers, short jacket and wooden clogs, there was an aura about Mitsu. Despite her unpainted face and tied-back hair, she appeared more than she seemed.

And right now, attention was the last thing Yoshima Mitsu wanted.

But she knew she need not worry. In some ways, the wars among the *daimyo* were a good thing. Though it was mid-morning, the streets were empty. Doors were locked, windows closed. None of the villagers even dared to peek at the unknown wanderers in their midst. Fear of attack, fear of yet another battle among the local feudal lords kept them indoors, hiding, afraid.

So much the better for Mitsu. She and her young attendant

passed through the streets without incident. The only immediate danger Mitsu felt at this point was succumbing to old painful memories. Truth to tell, she had grown up in the Gettoo but when she had left to become *shirabyoshi*, she had never returned. Until now.

Nothing has changed, she thought sadly. *It is still the same.* "Come, Shioko, do not dawdle," Mitsu said over her shoulder.

"Please, Mitsu-san," the girl, Shioko, said, puzzlement mirrored in her eyes. "Where are we going?" Mitsu's attendant was dressed shabbily, her baggy pants and jacket tattered, her face and hands dirty, her clogs worn thin at the heels. Mitsu had forbidden Shioko her morning bath and ordered her to dress like a common beggar.

It is for her own good. Mitsu continued staring straight ahead. *I must not falter,* she thought, recalling vaguely that the house she had grown up in had been located only a street or two away from this neighborhood. *I must do this, for Shioko's sake.* "Our destination is not much farther. Be patient."

She had seen this 'destination' in her mind's eye, her Dreamspace. Her sleeping visions had told her to bring Shioko here to the place of Mitsu's birthing. Her young attendant was in danger and though Mitsu could be a harsh mistress at times, she would not let any harm come to her little sister, who, against all tradition, Mitsu had learned to love as a daughter.

It had taken her and Shioko four days to reach Odawara. They had traveled what Mitsu's visions revealed would one day be known as the Tokaido Highway from Edo, stopping at the various post-towns along the way. Mitsu had worked her art, dancing and singing for the customers at the inns and tea-houses, accepting much-needed money, transportation and protection on the road as payment. Sometimes, more intimate types of entertainment had been required to allow them to continue their journey. To those who had asked, Mitsu had answered that their ultimate destination was the Ise Jingu, the Shinto Grand Shrine of Ise, to pay their respects to the Sun Goddess, Amaterasu. Yes, even in these times of perpetual war, there were still travelers and pilgrims on the road; she and Shioko appearing, on the surface, to be but two of many.

But at this particular fortress-city, this *jokamachi*, Mitsu would perform her true duty, the one closest to her heart, the duty of any mother to protect her child.

(*To realize the images in her mind; to admit, even to herself, that what she foresaw was real…*)

She had never seen so far ahead in the Dreamspace before. She could glean a little of what was to come—the rise to power of the Edo Shogunate, the building of the Tokaido Highway, the coming of the foreign barbarians and the fall of the samurai warrior class. Frightening yet fascinating events-yet-to-be but those far-seeing visions were as illusions to her, watched as if looking out of the corner of her eye. Fuzzy and indistinct, they appeared to her infrequently and, like most dreams, allowed her no control over them.

But this…though the images were faded and garbled as usual, she knew the journey she must send Shioko on would be one completely beyond her understanding. She wished she could know for a certainty what her attendant's 'ultimate destination' would be. But too much direct foretelling was forbidden even to her, she who possessed such a powerful though frustratingly inconsistent Gift of the Mind.

A gift? she asked herself for the thousandth time. *Or a curse?*

Mitsu turned to her right at a small intersection, moving unerringly as if she had trod this street a thousand times before. Indeed, as a child growing up poor and, in her family's eyes, unwanted as only another mouth to feed, she had. And once more, later as an adult, in her visions, her feet had followed this same path, over and over. She knew what she would find here — the narrow way ended in a circle of old shanties, garbage bins, privy sheds and boarded up lean-tos, the dead-end area littered with trash.

In such a place as this would miracles happen? she wondered. *Never could I have guessed this. The* kami *do work in mysterious ways.*

"Please, Mitsu-san, what…?"

Mitsu turned and knelt in front of Shioko, silencing her by lightly pressing a finger to the young girl's lips. Shioko's face shone with a beauty and pureness not found in other children her age. Her straight black hair, doll-like features and flawless complexion were visible even through the temporary cover of grime forced upon her by her elder sister. Such beauty, and the soul that it blanketed, must have the chance to blossom.

Was I that lovely as a child? Mitsu thought absently. *Perhaps. But that was so long ago.* "Attend me, Shioko," the *shirabyoshi* said softly but forcefully. "Listen to what I say."

The girl shook her head, her already large eyes growing wider.

"You know what the sisters of my profession call me, do you not?" Mitsu continued.

"'The One Who Sees', Mitsu-san."

"Yes. And do you know why they call me that?"

Shioko bit her lip. "You…you can tell which inn or government official will be the most willing to pay for your services. You know which client will be the most lu…lucrative? Sometimes, you know what others are thinking."

Mitsu smiled, an aching in her heart. "Yes. But it is more than that. I developed this 'talent' late in life, long after I had become *shirabyoshi*. I keep the true extent of my abilities a secret, even from you. Perhaps I could go further in this world if I used my foreknowledge for more money or power but, chances are, I would be deemed a *majo*, a witch, or one who is cursed. I would be persecuted, hunted down and killed if I showed the true nature of the power I possess. I have seen it happen before. People fear what they do not understand. And, besides, this gift of mine can only see so much. There is so much more that I cannot discern—"

"Oh, Mitsu-san—"

"Sshhh. Listen, little sister. I have witnessed your future, at least a part of it. And it lies here, in this filthy alley." Mitsu closed her eyes, taking a deep breath. What she was about to do was the hardest thing she had ever done, even more than leaving her family so long ago, sold by her father to the Guild of Courtesans who would raise and educate her as one of their own, the money exchanged to help the family she had left behind. But she had to be as strong now as she had learned to be then—this time for Shioko.

"But, Mitsu-san, how...?"

"I do not know everything. I only know what I have seen and only a small part of that. You are going on a voyage, Shioko, one you may never return from."

"No!" Shioko covered her mouth with her hands, a combination of shock at Mitsu's words and embarrassment at speaking in such a loud, unseemly tone to her elder sister.

But propriety and one's station in life were the last things on Mitsu's mind. Was she not *shirabyoshi*? A lowly courtesan in some people's eyes? "Please, little sister," she said softly, running her hand through Shioko's hair. "You must trust me. I see one who will care for you when you have gone and keep you safe from the purges-to-come of Omori Kadonomaro and his warrior monks, the *sohei*."

"Purges-to-come?"

"It has not happened yet but I see it coming to pass, and soon. The *daimyo* Omori is a rising feudal lord now but with the *sohei* as his allies, he may achieve dominance. Like all the other power-hungry warlords that have beset us these last many years, he will wage war and wreak havoc. He is bent on taking back Odawara from the Soun clan who had conquered Omori's own clan years ago. This is what warlords do, yes? Especially in these times of constant battle. Even now his forces lay in wait outside the gates of Odawara."

Mitsu looked away, knowing she must complete this task, no matter how difficult it was. But the fear rose within her. Was this the right thing to do? There was so much she didn't know. And Shioko was so young. What if she was wrong? What if her visions, no matter how reliable in the past, were not what she thought they were?

"But this lord is different," she continued finally. "It is rumored he makes pacts with demons and witches, that he consorts with monsters. In due time, he will search for children like you, the children of your years, to recruit for his brothels and slave dens, if he does not kill them outright. He will try to deter the prophecy—the telling of the One Child who will grow up to usurp him and his evil rule-to-be. Because you live with me, because we travel the open roads so frequently, you will be in danger. Not now, but soon, when his power grows, you will not be safe anywhere."

She stared hard at her little sister, her lips drawn in a thin, tight line. "I will not give you up to him."

"But...but..." Tears began to well in Shioko's eyes as the full import of what Mitsu said began to dawn on her.

"I know you don't understand," Mitsu continued. "I don't either, not fully. But you must believe me. I have seen what will happen or, at least, the fringes of it. I cannot protect you here when the purges begin, not for long. No matter where or how you'd hide, Omori or one of his warrior monks would find you out. And, most dangerously, he will unleash his shadow-trackers to scour the villages and the surrounding countryside in his mad bid for power."

"The shadow-trackers?" Shioko's lower lip trembled. "I thought the shadow-trackers were stories. Like the *nue* and the Ebon Warrior. I thought—"

Mitsu shook her head. "No. The *nue* are legend—creatures with the neck of a monkey, the body of a fox, the limbs of a tiger and tail of a snake; the Ebon Warrior is a black-clad hero invented to entertain children."

Mitsu closed her eyes. "The shadow-trackers are real. They are homunculi, creatures between, forged into being by Omori's alliance with those of the Left Hand Path. They are real. I have seen them." Mitsu concentrated. Her thoughts coalesced into a single thread of energy, sending a thin tendril of vision into the mind of her young charge.

(*An image of a man-beast, lean and powerful, running upright, eyes glowing yellow, fangs bared.*)

"Oh! Mitsu-san, please! Stop! It's a monster! A monster!" Shioko fell into Mitsu's arms, sobbing and trembling.

"I am sorry, little sister," Mitsu whispered, holding onto Shioko tightly. "Forgive me but you had to see what awaits you if you stay. But in this other place that you will travel to, you will be safe, even from such as them."

Mitsu paused at the first tremor—a slight shivering of the space around hers and Shioko's bodies. She glanced to each side of her as if she could see where the sensation was coming from, as if it was an actual physical thing, able to be measured and observed. She was sure Shioko hadn't sensed it; only because of Mitsu's sensitivity to such spectral matters would she even suspect anything untoward had happened at all. But it was there—a disturbance in the hollow of invisible thought she referred to as the Dreamspace.

And so, it was time. The Spirit Winds approached.

She grasped Shioko by the girl's thin shoulders, trying to still the hammering of her heart. She suddenly felt light-headed, short of breath. "I…I give you no weapon to take with you. Such a thing would only attract danger and self-inflicted harm. You must appear to be helpless.

"You are garbed as a pauper. Such an appearance will help you wherever you are going. It will appeal to the one who finds you, will garner sympathy and kindness."

Shioko frowned, wiping her tears with the back of her hand. "Who…who is it that will find me, then? Do they know I will be coming?"

"I cannot see that," Mitsu answered truthfully, the pain of it like a blade in her gut. "There are some things that remain hidden from me. All I know is that you will be found…and loved."

Shioko stared at her mistress, her eyes misting over again. "Mitsu-San, I don't want to leave you. I really don't understand."

"You will, in time, my child." *Perhaps we both will.* "Yes, I know that isn't much consolation now but, in the meantime, remember what I have taught you of the teachings of the philosopher Yira, he who was neither Shinto nor Buddhist but one outside of both. Now you must take Yira's wisdom into your own heart. Do you remember his primary credos?"

"The…the Five Precepts to Enlightenment?"

Mitsu nodded. "Yes. Recite them for me. Yes, yes, now."

Shioko nodded, took a deep breath and began speaking,

"Do not be afraid to open one door; be wary of the many. Embrace the darkness; our birthing springs from the abyss. There are no differences; only perceptions. The inner self holds the true power; the outer exists only as a vessel. The end is the beginning; the beginning has no end."

"Very good. Remember Yira's good words. Whenever you are troubled or in danger, their meaning, no matter how hard to grasp, will guide you. Hold them close to your heart as I have, adhere to them and you will be safe." Another tremor, this time stronger. "You will stay here, in this spot, do you hear?" Mitsu's mouth, despite its determined set, began to quiver. "You will not move from it no matter what!"

Fear now. "Yes…yes. But why? Please don't go, Mitsu-san!"

"Obey me! Believe me, Shioko, this is for your own good!" Mitsu stood up and walked back the way she had come. She stopped at the sound of Shioko's choking sobs. Her carefully built emotional walls crumbling, she turned, ran back and embraced the child.

"Please, Mitsu-San, please…" The girl clung to Mitsu, crying now, her tears flowing like water from a broken dam. "Why can't you come with me then? You will be in danger too if you stay! And why, if you know what will happen, why can't you stop it? Why?"

"I cannot come with you," Mitsu said, her voice breaking. "It is not the will of the *kami*. My visions saw only you and only fleetingly at best. And I cannot stop it; it is what must be, no matter what. I can only help in this small way as whatever happens is already written." Her own heart breaking, Mitsu released Shioko and backed up. "Goodbye, Shioko-chan," she whispered. "I love you."

"Mitsu-san!" At the sound of Shioko's last, wrenching cry, the ground spun out from under Mitsu. She fell against the privy shed to her left as a whirling dizziness struck. A roaring sounded in her ears, a shrieking from out of the grave. Light flashed behind her closed eyelids. Mitsu sank to her knees, covering her ears. She felt the breath sucked out of her, her body buffeted by pounding waves of force. She tried to scream, to call out for help…

And then it was over. She fell forward, stopping herself from falling flat on her face as she knelt on knees and hands in the stinking mud like a dog. Her breath came in ragged gasps, spots dancing before her eyes.

"Shioko!" She looked up to where Shioko had been standing; Shioko, her attendant, her little sister. As her visions had told her would happen, the young girl was gone, taken by the Spirit Winds to a far and distant place.

You will never get her now, Omori, the *shirabyoshi* thought, her own tears starting to fall. *She is gone from your cruel clutches. I only pray I have done the right thing.*

Yoshima Mitsu stood up, trembling, wiped her muddy hands on her trousers, turned and walked out of the alley and the Gettoo one last time, forever.

18

CHAPTER 2

Omori Kadonomaro, *daimyo* of the Omori clan, acting Warlord of Odawara and self-styled Eminent Lord of all the peoples of the eastern Kanto plain, stood at the overlook of the Pavilion of Black Dragons at the topmost level of *Odawara-jo's* main keep. Gloved hands clasped behind his back, he gazed outward at his city from the castle *donjon* and the rolling countryside which stretched west of Odawara.

The pavilion was a round, open-aired structure built with an elaborate, wooden frame; blackened silk tenting billowed overhead. Since Omori had taken the city, the pavilion had been hastily yet intricately constructed by hand-picked carpenters and artisans, overlooking Odawara and its accompanying environs.

Numerous flaming braziers revealed stone carvings of warrior spirits and delicate *ikebana*—flower arrangements set into small *tokonoma* alcoves built into each corner of the pavilion. *Bonsai* and trays of decorative bamboo lay strategically positioned throughout the inlaid wooden floor.

Enticing bowls of fruit, raw fish and sake had been placed on a large *kotatsu*—the wooden table situated to one side and surrounded by numerous decorative cushions. Colorful, streaming banners of the ever-present symbol of Omori Kadonomaro's own personal seal—a dragon swallowing its tail—fluttered over all. Here, in his castle-top retreat, Omori could comfortably plan his campaigns and survey the regions he had annexed for his empire.

But comfort was the last thing on his mind this morning. The rising sun illuminated Odawara, its fortress walls and winding cobblestone streets. To his back, at the eastern shore, lay the sea, its surface dancing with sparkling sunlight yet spotted darkly by his own victorious warships.

Smoke still plumed in the western distance from the battle two nights ago at the foothills of the Hakone mountains. The fading remnants of his land forces' campfires flickered in the morning light. The bloodied battlefield lay strewn with the dead and dying. The smell of death hung everywhere.

Let Soun Ujitsuna try to take back his city when he returns, he seethed. *I will break his army as I have done all the others who have stood against our clan.*

Dressed, even at this early hour, in his military gear, Omori stood in chain mail and leather armor, his long hair done up in a topknot. He had heard the whispering rumors that he slept fully clothed and adorned, always ready for battle, that he shunned the silk *kimonos* most samurai wore in the summer as too effeminate and weak.

His longsword, the *kitana* along with its accompanying shortsword, the *wakizashi* and knife-like *tanto*, were thrust through his belted *obi*. He knew some said these never left his person in any case. Feeling clogs or sandals were not a true warrior's garb, he still wore bearskin boots, though by this time they were considered unfashionable, even archaic.

A close-cropped, dark beard covered the lines, crags and scars of his battle-worn face. His black, unblinking eyes pierced the smoky air, ablaze with anger and fanatical desire. Some of those rumors were true. And some were not. *Let the fools think what they want*. Anything that added to his power, his mystique, was good and helped him maintain his hold on the region and his armies.

"Lord."

Omori gritted his teeth in irritation at the sound of that silken voice but did not turn. He knew who stood behind him. He could smell him. "What is it?"

"I do not mean to disturb you, Lord, but there is something you should see."

The warlord turned then, finding the *majo*, Eela, bowing in his usual posture of obeisance. *A sham*, Omori thought. *The witch knows no masters but his own black* kami.

Standing on either side of Eela were two of the *sohei*. Their broad, powerfully muscled bodies were covered alternately with armor plates and chain mail over black robes. Winged vests overlaid their shoulders while balloon breeches billowed around their knees, revealing armored shin guards glinting in the light. Wooden clogs adorned their feet, which were, in turn, covered in two-toed socks. A long, flowing turban/scarf swathed their faces and necks.

Each held a spear-length weapon, a *naginata*, clenched in their hands. A gleaming curved blade sprouted from the end of each weapon, connected to a long, black and bronze lacquered handle.

Impressive and powerful looking, and in marked contrast to Eela's long, braided hair and flowing, belted black robe, the warrior monks stared straight ahead, straining to avoid even glancing at the *majo*.

Though Eela had been extraordinarily useful with his magic, helping Omori win key battles and unveiling the Prophecy of the One Child, Omori's men still feared the witch.

Truth to tell, even Omori was a little uneasy in Eela's

presence. But for a different reason—the *majo* had power and an alliance with the Left Hand Path, which, in reality, had served the warlord well as long as that black magic and supernatural prowess weren't turned against him.

"You have news of the Child?" the warlord asked.

Eela nodded. "Perhaps," he whispered. His eyes, one green and one blue, held no hint of emotion in them. They blinked back at the warlord as two bottomless pits. "But you must see this for yourself, if you please, Lord."

Checking his impatience, Omori followed the *majo* to the steps at the back of the pavilion, the two *sohei* bringing up the rear. There, at a lower level stairwell, were two more monks, standing guard over a crumpled body.

"What is this?" Omori demanded. The body was that of one of Eela's freaks—a shadow-tracker—an unnatural beast that was part dog and part man and who knew what else. Yet, this one was different. Oh yes, it had the tall, lean, close-furred body that stood on two legs like a man, the short-snouted face with a mouth full of sharpened fangs, long braids of tightly wrapped hair and the yellow eyes that normally reflected an animal instinct. Now those eyes were blank and staring into a middle distance.

This one lay dead, blood pooling from several small wounds, its body covered in a strange, tight-fitting garment made of some material Omori didn't recognize.

The *majo* looked sideways at his lord. "This is a messenger, I think," he said softly. He looked towards one of the *sohei* standing guard. "Tell him," he commanded.

The monk bowed. "Lord Omori, I saw it. Earlier this morning as I stood guard here, there was a rumbling as if the earth moved and a terrible flash of light, like the sun, blinded me. When all had cleared, this one was lying here."

"What tale is this?" Omori snapped. "I heard or saw nothing and I slept last night in the pavilion itself!"

"I swear, Lord, it is true."

"You *were* asleep, Lord," Eela interjected. "The battle had taken much out of you and you had drunk much sake in celebration of your victory. Nothing could have awakened you."

It wasn't victory I was celebrating, the warlord thought with a shivering thrill, ignoring the reproach in the *majo's* voice. *I would have gone on killing if not lulled by drink. The thirst for blood, for death, as usual, was unquenchable.*

The *majo* looked back at the body. "I came instead as I do not require much sleep. The shadow-tracker was still alive when I got here. I believe he comes from our future."

"What? What did you say?"

Eela stared back at him. "Our future. I believe it to be true, Lord. Before he died, he spoke of events to come—yes, he *spoke*, Lord, like my Prime Breeder, the Source of All Things speaks—events I too have glimpsed in far-seeing visions. Plus, he described one who may know of the Child—one who may be here in Odawara in our own time even now."

"How? How can it…he be from the…the future?"

The *majo* looked away, a knowing smile on his face. "There are ancient tales…but the evidence is before us—observe the garment he wears, Lord. Have you ever seen anything like it? And before this one fell into darkness, he told me he had found the future protector who would help the One Child—he called her the Yomitsu. As he battled this Yomitsu in his own far-flung time, he suddenly appeared here, wounded and dying."

Impossible! And yet…"Who did he speak of, this one who would help the Child? This Yomitsu?"

"A woman of the future. But, in our time, she exists in a

different life as a *shirabyoshi*, a wandering courtesan, yet to be reborn as the one who will protect the Child. In this shadow-tracker's time and place, your future agents were looking for the Yomitsu. But, according to our reports now, one such may have entered the city a few days ago and is still here. She may indeed possess information about the Child, no matter how twisted this tale is. We should seek her out, for the future has many outcomes, many paths. This shadow-tracker lying here may be from one of these alternate times. And this *shirabyoshi* may be the one who can tell us about the Child now in our own time. The purges have begun as you ordered but we must examine every reference to the Child, no matter how incredible."

*The future? The Yomitsu? Another shadow-tracker like the Prime Breeder who speaks? The witch has been valuable but this talk is madness. Still...*Omori breathed deeply, not wanting to show his confusion. "Very well. I agree. Find her then. Let us see if this is true. Release the shadow-trackers to sniff her out. Bring her to me." He took a step towards Eela, his eyes burning into the *majo's*. "And next time, I *will* be awakened when something such as this happens, no matter what. Do you understand?"

Eela bowed. "Yes, Lord."

He turned back towards the pavilion but paused as he barked one more command over his shoulder, "Clean up this mess and burn that freak!"

CHAPTER 3

It had finally happened.

Perhaps it had been the encounter with the Spirit Winds. Perhaps it was the shock of losing Shioko. Or maybe it was simply that her time had come and she had finally been allowed to glimpse her own future. The magnanimous nature of the *kami* could be a two-edged sword indeed.

Whatever the reasons, Yoshima Mitsu had dreamed of what lay ahead on her own life's path. Always before, it had only been the future of others she could discern—people, events, situations. She had never envisioned her own destiny but now, in her dreams the last two nights, she saw nothing else.

Mitsu was not a religious person. Zen Buddhism did not appeal to her and Shinto could not answer all of the hard questions of life. Perhaps that was why she felt drawn to Yira's teachings—to live one's life simply and independently of others, to take pride in one's work no matter what it was, to stand up for what was right no matter how difficult it was. Yet even Yira could not address the dilemma Mitsu now faced.

She stood alone in a shadowy doorway at the far end of the main street of Odawara. A long, voluminous pilgrim's cloak and hood covered her elegant features and slender body. She cradled a cup of sake, long since gone cold, as she scanned the crowd around her.

A *matsuri* was in progress this mid-afternoon. The festival procession lined the street with pageant wagons, the smaller *hoko* and dancers, acrobats and musicians. The crowds were thick in this part of town but only the children projected looks of joy and wonder. The adults seemed reserved and quiet. This celebration decreed by the priests of the local temples, with the conquering warlord's surprising assent, seemed to be doing little to take the Odawarans' minds off of the tyranny that now enshrouded them. Some of their children had been taken from them already. A distinct layer of fear and dread hung over the city.

If only Soun Ujitsuna, the rightful ruler of Odawara, would return! Perhaps Mitsu wouldn't have to go through with her dangerous plan.

Mitsu walked closer to the street, watching as the sacred palanquin was carried by, occupying its place of honor in the procession. Octagonal in shape and covered in black lacquer and golden edging, the palanquin resembled a small shrine complete with a base, walls and roof. Four acolytes shouldered the palanquin, each young man representing one of the city's temples as they made their way to the largest of Odawara's Shinto shrines. There, the local deities, or *kami*, in whose names the *matsuri* was being held, would be honored.

Following close behind the palanquin were several *hoko*, the brightly-decorated, four-wheeled, rope-drawn carts that served as traveling stages for actors and musicians. Even now, the lilting musical productions of the *dengaku*, performed with flutes, drums and wooden blocks, drifted throughout the city street.

But even amidst all this pageantry, Mitsu saw with only a partial eye. Her mind, too, was preoccupied with other matters. She had successfully put Shioko out of danger. Now she must try to do the same for herself. In the sake bar behind her, as in similar establishments she had searched the last two nights, she had hoped to find one who could help her—one who wasn't afraid, who had nothing to lose.

Her nightly visions had been clear yet incomplete—she and the warlord, Omori, struggled together in the Dreamspace. She knelt on the wooden floor of some outdoor structure atop Odawara-jo, injured and a prisoner, the mountains ringing the Kanto plain serving as a dark, forbidding backdrop to the castle. The *daimyo* was standing over her, striking her, his face an emotionless mask. She felt fear and pain.

The scene was so clear and sharp in her mind yet there existed nothing specific beyond that, no details, no further actions to draw any lasting conclusions from.

She shivered, but not from the cold. Would she die at the warlord's hands? Would he or his evil minions silence her forever? Mitsu felt certain something important would happen, some finality that would have to be faced. Why else would she be granted this vision now? But if such a scenario would help to stop Omori's reign of terror, if it would keep the remaining Odawaran children from being rounded up like wild animals and the rest of the city's populace safe, then she would gladly submit to it.

But she didn't want to die. Not just yet.

In light of her dreams, was it senseless then to stand here now waiting to put this reckless, new plan of hers into action? What hope did she have to change her future?

I must try, she thought. *I cannot just stand idly by and wait. If there is something else I can do, then I must do it! I am not just* shirabyoshi *anymore. I am a participant in something bigger than any one person. The Spirit Winds proved that! This gift that I possess, I must use it now for something other than my own self-serving desires.*

Through the smoky haze of fireworks, the dust raised by the passing procession and the jostling of the crowds, she became aware of someone markedly different from the other spectators, someone angry…more dangerous. *There*! He had just become visible across the street.

He was unlike the other onlookers. Yes, he wore a worker's garb, his face hidden beneath a large, wide-brimmed hat. *But that is just a façade*, Mitsu reasoned. She could feel it—a certain disenfranchised aura surrounded him; a feeling of loss and betrayal were picked up by, and permeated, her mental senses—a longing for retribution and a desire for personal justice. Yet a certain power lay there as well, one that had been instilled by training and relentless conditioning. It could be a very great power, she realized, one that could accomplish the task Mitsu contemplated.

He is ninja, she thought in surprise. *But an outcast, not allied with any master or guild—a ronin.* She pursed her lips. Dangerous and unpredictable, she knew, but this could very well be the one she was searching for.

The ninja moved back away from where he had been standing, only his hat visible above and through the line of spectators as he turned and began walking away. Mitsu darted a look down the street and ran across in front of an oncoming *hoko*, getting an angry earful from one of the four men manning the cart's pulling-ropes.

"Excuse, please," Mitsu mumbled, her head down. She reached the opposite side of the street and turned, a sudden urge stopping her. The *hoko* was stage to a handful of actors, painted and lavishly costumed, as they performed a scene from a favorite local play. One of the actors was dressed as a furred animal, a giant dog, who turned his masked gaze toward her.

Mitsu returned that look as a shiver ran up her spine. There was a movement in her Dreamspace (*though she was fully awake and in the light of day*), a flickering of vision…

(*She saw this dog-creature, one of Omori's shadow- trackers… It was a female and she was somewhere else, somewhere far away, both in place and…and time, a time not yet come. Like Shioko. The she-beast lay wounded and bleeding with someone kneeling over her, someone who looked just like Mitsu…*)

Mitsu blinked and shook her head. The actor had turned away as the *hoko* continued down the street. Mitsu licked her lips. *How strange,* she thought, trying to clear her mind of the unbidden image. *How very strange.*

And then she was off, pushing through the throng of onlookers to follow the ninja. She could just make out his hat bobbing above the heads of the crowd in the distance. She fingered her money purse hanging from the *obi* beneath her cloak. She had managed to save a little from all that she had earned and spent on her and Shioko's journey from Edo, and had gleaned a good bit for more personal services rendered since arriving.

She hoped it would be enough to buy the ninja's expertise. If not, she realized grimly, she would have to perform this task on her own; she would have to kill Omori Kadonomaro herself.

CHAPTER 4

The attempt on his life had been an act of desperation, he knew. The battle was lost, the opposing forces broken and scattered. Without the inspiration of Soun Ujitsuna, the Odawaran armies had been routed. Omori Kadonomaro had vanquished those foes who had defended this city as he had crushed everyone else who had ever opposed him. Even now, most of his own army and all but a few of his warrior monks were rounding up prisoners or putting to the sword any who offered even token resistance. But the assassins' threat had been real enough, though for a different reason entirely.

He had led a small party of his warrior monks and a trio of shadow-trackers in the hunt for the *shirabyoshi* spoken of by Eela. He had no desire to sit and wait, to allow others to do his work for him. He had always been a man of action and the Prophecy of the One Child concerned him greatly.

Though the shadow-trackers had no real scent or clue to rely on, through the magic urging of the *majo*, one of them had led Omori and his men to the market district of the city. The creature's manner was agitated yet focused; the beast appeared like something out of a traveler's tale. Naked, it moved like a ghost, spiriting almost invisibly in and out of the smallest places as it used the shadows as cover.

Omori had never gotten used to them but the creatures did

serve his purpose. Whatever magic the witch called upon to create such monsters was the warlord's to control. At least for the moment.

And he meant to keep it that way.

Located near the lower west gates, the marketplace was the one area his attacking land forces had been able to breach. Parts of it lay in smoldering ruins; the remaining residents hiding fearfully behind closed and latched doors.

The city's defenders had been beaten but the fear of Omori and his allies—the *sohei*, the witch and the shadow-trackers— still hung thickly in the air. To most of the downtrodden Odawarans, it was their worst nightmare realized.

Eela rode by the *daimyo*'s side. Both men's armored horses picked their way among the scattered rubble and trash that lay strewn about the streets. "My pet seems sure the one we seek is here, Lord," the *majo* said silkily. "He is the best of the three and can discern his prey with very little assistance."

His pet. Omori frowned. Eela's skills had extended to supervising the breeding, raising and training of the shadow-trackers, skills Omori appreciated but which gave the *majo* another point of power in his favor. "Just make sure your *pet* finds her," Omori said distastefully. "I will stop this child once and for all."

Though he distrusted the *majo*, the tide of conquest had definitely turned in Omori's favor since Eela's arrival. The warlord was a superstitious man, and so he had eagerly recruited Eela rather than have the *majo* lend his dark powers and his skills with the shadow-trackers to Omori's enemies.

But still…

"Here, Lord! The tracker has found something!" One of the monks gestured sharply to Omori from several yards away. The warlord spurred his mount forward but then stopped, allowing Eela and the rest of the monks to go on ahead. He watched impassively as his men followed the shadow-tracker below street level into what appeared to be a collapsed, burned-out cellar.

Alone, Omori slowly looked around him. His horse nickered impatiently as it stomped its feet and tugged at its bit. The smell of burnt wood and flesh assailed the warlord's nostrils. Small fires still flickered around him as the skeletons of once thriving shops appeared and disappeared in the smoke like withering mirages. Here and there, a corpse showed its death's-head, hands clutched stiffly in the air as if begging for mercy. The enemy had been ruthless but Omori's army had been more so.

Yet now the warlord felt that something was not quite right. He had risen to power by utilizing many skills, not the least of which were simply by being careful and suspicious. The hair on the back of his neck tingled. There were shadows on either side of him, pockets of darkness that could conceal—

In that moment, the assassins struck.

A whirring sound like a hummingbird, a slight glint of light...Omori ducked as a multi-bladed *shuriken* whizzed through the air where his face had just been. Another one flew out of those self-same shadows and struck his horse in its exposed flank. Screaming in pain and fright, his mount reared, toppling the surprised warlord to the ground.

Shaking off the shock of his fall, Omori leaped to his feet and drew his *kitana*. A black-garbed figure rushed at him from his right, his own gleaming sword in hand. *Ninja*, the *daimyo* thought, as he parried his attacker's sword thrust. Only the ninja's eyes were revealed through his black face-wrap, and they were dark, hard and cold, his intention clear.

Omori slashed back at his attacker. The ninja leaped above

the warlord's blade and kicked out at his face while still in mid-air. Omori barely dodged the expert blow, whirled and brought his sword around in a wide arc. The ninja blocked Omori's sword with his own fine blade but, as he sidestepped, slipped on a piece of broken brick. He recovered his balance almost instantly but that small distraction was all that Omori needed. His sword was already slicing through the air as it connected with the ninja's neck, neatly severing the assassin's head.

The blood-spurting, headless corpse stood swaying for a moment and then crumpled to the ground. As the body lay twitching, its head rolled away and stopped, eyes wide and staring as if wondering how this could have happened.

"Kyaa!" Omori cried aloud, reveling in the kill as he slashed at the headless body, again and again. Spittle flew from his mouth as, laughing, he kicked the assassin's head back into the shadows. *Try to kill me, would you? Try to kill Omori Kadonomaro!*

Another noise…Omori whirled to see a second black-clad assassin charging him from the opposite side of the street. This one brandished a *wakizashi*, but this…ninja seemed smaller, more delicate. The second attacker had waited while his fellow initiated the assault—*too much faith in the first ninja or lack of experience on the part of the second?*

No matter. Omori rushed forward to meet this new enemy, eager for more blood. He would take this one slowly, would give him such pain as he had never experienced. He would—

Like a demon falling from the sky, a hellish, taloned figure dropped down on the attacking ninja. The shadow-tracker knocked the assassin to the ground, tore the shortsword away and gripped a clawed hand around the ninja's throat. The creature's fangs dripped saliva, his furred body trembled with anticipation of the kill.

THE SIXTH PRECEPT

"No!" Omori shouted at the beast, forcing himself to slow down, sword outstretched in a trembling hand. The creature shot a hardened glare at the warlord. A warning growl rumbled from its throat. Omori knew how the beast felt—to be denied the kill, not to be able to quench the thirst for blood—in this they were much alike. He almost stopped to let the creature have his way.

But no—there was more at stake here than the warlord's murderous lust. He must exercise control. Now was not the time to allow his urges to control *him*. Omori met the shadow-tracker's red-eyed stare straight on. "Do not kill him. I would question this one. Do you hear, dog? Obey me!"

"Lord! Are you injured?"

Omori turned to see Eela and his warrior monks rushing towards him. Is *that actually concern written on the* majo's *face*? Yes, concern that he might lose the money and prestige the warlord provided for his services if Omori had been killed. Nothing more.

Omori grunted in response and stood over the trapped ninja. "So much for your 'pet's' skills," he taunted the *majo*.

Eela looked down. "Rotting animal flesh lay in the cellar, Lord. It's strong spoor confused my tracker."

The shadow-tracker growled in anger, its animal stench strong. The *daimyo* reached down and ripped the face-wrap from the supine figure's head.

"A woman!" Omori exclaimed. Soft, elegant features were revealed beneath the ninja's guise. Green eyes filled with fear and hatred stared up at him. Full lips twisted into a grimace of defiance.

Eela approached, rubbing his chin. He had an odd expression on his face. "Not just any woman, Lord," he murmured. "This is she, I think. The *shirabyoshi* we seek. She fits the description your agents supplied us."

A shirabyoshi *ninja!* A grim smile spread across the warlord's face. "You would try to kill me?" he asked the woman. "Is this great courage or wanton stupidity? Surely you knew you would fail."

At a motion from Eela, the shadow-tracker released the woman. The creature backed off reluctantly, snarling, hackles raised. "It is my fate," the woman answered hoarsely, rubbing her throat, her voice an edgy combination of anger and reluctant acceptance. "No matter what I do or where I go, I...I have finally seen my future for the first time and it is always here with you...*Lord* Omori."

"Ahhh." Omori nodded, amused and suddenly curious, his anger and homicidal desire waning. "I am honored." He turned back towards his wounded mount. "Bring her!" he commanded his monks. "I will get the answers I need back at the castle. Now!"

CHAPTER 5

The young girl, Mitsu, sat on the bank of the river, behind the small, wood and plaster house where she had been born and had lived all of her short nine years. The smell of garbage and waste permeated every nook and cranny of the slum called the Gettoo; the marks of poverty and despair were everywhere. Every day was an uphill climb, yet this was the place she called home.

Though her parents were poor, the meager abode they lived in was clean and possessed a semblance of a yard. Here she could sit on the riverbank and watch the boats drift in from the bay, the fishermen working their nets, and the larger sea-going craft plying the dirty inland waters. Every now and then a squidder would smile and wave at her. Sometimes, if his catch was good, he would stop and give her several squid and some seaweed. Those were the times she and her family ate well.

In small ways such as this, she would show her father that she could help provide for the family, that she wasn't just an extra mouth to feed, that she was needed. Surely the whisperings she had heard late in the night from her parents' bed couldn't be true! That they needed money; that they would sell her to the Guild of Courtesans.

Fluffy white clouds floated across a rich blue sky. The sun felt warm on her face. If she closed her eyes, she could imagine she was not the youngest of six brothers and sisters and that sometimes, there was enough to eat. She wore the ragged hand-me-downs of her siblings and went barefoot. But on days like this, she could pretend to be happy.

She turned to see her mother, her tired back bent as the older woman ran a hoe in the dry dirt, trying to work the ground for vegetables. Not much would grow here but her mother always tried and sometimes even succeeded. Perhaps if Mitsu asked, her mother would allow her to go to the marketplace. There she could steal some fruit and perhaps a chicken for dinner. She could be useful in that way too. Surely they could see that!

She got up from the bank and walked towards the older woman. "Mother," she said, smiling. "May I help you? You have so much work to do."

"Yes," her mother said, her voice oddly deep and gruff. The older woman suddenly stood up straight, her back muscles rippling oddly beneath her coarse, cotton shirt. She dropped the hoe at her feet. "You may help me." Then her mother laughed, a strange, dark sound, not like her mother's laugh at all.

Puzzled, she tugged on her mother's arm. The woman standing there turned around but the ravaged face that stared down on her wasn't her mother's face at all.

It was the face of a monster.

She tried to scream, tried to run but she couldn't move, couldn't breathe. "Mother, Mother," she croaked. "What's happened to you?" Angry yellow eyes glared at her out of a furred, dog face, and from its grinning mouth, slavering fangs glinted in the sunlight. Clawed hands reached out to her.

Her body suddenly felt limp as she tumbled to the ground. The thing that had been her mother knelt over her. Mitsu wet herself in the terrible terror that gripped her. Her body began to shake uncontrollably. Tears welled in her eyes.

The monster laughed again but this time it *was* her mother's laugh.

"No, Mother, please! Please!"

"Ugh!" Yoshima Mitsu shook herself awake, gasping for breath. She blinked her eyes; her head hurt; she felt nauseated and weak. A dream. It had all been a dream.

But there was something else. She bent forward, retching. What had happened to her?

As her vision cleared, she found herself kneeling on a hard, polished wooden surface. Black tenting billowed above her in the wind. In the distance, the familiar Hakone range west of Odawara rose like rocky sentinels. Mitsu found herself in some kind of outdoor pavilion. In the castle? At Odawara-jo itself?

"Observe, Lord, she awakens."

She squinted towards the sound of that voice, somehow recognizing it. Several shadowy figures stood a few feet in front of her. Who…? Yes! The dark warlord, Omori, and his witch. The *majo* was the one who had spoken. Some of the *daimyo*'s warrior monks were with them and—

There was a snuffling, scrabbling sound. As the wind shifted, an animal musk assaulted her senses. Mitsu turned to her left and then to her right. Three of the monstrous shadow-trackers were chained by the neck at separate locations within the pavilion. All were growling and straining to break free; all were struggling in her direction.

Omori walked closer, his arms folded at his chest. So this was the famed *daimyo*. An impressive-looking soldier, clad like a warrior, rugged and fit, his weapons hanging from the black *obi* that belted his waist. But she shivered as she looked into his dead eyes, remembering how ruthlessly he had killed the ninja. She tried to peer into his mind but found nothing but a wall of hatred and desire. What could turn a man into such a thing?

"You extracted no knowledge from her?" he asked the *majo*, while returning her gaze.

"No, Lord," the *majo* replied, his manner smooth and confident. "She is stronger than she looks. She fought the interrogation I used on her and the spells I cast, as well as the truth potion I forced her to drink. She revealed nothing about the Child."

The warlord nodded. "Impressive," he said softly.

The Child! Now Mitsu remembered. She had been drugged and subjected to the *majo's* vilest questioning techniques. But her gift had protected her. The mental wall she had thrown up around her mind had enabled her to reveal nothing about Shioko. If only she could use her power as a weapon!

But it would do no good. She had told Omori the truth— she had seen her future in a series of recent dreams after being denied such visions for so long and, in those dreams, she had always been with the warlord. That was why she hadn't left Odawara. What good would it do? She had tried to change that future instead, hoping that the philosopher Yira had been right, that there could be more than one outcome to one's life; that it only depended on the choices one made.

She had haunted the bars, teahouses and night places of Odawara until she had found the ninja. Money had bought him and the plan had been devised to kill the warlord.

The plan had failed. And now there was no turning away from the future she had envisioned in the Dreamspace. Somehow, she must face and accept that outcome without fear.

THE SIXTH PRECEPT

But the shadow-trackers were unnatural. She *did* fear them. They were born of the Left Hand Path and one of them had attacked her! Mitsu shuddered as she remembered its vile touch, it animal stench. She tried to curb the fear that threatened to envelop her.

A frantic urge to pray engulfed Mitsu. She had never put much assurance in any deity. Whatever trickster *kami* had endowed her with her 'Gift of the Mind' was not one she had ever wanted to pay allegiance to. But now, in the face of such unnatural horror, she reached out…

Please, Amaterasu, great sun goddess, ruler of the Plain of Heaven, protect me! Let me accept death, if that is to be, with honor.

Omori approached her closer still, a scowl on his hardened face. He pulled a metal object from his *obi*, a *gunsen*, a folding metal war fan. "Could she be the wrong one?" he asked the *majo* as he spread the fan and held it close to his chest.

The *majo* moved by his side. He was like a snake, fawning and slithery. Mitsu sensed that he might be the more powerful of the two. "Unlikely, Lord." His voice sounded low and whispering. "She possesses a certain power and, her face, well, let us say that she looks the part. It is a look I know."

A look? Mitsu wondered, puzzled. *What does he mean by that?*

But her unspoken question was not to be answered as, without warning, the warlord lashed out, backhanding her across the face with the now closed, stiffened fan. Mitsu fell on her side, blood welling in her mouth. The shadow-trackers went wild, the smell of blood igniting their killing instincts.

She raised herself up on trembling arms, looking wildly at the beasts, her heart pounding. *Not the shadow-trackers*, she thought. *Please, not them!*

"Lord," the *majo* said, knowingly. "She fears the shadow-trackers. More than most, I think."

"Ah." Omori knelt in front of Mitsu and cupped her bloody chin in his hands. "You will tell me about the child that was with you or I shall set my shadow-trackers loose. Do you hear?"

"Never," she said, trying to summon up her courage. She tried to look into the warlord's mind again. There must be something there she could appeal to! "Never."

The warlord unhanded her and nodded. "So be it," he said, standing up and fanning himself casually with the metallic *gunsen*. "Release them," he ordered the *majo*. "But stop them before they kill her. If she has some power, as you suggest, it might prove to be useful. Hopefully more so to me than it is to her."

Help me, Amaterasu, I beg you! Give me strength and dignity. Do not let me betray Shioko! Mitsu closed her eyes. As if she was dreaming again, she saw her mother clearly, this time as she remembered her, smiling and beautiful. Like a vision, her mother nodded to her and opened her arms. *Mother, mother, why did you let father sell me? I could hear you talking. Why? Why?*

There was a sound of chains dropping to the floor. A chorus of blood-curdling shrieks. *I will not falter,* Mitsu thought. *I must not!*

At that moment with her eyes still closed, Mitsu saw another in this Dreamspace, standing behind her mother. She gasped at the intensity of the image. *It is me,* she thought in wonder. *And yet it is not me—the same one I saw with the dying shadow-tracker in my vision. She has my face…Is this what the* majo *meant by…by my look?*

What she did know was that the Dreamspace illumined another part of her future. One she now understood.

Mitsu opened her eyes and threw back her shoulders. The shadow-trackers loped toward her, grinning their feral grins. She smiled at them now, her fear gone. There were many futures as Yira said, but only one she could play a part in. She knew now she had to tell the warlord what he wanted to know, no matter what happened to her. The Dreamspace had showed her that it was the only way to set in motion those events that would end the *daimyo's* tyranny. It was the only way he would be defeated.

Shioko *was* the One Child. And the girl must be allowed to follow her own path.

"You cannot hurt me, Lord Omori," she said pointedly, looking straight at the warlord. "For, though I may break, I will return, stronger than ever, and as surely as the sun rises I will defeat you. And, no matter what I tell you, you will never, ever, get Shioko."

In a heartbeat, the monsters were upon her.

CHAPTER 6

The sky over Odawara-jo was devoid of life—no bird could be seen, insects were absent and quiet, even the clouds overhead parted as if to run from the terrible act that had transpired on the blood-stained pavilion below.

The wind had stopped. The city itself, its inhabitants and the intermittent hum of activity they created at their daily tasks, seemed to hold its breath, suddenly quiet and still. Time itself seemed to pause, as if waiting. And then, a piercing cry shattered the momentary stillness.

"She was not to be killed!" Omori screamed. He knew better than to touch the *majo* or threaten him in any overt way but his fury almost betrayed him. He unsheathed his shortsword, the *wakizashi*, and held it at Eela's throat, barely able to control the trembling in his body. "I told you…"

Eela faced the warlord, eyes downcast but Omori was not fooled. The *majo* only served his 'Lord' for his own purposes even though Omori had benefited from Eela's powers. Omori needed the *majo* and Eela knew that. There was no real threat here.

Still, Omori's anger had made an impression.

"Forgive me, Lord," Eela murmured. "The blood-lust was upon them. There are times even I cannot control them."

"You liar. You—"

Eela's blank, bi-colored eyes rose to meet the warlord's. "But we did gain the information you desired. She did talk."

Omori backed off a step, lowering his weapon. The warrior's code dictated that once one's weapon was drawn, blood must be shed. But Omori had never been a strict follower of such structured dictates. He had made his own set of rules and knew he would never have gotten this far without it. Though he hungered for the *majo's* blood, as he did for anyone's when his perverse need arose, there was prudence in hearing Eela out.

Omori had walked away from the pavilion when the shadow-trackers had been released. His superstitious nature would not allow him to witness such brutal acts of any of the Left Hand Path even though he had aligned himself with them. They were necessary and useful to his grand plan but he need not be present at all of their hideous deeds. Though he could stomach such bestial brutality, even relish it, he could not let his men see him in such a state as he had been when he killed the ninja assassin. It was one thing to be observed as weak, another to show what most would consider an unnatural affinity for such violence. Even a powerful *daimyo* like himself must set limits. History had proven to him that some secrets must not be too widely known.

Yet the hissing snarls of the beasts as they set upon the *shirabyoshi*, the ripping of her clothes, the rending of her flesh… These sounds would be forever imprinted in his memory. As so was the fact that the woman did not scream or cry out at all.

Damn her—she was strong indeed! But the beasts had gone too far and killed her. *Stupid bitch,* he thought. *She died what she presumed was an honorable death but what good will her honor do her now? No matter. I will have the Child, regardless!* For a moment an unwanted memory intruded on his thoughts—he saw again his father, a minor feudal lord who had run a fanatically strict household. There had been beatings, many of them. His father had been cruel and unjust, ruling his family with an iron fist. And, every now and then, his father had done other things to him as well. Forbidden, obscene things.

Things Omori had to finally admit to himself that he had enjoyed.

Yet he hated his father and, when he had eventually killed him, running his father's own sword through the man's bowels, he had left laughingly and eagerly to find his own way. An appetite for domination and the determination to rule and empower by any means had been his father's gift to him. He would do what was necessary to take back all that had been driven from him and his clan.

"What is it then?" he questioned the *majo*, still holding the *wakizashi* in front of him. "Where is the Child?"

Eela placed both hands together in front of him, hidden within the folds of his robe, turned and walked a few steps away from the *daimyo*. "The *shirabyoshi* had great will and courage, Lord," he said, a slight hint of admiration in his voice. "But, at the end, the pain and terror inflicted by my pets were too great. Her mind broke and I was able to discern what we needed to know." He turned to face the warlord. "There are great cosmic workings taking place here, Lord. Wheels within wheels, mysteries we do not understand."

Omori waved his sword in front of him. "Get on with it! What are you talking about?"

Was that a glimmer of a smile on the *majo's* face? "Do you remember the clothed shadow-tracker we found who I said may have been from our future?"

"Of course! What has that freak and that insane fairy tale to do with this?"

The *majo* began to pace, his eyes closed. "The *shirabyoshi* had a gift, Lord, a Gift of the Mind. She could see what was to be. She foresaw the temporal winds carrying this child of hers into a future time and place. She brought her to an appointed spot to save her from you."

"Temporal winds? You speak of madness!"

Eela shook his head, his eyes glowing with some inner light. "No, Lord. Trust in what I say. Did you not find me and my three original shadow-trackers, including the Source of All Things, as if by accident? Another might consider that story and what we have accomplished so far as madness. The child you seek, the one who may bring you down according to the prophecy, is now far out of our reach."

The *daimyo* gritted his teeth, frustration threatening to overwhelm him. The cursed *majo* had a point. "So…so what danger is she then?" he sputtered.

"She may return to fulfill that prophecy the same way she has escaped us, and we must be ready for her. My pets have taken pieces of the *shirabyoshi's* body and samples of her blood. We will need them if the Child does return and succeeds."

"I understand none of this! What magic is this you speak of now?"

"It is a magic called genetics, Lord. We must be patient, even if takes many centuries."

"You talk in riddles! Speak plainly."

"If we are defeated…"

"Never!"

"If we are, and there are some future records that confirm that, then we must carry the fight into that future. We must hunt down the Child and whoever would be guarding her, this Yomitsu perhaps, to prevent her from returning here."

Future records? "Pah! If she does return, then that means we will have failed!"

THE SIXTH PRECEPT

The *majo* held up a long nailed hand, as if lecturing an unruly student. "Not necessarily. You see, Lord, I come from a future time as well and there are many paths to follow within the timelines, many chances to change what will be."

Omori felt a rush of unreality envelop him. The look on the *majo's* face unsettled him. "What? What do you mean, you are from a future time?"

The *majo* smiled. It was not a pretty sight. "It's true. How do you think I've been able to help you? To know when and where and how to attack your enemies? To recognize the dead shadow-tracker? To breed them? In my time, I tried to control the Spirit Winds, to gain entry into your world. I fell victim to them instead but here, in this place and time, I could escape and hide from those who sought my death. Now I know there is a way we both can win. I know now that I'm the one who will start the sequence of events that will end with the creation of the *Totou*. A paradox, I suppose, but it does make me feel like a sort of god, you see?"

A god? The Totou? For the first time, Omori Kadonomaro, *daimyo* of the Omori clan, Warlord of Odawara, Eminent Lord of all the peoples of the eastern Kanto plain, felt true fear. The *majo* Eela stood in front of him, eyes blazing like cool fire, no longer just a follower of the Left Hand Path, but the manifestation of a black *kami* itself. His words, with their mad emphasis on gods and cabals, struck the warlord like sharp knives. He knew Eela spoke the truth.

At that moment, the wind kicked up. The banners flying above the castle roofs snapped in the breeze. The *sohei* looked around as if anticipating an attack. Omori felt a prickling at the base of his spine. Even the look on the *majo's* face became uncharacteristically wary as the very air itself seemed to quiver.

A blinding flash of light exploded in front and around him.

Like a star falling to earth, all sight and sound was blotted out. The warlord blinked, raising his sword as the fiery resonance dissipated. His mouth fell open in surprise and wonderment.

Above him and the *majo,* on the steps leading to the tower level of the *donjon,* stood a woman unlike any woman he had ever seen. She was dressed in strange, alien clothes, her short hair and face unadorned, her feet shod in shoes the like of which were unknown to the warlord.

She looked confused, staring down at the warlord and his men as she held some unknown object with both hands straight out in front of her, an object that seemed to be constructed of metal. *She looks like the* shirabyoshi, he thought, staring in amazement. *Despite the differences, she has her face. Who…?*

Another explosion of light and the woman was gone.

The *majo* looked shaken as he turned flickering eyes to the *daimyo.* "She had a gun," he said, talking as if he had become someone else, using words Omori had never heard before. "That freaking cop! Just like the shadow-tracker. How…?"

'Cop'? "I would use these Spirit Winds you speak of," Omori said, quickly assessing the situation realizing he could swing the advantage back to him. Here was a chance to regain the upper hand. He would still use this *majo,* dark powers or not.

"Lo…Lord?"

"In case your plans do not work, I would use these winds to bring weapons here from the future to help me. Yes? Would that not work? Is that not what we have just seen with our own eyes—someone from a distant time appearing before us?" The warlord quelled the beating of his heart and hid the trembling of his hands. Madness, madness but an insanity that might work in his favor. Once again he raised his *wakizashi.* "And now," he said, reassured by the *majo's* unexpected display of fear and apparent loss of confidence. "You will tell me all about yourself and this future you come from, the weapons that can be obtained there. You will tell the truth of how you and the three shadow-trackers that were with you arrived here in Odawara. You will tell me about this…cop. You will tell me everything."

PART TWO

A Glimpse of Shadow

CHAPTER 7

Pittsburgh, Pennsylvania, 2010 C.E.

Give me a bricks-and-mortar store and a real person anytime! Kim Yoshima shook her head as she attempted to navigate her way through an online website that specialized in classic video games on compact disk. She'd finally managed to order copies of *Pac Man* and *Donkey Kong*, added them to her virtual shopping cart and keyed in her demographic and credit card information.

Phew! It's easier filling out crime reports! she thought, laughing. But at least it was done. Bobby would get his birthday presents on time.

With a sigh, Kim leaned back in her chair, rubbing her eyes and running her hands through her short, dark hair. She threw a guilty look at the jumbled mass of paperwork on her desk. Several empty coffee cups and a couple of bottles of *Aquafina*, a carton of half-eaten black bean chicken, and assorted reports relating to the cases she had been working on rounded out the disarray.

The usual brand of job-related material found on the desk of a police officer, Kim knew, but she shook her head, finding a certain amount of irony in her present real-time state. *Here I am sneaking in some personal stuff on company time.* She glared back at the monitor defiantly, knowing, at least in theory, that she was allowed a break once in a while, despite the workload. *I promised myself I'd get Bobby these gifts for his birthday. Show him what real video games are like!*

When she had been younger, Kim had time to indulge in such diversions. Though entirely focused on what she had wanted out of life even then, she still had managed to take a break periodically. Lately, her personal life had been pretty much on hold. Work, once again, had consumed most of her time. Particularly with some of her recent cases—politically charged, high profile with their accompanying media circuses and public outcry.

She got up and stretched, yawning ferociously, and glanced through the glass partition on the office wall opposite her desk. In the adjoining room, Officers Hewlett, Lesky and Posmoga sat at their desks. It had been a slow evening for a change, especially since South Side and the West End station had to merge because of the city's recent financial problems. South Side precinct wasn't too busy at this time of night. The afternoon shift was mostly engaged in catching up on overdue paperwork and answering phones. Any peripheral movement at all was mostly directed towards going to the rest room or water fountain. It was a rare moment of calm that Kim and her fellow officers appreciated.

She moved around her office, suddenly restless despite the welcome respite. She had tried to make her professional space as comfortable as she could, an extension of her home and her own personality. A couple of Japanese prints (two reproductions of Hiroshige's "53 Stations of the Tokaido Highway" and a copy of "The Great Wave Off Kanagawa," by Hokusai (as stereotyped as it may be to someone of her pacific rim heritage—Kim just liked them) hung on the walls. The placement of her furniture adhered to the concept of *feng shui* as much as could be allowed in such a confined area. One or two houseplants reached for the fluorescent light while a bonsai of a Japanese maple sat on her desk, its miniature branches and delicate red leaves poking up behind the encroaching piles of paper and books.

Her gaze roamed her small bookshelves, stacked with her own personal choices as well as professional. Sensational best sellers on the occult and the supernatural sat side-by-side with cut-and-dry police procedural manuals. Scientific and medical journals shared space with bound, collected reports and studies on UFOs and Cryptozoology.

Her eye caught a specific title in gilded Japanese script, the abrupt incongruity of it almost jarring—*The Teachings of Yira: The Five Precepts to Enlightenment by Samuel Kim* it read in her native tongue, almost seeming to jump out at her. *Yira?* Kim frowned, momentarily distracted. *I don't remember ever buying that book...Grandmother must have given it to me. I wonder why I kept it here, in the office?*

Grandmother. She smiled fondly at the memory of her Grandmother Mitsu. Kim could hear her father's mother now—"You must take some time for yourself, Kimmy-chan," Mitsu would have said. "Life is a slippery circle but that doesn't mean you shouldn't try to stop along the way once in a while."

Yet, if Yoshima Ayako Mitsu had lived into the twenty-first century, Kim knew she would have been proud of her "Kimmy-chan." A slim, forty-two year old, very youthful-seeming Japanese-American, Kim was the only female of her rank and ethnicity in Pittsburgh's South Side precinct. She had worked her way up to lieutenant by taking on any case that had come her way, playing by her own rules and getting the job done. A doggedness, dedication and interest in the oddball side of life, inherited from her grandmother, had allowed her to look at every situation from a slightly different angle.

Of course, Kim wouldn't have it any other way. It was her *karma. I miss you, Grandmother. You and your age-old philosophy.*

The ringing of her cell phone brought her back to her present situation. *Hmmm,* Kim thought. She reached into the pocket of her suit jacket, which hung over the back of her chair. Only a couple of people would call her at work on her cell phone. "Yoshima," she said. "And this better be important."

"Yo, Kim," a deep familiar voice rumbled from the receiver. "It's Lazo. And you know I'm good for it."

Kim smiled. "Hey, Laz," she said, lightening up, and then, in a mock-menacing tone, "*Konichiwa,* big guy. I thought I told you never to call me at this number."

A hearty chuckle. "No, that was your phone sex line, remember? I need to talk official business here. And good day to you too."

Kim laughed. Lazo Sibulovich was an old friend, a fellow officer, in fact, who had retired a year and a half ago to open his own business—a private library and research facility. Kim had taken advantage of Lazo's *Old Books and Research Haven* on more than one occasion. Hoarded in his retrofitted underground storage shelter was information not even accessible through the Internet. He had parlayed a life-long hobby of rare-book collecting into a unique and valuable service.

"Got a sec?" Lazo asked. "I know you're up to your butt in paperwork."

"That's OK," Kim replied. "I was zoning out a little, letting my mind take a little break. Actually, I was thinking about my grandmother. What's up?"

"Well, *that* is." Lazo's tone became a little more serious. "That's why I was callin'. You had asked me a while ago if I had any information regardin' some historical anecdote your grandmother used to tell you. Had to do with an ancestor of your family's. Remember?"

Kim blinked and looked back at the book about the philosopher Yira that she had noticed. "Yes," she said slowly, her green eyes narrowing. "I remember. Grandmother never gave me many details—her story was always thrown in as a little aside. Kind of mysterious, you know? That always impressed a little kid like me." She paused, remembering. "Father never believed it; always said Grandmother was a little around the bend. Of course, he never tried to prove or disprove it, one way or another. He was too involved in business, being on the fast track, you know?"

"Well," Lazo said. "I may have found somethin' that might help in that area, if you want to dig for it. Brand new acquisition, in fact, a pretty old tome but in fantastic shape, near mint. Just let me know when you can come over. Your convenience."

"Thanks, Laz. I appreciate it. I'll try to stop over as soon as I can."

"Whenever. I know you're busy. How's it goin'?"

"Ah, you know. The usual."

"No rest for the wicked Kim Yoshima, huh? Hey, I keep tellin' you. Do like I did. Be your own boss. You only have to put up with yourself."

"I'll keep that in mind," Kim chuckled. "Gotta go, Laz. I've got a meeting with Aiello shortly. Thanks. I'll call you and, as soon as I can get away, I'll drop by. And tell Jenny I said hi. I liked that last book of hers. It was a real treat!"

"My wife, the cosmologist!" A short chuckle. "Yeah. Who would've thought quantum physics could be so much fun, huh? Later. And give the commish my regards."

She switched off her phone and ran her hand down the

spine of Samuel Kim's book, looking up at the clock on her wall. Enough of that. Back to work. She sat back down, closed out of the Internet and reached for the topmost folder from the dog-eared pile on her desk. Her meeting was in a half an hour but she felt ready.

Commissioner Aiello was one of the few top men who didn't adhere to that old white boy's network and appreciated her work. He had stuck by her in the old days when being a woman and of Asian descent had been more than just a little detrimental to her career. Kim had maintained a good working relationship with him ever since.

(*Concern, fear, a crackling of energy…*)

She looked up, tapping her lower lip—something had changed—there was a sudden electricity in the air outside her office. Perhaps it was that vaunted 'sixth sense' or 'gut feeling' criminal investigators are said to develop. The muted conversations and myriad noises of computer keyboards, ringing phones and shuffling papers had settled into the background while a more pronounced sense of…Excitement? Apprehension? had asserted itself. That's when she saw officer Hewlett marching toward her office, the tight look on his face, the 'ready for action' body language written all over his chunky frame.

Aiello's going to have to wait. She was on her feet, strapping on her shoulder piece, donning her suit jacket and heading for the door even as Hewlett stuck his head in her office.

"Lieutenant," Hewlett said worriedly, his dark brown eyes flashing. "There's a…"

"A hostage situation," Kim interrupted, surprising even herself as she knew absolutely this was the case. "And right down the street. Yes?"

An open-mouthed expression stared back at her. "Yeah,"

Hewlett said. "How did you—?"

"Hold on." Kim turned on her heel and marched back toward her bookcase. She grabbed the book on the philosopher Yira and stuck it in her briefcase. *I need to read this,* she thought. *I don't know why but…*

"OK," she said to Hewlett, rushing past him. "Let's go!"

CHAPTER 8

Why can't these people settle their differences on their own? Wayne Brewster thought, fear and anger coursing through him. *Why can't they just move on instead of instigating this kind of senseless violence?*

No one, including Brewster, was sure how 'Mike' had managed to get the gun. His girlfriend, Loraine, a waitress at Lilly's Restaurant, was as confused and afraid as anyone. What seemed certain, however, was Mike's resolve to kill all seven hostages if his demands weren't met. "I want you back!" he cried, wild-eyed at Loraine, as he brandished the .357 magnum over his head. "I want everything to be like it used to!"

Lilly's was a mid-range, family-style establishment located in the back end of Pittsburgh's South Side past the Birmingham Bridge. Like all of its cookie-cutter ilk, it was imbued with the requisite tacky decor—framed posters of wide-eyed cats and generic landscapes adorned the walls; plastic house plants hung from the ceiling while the worn red wall-to-wall carpet hosted the stray remnants of last night's tuna fish special. The second-shift crew had just finished the dinner hour when Mike rushed in out of the rain-misted early evening like a tidal wave.

Raindrops dripping off his Pirates baseball cap, Mike had stood in the doorway, a young man in his twenties sporting a soul patch and a dull glaze to his eye. His scruffy, unkempt appearance, gravely voice, and, of course, the gun had certainly got everyone's attention.

"Mike!" Loraine had cried, almost dropping an order in a customer's lap. "What are you doing? For God's sake—"

"You're coming home with me!" Mike cried. "Now!"

But someone had called the police—an alert passerby, someone in the kitchen out of Mike's immediate sight, or maybe one quick-acting customer with a cell phone. Now it was more than just a violent domestic quarrel. It had become an even more dangerous situation.

Brewster and the other members of his reluctant group were herded together and forced to huddle in the back of the main dining area near the kitchen. Mike paced back and forth like an expectant father, muttering under his breath while he kept his perpetually darting eyes ever-shifting to his 'captive audience'.

"OK, Mike?" Over the restaurant speakerphone, the hostage negotiator's voice actually sounded a little bored.

Brewster felt another rush of anger. Was this just business as usual for the police?

"Just calm down. Please. There's no reason to hurt anyone. We can work this out peaceably." Rote, as if memorized, no emotion whatsoever.

"Yeah?" Mike retorted, pointing his gun at Loraine. "Tell that to her! She's the one that left me! And for a goddamn Cleveland Brown's fan!"

Brewster had gone into Lilly's for a late supper and to peruse the local newspapers. It was a habit he had gotten into whenever he worked a little overtime. He was a software analyst and always considered himself mild-mannered and non-confrontational. Some of his more less-than-understanding co-workers had dubbed him 'Tame Wayne'. So this kind of violent encounter would be considered clearly out of his league. Except here he was.

"You always think this happens to someone else," an elderly woman said, giving voice to his own thoughts. "You see it on the news all the time." Brewster, along with the woman and a small child—her grandson perhaps—were part of only a handful of customers at that post-dinner hour of the evening. Lilly's second-shift manager, fiftyish and sweating profusely, looked extremely nervous. Still, Brewster noted with approval, the man had calmed his employees down, especially placating Loraine who was crying and close to hysterics.

Brewster sat at a table with the grandmother, doing his own best to reassure her everything would be all right. His outwardly calm and soft-spoken demeanor helped allay her fears, at least for the moment.

"We were about to call a cab to take us to the bus terminal," the woman said, her eyes darting from Brewster to Mike and back again. "We have relatives in Philadelphia we had planned on visiting. I never dreamed we'd be in this type of situation."

"Are we going to be on TV, Grandma?" her grandson asked hopefully.

"If we are, son," Brewster said, squeezing the boy's hand, "it'll be after we're rescued." *Where did that come from?* he thought. *God knows I'm no hero!*

Except in his dreams. Except when he fell asleep.

The woman gave Brewster a brave smile and held the child closer. The little boy couldn't have been more than five or six and, much to Brewster's relief, didn't seem to comprehend the seriousness of the situation. The adults, however, were all understandably frightened and bewildered but it could have been worse. By a stroke of good fortune, the restaurant had been practically empty when Mike had begun his irrational stand.

"Shut up!" Mike shouted. "I'm trying to think!"

Brewster's mind suddenly shifted; a spark deep inside him flickered. He had to help these people.

He knew, he reasoned, he deduced, that at some point Mike's guard would weaken. A moment of indecision would emerge that Brewster could exploit to his and the others' advantage. He just needed to stay alert and wait him out, which, from the look of things, might not be for too much longer. In his mind's eye, he visualized the hostage-negotiating team, SWAT personnel and sharpshooters consolidating their positions. Through the wall-mounted speakerphone, Mike had been talking to the police though his demands, and conversation had become more and more incoherent.

Now. Brewster took a deep breath, his dark eyes hard as steel. "Excuse me," he said as he slowly got up from his seat. "Mike? May I have a word with you?"

"What?" Mike shot Brewster a vicious glance.

The elderly woman gasped in shock. "No," she hissed at Brewster. "Don't. Please sit down!"

"I have a suggestion." Brewster took another step closer, his arms and open hands spread wide in front of him. "Why not let everyone go but me? I'll be your hostage. Just let everyone else go. I know you really don't want to hurt anyone and I'll do whatever you say." Another part of his mind shouted, *I can't believe I'm doing this!*

"Sit down, asshole!" Mike took a few steps closer to Brewster and raised the gun. That's when that other part of Brewster, the one he became in his dreams, took control.

Brewster kicked out with his right foot, knocking Mike's gun hand up toward the ceiling. A shot fired wildly into the air, causing the hostages to dive for cover. With some other sense, Brewster saw the grandmother quickly grab her grandchild and run into the kitchen.

THE SIXTH PRECEPT

Good! Brewster spun off the floor and landed another kick, this time knocking the magnum loose from Mike's hand and sending it flying. Mike recovered and swung a hard right at Brewster's head. Brewster ducked under the punch, sidestepped around the enraged young man and hammered his fists into Mike's rib cage—once, twice, three times.

A final punch to Mike's jaw put him down on the floor. At that moment, alerted by the gunshot and sounds of the struggle coming over the speakerphone, the police and SWAT teams swarmed into Lilly's.

"Everyone stay down!" shouted the officer-in-charge. As Brewster backed up toward the kitchen, he saw the speaker was a police officer known to him, one he had seen on television news reports many times—Lieutenant Kim Yoshima, her own gun (a luger—a Sig P228, he knew from somewhere) sweeping the room. "You!" the lieutenant cried as she noticed Brewster not complying. "Stay where you are, please!"

But Brewster was already on the move, sprinting into the kitchen. He bolted through the surprised group of police officers converging through the back door and huddling around the grandmother and child and quickly lost himself in the crowd that had gathered outside the restaurant.

He ducked down a side alley further up the street and stopped, risking a quick glance back toward Lilly's. *Good, no one's seen me.*

He leaned back against the alley wall, cradling his head in his hands. *How did I do that?* he asked himself. *Why did I do that?*

But he knew. *Those dreams,* he thought, gasping for breath. *Those cursed dreams!*

CHAPTER 9

In all this stench and decay…a sprinkling of perfume, a slight whiff of body lotion. Ahhh. And under that…

The shadow-tracker raced through the rain-slicked back alleys of the city's North Side, slipping in and out of the streetlight-cast shadows like a ghost. Almost invisible in a black, form-fitting jumpsuit, he flitted amidst the battered hulks of buildings and garbage-strewn streets of the darkened slum district as easily as wind through trees, his bare feet whispering over the pavement.

His presence was unseen—no one caught a glimpse of the shadow-tracker unless he allowed them to. He stopped for a moment, raising his nose to the night air. If, by some unseen miracle, someone did catch sight of him, he would appear as merely a silhouette, a glimmer out of the corner of one's eye, perhaps, at most, another inhabitant of the fringe lurking in the darkness.

But upon closer inspection…

No. The shadow-tracker smiled. No one ever got *that* close to him. No one but his teachers and handlers had in the twenty three years since his birthing; no one outside the *Totou* and his huntmate, had in the nine years since he had been activated as a shadow-tracker.

No one ever would.

Rot, mold, human waste. But there, again, something quite remarkable in this area's grid—the spoor of his target, faint but present.

Death, decay. But life, yes, *that* life!

He sniffed again, to reaffirm, to make sure this was not another false lead, like so many others had been over the centuries. His target's spoor, *the* target's spoor, was indeed evident even among the myriad smells confined to this back street, though the still-falling rain washed most scents from the air.

The particular scent he followed had been imprinted in his DNA, as it had been in all the shadow-trackers before him, harvested from one of his target's ancient ancestors. There was no mistaking it.

It was her. After all this time.

She had gone in this direction, perhaps three or four hours ago. The shadow-tracker's yellow eyes narrowed, he licked his lips, running his tongue over sharp, pointed teeth. He extended and retracted his claws in anticipation. The very flesh on his lean, powerful body quivered.

Tonight would be the night. After centuries of searching, he would finally find the target generations of shadow-trackers before him had failed to do, she who his masters had sought for so long—the female known as the Yomitsu, the Great Enemy.

The very sound of that name held him in awe, even he, who knew no fear. But in the world of his masters, they who had bred him and his kind for this one purpose, the Yomitsu was almost like a goddess to him, second only to the other one, the one the Yomitsu would eventually send forth into the Void to destroy the Eminent Lord, she who the Masters called Ko the Little.

But, according to legend and the masters' historical data,

Ko's time had not yet come to maturation. And would not if the Yomitsu were stopped first.

And with the information he would glean, those he served would put an end to her, here, now. He frowned at the thought of his huntmate, searching another of the city's grids, missing out on this glorious opportunity. *The glory should belong to both of us,* he thought, knowing she would wait for him if the situation was reversed. *But…*

He grasped the small silver amulet he wore around his neck, caressing its finely wrought curves. *Yes,* he thought. *The masters will be pleased.*

He loped into the adjoining street, clinging to the shadows as he avoided the occasional nocturnal inhabitant of this grid. Tonight, the streets were not so crowded, the rain and unusually high summer temperatures keeping most everyone under cover.

So much the better.

He moved across the street, seeming to dodge the very raindrops themselves, quickly, economically, following the invisible trail as if he were indeed the shadow his name implied.

Tonight, he thought, licking his lips, anticipating what was to come. *Tonight everything will change.*

"Hey, how 'bout a break?" A rich baritone broke in on Kim Yoshima's thoughts, making her jump. "You've been at it now almost three hours. Is this all you came over for? What about *my* needs? *My* wants?"

Kim smiled at her friend, Lazo Sibulovich, as she rubbed the back of her neck. "Sorry, Laz," she said. "I didn't mean to ignore you, you poor baby. Has it been that long already?"

Lazo nodded, placing a cup of fresh coffee in front of the lieutenant. "Yep. Time flies when you're cruisin' the Web. That is, for those of us who don't surf. It is now…" the big man glanced at the clock on the fireplace mantel adorning one wall of the main reading room, "…almost ten-thirty PM, my sleepy-eyed Ms. Yoshima. Time for all good cops to be in bed. Besides, it's way past our closin' time for a weeknight."

"I know. And I appreciate you letting me stay," Kim said. It *had* been a long evening. Of course, the comfort level of the reading room—thick hand-woven carpet, antique furniture accented by fresh flower arrangements and assorted works of art (some original)—could be a little too relaxing at times. But that ambiance, aside from the wealth of knowledge stored here, was one of the attractions of Lazo's facility.

She took a sip of the coffee. "Mmm, delicious," she said, stretching the kinks out of her jean-clad legs. "Your coffee-making has always been your best trait. But you know what? I found more info in this book than in any web site—*Roots of Ancestral Geishas* by Razan Endoso. Pretty interesting. Where did you find this edition anyway? As well as the rest of your collection? Pretty rare stuff, yes?" Kim waved her hand to encompass the richly adorned reading room that contained a part of Lazo's library—floor to ceiling bookcases on each wall that held just some of his unique reference collection. Countless matters of science, history, mathematics, geography and assorted ephemera could be found within the pages of the old volumes ensconced here in his 'Old Books and Research Haven'. The rest of Lazo's collection was housed in the other archival-designed climate-controlled rooms located in his specially renovated apartments. With its combination of a strict library atmosphere and a design motif straight out of Victorian England, Kim had always kiddingly referred to the restored underground storage facility as Lazo's "intellectual bomb-shelter."

"How many times have you asked me that before?" Lazo said, sitting down next to Kim. He leaned back in the chair, stretching his own long legs under the antique claw-footed oak table. His brown eyes twinkled beneath a long, scraggly crop of gray hair. "And how many times have I told you…?"

"I know, I know," Kim smiled, shaking her head. "Trade secret of the 'Loyal Order of Bibliophiles' or some such mysterious organization." She sighed, suddenly feeling tired. "I swear you're a damn time traveler or something. I mean, how else do you explain a copy of *The History of Atlantis* by someone named Septus Monimus? I mean, where did that come from?"

"From his publisher, of course!" Lazo chuckled, his ample belly jiggling. "OK, OK, enough about me. What did you find?"

Kim ran her fingers down the pages of the large open book facing her. "Well…it looks like Grandmother was right after all. One of the distant ancestors of the Yoshima clan was a *shirabyoshi*, who were minstrel/courtesans, I guess you could say, sort of precursors to the geisha."

"Hubba hubba," cracked Lazo. "I always thought you'd look good in a sarong."

"Wrong culture, as if you didn't know," Kim said with a laugh. "But thanks anyway. This particular geisha wannabe was named Mitsu, Yoshima Mitsu, which, by the way, was my grandmother's name. The *shirabyoshi* Mitsu lived in the sixteenth century in Tokyo, or Edo as it was called then, around the time of Omori Kadonomaro's reign of terror during what is referred to in Japanese history as the Muromachi period. Within *that* was this timeline of feudal warfare called—"

"The Epoch of a Warring Country." Lazo nodded. "Or the Warring States Period."

"Right." Kim gazed at her friend. "What do you know about that?"

Lazo shrugged. "Oh, a little. The Warring States Period lasted about a hundred years, from around the early-to-mid-fifteenth to mid-to-late sixteenth centuries. Omori's so-called Great Purges were just a small footnote on a back page of a particular local history."

"But the violence of the purges was supposed to have been pretty widespread at one point," Kim interjected. "Spreading out from the fortress-city of Odawara (Pittsburgh's current sister-city, by the way) and the Kanto plain region into much of the surrounding countryside. All the local *daimyos* or warlords were jockeying for power then. A pretty chaotic time apparently."

Lazo nodded. "Right. And, in this particular case, if I remember right, the purges began with your man, Omori. He was a friendly, neighborhood Japanese *daimyo* himself who had briefly conquered Odawara, taking the reins of leadership from another warlord called Soun Ujitsuna. Omori wacks out and decides to kill or imprison all children of a certain age because of a prophecy that decrees one such child will overthrow him."

"Yes. Seems like a lot of cultures have some kind of prophecy/myth angle concerning children."

"And, like all those others, this was the usual frenetic power-mad melodrama replete with murder, mayhem, magic and eventual heroism. Thank you very much."

"Well put, I think." Kim frowned. "It seems you know a little more about this than you originally let on. Why didn't you tell me before I started all this research?"

"I didn't know anything about your ancestor, I promise," Lazo said, holding up his hands. "I just thought this volume might be able to help you in your search. Hey, you know what they say—'The reward is in the journey itself'."

THE SIXTH PRECEPT

"Well, I'm not sure that *is* what they say but it's the heroism that interests me in this story. According to my grandmother, this *shirabyoshi* was supposed to have helped to bring down Omori but there's nothing here on the record that refers to my ancestor's participation in his defeat."

"Still, that *is* interesting." Lazo leaned across the table, glancing at the upside-down text of the book. "Such historical asides often have a basis in fact. I know the *daimyos*, in general, kept sluggin' it out until, finally, the Edo Shogunate stepped in and cleaned everything up but as far as your guy is concerned…" He shot Kim a knowing glance. "I may have some other stuff that might be helpful in the other rooms. Sometimes that's how these searches go, you just get enough information to want to know more."

Kim glanced down at the pages of the thick tome, tapping her lower lip in concentration. Not much existed in the way of illustrations but there was a drawing of the personal seal of the *daimyo* Omori in an adjoining sidebar—a dragon swallowing its tail, stylized in an ancient Japanese configuration. *The Ouroboros,* she thought. *An ancient symbol in a lot of cultures. But what's it symbolizing here?*

Kim stretched again and stood up. "Thanks, Laz, but I'd better be going. I've still got some papers to go over for this case I'm working on. I just started thinking about Grandmother Mitsu earlier and remembered you had called so I decided to check up on that old story of hers. It's something I've thought about doing before but reality has kept getting in the way, I guess."

"Had nothin' to do with visitin' an old friend?"

"Nope. Nothing in my *karma* for the day about that at all. Too busy!"

"*Karma*, huh?"

"I know, I know. I'm not a Buddhist but do like the word."

Lazo stood up and grinned. "Yeah, well, I remember when we were both busy."

Kim returned the grin knowingly. Lazo had been a police officer himself for almost three decades before he retired and set up his *Old Books and Research Haven* under the streets of the North Side. It helped that the big man had made some shrewd investments despite the economy tanking and had done very well under the circumstances. This wasn't the first time Kim had perused the arcana housed here.

"Hey." Kim shrugged. "Police work is my *gei*, my art. Don't really have time much these days for anything else."

"Tell me about it. Say, find that guy who took out the perp in the restaurant?"

Kim shook her head. "No. Can you believe it? We have a very good description and the press has been playing it up but he seems to have just vanished. And he was a hero, yes? He saved those people. In this age of reality TV, Twitter, and fifteen-minute fame at any cost, he's certainly not the norm. Very *hen desu nee*…strange, yes?"

Lazo shrugged. "Sort of refreshin' actually. Not like our Lieutenant Yoshima who's on TV almost every night."

"Please," Kim laughed, rolling her eyes. "I've always loved the work but the politics and attitudes and BS and paperwork really get me."

"Know what you mean. Hang in there."

As Lazo got to his feet, Kim picked up her briefcase, shouldered her backpack and embraced her friend with her free arm. She had to stand on tip-toes to reach the big man's shoulders. "Thanks again," she said. "The department isn't the same without you, you know. And let's you and me and Jenny do lunch sometime."

THE SIXTH PRECEPT

"It's a date."

Kim walked through the door into the outside foyer. She stepped into the waiting elevator that took her up to the small, private garage reserved for Lazo's 'clients', two stories above at street level.

Kim stood for a moment, relishing the secret quiet this little 'enclave' of Lazo's provided. Though located in a pretty rough part of the city, the location did provide her friend with a certain degree of autonomy and anonymity. The so-called dangerous surroundings here were, in fact, the 'moat' to Lazo's 'castle'. He had renovated and recycled some more use out of the sixties' era underground storage facility—usage that definitely provided a service to law enforcement and government officials, scholars and information junkies alike.

The idea, in theory anyway, was, like in other 'bad' parts of the surrounding area like Homestead, to start slowly with a kind of 'creeping' renovation or gentrification that would allow other businesses and positive influences to sneak in and set up shop. Though hidden from most of the public eye, Lazo's reference library was a beginning and had begun to attract more than a passing interest from the public.

Still, one had to be careful. That's why Lazo employed a small security force, mainly on the surface for the parking garage. Just in case.

Kim paused briefly, again rubbing the back of her neck. The paperwork she needed to review was, in reality, routine documentation. Things had been a little slow since her last case—despite the investigations, interviews and meetings consuming a lot of her time. Yet she was reminded of something that had been scratching at the back of her mind for some time. Kim realized, despite everything, that she was getting a little bored, a little restless—the worst thing that could happen to someone as motivated as she was. She sighed and walked toward her car.

There were three of them—furtive, shadow-like in their own right—gang members from the looks of the clothes and colors they wore, all huddled around a small trash fire at the back of an alley. It had stopped raining and some of the human refuse were surfacing like worms, going about their wasted nocturnal rituals.

Drugs, the shadow-tracker realized, watching them from a safe distance, hidden in the dark. He could smell their sweat, hear their mumbled whisperings. Even now, one shot up with some substance, heroin, no doubt. He visualized the prick of the needle, the user's shudder, heard his ecstatic, breathy exhalation.

Fools. The threesome and their inane activities were unimportant; only their proximity to his target's position concerned him and, that, only a little.

Across the wet, littered street sat a newer, more modern-looking structure. Unlike its neighbors—abandoned tenements, their outward appearances broken, boarded up and scrawled with graffiti—this one seemed to have been recently built or renovated. An ornamental security fence surrounded an area of perhaps a quarter-block square with tall lighting stacks set up at each corner. The one-story building had no windows or visible doors but the shadow-tracker could discern the hidden shapes of security cameras placed strategically about the building. A newly-paved driveway led up to the front gate with another side-road running off around the back.

The shadow-tracker had followed his target's spoor to

this spot. His keen hearing and eyesight picked up nothing as yet but there was something about the building itself, its construction, design.

A façade, he decided. An intriguing yet openly innocuous exterior that, in reality, hid something else.

Interesting.

His target would have to exit the structure at some point. Once he made visual contact and positively identified her, he would inform his masters. His duty to the *Totou*, the duty of all shadow-trackers, past and present, was to report the location of the Yomitsu as soon as contact had been made. His masters would then do the rest.

His chest momentarily swelled with pride at his accomplishment; a sense of wonder at the history being made this night almost overwhelmed him. He would be the one future generations of the *Totou* would remember; the one they would talk about; he who had found—

Laughter sounded from the alley. Curses, shouts. He peered closer, his heightened night vision piercing the murk. One of the three gang members had drawn a gun.

The shadow-tracker didn't care if these three killed one another or anyone else for that matter. Why should he? Why should he care about such insects?

But if the one who possessed the gun decided to fire it, the noise might alert his target. Thus on-guard, she might take another route out of the building, and make it harder for him to accomplish his mission.

They would have to be dealt with.

The shadow-tracker approached the alley, moving silently yet quickly, his feet skimming over the surface of the wet street like a water spider's. He hit the side street's opening at a run, banking off the wall to vault into the air above the gang members.

He fell on them like a raptor, claws unsheathed.

He struck the one holding the weapon first, his claws raking across the man's throat and opening it to the bone. Before the first gang member even hit the ground, the shadow-tracker whirled on the other two. They were just now realizing they were under attack, their drug-riddled brains slow, uncomprehending, oblivious. He could see the alarm slowly building in their narrowed eyes.

He moved forward and, bent at the knees, brought his right hand upward in a slashing arc. His claws slit the second man through the ridiculously thick bulk of his layered clothes from stomach to neck. Gurgling and convulsing, the man stumbled backwards jerking like a marionette, blood gushing from his wound.

A thrill rushed through the shadow-hunter. Though bred for offensive action, he and his brethren were rarely allowed to follow the hunt through to its most satisfying conclusion, tracking being their primary function. The occasional kill was allowed if deemed necessary but he had almost forgotten the feeling when the bloodlust was on him. Besides, if he couldn't be permitted to terminate the Yomitsu, these three would have to fill that sudden need.

He took his time with the third. Time was of the essence, yes, his target was near. But he grinned as he slowed down, approaching the third man at a more leisurely gait. He would break this one's neck. Yes, that would do nicely, allowing him to savor the moment.

The third man tripped on his own feet and fell back against the wall. His hands fumbled in his coat, his eyes wide and staring. The shadow-tracker smelled the urine in the man's soiled pants.

He reached out and grasped the man on each side of his head and twisted.

THE SIXTH PRECEPT

A shot rang out, muffled by the man's coat yet still ringing clearly as a bell through the night air. The shadow-tracker leaped back as a burning flame arced across the side of his head. He fell back into the shadows, a blackness of another kind enveloping him.

Idiot! he thought. The third man, now a crumpled heap on the other side of the alley, had been holding a gun too. The shadow-tracker realized he had been careless, too caught up in his attack, too overconfident.

Blood trickled down the side of his head. The bullet had grazed his temple. He touched the blood, tasted it. He felt dizzy, disoriented. He hung his head, panting heavily. He closed his eyes, trying to overcome the pain and sudden weakness.

There was a noise. His head snapped to the left, the sudden motion making him swoon. He looked through mist-shrouded eyes. There...his target had exited onto the street.

Kim heard the shot just as she was putting her briefcase into her car. She didn't think twice, her instincts taking over. She pulled her Sig P228 and an extra clip from her backpack, threw the pack into the back seat and headed for the lot's exit door.

The door had a special keyed locking system on the outside to keep possible intruders out. From within the parking lot, it was essentially an emergency exit. She looked up at the security camera stationed above the door and thought about contacting Joe, Lazo's security head. *No time,* she decided. Besides, there was no need for two people to be in a possible line-of-fire. Once she took stock of the situation, she'd call for backup on her cell phone. She punched the button and as the door shussed open, exited the lot.

The humidity was all over her; heavy, moist air settling on her skin like a hot towel. It had stopped raining but the streets steamed; the glow of the streetlights cast an eerie luminescence throughout the empty block. She blinked, creeping into the shadows at the side of the garage and then, quickly, opened the section of gating outside the emergency exit and jogged out into the street.

No sounds. Nothing. The street was devoid of life.

That was when she saw the figure walk out into the light.

It's her. The Yomitsu. The Eminent Lord be praised!

The shadow-tracker felt a thrill of another kind as he saw his target, gun in hand, crouching across the street. Her scent, even at this distance, filled him to the bursting.

I can take her, he thought, his head throbbing as he blinked the spots from his eyes. *I can bring her back to the masters myself!* The hell with their rules! The situation had become something entirely different. She was so close! Why shouldn't he take advantage of this? The masters would know then, that despite his miscalculation on the three gang members, despite the wound he had incurred as a result, that he had still served his purpose.

Yes, he thought, rising to his feet. He would make his mark, no matter what. He walked out of the alley.

The silhouette was tall, lean, moving like a dancer, sinuous and mincing. The muted light revealed some kind of tight-fitting garment clinging to its body. Its hair was long, knotted into thin corn rows. Its eyes reflected the light as...yellow?

Something sharp glinted from the tips of its fingers.

What in heaven? Kim raised her gun. The figure stopped, its form backlit by a wavering glow from the alley behind it.

Trash fire? This one doesn't look like your typical street person.

The figure began to move again, loping (yes, *loping* was the right word) toward her, its motion controlled and precise like a gymnast.

"Stop right there!" Kim cried. "Police officer!"

The figure entered a pool of streetlight, its face briefly illuminated.

It was the face of an animal.

"Freeze!" Kim yelled, a chill running up her back. "Stop or I'll shoot!"

The creature speeded up, suddenly charging like a sprinter on overdrive. Kim fired once over its head. No effect. It was only a few feet away now, its arms and legs moving in a whirlwind of motion. *My God!* Kim thought, her fear building. She aimed a kill-shot, straight at the creature's head.

The thing shifted to its right, dodging the bullet as if the deadly projectile was moving in slo-mo. It reached a clawed hand out toward Kim, its suddenly visible face stretched into a ghastly parody of a smile.

Kim threw her body sideways. She fell, rolling on her side, the pavement smacking her hard. She felt a crunching pain on her waist.

She pulled herself to her feet, breathing fast, holding her luger with both hands extended in front of her.

Her breath caught in her throat. The creature was down.

Kim blinked. The thing was fast, unnaturally fast. It should have had her. She was positive it had dodged her bullet.

Yet, it lay facedown on the street, struggling to get up. This close, Kim could see the blood on the side of its head.

And that face. Inhuman features glared up at Kim. Man? Dog? It looked a combination of both—exaggerated bone structure, sharp teeth, high cheekbones, sloping forehead, yellow eyes.

Kim fell back a step, a sudden, unreasoning fear taking control. *What is it?* Both her hands shook as she tried to hold the gun steady. *What—?*

The creature suddenly leaped to its feet and flung itself at her, arms wide, mouth open. Kim fired and fell back, flinging her arms up over her head.

What? Kim looked wildly around her. The thing was gone. Where had it vanished to?

Have to call for backup! she thought frantically. *And surely Joe saw what happened on the security cams!* She started back towards the garage, hoping the gate would open again as she fumbled at her belt for her cell phone, looking over her shoulder. The fear was like a burning fire running through her system.

A low moaning floated through the night air. Kim stopped and turned back towards the alley. *Someone's hurt,* she thought, licking her lips. *Probably by that dog-thing.*

Taking a deep breath, she jogged back toward the alley and stopped at its entrance, the skin between her shoulder blades tingling. *If this dead-ends, I'm trapped. And yet I just can't leave someone in there if they've been injured.*

The moaning increased, a desperate sound radiating pain and confusion. Kim got her cell phone off of her belt. *Got to call Lazo,* she thought. *Have to get—Damn!* She stared dumbly at the cracked casing of the now-useless phone. *That's what I felt breaking when I hit the street. Cheap shit! The Captain's going to hear about this!*

THE SIXTH PRECEPT

She snorted. *Listen to me. Come on, Yoshima, get your act together!*

Darting another look back towards the street, Kim took a few tentative steps into the alley. "Who's there?" she called, her mouth dry. "Are you hurt? I'm a police officer!"

A gurgling, wet sound answered her, a barely recognized imitation of speech. Gritting her teeth, Kim entered the alley.

Across the street from the alley opening, the shadow-tracker knelt, trying to quell the aching in his head. He gulped air, his heart hammering in his chest. *I had her! She was mine!*

But his head—the pain and blood had disoriented him, which caused him to falter, something he had never done before. *Curse that insect and his gun!*

By now, his huntmate would have sensed his distress and started to look for him. They had been raised together since their birthing, both attuned to each other's emotions and instincts. Like all matched huntmates, the two of them had always shared everything. It was only right and honorable that she be a part of this moment now. Again, he knew he should wait for her; he should report back to his masters the location of his find.

But what if this glorious opportunity was lost? He was here, now! How could he resist? He growled softly, his claws scraping the pavement. Yomitsu or not, he was still the greater. He would finish what he had started, using the abilities he had been born with and had honed through a lifetime of training. If he could bring the masters of the *Totou* the body of his target, he would be forgiven his mistakes and his name could still be written in glory.

He tore a piece of his jumpsuit off of his leg and wrapped it around his head, stanching the still-flowing blood from his wound.

His yellow eyes followed the movement of his target. He sensed her fear, watched her indecision. He almost felt disappointed. Surely she should be a more worthy opponent. This was the Yomitsu after all, the vaunted Great Enemy. *So be it,* he thought. *This is where it ends.*

Following a line of shadows cast by the building behind him, he flitted once more into the street.

Three bodies. Young African American men, possibly members of a gang. Two had been horribly mauled as if by an animal, the third appeared to have had his neck broken. The one with the stomach and chest wound was still alive.

Kim knelt over him, keeping the alley entrance in sight, knowing, at this point, there was very little she could do for this victim. Considering the extent of his wounds, she was surprised he was alive at all. "What happened?" she asked softly, knowing already. "Who did this to you?"

The boy was trembling, breathing rapidly, almost hyperventilating. Blood pooled around his body and dribbled from his mouth. His glassy eyes were blank and staring. His body twitched. He tried to speak. "De...Dejuan got 'im," he said, his words thick and slurring. He jerked a thumb to point behind him. "Dejuan popped the motherfucker. Yeah... yeah..."

Kim saw one of the dead men still held a gun in his hand but the one still alive had pointed to Broken Neck. "Hang on," she said. She went over to the third man. There was a hole, possibly a bullet hole, in the front of his coat. Yes, Kim felt the gun still held in a claw-like grip beneath the heavy garment, incongruously worn even in this humid weather.

It was surprised, Kim reasoned, remembering the blood on the face of the creature. *It didn't think this one had a weapon.*

She knelt back down beside Stomach Wound. "I'm going to get help," she said and then stopped. The boy was dead. In just those few heartbeats—*No!* she thought, smacking her hand against the pavement. She looked back to the alley entrance. Nothing.

It took out these three easily enough. It should have killed me with no problem but it was wounded. She again pictured the blood on the side of the creature's face, the discharged weapon in the hand of the dead gangbanger. *Shot in the head, probably grazed, and that head wound is slowing it down.* Kim nodded to herself. *Looks like I've been given a little bit of a break. Now if I can just take advantage of it.*

She looked back out into the street. No movement. No sound. The city block seemed almost like a ghost town. If anybody was out and about at this hour, the sound of gunfire, no doubt, was keeping them safely out of sight.

She grasped her gun tightly, her hands shaking and slick with sweat. *Why am I so afraid?* she wondered again. *Yes, yes it's some sort of…of freaking monster but it's…it's as if I know that thing; as if I've seen it before.*

She paused at that realization. *As if she'd seen it before.*

But that couldn't be.

She pressed her back against the wall, gun held securely in both hands. Taking a deep breath she slowly started inching her way back towards the alley entrance.

(There was a movement…Kim felt something…a tingling in her head…)

Startled, she looked up. The creature was above her, clinging to the side of the alley wall like a spider. It let go, flipped its body around and dropped downwards, claws extended, fanged mouth open.

Kim cried out and jerked her hands upward, firing, once, twice, three times. The creature twisted in mid-air, impossibly dodging all three shots. It landed clumsily yet slashed out at Kim, its razor-sharp claws raking her shoulder.

Kim screamed and stumbled backwards. She fell onto the pavement, her gun clattering across the alley. The creature crouched on all fours, its muscles tensed as it readied to pounce. It grinned at her like a deformed circus clown. Uttering a small cry, Kim kicked out at the thing's face, the upper part now wrapped in a piece of ragged black cloth. Her tennis shoe clipped it on its bloody temple.

The creature howled in pain (the first sound Kim had heard it utter). It backed off, holding its head.

Kim scrambled to her feet. Her right shoulder burned like fire where the thing had cut her. She felt hot blood coursing down her arm.

The gun! The gun! She ran, scooped up her weapon, whirled — but again, the creature was nowhere to be seen, vanishing as if into thin air. Her feet pounded against the pavement as she headed towards the back of the alley. Fear drove her now, her training and survival instincts forgotten. *Have to get away, have to get away...*

The light from the dying trash fire outlined a door on the back wall of the alley — an old wooden door with a simple lock and hasp. She fired at the lock, the rusty metal practically disintegrating with the force of the bullet. She kicked in the door to the long, one-story building and bolted inside.

The glow from the fire, the outside streetlights and a large skylight looming in the ceiling above her shed a soft light throughout, illuminating the interior of the building. From the quick look Kim gave the room she found herself in, this area appeared to be part of a warehouse, stacked high with crates and boxes; empty shelves lined the walls; bags of some type of supplies lay piled in corners.

No alarm, probably no security here. Christ! Where's the freaking light switch? She ran behind a pile of crates, her lungs burning, a terrible pain shooting through her shoulder. *Stupid, middle-aged...*She took deep breaths, trying to calm herself. She pressed her gun hand against the bleeding slash marks on her shoulder. *Come on, Yoshima, remember your training! Remember what Grandmother taught you!*

Ancient rites of self-discipline, the natural order of the universe. Even to someone as young as Kim had been thirty years ago, a girl of twelve, a third-generation Japanese American visiting in Japan, the tales and advice proffered by her grandmother had always remained with her. She had been awed and impressed then and had tried to live her life by such tribal but powerful philosophy as much as she could.

But now she struggled for control, fought with the rising panic and desire to run that threatened to engulf her. The creature, whatever it was, had touched something deep within her, pressing some heretofore hidden fear-of-the-dark button she never knew she possessed.

And again, there was that nagging, inexplicable thought—*I know this thing. But how?*

She snapped her head towards the doorway. There had been a noise, slight, almost a whisper. The creature was inside.

She is *good,* the shadow-tracker thought approvingly. But if he had not been shot, this farce would have long been over. Even the Yomitsu was no match for the powers of the *Totou.*

Still, he *would* kill her. History *would* be changed. It was his destiny to be the one!

He paused within the doorway to the building, his nostrils flared. Her scent was now mixed with something else—fear. He smiled through the throbbing in his head. He had made the Yomitsu afraid. He fondled his amulet, gaining strength from its gleaming touch. Ah, the stories he would tell the others when this was over. They would beg him, plead with him to tell the tale one more time, the tale of the downfall of the Yomitsu and Ko the Little and the victory of the Eminent Lord.

Grinning, he padded into the building.

There! He sensed her immediately, standing behind a pile of crates. *Is that the best she can do?* he smirked to himself. Softly, he slipped behind the boxes…

Where are Lazo and Joe? Surely they know by now I'm in trouble! Kim Yoshima backed up against a pile of boxes, berating herself. She had made a grave tactical error in going out to investigate the shot by herself. Someone with her experience should have known better. But she had been impatient, of perhaps wanting to make a change, to do something different with her life. Here had been a chance for action! What a fool!

Time to kick herself later. Her attention was suddenly and joyously diverted as hope began to replace her fear. Sirens! Getting closer. Finally! Lazo must have called the police.

She ejected the spent clip and loaded the extra one into her weapon. She breathed in and out, keeping the luger pointed in front of her. Her shoulder throbbed. Her legs buckled, just a little. *Getting weak. If I can keep it at bay for just a little longer…My god, maybe I'm just too old for this.*

And then it happened again. A tingling sensation ran down the left side of her head, causing her to jerk in that direction. But more than that, there was an image, a picture…in her mind?

(*The creature—leaping over the pile of boxes directly behind her, silently, its body lean and sinewy, built like a deadly machine. No noise, no warning. She could see it happening, like a movie, like a—*)

"Aaagghhhh!" Kim screamed and brought her gun up shooting, firing straight above her. "Eat this, you freak!"

The creature twisted again, but this time not because of its agility. It shrieked as it was hit, flailing in mid-air and flopping like a fish out of water. It came down hard, still reaching out desperately in Kim's direction as the lieutenant barely jumped out of its way.

The thing lay on its back, gasping for air, its yellow eyes glaring at Kim. The lieutenant stood, legs apart, still holding her gun out in front of her as if the weapon was connected to her body. She shook all over. Her arms ached. She felt like she was going to throw up. Despite the terror and revulsion coursing through her, she couldn't take her eyes off the creature.

It spoke then, its voice smooth and silky, sounding more like a human than a beast.

(*Like something out of a nightmare, like something she had heard before—somewhere else, in some other time…*)

"Yomitsu." It pointed a taloned finger at Kim, its already ravaged features contorted in pain. "Great Enemy…" It convulsed once, its eyes clouding over. "It was not meant to be. I was not the one. You…will still send Ko into the Void unless… there will be another…like me…" It lay still as its chest heaved with weakened breath. Its eyes closed.

Jesus, Jesus. Kim moved closer. Dead. It *was* dead! No, not yet. It was still breathing.

Yomitsu? Ko? Another like it? And what the hell is the Void?

Abruptly, her scrutiny shifted to the thing's neck. *What?* Something silver glinted there against the black clothing of the creature. A necklace of some kind, no, more like an…amulet? Its design…a dragon swallowing its tail.

Kim's breath caught in her throat. She stared at the amulet. *What in heaven? It's the* daimyo *Omori's personal seal. How…?*

She shook her head, trying to clear it. A whirlwind of thoughts and images collided in her mind. It came to her then, bubbling up from the depths of her subconscious—*Embrace the darkness; our birthing springs from the abyss.* The voice inside her head reciting that odd combination of words was hers but… but…

The sirens. The patrol cars were close. Kim turned and bolted for the open back door, more than anxious to get as far away from the creature, wounded or not, as she could. She should shoot it again, she knew, but she had to get out.

The patrol cars' lights were visible through the alley's narrow opening, swirling like a rainbow in a blender as they reflected off the wet pavement. As she ran outside Kim fought the panicked urge to fire another shot into the air. "Over here!" she shouted, pulling out her badge and waving it above her head.

But, rather than uniformed blues coming to her rescue, two familiar figures came running into the alley—Lazo and his security head, Joe. "Kim!" Lazo called out, a gun in his hand. "Are you OK? What's happened?"

"I…I was attacked. Where were you? Couldn't you see…?"

Lazo shook his head. "We heard the shots—that happens periodically here—but it looked like something was wrong with the security cam film…we really couldn't see anything but you and, I don't know, a blur, a shadow. What—?"

"In here!" Kim turned back toward the building and thought she heard a noise from its darkened interior. Something…a blast of wind? Some kind of roaring sound accompanied by a brief burst of light. She felt disoriented then, as if she had looked down from a great height.

She stopped, the fear returning, her mind suddenly on guard. "It's…it's inside," she muttered, as Lazo ran to her side. Joe had stopped to check on the dead gang members, speaking into a cell phone.

Kim was shaking again. Something had happened inside the old warehouse just now. She could feel it. Something elemental.

"Kim?" Lazo put a meaty hand on his friend's shoulder. "What's happened?" he asked again, then pulled back, his fingers covered in blood. "Shit, you're hurt!" His face hardened, creasing with worry. "Joe!" he called over his shoulder. "Call an ambulance!" Kim shook her head and ran back inside the storage facility.

The creature was gone. A vague blurred outline drawn in blood lay pooled on the floor. But the creature itself was nowhere to be seen.

"It was right here!" Kim shouted. "I shot it!"

A sound. Kim whirled to face a pile of boxes lying in a corner of the room. Behind them a shadowy movement. Slowly she approached, her gun trained on the boxes with Lazo right behind her.

"Come out," she commanded. "You know damn well I have a gun."

Another…sob? Kim quickly rushed around behind the crates. There, huddled on the floor in the dark, her back to the wall, crouched a young girl, a child really, not more than seven or eight years old. Dirty and dressed in ragged clothes and worn clogs, she sat shivering, her eyes wide with fright.

*Her eyes...*Kim stopped, startled. The girl was Japanese. Through the soot and grime covering her tiny face, her Asian features were unmistakable.

"Kyaa! Tasukete, Oneesan! Oneesan!" the girl cried suddenly in Japanese, reaching her hand towards Kim.

Help me. Elder sister. Kim lowered her weapon and knelt down in front of the girl. "Mitsu-san," the girl said, tears welling in her eyes. "Mitsu-san."

"What the hell?" Lazo exclaimed, and then more gently, "Kim, the squad cars are finally here."

"Laz," she said weakly; fear, fatigue, loss of blood and spent adrenaline were catching up with her. Her eyes never left the girl as she grasped her tiny hand. "I killed it. I know I did."

"Don't talk," Lazo said. "The ambulance is on its way." The girl's face began to swim before Kim's eyes. She blinked furiously, struggling to stay awake.

"Have to find it," she whispered. "Before it gets away. Laz, the dragon...Omori..."

Darkness settled over Kim Yoshima then as she fell floating into unconsciousness.

The shadow-tracker's huntmate eased the manhole cover back into position above her. She stopped and listened, her nostrils flaring at the cover's seal.

Nothing yet, no sounds or smells of pursuit. But soon this area would be swarming with police, searching for her huntmate. She looked down from the topmost rung of the service ladder to the catwalk below her. Her lips curled in a silent snarl.

She had been there at the end. Her huntmate wasn't dead. But the Yomitsu had tried to kill him. And then…and then…

It was *her*, she thought in wonder, despite her grief and rage. Who else but the Yomitsu or Ko the Little could have stopped a shadow-tracker? Could have called the legendary Spirit Winds to carry him off? And the scent the shadow-tracker had picked up on as she neared the storage area confirmed it.

The Yomitsu. Within reach at last. The Eminent Lord be praised!

She slid down the ladder and knelt, as if praying, her shoulders hunched. She placed her hands on the floor, her eyes closed. *Why didn't you contact me?* she thought, though she was certain of the answer. Her huntmate had always been proud and overconfident—traits the masters had failed to breed and completely train out of him. He wanted the glory of the kill for himself. Of that she was sure.

And that vainglorious attempt had destroyed him.

She reared her head back, hungry to howl her fury. But no, that would alert those above who would be searching. She must temper her grief until she was far away from here, back in the safe confines of the *Totou's* secret quarters.

But all was not lost. The Yomitsu was here, in this time and in this place. When the shadow-tracker had sensed her huntmate's distress across the many city grids that separated them, she didn't know exactly what was happening, only that he was in trouble. But now…even though she had been too late to help her huntmate, what news she would bring the masters! It would be a simple matter to locate the Yomitsu again. The hunt would be concentrated here. Oh yes, the masters would require all shadow-trackers to pull back for a while, to cease operations until this incident had blown over. No undue attention must be attracted for too long.

In a few days, weeks, months, the hunt would start again. And the shadow-tracker would find the one who not only was partly responsible for the fall of the Eminent Lord but who, now, had left her huntmate to die.

She lightly maneuvered down the catwalk stairways, her bare feet picking out toeholds in the damp metal. Her yellow eyes glowed, her long ponytail of coarse hair swung down the middle of her back, her supple body tensed with the memory of what she had seen.

Her huntmate—one minute he lay on the floor, the next, he was gone. The wind, the light.

As she made her way under the streets, deeper into the bowels of the city's sewer system, she began to croon softly to herself, a low, animal keening, a singsong cadence of grief and something else. She now understood her huntmate's desires. Those desires had become her own.

When the time came, she would be the one to find the Yomitsu. She would be the one to track her down and kill her. The glory would be hers.

And the vengeance.

Lying on the emergency room bed, Kim Yoshima stared at the ceiling, a sudden nervousness settling over her body. Her wound had been cleaned and dressed and she was being pumped full of antibiotics. Despite her condition, the fatigue and weariness of an hour ago were gone. She felt energized.

But that was not necessarily a good thing.

That creature, she thought again for the thousandth time.

THE SIXTH PRECEPT

It acted like it knew me in some way. It called me the Yomitsu. A shiver ran through her body. No Japanese word like 'Yomitsu' existed that she knew of. But Mitsu was her grandmother's name as well as that of the ancestor she had referenced earlier in Lazo's library (not to mention what the mysterious little girl had called her). The 'Yo' part of Yoshima could easily be the first part of that name with Mitsu as the second part. Was that a fluke or a desperate reach in logic on her part? But there was more about this incident that bothered her.

The amulet around the creature's neck—its design was definitely that of the *daimyo* Omori Kadonomaro, the ancient feudal warlord who had succeeded in breaching the walls of Odawara. How much of a coincidence could that have been?

And the 'warnings' she had perceived during the creature's onslaught. They seemed to be images she could see, without actually seeing—some kind of prescience?

As a kid, I used to have such…hunches, she remembered. *Grandmother said I had some kind of talent, some…gift but I've not experienced anything like that in years. Mother and Father said that was all bullshit; that Grandmother was living in a fantasy world.*

And Ko…who was Ko?

Kim gripped the arm rails of the bed. She felt like she had slipped into a dream. *No,* she thought. *Not a dream, a nightmare.*

Her brow furrowed in confusion. She moved restlessly, anxious to get back to her office, home, or even back to Lazo's library. She needed information!

But here, in the hospital, surely she was safe! All these people surrounding her…she could hide, be protected.

The tears came like a pipe bursting within her. Kim wrapped her arms around herself and let the fear and horror of the last two hours vent themselves from her in a torrent of pent-up emotion. She shook uncontrollably, gasping great gulping sobs. *What happened back there?* she wondered. *What in God's name happened?* Finally, when she thought she would never stop, when she thought she might cry forever, she lay back against the pillow, drained, and suddenly calm.

She took a deep breath, inhaling like it was the first time. The image of the young girl she had found came back to her. The doctors had no information about her when Kim had asked. Why was she hiding in the warehouse? Where was she now? There was something about her.

"Hey, Kim, how are you feelin'?" Kim jumped as Lazo ambled into the room, his bulk taking up most of the small space.

Kim managed a shaky smile, wiping her wet face with her hands. "OK, I...I guess. Surprisingly good, in fact. When... when can I get out of here?" *I won't be afraid. I won't cry again. That dog-thing can't hurt me anymore.*

Lazo folded his arms, his lips pursed in thought. "I guess you can make the decision to leave yourself," he said. "You've lost a lot of blood but they can't keep you if you don't wanna stay. But, you're gonna have to make a statement. Now, if you're up to it. There's an officer waiting outside to talk with you."

Kim nodded. She'd be on the other side of the desk on this one. What would she tell the interviewing officer? A strange creature with inhuman powers had attacked her, spouting fantastical nonsense? That she had mentally visualized its attacks? No, no, she already had a reputation of being a little left of center in the precinct. In this case, there was no body, no witnesses (none left alive anyway but her), nothing to corroborate her story. A forensic investigation of the three gang members might turn up some abnormalities about the wounds that had killed them. And what about the analysis of the blood found at the scene in the storage warehouse? What would that reveal, if anything?

A wacko with a knife, or knives, hopped up on PCP and Ecstasy. That would have to be her story. She'd always played by the rules; always tried to be the good cop. But this, this one time, she might have to bend them a little.

"The little girl, Laz—"

"She's gone," Lazo said, frowning. "When the EMTs and the officers got there, she must have slipped away. I couldn't find her."

"We've got to look for her," Kim said, suddenly agitated. "I don't know why but it might…it might be important."

"Sure, Kim, we will. But listen." Lazo moved closer. "One thing. Back in the alley when Joe and I got there; you said 'it'; you said '*It's* inside', 'I killed *it*', '*It* was right here'. Not 'him'. *It*. And then this stuff about a dragon and that medieval *daimyo* we were talkin' about earlier." Lazo's gaze became that of the interrogator, the professional he once used to be.

And of a concerned friend.

"I was just babbling," she said slowly, calming herself. "The wound…shock. I don't know…just caught up in that moment, I guess. The guy was a maniac, you know?"

Lazo stared, obviously not convinced. "You sure you're OK?"

"Yes. Yes. I promise. Thanks."

Kim sighed and closed her eyes. Not much paperwork would get done tonight. But then, she realized a new feeling had manifested itself, a sudden excitement brimming just below the surface, the anticipation her work brought at the beginning of a new case, no matter how grisly or brutal.

The thrill of the chase, the deduction, the putting together of facts, clues and theory. There was nothing like it. It was all there, ready to take her away.

But something was suddenly missing from her life as well.

Oh, yes. She smiled. That restless, bored thing. Right now, at this moment, Kim Yoshima was not undecided about her future any longer. And she had a feeling she wouldn't be for quite some time. Whether that was good or bad, time would tell. In the meantime…

"OK, Laz," she said. "Call the doctor, will you? And tell that officer I'm ready! I want to get the hell out of here!"

CHAPTER 10

Wayne Brewster's hands were trembling. He leaned back in the bus seat and closed his eyes though his current discomfort was more mental than physical. The events of the last three months were beginning to take their toll. First there was that trouble at work—the layoffs and benefits cuts and added work burden, then his parents had died within two weeks of each other and the trouble with his brother over their wills. Then his dreams started and now this confrontation at Lilly's.

What was happening to him? Were these dreams stress-related or something else entirely? He'd always been able to avoid most types of personal conflicts before but now everything had been hitting him at once.

Outside, the city rushed by in a blur of neon, steel, glass and concrete motion. Gray pavement gave way to more gray pavement. Buildings and storefronts merged into an endless stream of street corners and moonlit alleyways. *The city,* he thought, as he stared at the skyscraper skyline. (*No matter where I am, it's always the city*).

He blinked. *What's that supposed to mean?* he wondered. *Where did that thought come from?*

Brewster got off at the next stop on Centre Avenue and, under cover of darkness with his recent 'disguise' of baseball cap and dark glasses, walked to the back of his apartment building.

The police were looking for the "unidentified man at Lilly's Restaurant" who had disarmed the gunman, but Brewster didn't want to be found.

He swiped his card key through the rear exit security box, opened the door, and started running. Taking the steps easily two at a time, he shot upward—one floor, two, three, all the way to the twelfth. Barely winded, he walked down the hallway, unlocked the door to room 1204, and entered.

It was only then that he realized the athletic feat he had just accomplished.

He started shaking again as he walked into his kitchenette and leaned against the counter. *I need a drink,* he thought, but he didn't drink. Now, he realized, might be a good time to start.

A chatter of buzzing conversation turned him around.

Only last week, Brewster had purchased a police scanner. Somehow, it seemed like a good idea. Tonight, like every night, like some obscene Muzak accompaniment, the scanner blared out a running list of the evening's criminal activity.

It was as if, suddenly, he needed to know what was going on in the dank underbelly of the city; what evil Pittsburgh's dark side was capable of.

This is crazy! Angrily, he stormed into his bedroom and turned off the scanner. He tore off his cap and glasses and threw them against the wall. *Maybe I should see a dream therapist,* he thought, sitting down on the edge of his bed. He raised his head, his brow suddenly furrowed. *Yes. Maybe I should stop being afraid and try to find out what's really going on.*

CHAPTER 11

From the Mount Washington overlook, the city spread out before Kim Yoshima, the confluence of its three rivers a sight that always inspired her with a kind of awe. The fountain at Point Park blossomed skyward; a few boats drifted lazily on the calm river waters while Pittsburgh's many bridges, connecting the downtown area with its North and South Sides, presented a series of interwoven spans that vanished into the distant haze.

It was almost noon, not quite as hot today as it had been even though most of the summer of 2010 had been cooler than usual. Kim stood dressed in shorts, sneakers and sleeveless blouse. The sun was bright in an almost cloudless sky but a slight breeze compensated.

Pittsburgh was a 'big small town', made up of several culturally, ethnically and economically diverse neighborhoods. Downtown, nevertheless, still provided an impressive skyline.

Kim had grown to love it here. Pittsburgh had become her town. Her parents had emigrated from Japan when she had been only five years old, her brother, Ken, seven. Her mother and father had been eager to climb the corporate ladder in this 'new world' and had ended up in Pittsburgh because of some distant family connections.

Ken had become a businessman, just like their parents,

cashing in on the early dot-com boom of the late nineties and the stock market before it had nose-dived. Kim had become a cop, driven by something deeper, eager to be of service to her adopted home.

A damn good cop too, she thought, without a trace of hubris. *Except for this last incident.* Absently, she scratched her left shoulder. It had been two weeks since the attack and the wound had been healing nicely. Despite the raggedness of the cut, only a few stitches had been required and the doctors said there would only be a small scar.

No trace of her attacker and the killer of the three gang members had been found. The press had played up the incident for a while ("Mystery Slasher!" "Gang Related Killings"). But the initial furor had died down and, as yet, there had been no new leads. The results of the creature's blood-sample had been inconclusive.

Sometimes it worked like that, much to her and every other cop's frustration. The good guys only won consistently in the movies, it seemed, and a lot of the time not even then. But the reality of that encounter still haunted her. God knows, she didn't experience something like that every day!

(*But maybe in another lifetime?*)

She closed her eyes momentarily. Yes, it was still there—the fear. Not the fear she and everyone else felt in her line of work. You had to be afraid; that emotion was your pressure outlet, your safety valve, the thing that kept you alert and, ultimately, safe. You couldn't do the kind of work she did without it.

But this fear she felt was different. Ever since her encounter with the dog-man, she couldn't shake the nervousness, the anticipation of her life being in danger, of some unknown adversary stalking her. She had requested and had been granted some time off from work to try to figure out what was happening to her. Post-traumatic stress was a good guess. She hadn't seen the department shrink yet even though that had been part of the deal. *Not yet,* she thought defiantly. *I need to examine this 'fear' from all angles first. I need to figure this out myself.*

Still, some nights she couldn't sleep, couldn't stop shaking, couldn't turn on enough lights when darkness fell. She found herself praying, not to any Christian deity, but to her Grandmother's ancient gods, something she hadn't done in a very long time.

Because of the hard work and pressure put on her during her most recent investigations, her superiors, particularly Commissioner Aeillo, thought a short leave of absence was a good idea. There were other people that could take over her workload temporarily and they didn't want the work she had done to be compromised in any way.

As much as that galled her, Kim was pressing on regardless, researching the dog-man incident and any ideas she came up with on her own time. She knew this fear would pass eventually—she had been a cop for too long. The excitement generated from the mystery of the attack was still alive, though, despite the fear.

How could it not be?

Still, she wasn't used to so much time off. Since her divorce from Jonathan, she had buried herself in her work. They hadn't had any children; her nephew, Bobby, had become an emotional center for her, whenever she could find time for him. Now, restless and preoccupied, Kim needed to slip out for a while. She needed time to think in a neutral place. Even her own apartment seemed smothering to her.

She turned away from the view, normally so comforting to her, a reminder of her goal to bring some kind of order out of the chaos of her world, and walked quickly to her car. There was one other place she needed to go. Now was the time. No sense putting it off any longer.

She drove to the warehouse where she had fought the creature. The North Side rushed by her in a blur, her attention focused only on her destination. In broad daylight, the slum district appeared more desolate, its people more hopeless. Sometimes Kim thought Lazo was wasting his time.

Parking across the street from the *Old Books and Research Haven*, she sat in the still-running car, gripping the steering wheel tightly. Finally, with a sigh, she turned off the ignition, checked to make sure her gun was in her purse and slowly got out. A couple of street people ambled up to her, wanting money or drugs. But the look on her face was like an invisible wall, causing them to back off.

Kim locked her car and, ignoring the stares she got from the few bystanders loitering in the 'hood', crossed the street. The area of her back between her shoulders tingled; her eyes darted back and forth. Even after two weeks, this part of the North Side still seemed to be a hunting ground, an abattoir that had her name written on it in blood.

Why was she so afraid?

Kim shivered and stopped in front of the alley that led to the warehouse. This was where she had found the three dead gang members and where the dog-man had attacked her. The side street was officially clean now, the investigative and forensic teams had moved on to other areas of inquiry.

That's not to say there didn't appear to be the usual signs of drug and alcohol usage littering the alley. Probably partying here now was a badge of some kind of sick honor, the deep urban equivalent of a rite of passage.

Kim walked into the alley, avoiding the loose garbage and broken glass, ignoring the graffiti. She glanced up, expecting to see a monstrous creature clinging to the wall.

THE SIXTH PRECEPT

At the warehouse door, she saw the new lock put up by the building's owners had been broken, the boards nailed across the threshold torn off, the door battered in. No surprise there. Like a challenge, a 'double dare', this was the place to be hanging out now especially since the owners apparently still didn't feel it was worth it to hire any security.

She took her gun out of her purse and entered. Dirt, cobwebs, a dusty, old smell greeted her. Oddly enough, a faint odor of cloves drifted within the gamy mix. The marks of several footprints lay outlined in the dust on the floor, no doubt from the investigating teams as well as looters, and vagrants and squatters who may have recently made this building their home.

She took a few more tentative steps and then turned, sensing…something. Cautiously, Kim moved deeper into the warehouse, all instincts firing. There was someone up ahead, near the other end of the building. Crouching behind an old fork lift, she cautiously peered ahead.

There, standing at the far end of the large room, almost hidden in the muted light, and clinging to a vertical wooden support beam, was the little girl.

My god. Kim ran to the girl. She knelt beside her, instinctively reaching out to push the girl's greasy hair back from her face. The girl grasped the beam as if her life depended on it. She looked thinner and weaker since Kim had last seen her, as if she hadn't eaten in days. Her clothes and body were filthy. Her eyes reflected a fear and shock Kim had rarely seen.

"On…*Oneesan*," the girl croaked from between cracked lips. "Mitsu…"

"You poor thing," Kim murmured. "How in heaven have you survived? Have you been hiding here these past two weeks?" As she gently pried the girl's hands from the beam, whispering soft reassurances in Japanese, Kim recoiled in shock.

She grasped the beam herself as a burning pain spread quickly through her head. She closed her eyes, dizzy, suddenly nauseous. She gasped as she saw them—distinct images, pictures that seemed to float in front of her, as if she viewed them from somewhere outside of her body…

(*She floated above and within an elaborately constructed structure, high on the summit of a mountain. A…a samurai? stood waiting below, his sword at the ready, hate and fear etched on his cruel face.*)

(*Another alleyway—she knelt in front of…this girl—but somewhere else, sometime long ago. A roaring wind, a blast of white light—and then the girl was gone.*)

(*Here, in the warehouse—a small storage area near the back of the ground floor…the girl, Shioko? Yes! Shioko was her name—sleeping there, curled fetus-like, crying, eating whatever she could find…too afraid and confused to leave.*)

The words came to her then, like before with the dog-man, from somewhere deep in her mind—*Do not be afraid to open one door; be wary of the many.*

*Oh…*Kim pressed her head to the beam, gulping air in great gasps. *What in heaven…?* She opened her eyes to see the girl lying on the floor, eyes fluttering closed. Her face was so pale. *She needs medical attention,* the lieutenant thought, as she put her weapon back in her purse. *I've got to get her out of here.*

And then, as when she had sensed the dog-man about to attack, a tingling feeling of anticipation enveloped her—Kim knew someone else was in the building. *No,* she thought, her skin beginning to crawl, *not again.*

As if looking through a thin piece of glass block, Kim could 'see' three men on the floor above her. Guns held tightly, they were descending the stairs to the first floor, quietly and with purpose, not like any gangbanger or street person at all. There was a definite vibe of subtle, purposeful malevolence and directed intelligence emanating from them.

Whoever they are, they heard me talking to…to Shioko. Kim's mind raced. *I've made us targets.*

She scooped up the girl and bolted for the door. *She barely weighs anything,* Kim thought absently as she reached the doorway.

Something intangible grabbed hold of her, a feeling of danger so strong it whirled her around. From out of the shadows at the far end of the room, three figures emerged into the muted light. Through the broken roof skylights, widening shafts of sun spotlighted the dark trio like surreal stage performers. Dust motes from the ceiling rafters whirled around them.

All three were dressed in black jeans, sneakers and T-shirts. The one in front, who radiated authority, also wore a thin black jacket and had some kind of amulet chained around his neck. Short and well built, with shoulder-length dark hair tied into a ponytail, he also looked to be Japanese. A random beam of overhead light briefly illuminated his face. Oddly, one of his eyes was blue, the other green. He held a gun pointed straight at Kim.

Those strange eyes widened. He seemed surprised. "That's far enough," he said softly, his voice as velvety and smooth as water. "Step back inside and out of the doorway please."

His amulet, the *ouroboros*—it was the same as what the dog-man had worn!

NO! Kim screamed in her mind. She felt her senses open up, a rising force of energy exploding within her. She stumbled backwards, a sharp pain in her head as she gripped Shioko tighter. As if a great wind had kicked up, boxes, crates and trash lying on the floor suddenly flew into the air directly at the three men.

As the men ducked and cried out, Kim turned and ran outside into the alley. Holding on to Shioko, she reached the street and risked a quick backward glance. No pursuit. The assorted junk from the warehouse had hit the men squarely, certainly knocking them off-balance, if not injuring them outright.

How did I do that? How?

Time to figure that out later. It was certain the three intruders had meant her and the girl harm. She had acted out of instinct, her street-smarts fading into the background. Something had just…happened.

A group of four young men were gathered around her car. A Toyota Prius probably didn't show up in this neighborhood very often. *Fuck off!* she shouted in her mind. With surprised looks, the men backed away, as if they had been slapped. As they watched her warily from the sidewalk, Kim fished her keys out of her pocket and remotely unlocked her car doors. She approached her vehicle and gently lay the girl in the back seat. *There's a clinic not far from here,* Kim noted, immediately vetoing going to Lazo's. They would be safer there but Lazo's medical supplies consisted of a first aid kit at best.

She jumped behind the wheel, started it up and roared into the street. As she sped away, a figure loomed within her rear-view mirror—one of the three men, the leader, appeared at the entrance to the alley, watching her retreating taillights.

He's got my license number, Kim thought. She smacked her hand against the steering wheel. *What in heaven is going on?*

CHAPTER 12

Wayne Brewster sat at his PC, nursing a cup of coffee, surfing the Internet and trying to differentiate between what was real and what was not. He had finished arranging his 'virtual office' just in time, it seemed. Working from home four days a week would give him a regular long weekend and he wouldn't have to put up with the jibes of his co-workers.

Of course, now, everything had changed. Holing up in his apartment since the incident at Lilly's Restaurant, only going out when absolutely necessary and only in his disguise, he had been waiting out the search for the hostages' 'savior'.

I can't believe no one recognized my description, he thought for the hundredth time. Probably anyone who knew him couldn't quite believe that the one who disarmed and overpowered the gunman could have been 'Tame Wayne'.

Judging from the latest news reports, the search was finally winding down. People didn't really care in the end and just went back to their own lives. Had it been some grisly murder or kidnapping, well…

Brewster was just glad he had been able to help but to be in the limelight and public eye—No way. Still, he was starting to get stir crazy. It had been two weeks after all. And lately, ever since Lilly's, he had been having trouble getting his realities straight. Sometimes he felt as if his dreams were taking over.

A web site description caught his eye as he surfed the net, an activity that now, out of boredom, kept him more occupied than usual. Thank God he hadn't gotten a Facebook account! "Old Book and Research Haven", the text read. He called it up.

Hmmm, interesting. Underground facility. Large unique collection. Comfortable and private reading rooms. Brewster had decided to hold off talking to anyone about his dreams for the time being and research them himself. He wasn't ready to reveal such a strange side of himself yet and, anyway, he was afraid what they might find out. Surely there was some rational explanation for what had been happening to him. Look what he had done at Lilly's! Again, it had almost been like something had taken him over.

Or someone.

His dreams had been powerful, so real. They had taken him on a journey through someone else's eyes in a world like his own yet very different. He was a hero in that other world, performing feats of strength and agility he could only, well, dream about. He was everything there that he was not in reality.

(*In* this *reality*.)

And yet, at Lilly's, he had become that hero.

OK, he thought. *I don't want to be labeled a lunatic yet. I need more information before I talk to anyone. This research haven might be a place to start.*

CHAPTER 13

She looked like an angel.

Kim turned away, caught off-guard by her sudden emotional reaction. She hadn't told the police about the incident with the three men in the warehouse yet, not sure exactly how she should report it. Right now, her main concern was Shioko, who she had brought back to her apartment. The young girl lay in Kim's bed, peacefully asleep. Shioko had been treated at the clinic--the nurse practitioners determined that she was dehydrated and needed some good, solid food, but otherwise was surprisingly fine. Antibiotics had been prescribed just in case.

Shioko's reaction to being in Kim's car, the streets of Pittsburgh, and the clinic itself, had been puzzling. She seemed either paralyzed with fear or completely unaware of anything around her. She had remained silent during her examination by the NP, her eyes closed and both trembling hands grasping Kim's with a steely grip.

Afterwards in Kim's apartment, she had allowed Kim to bathe and feed her (eating and drinking ravenously) and then immediately fell asleep as if completely exhausted.

It's like she fell out of the sky, Kim mused, gently touching Shioko's face. *Where did she come from?*

Now three weeks later…

The *Horowitz Box Factory* complex stood boarded up and neglected, most of its windows broken; its three multi-storied, brick structures connected by covered walkways; a tall smokestack tower looming over it like a giant stone overseer. It stood a forgotten industrial island in the middle of a sea of overgrown weeds, rubble and dust on the outskirts of the city's Strip District.

Spider webs of temporal lightning arced wickedly overhead. An aura of blue inter-dimensional iridescence surrounded the structures and their accompanying fenced-in parking lot with an astral pallor—at least that's what Kim Yoshima's mysterious caller had told her to expect. Surprisingly, those odd terms did mean something to Kim, having read similar theoretical descriptions in her friend (and Lazo's wife) Jenny Sibulovich's latest book on the 'quantum metaverse'.

"I have some information about the little girl," the voice had said over her cell phone (*how had he gotten my number?*). "I know you've taken her into your home. I know you're protecting her."

Kim's cover story was that Shioko was a 'visiting cousin' from Japan who had been ill. That seemed to ward off any undue questions. But, somehow, this caller knew.

Shioko was still painfully shy and fearful of almost everything and everyone except Kim. She clung to the lieutenant as if afraid Kim might literally vanish at any moment. It had only been in the last few days that Shioko had begun to calm down a little, allowing Kim to leave her in the temporary care of the Sibuloviches so Kim could meet her mysterious caller.

"And about your ancestor, Yoshima Mitsu," the voice had

continued. "Come alone. I know you're a police officer. Please don't inform anyone of this meeting. I'll know if you do and will be gone before you even get here."

Kim stared with a combination of fascination and bafflement at the display of blue spectral fireworks surrounding the factory. *Temporal lightning?* she thought in wonder. *Why doesn't anyone else seem to notice it?*

An early summer evening spread a cooling layer of air over the city. Wearing a light jacket and dressed in jeans and jogging shoes, Kim found the drop in temperature a welcome relief from the recent heat wave.

The rusty gate to the complex stood unlocked. Once the biggest and most productive factory of its kind in the country, *Horowitz*'s had been vacant for decades. Many would-be entrepreneurs had attempted to renovate it over the years but nothing, not apartments, not office space, not artists' studios, had ever worked out. And so, here it stood—dark, empty and eerily foreboding.

There's something happening here. She tapped her finger against her upper lip. *There's—*

Something clicked in her mind, directing her. She turned to her right and walked towards a pile of rubbish heaped beside a dilapidated parking attendant's booth. From under a batch of newspapers, she reached down and pulled out a banjo-like object. It was a beautiful piece of work. About four feet long, wooden with mother-of-pearl inlays, the three-stringed artifact felt like satin in her hands.

"Superb craftsmanship, don't you think?"

A man stood a few yards away, watching her. Tall and thin, dressed in green cargo pants, a thin cammo jacket over a black T-shirt and ankle-high black sneakers, he stared at Kim out of dark, piercing eyes. Short dirty blond hair crowned an angled, lined, thirty-something face—a face full of a calculating intelligence.

"But I've forgotten…It's a…?"

"A *samisen*," Kim finished his sentence, puzzled and surprised. "A musical instrument Japanese geishas utilize for their art. And it looks brand new." *What in heaven is it doing here?*

That same feeling of déjà vu that had gripped Kim in her encounter with the dog-man washed over her again. *I know him,* she thought with a chill as she refocused her attention on the stranger. Yet, despite the sudden apprehension starting to edge its way through her, she put the *samisen* down, rose to her feet and took a few steps closer.

As if reading her thoughts, the man smiled and said, "Yes. We knew each other once. Long ago." His voice was deep and gravelly as if he had been a heavy smoker all of his life. It was the voice she had heard on the phone.

"Impossible," Kim retorted. "I would remember."

The man nodded and looked away. "As I said, it was a long time ago."

"What's this all about? What do you know about—"

"Shioko?" The man turned his gaze back to her. "That is her name, you know."

Now it was Kim's turn to nod. Reluctantly. "And how do you know that?"

"Let's just say I have an interest in both you and the girl; that I've taken the time and resources to find out as much as I can about you and that it may be fortuitous for us to work together."

"Work together? What—?" At that moment, the blue aura surrounding the Box Factory flared up, its fiery radiance undulating wildly.

"What's wrong with it?" Kim said, her eyes widening in alarm. "What is that?"

The man jerked a sudden satisfied gaze toward her and then back to the building. "So you *can* see it," he said matter-of-factly. "The temporal energy surges? Are you familiar with that phenomenon?"

Kim found herself caught up in the incredible sight. "Yes, I think so, a little; only enough to know that they're just a theory. Is that what they're supposed to be?" Kim shook her head as she placed her fingertips to her temples. "It's more of a feeling I'm picking up on. Something…is wrong. The harmony of this place has been disrupted. It's as if the fabric of…of this space is being pulled apart."

The man pursed his lips in thought. "This is what we believe to be the epicenter of a temporal distortion, a rift in space-time." He paused, as if for effect. "Only those like myself who know what to look for or specialized telepaths can detect such an anomaly."

A rift in space-time? "What is this? Some comic book adventure? I don't have time for—" Kim stared straight ahead, her attention suddenly diverted. There was that tingling sensation in her head again. It forced her to look closer. "I see and feel…this anomaly a little more completely now," she said slowly, almost as if talking to herself. "It's blurry and indistinct, but it's there." She turned a concentrated, intense look back towards the man (*visions of her encounter with the dog-creature and the accompanying flashes of prescience came back to her, the way she apparently levitated those boxes in the warehouse, the psychic 'talent' her grandmother had always told her she possessed*). "You said telepath—"

"You're good, lieutenant. I started researching the city's law enforcement zones a few days ago based on some information we had recently obtained and your name just kept popping up. Your exemplary record caught my eye, among other things."

Kim shrugged, not knowing whether to be flattered or creeped out. "It's what I do. Get to the point."

"You have a gift, you know."

Kim cocked an inquisitive eyebrow. "Oh? What is that, a pickup line? Surely you can do better than that."

"You're a borderline telepath, no more than that—a possessor of many esper or psi powers. Possibly of a very high caliber. Ever get any hunches?"

"All the time." A pause. "Especially when I was a kid. What are you saying? That I really am telepathic?"

"Yes. Just like your ancestor, Yoshima Mitsu." A crooked smile. "It must run in the family."

Kim felt as if she were falling. "Enough! Tell me what this is all about and why we're here!"

"Of course. I did ask you to come here, after all." Again that pause. "My name isn't important. At least not in this life. Call me Parker for lack of anything else. My associates traced your license number. That's when I started checking up on you."

Kim moved another step closer. "Those men at the warehouse work for you?"

A shrug. "You might say that. Actually, I'm more of a consultant, I suppose. My unique knowledge and first-hand experience happen to be very valuable to a certain group of people at the moment. But I'm not here as a representative of that group but for myself. I have an offer for you."

He's serious, Kim thought, using her ability to read a person's face, their expression and body language. Plus there was something else, something she could sense, something dangerous. "Which is?"

Parker smiled again, cruel and calculating. "I'll show you.

My mind is completely open. Look inside it. You have the talent. See for yourself. You'd never believe me otherwise… about the *samisen*, you, Shioko, or your ancestor."

Kim snorted. "You think I'd do that? Do you think I'm that stupid to leave myself wide open for an attack? As if I would even know how in the first place!"

"Oh, but you do know how. The way of it is right there within you." Another shrug. "And don't forget the shadow-tracker. You'd like to know about him, I suspect."

Shadow-tracker? Kim backed up a step, drawing her weapon. The dog-man! "Who are you?" she hissed, pointing the gun at the man. "No more snide remarks and cryptic asides. Tell me!"

Parker held his hands at his sides and closed his eyes. "Come in and find out."

Maybe it was the fear and anger raging through her that allowed her instincts to waver; maybe her confusion about Shioko and the shadow-tracker caused her to lower her guard. Maybe Kim Yoshima just wanted to know.

In any case, she just let go, some latent talent uncovered. She opened her own mind to whatever forces had been released within her.

It was like opening a door, slowly and carefully, onto a rushing river. A mental buzz of voices and assorted neural noise assaulted her like a whirlwind.

She felt as if she were swimming underwater with her senses scattered. She was aware of a blank texture surrounding her, a roiling grayness. Within this ever-shifting layer ribbons of wispy, green matter rose and fell in a dizzying undulating rhythm, writing and coiling like snakes. Multi-colored bubbles shot past, moving in an oddly regimented formation before breaking apart and shooting off in every direction. In some imaginary distance, flashes of light flickered like the violent afterglow of fireworks.

There were voices too. A constant background babble of conversation rose and fell as if a million people were whispering and murmuring at once.

There was no warmth here in this mental never-never land, no cold, no physical sensations at all. Her senses seemed outside herself, observing as if she were floating above the world, if that word could indeed describe this environment. *Interesting,* she thought, trying to maintain an investigator's detachment. *Where exactly am I, anyway?*

Now and then an image appeared, briefly, like a patch of blue in a cloudy sky—people, places, objects—all from some file of memories, perhaps?

But she seemed to be going nowhere, her forward progress abruptly impeded. Sudden fear and confusion surrounded her. One of those patchy images widened and became a whirlpool of shredded colors, opening a jagged maw to suck her in.

A warm, fuzzy tingling enveloped her, a cocoon of white light, a pulling on her mind as if something had grabbed hold—a complete immersion—

Rage, anger, hatred. Lust, terror, madness. A black shape, indistinct yet powerful, lunged at her; a fanged slit of a mouth, piercing eyes that glowed with hunger.

NO!

She was standing in a field of waist-high wheat. A rolling meadow of amber grain stretched to the horizon, broken up into jigsaw patterns by a series of small vernal pools. The largest, a lake-sized body of water, glistened mirror-like in

120

front of her. Blue sky, almost cloudless, formed an endless roof over her head. She looked at her hands, her feet; she touched her face, rubbed her eyes.

This seemed like her body. She felt the warmth of the sun, the whispering of a warm breeze on her brow. Where was she? What had that thing been that had tried to attack her? *My god,* she thought, licking her lips, her body suddenly trembling. *If only grandmother could see me now.*

A sound of crashing timbers caused her to whirl around—a short distance away, a house and the field beyond it were engulfed in flames. Smoke curled into the sky, the smell of charred wood and burning earth filled the air.

Kim ran toward the house, her instincts back in gear. As she got closer, she was able to see behind the curtain of smoke and fire that billowed upwards.

Several naked bodies lay strewn around the outside of the house—four men, three women. All were blood-spattered and burned. What was left of their faces stared wide-eyed at some unseen horror.

Kim's mind raced furiously. Her heart was pounding, her hands started to sweat. She felt exposed and vulnerable, open to whatever danger this strange world might hold for her.

Was she in the mind of the mysterious Parker? Was this 'landscape' and these 'characters' some natural part of the imagination? Subconscious creations of some kind? Hallucinations on her part?

She whirled at a sound, like cannon fire but something more.

On the horizon, a line of darkness had inched closer. Lightning flashed out of mountainous thunderheads while a cold wind suddenly kicked up, blowing right through Kim. As the lieutenant watched, fascinated, the clouds twisted and roiled, swirling into a giant dark shape.

A dragon dropped from the sky, giant wings outstretched to blot out all light. Its red eyes gleamed as it flew straight for her.

(*a quickening darkness, a collapsing of the harmony that held this "world" together, a sudden surge in...evil*)

"Where are you?" she shouted. "Damn you, Parker! You said I could get the information I needed!" The dragon roared, emitting a blast of sound like exploding thunder. Kim looked up to see a wall of flame descending, a veritable pillar of fire spewing from the monster's mouth.

Kim gasped. She stood in the middle of an inferno. Columns of flame leaped and danced all around her. She felt the heat but stood impervious to the burning as if she had suddenly become fireproof.

"*Konichiwa*, Yoshima Mitsu."

Kim's heart caught in her throat. A figure out of ancient history stood before her, entwined in flames that coiled around his leather and chainmail-covered body like writhing, fiery serpents. His dark, almond-shaped eyes glinted as brightly as the surrounding inferno. A glimmer of a smile pinched his bearded, pock-marked face.

A samurai? She remembered the vision she'd had in the warehouse. *How?*

The warrior laughed then, a low mocking sound. His voice echoed something dark and sinister. His eyes shone like glistening, fathomless pools—older and more menacing than any human being's had a right to be. It was easy to see that the thing standing in front of Kim wasn't really a person at all but some manifestation, some mental doppelganger, created for this encounter.

"How?" the samurai-creature echoed. "Magic. A magic of the mind. A magic passed down to you by those that came before."

THE SIXTH PRECEPT

Despite the seeming reality of scorching heat, Kim shuddered with an icy fear. He looked like the samurai she had seen in her 'vision' when she found Shioko in the warehouse. "What...are you?" she asked though she already knew the answer. This was the thing she had seen earlier, the black shapeless thing. "Parker? The man in the parking lot?"

The samurai-creature nodded. "Parker is the entity whose body I inhabit in this modern world. But here in this ambient mental plane, I revert to my true form. I've been away a long time. Now I've returned and am ready to take back what is mine."

Ambient mental plane? "Who were those others? Those people at the burning house?" Kim's thoughts raced. This situation was so unreal, like a nightmare. How could you fight a nightmare?

"Them?" the samurai snorted. "Call them a last line of defense—avatars or incarnations of certain personality traits. Parts of the Parker entity that tried to fight my true nature, tried to stop what will be."

Poor bastard. The real Parker has been consumed by this thing. Kim felt the flames getting closer, the heat burning her skin. "Why are you doing this? What do you want?"

"You don't know who you are, do you, Ghost?"

"Ghost?"

The virtual warrior shook his head. "You don't realize how we have come to the beginning of the circle, you and I and your little girl. I didn't know either until the *kami* enlightened me, allowed me to see the being I had become in this...future time. I became empowered and was allowed to realize my past life, allowed to understand the destiny I had to follow as a modern western barbarian."

The samurai paused. "I am the Eminent Lord, Yoshima

Mitsu," he said, his eyes shining. "Do you not recognize me? I am, as you might say in these contemporary times, a reincarnated soul. And I have come back as I promised I would that day, so long ago, at the Pavilion of Black Dragons."

"Yoshima Mitsu? That's my ancestor, not me!" The Eminent Lord. She had heard that name before! And the Pavilion of Black Dragons. Why did that sound so suddenly familiar?

"Not so. You have certain powers of the mind. Just as you did so long ago. Make use of them. Look deep inside yourself and you will see. Learn who you really are so you and your little girl can—"

"Shioko? Never! You leave her out of this!"

The samurai cocked his head. "Shioko. Yes, I remember. That was her name. My shadow trackers ripped that knowledge from you, Yoshima Mitsu. "

A burning smell assailed Kim's senses—a smell of death and decay. She, or whatever this image of her was, gritted her teeth, her body shivered with an intense cold. This was a sickness facing her, a foul abomination of the human spirit. *God, help me.*

The warrior shook his head. "No one can help you now, Ghost," he said with a twisted grin.

"Quit bullshitting me. And stop calling me Ghost! What do you want?"

A laugh, cold and harsh. "What do you think? To be free. To practice my *gei* of conquest. I was reborn to kill you, to stop you from sending the girl back into the Void through the Spirit Winds. However, I have a proposition for you instead. Perhaps we can work together."

The Void again? Spirit Winds? What is he talking about? Kim's control started to falter. Anger and disgust filled her. "Work together?" she growled, her heart pounding. "I don't think so."

THE SIXTH PRECEPT

The samurai stared at Kim, a thoughtful expression creasing his terrible face. "I thought I could recruit you to our cause. Rather than kill you, why not employ your talent for the *Totou's* own ends. Working together we could build an empire."

"An empire? With you as *Shogun*, I presume. You're insane! This whole thing is insane!"

"Perhaps. But my associates are near to perfecting a method of traveling the Spirit Winds—temporal displacement tremors they call them, complete with aftershocks just like earthquakes. How do you think the *samisen* came to be where it was? A failed test but they are close to success now. Imagine the possibilities of traveling through time, the chances of perhaps rearranging history to our benefit."

Kim stared at him, her mind racing. *The samurai is from the past?*

"Ah, I see you're not interested, my Great Enemy. Or perhaps you just don't believe me." He sighed then, almost as if resigning himself to an inevitability he knew he couldn't, wouldn't be able, to change. "Very well. I'll stick to my original plan then. It's much simpler in the end. I will kill you and Shioko."

(*The inner self holds the true power; the outer exists only as a vessel.*)

"Like hell you will!" At that moment, Kim felt that surge of power again as if those words in her head had ignited a hidden fire. From somewhere deep in her mind, something clicked. Whether spurred on by her rising anger and fear or the powerful mental environment she found herself in, it coiled deep inside her.

Without even thinking she aimed that rising force straight at the one who called himself the Eminent Lord.

The flames around her and the samurai-creature leaped

and wavered as if blown by a giant gust of wind. The Eminent Lord started in surprise, its samurai façade withering as it put its hands up in front of its face.

Its true nature stood revealed now, its features twisted into an animal's rage. A dragon once again, the beast reared its massive body to its full height, wings unfurled., anger and madness flashing in its red eyes. The mythical creature opened its jaws and arched forward, shooting its fiery breath straight at Kim. *Stop!* Kim shouted into the mental slipstream. She raised her hand as if to ward off the approaching flame and felt the power that had enveloped her whirl her around in an ever-tightening grasp.

"Ugh!" Kim fell to her knees, the hard concrete of the parking lot slamming into her. Her head felt as if it had been clamped in a vice; her vision swam. She gasped, pulling her gun up to sight it at the back of the retreating "Eminent Lord." Her arms shook, the gun felt like it weighed a thousand pounds.

"Stop!" she cried hoarsely, this time aloud. "Stop or I'll shoot!"

But the man, Parker, vanished through a hole in the fence, staggering as if drunk. Apparently, Kim's mental defense had worked, both in and out of the killer's mind. But not enough to stop him from escaping.

Breathing deeply to relax and calm herself, Kim rose unsteadily to her feet. *How did I do that?* she thought. *How did I fight that thing?* She felt weak and drained and her head hurt. Before she turned to walk out of the parking lot, she noticed that her nose was bleeding.

THE SIXTH PRECEPT

A few minutes later, Kim approached Penn Avenue, the main artery of the Strip District. She held the *samisen* gingerly under one arm. The gentrified mercantile area was crowded, as was usually the case on a Saturday morning. Visitors came early to take advantage of the fresh produce that had been delivered before dawn at the adjoining Mon Wharf.

Street corner vendors and outdoor food stalls competed with an eclectic selection of restaurants, bars, fresh fruit and vegetable stores, fish markets and various merchandising outlets. Live music reverberated from the street, reflecting a multitude of cultures and ethnicities.

Kim had left Shioko with Lazo and Jenny at *DeLuca's* restaurant—a popular diner-style establishment and home of the "Best Breakfast in Pittsburgh"—so she could, ostensibly, meet with one of her 'underworld contacts' regarding the case she had been working on before her leave.

She stood in front of the *Pennsylvania Macaroni Company*, across the street from *DeLuca's*, and dialed Lazo's number on her cell phone (a replacement for her damaged one from Captain Mousadis). She had asked the Sibuloviches to join her and Shioko on a little outing in the city to give the young girl a kinder, gentler view of Pittsburgh. Shioko had seemed tentative and nervous at first but then became wide-eyed and excited, almost as if she had never seen a big city before. Again, she had clung to Kim yet still drank in all the sights. Kim had felt this was a breakthrough of sorts but the young girl's seeming ignorance of the modern world was worrying.

After only one ring, the big man's voice said, "Sibulovich, and this better be important."

A smile, despite herself. "Yo, Laz. It's me. No, don't say anything. It's bad manners to talk on your phone in a restaurant anyway, you know. Listen, I'm on my way in but I need to talk to you and Jenny later."

"OK. What's up?"

"I'm not certain. But I need to talk to someone and I'm not sure who I can trust or who would even believe what I have to say—even the guys on the force. Except for you two."

A pause. "Thanks. That means a lot. No problem."

"Great. Save some of that omelet for me, yes?"

Kim turned off her phone, closed her eyes. *I hope I'm not making a mistake telling them. I don't want anyone else put in danger but I don't think I can do this alone.* She took a deep breath and crossed the street.

PART THREE

Another Life

CHAPTER 14

Pittsburgh, Pennsylvania, 2010 C.E.

You are too involved. You, like your huntmate, would allow emotion and personal feelings to mar your judgment."

The shadow-tracker crouched in a corner of her cell, listening. Not all of what she heard had pleased her but it was one of her masters who spoke and all shadow-trackers had been bred to be obeisant to them. To act otherwise would be to face the displeasure and curse of the Eminent Lord and eventual death. That was one of the tacit imperatives of the *Totou*.

The man, short, stocky and dark, paced her cell. "Our agents are monitoring that city grid," he said. "If it is the Yomitsu you sensed there and she turns up again, we'll get her." He stopped to face her, his features unreadable, his strangely colored eyes boring into hers. She choked back a growl. Yes, this one was her master and she would obey but, sacrilege though it may be, her loyalty only went so far. He had been her and her huntmate's handler and had been cruel to both of them. They had been treated differently over the years, not like the other shadow-trackers. She had always wondered why.

And now her huntmate was gone. Wounded by the Yomitsu and taken into the Void.

"You have done well, my pet," her master said finally with a nod, and a rare smile quivering on his face. "But you must not be a part of this further because of your huntmate's involvement. We're still trying to confirm there was a rogue temporal displacement tremor at that location and our Mr. Parker is following up some leads of his own." He smiled again, clasping his hands behind his back. "Yet I feel we're close. I myself saw who I think may have been the Yomitsu and Ko. We went to the warehouse where your huntmate was killed to investigate and there was an incident."

He paused, looking troubled for a moment. "That cop did something. Something almost supernatural. But that kind of power won't help her. Killing her and possibly the young girl will be a glorious accomplishment and nothing must go wrong! Do you understand, dog?"

She nodded slowly, her body tight as a drum. As the shadow-tracker had suspected, the *Totou* had pulled back its operations after she had reported what she had seen and sensed. The attack by her huntmate and the possible appearance of the Spirit Winds had brought matters enough to the surface that the *Totou* might be noticed, something its members could not afford. Oh, as her master had indicated, inquiries had been made by the *Totou's* agents; a covert investigation had been instigated. She had not been told everything—most information was not deemed necessary for her or the others of her kind, they being bred and trained for one purpose only. But she suspected the *Totou* knew more than they were revealing.

How frustrated the shadow-tracker had been! The *Totou's* Great Enemy was so close! So close. What were her masters waiting for? The correct omen? This confirmation of the Spirit Winds her master had spoken of? Or was it something else? Politics also played a part in the *Totou's* machinations. Power struggles. Clashes of egos. Those self-defeating traits existed even within the ancient cabal.

THE SIXTH PRECEPT

Emotion and personal feelings, her master had said. Well, if emotion would end the life of the Yomitsu, then she would allow her judgment to be so tainted. The masters were too slow! Here was the object of their centuries-old search and they delayed the final outcome!

She realized the irony of her feelings. Such an attitude had killed her huntmate. But she couldn't help herself. And she found that she didn't care.

"I will keep you apprised," her handler said. "You do, after all, have an investment in this situation." He turned and walked out of her cell, locking the door behind him from the outside.

Investment? Words! Only words! The shadow-tracker shot from the corner of her cell, picked up the cot she slept on and smashed it against the floor. She howled then, head back, claws extended. All the pent up rage since she had lost her huntmate burst forth in a piercing shriek.

The Great Enemy had hurt her huntmate, causing him to be swept up into the Void. Curse the ages-old plan! She didn't care about the *Totou's* goals anymore. She had her own goal now and she *would* kill the Yomitsu!

CHAPTER 15

The book floated across the floor as if on butterfly wings, hovering over the *goza* mats that served as throw rugs in Kim Yoshima's apartment. Kim concentrated, adjusting the mental beam of energy directed at Yira's tome. Slowly, the book spun in mid-air and gently lighted on her custom-built *kotatsu* table, the traditional heart of any Japanese home.

Asian hanging scrolls, lush houseplants, and a brass *kirin* sculpture bore silent witness to her psychic testing.

OK, Kim thought with a triumphant smile, a bead of sweat creeping down her temple. *A little at a time. I've got to walk before I can run.*

She lay back on one of her two *zaisu* floor chairs, letting out a long, slow breath. The comfortable trickling of her rock fountain echoed softly in the background. The smell of green tea brewing wafted in from the kitchen. A typical enough home setting for the lieutenant except for her very unusual 'practice session'.

Tele or psychokinesis—that psi ability associated with moving physical objects—was one of the new powers she had discovered she possessed. The research she had done on psychic/telepathic skills had given her a starting point at discovering what she could do and, at least, a modicum of understanding since the incident at the warehouse. At first, utilizing those abilities had tired and frustrated her. Now she thought she might be getting the hang of it.

It's like I've awakened from a long, long dream. Or been reborn. Now she knew how some of those comic book heroes felt when they discovered they could fly or flame-on or see through walls. All this time she'd possessed these powers but, apparently, they had been latent, lying in her mind just waiting to be awakened. The attack by the dog-man had to have been the catalyst that brought them to the surface.

A smile as she picked up the book—"*The Teachings of Yira--The Five Precepts to Enlightenment* by Samuel Kim". *Grandmother knew. And she tried to tell me. Through this book. I'm sure of it but it's all so convoluted!*

All Kim had ever really wanted to do was to help people— to restore the harmony of those who had lost it from their lives. Her grandmother had inspired her to such thinking. Though Kim had left Japan with her family when she was only five, she had reestablished contact with her father's mother in later years before the old woman had died. With her simple ways, Grandmother Ayako Mitsu had filled Kim with her ancient stories and strong philosophy of life. It was Mitsu who had first told Kim she possessed this gift.

"A gift of the mind and spirit," Grandmother had said, her rheumy eyes sparkling. "A gift of wonder. It lies hidden from you now but use it well when it becomes known to you, Kimmy-chan, when it reveals itself to you at last. Use it to help others and you will forever live in harmony."

She had never really known what Grandmother had meant then but now…Being a cop had fulfilled Kim's desire to be of service to a point. But now she had an opportunity to do something more.

If only she could figure out how to accomplish that. These

psychic abilities were like something out of a movie!

She put the book down, got up and crossed her living room to the spare room, opened the door and peeked in. No longer her work area, it had been refashioned into what it had been originally intended for—a bedroom. Gone were the PC and printer, filing cabinets, fax machine, written notes, and mountains of news clippings. A young child now lay asleep on a futon surrounded by stuffed animals. Posters of the Japanese countryside and hanging scrolls of cherry blossoms and Japanese script hung on the walls. A decorative rice-paper *shoji* screen stood in front of the closet door. Kim had moved her small marble lion-dog sculptures (protectors against evil spirits) from her living room to stand guard on Shioko's bedside table.

The *samisen* stood cradled on a guitar stand in a corner of the room.

Not like a normal eight-year-old girl's room would look like, Kim knew, but this certainly seemed right for Shioko.

Kim paused a moment to gaze at the slightly troubled, sleeping face of Shioko. In the three short weeks she and the young Japanese girl had been together, they'd formed a bond, perhaps not yet as sisters or friends but close, despite the cultural and linguistic barriers. Kim smiled, blinking back sudden tears. She had always wanted children but had never thought she'd acquire one the way she had Shioko.

The guardianship process she had set in motion was going slowly since no one could contact any of the girl's relatives. An identity and fingerprint search of Shioko had revealed nothing. It was as if Shioko had just appeared out of thin air. Kim was just barely holding off the social services people and their questions. Luckily, Lazo had some contacts in the system who owed him some favors (was there anyone who didn't?).

They had helped keep the proverbial wolf from the door.

Kim tip-toed softly to the bed and knelt on the floor. Her hand gently touched the child's silken hair, a far cry from the dirty, lice-infested mess it had been. Shioko moaned and rolled over on her side. "Having trouble sleeping again, I see," Kim whispered. *Maybe I can help.*

Kim closed her eyes and focused. She was tentative with certain aspects of this mental telepathy or esper stuff or whatever it was called. She knew there was power there but controlling it, even realizing its limits and potential, were the hurdles she faced now.

Just like scuba diving and mountain climbing, she thought. *Never do it alone. Always have a partner. That's what I need now. Someone to help me navigate my way through this.*

That's the part she hoped Lazo and Jenny would play. The three of them had arranged to meet at the research haven to talk later. Kim knew it would be hard to tell them what had been happening to her but if she could demonstrate her powers.

Sleep, sweetie, she thought as she tentatively reached for Shioko's mind. Kim had discovered that certain regions of the mind could be accessed and massaged. Though Kim couldn't actually 'read' anybody's mind as yet, the gist of what that person was thinking or what emotions they were feeling could be gleaned.

And she had been able to utilize her blossoming mental abilities in other ways. Levitating objects, like Yira's book and the crates and boxes in the warehouse, and 'sensing' events before they actually happened, had become stronger.

And then there was the incident with the dragon in the 'ambient mental plane'. Kim still wasn't sure how she had managed that!

In the meantime, Shioko had served as a test subject, in a

way, giving Kim a lot of practice in using her psi powers. Kim tried to augment her attempts at communication with the girl with mental nudges and hints. The learning process had been slow and arduous between the two. In the beginning, Kim's fluent Japanese had allowed her and Shioko to converse on a basic level. But Shioko's odd dialect and phrasing hadn't always matched with what Kim understood.

But was it more than that? There were other missing picccs to the young girl besides her lack of identity and strange speech patterns—Shioko's mannerisms, her non-recognition and fear of so many commonplace things, the small bursts of mental images Kim managed to pick up from the girl—all hinted that Shioko might be someone radically displaced.

There were these Spirit Winds (the temporal displacement tremors the mysterious Parker had alluded to?) Shioko had spoken of. As incredible as it sounded, could Shioko, like the *samisen*, be from the past?

It would explain so much. But to accept that possibility, like the existence of the shadow-trackers and the 'ambient mental plane', well, it would mean the world was so much different that anyone had imagined.

To make matters more difficult, the girl had been frightened and disoriented after her somewhat disheveled arrival. She was reluctant to say much about herself. She continued to sleep fitfully, experiencing disturbing nightmares, waking up screaming in ancient Japanese. "Mitsu-san!" she had shouted into the dark on more than one occasion. "Mitsu-san!"

Mitsu. Surely a common enough name in Japanese. But Kim couldn't help but wonder again—Mitsu was what everyone had called her grandmother. And then there was her ancient ancestor—the shirabyoshi, Yoshima Mitsu, not to mention the 'Yomitsu', the title uttered by the dog-man that had attacked her outside of Lazo's reference haven. An unsettling set of coincidences.

And that had been what Shioko had called her when they had first met—"Mitsu-san," she had said. "Help me, elder sister!"

Why is she here now? With me? she wondered, as she recalled another old philosophical adage her grandmother used to recite to her. "There are no coincidences, Kimmy-chan," Grandmother Mitsu used to say. "Everything is connected."

Satisfied now that Shioko would sleep peacefully, Kim got up, gently closed the bedroom door, and went back into her living room. Not much would bother Shioko now for a few hours; an undisturbed rest part of what she needed. In the meantime—

She sat down on the futon and abruptly looked up.

(*Someone is right outside my apartment building.*)

"Lieutenant Yoshima, sorry to disturb you—"

"Hey, Joe. What a surprise. And isn't it about time you started calling me Kim?"

A nervous laugh on the other end of the intercom. "Yes, ma'am. Do you mind if I come up? I was headed this way and Mr. Sibulovich had a new book he wanted me to drop off. Said you'd probably be interested."

"Oh! Great. Sure, I'll buzz you in." Kim smiled. A middle-aged African-American and ex-marine, Joe Martin cut a pretty impressive figure whether in his security uniform or street clothes. Tall with an athletic build, he exuded authority and a certain quiet strength. Kim had liked him from the first moment they had met though he could be a little too formal at times.

THE SIXTH PRECEPT

She strode toward the door when her bell rang, distracted, thinking about Shioko and the strange events of the past few weeks. Without a second thought, she reached for the door's deadbolts and slid both aside. She unhooked the privacy chain and only then did her mental alarms go off.

The door slammed inward from the outside, knocking her off-balance. Two people stood in the hall beside Joe—the man-in-black from the warehouse and one other—Parker, the so-called Eminent Lord. A waft of clove drifted in from the hallway. Joe was pushed forward, a gun at his head.

The dark one lunged into her apartment, the hand at the end of his outstretched arm holding another weapon.

There was a popping sound. Kim felt a stinging sensation on her neck. She stumbled backwards a step as Parker followed the dark man into her apartment, shoved an anguished-looking Joe further into the room, and closed and locked the door.

Kim's legs buckled as a fierce heat spread throughout her body. Her arms suddenly felt as if they each weighed a ton.

Drugged! She thought. *Shioko!*

She turned towards Shioko's room, her body feeling as though it were made of stone. The *tatami* mats on the floor rose up to meet her as she fell, her head thick and cottony. She put her hands out to break her fall; they crumpled under her like cardboard.

Stunned, rapidly losing consciousness, her breath coming in slow gasps, Kim managed to roll over on her back. Her attacker stood over her, dressed in black, long dark hair curling over his shoulders, Asian features, one green and one blue eye.

Shioko! Kim cried in her mind. *Have to...*

Parker's face floated in front of her. "We meet again," he said, his voice thick and hoarse, his manner agitated, excited. "Do you know how long I've waited for this, Ghost? I told you

I would come back for you."

Ghost again? Kim's eyes fluttered and she was pulled into darkness.

It was different this time. She felt a tightening rush, as if drawn inexorably forward toward some actual physical destination; a flash of white light encompassed her.

She stood in a wooded glade, surrounded by delicate Japanese maples and stylishly trimmed topiary. A brilliant blue sky arched overhead, dotted with clouds and flitting birds. A gentle breeze carried with it the scent of fresh cherry blossoms. Sunlight, like a comforting blanket, spread a lambent brilliance throughout. Lying in front of her, an inset stone path led up to an ornately carved wooden dais.

On that dais stood a woman, her back to Kim as she looked outward onto a vast ocean, its calm waters a crystalline green. She turned slowly to face the lieutenant.

The woman was Japanese, dressed in ancient Japanese clothing, in the formal *jyunihitoe* style once worn by the more affluent women of that centuries old, medieval time. A red split skirt with its train of white silk fitted beneath a red over-garment. An open green and gold robe reached floor-length to set off the other colors in a burst of woven radiance. Silver *soris*, or slippers, peeked out from beneath the robe.

A circlet of gold, a *saishi*, had been placed over her hair which was done up in an elaborate topknot. Kim blinked, her breath catching in her throat. She was beautiful! But men, two men, had invaded her apartment; Shioko and Joe were at their mercy. She had to help them!

How and why was she here?

THE SIXTH PRECEPT

"You will experience this place in but the blink of an eye." The woman cocked her head, her features white with face paint, her lips a ruby red, her eyebrows plucked. Her hands were held together in front of her within the folds of her robe.

She bowed to Kim and said in clear English, "But first, I will tell you why you are here. You follow the path I once did. I stumbled and fell from that path. You must not."

"I...I don't understand. Where am I? Who are you?"

A slight smile. The woman moved towards her, not walking exactly, more like floating. Her every movement was filled with grace and beauty and the most minimal of motion. She stopped within inches of Kim.

"I am Yoshima Mitsu," she said, matter-of-factly.

Kim felt her mouth drop, if indeed she possessed a mouth in this ghostly realm. "My ancestor," she breathed. "How can this be? Am I dreaming? Am I dead?"

The woman shook her head. "Neither," she said. "You are very much alive. And I am more than just your ancestor. I am you, Kim Yoshima. And you are me—in another incarnation."

Kim knew she should be dizzy with disbelief, that she should be screaming to get out of this place. But she stood, entranced by the woman in front of her, transfixed and waiting to hear what she would say next.

"I am not permitted to tell you everything," she continued. "Such are the laws that govern this spectral realm. We have little time here and there is much you must discover for yourself. This part of the psychic milieu we exist in now, this Dreamspace, is a place between, a place where those who have crossed through the Veil of Life to the Plain of Heaven as I have can meet with those like you who have not. There are other levels within the ambient, some of which you must discover for yourself, levels of mental energy and thought, of physical manifestation that rivals what you know as reality. Suffice to say that we have been brought together on *this* level so that I may help you."

So there is life after death? Kim thought in shaken wonder. Or was this all some kind of elaborate dream? "The shadow-tracker and the…the Eminent Lord—"

"Yes. I faced them in my time. Now you must face them in yours."

"But how?"

"You have the powers of the mind as I once did but do not know fully how to employ them. I will help you to breach the walls in your mind that block the knowledge of those powers from you. And, thus, you will be able to employ your gift in any situation. But you must use that knowledge to help Shioko, to defeat the Eminent Lord and his minions."

"Of course! But how can I do that?" Kim asked again, her head spinning. "What is this all about? And who *is* the Eminent Lord?"

"One who bodes ill for more than just you and Shioko, one whose identity you must discover for yourself." Mitsu looked away, her gaze focused somewhere distant. "I sent Shioko away so long ago, knowing someone would find her; not realizing it would be you." A smile. "Or me."

She focused that gaze on Kim. "Shioko is from your time's past as I think you have already guessed. The time I lived and died in. She was my attendant and holds the key to defeating the Eminent Lord."

"Impossible!" Kim felt herself shaking, whether with fear or anger, she couldn't tell, even though she had suspected what Mitsu had just told her. "This isn't real! It's the drug they shot me up with. This is all just an hallucination brought about… brought about by what I read in Lazo's library."

"No." The Mitsu figure looked sad for a moment. "You are indeed like I...*was*—strong-willed with a need to see things for yourself. Very well. I will nullify this drug's effects. There is a place in your mind I can strengthen to block the drug's weakening powers. This much have I learned in this realm and am allowed to do for you. You must return and help your friends with the new knowledge of your psychic abilities. You must talk to Shioko—touch her with your mind. She may still be fearful of revealing her memories but you must try."

Kim felt herself wavering, her body being pulled again. "Wait!" she shouted. "Not yet. I have so many more questions—"

"Use the gift you have been given," Mitsu said at the last. "It is greater than what I possessed. You cannot turn away from it!" And then right before Kim dematerialized, "And remember the teachings of Yira! The words in your head..."

My god! Kim thought, as she jerked spasmodically. She was back in her apartment, trembling and out-of-breath. She sat down on the floor, drawing her knees up to her chin, breathing slowly and blinking the tears from her eyes. *God in heaven,* she thought. *It feels like my head's on fire.*

A murmur of voices from her kitchen grabbed her attention. Slowly, she got to her feet, her knees weak and her head still throbbing. Joe lay near the balcony windows. He was bound and gagged with duct tape; even his eyes and ears were covered. Somehow he had managed to scrape off the tape masking one of his eyes. Seeing Kim wake up, he struggled to a sitting position and nodded frantically towards the kitchen with his head.

Damn them! she thought, as she motioned for Joe to lie still.

She tiptoed over to the far wall near the hallway to the kitchen and leaned against it, listening.

"You've been paid," a vaguely familiar voice said, cool and edgy. A slight inhalation as if the speaker was taking a drag from a cigarette. That clove smell again. "I took a chance listening to you and allowing you to come with me. But you've been right every time, I'll give you that. She's the one I encountered in the warehouse and, no doubt, the one my lost shadow-tracker found. I'll handle it from here. Now take the money and go before I change my mind."

His *shadow-tracker?* Kim felt a chill in the pit of her stomach.

"I'll go. And you can have her to do with what you will." Parker. "But I need to do something first."

"Which is?"

"It will only take a few minutes."

"Look! She's already beaten one of my shadow-trackers and the Eminent Lord only knows what else she can do! It looked like she actually caused that junk in the warehouse to freaking levitate!"

"Yes," Parker agreed softly. "I imagine she did."

"The sedative will keep her out for at least another hour but she's not to be underestimated in any case. Whether she's really the Yomitsu or not! That's why I didn't shoot the security grunt—he'll be easier to handle and I want to keep these darts reserved specifically for her, just in case. I need to interrogate her first before I bring her to the *Totou*."

Kim closed her eyes. *The Yomitsu!* Her skin crawled. *That's what the shadow-tracker called me.*

"Oh, she's formidable, all right. And she *is* the Yomitsu. And who do you think *I* am?"

Shrewdly, "Someone with information he's not supposed to have. Normally you'd be dead by now but—"

THE SIXTH PRECEPT

"You can't afford to kill me. Believe me, not with what I know. I thought about revealing my true nature to you but that may not be wise at this point. I can see now how this works out. I see what part you will play in the future, or I should say the past, of this little drama. That's how I knew how to contact you, how to find you and the rest of the *Totou*. Interesting. But maybe I *can* change things a little. Just a little."

"What the hell are you talking about?" Another pull on the cigarette. "Is it more money you want? No problem. Once I bring her back to my superiors, I'll be set for life. And you can have anything you want as long as you keep your mouth shut."

"Ko is the one I want. She's here too, you know."

Ko. The Totou again.

A pause. "Ko? The little girl I saw in the warehouse? How the hell do you know all this? And you better be telling the truth."

"Come. Now I'll show you Ko, brought to this time and place by the very temporal displacement tremors you seek to harness for your own ends."

He's talking about Shioko! Kim glanced down the hall toward her own bedroom. Her gun was there. She'd waited too long; she wasn't going to have time.

Parker was the first to enter the living room. Kim grabbed him by his shirt collar and threw him forward. The man grunted, tripped up by Kim's outstretched leg, and fell onto the floor.

Kim whirled and faced the surprised dark man. Before he could get off another shot of his dart gun, Kim spun and landed a high kick on the man's outstretched arm. The dart gun flew in the air back into the hallway behind him.

The dark man responded with a kick of his own. Kim blocked it with both hands, leaped up and slammed her foot squarely on the man's black-clad chest.

As the man fell backwards, Kim turned and sprinted for her bedroom. A shout behind her—she turned to see Parker on his knees, his gun drawn. There was a crashing noise—Joe had managed to knock her standing lamp over. It was enough to momentarily distract Parker.

She dove through the open doorway of the bedroom, kicking the door shut and locking it behind her. As she ran to her dresser, the door thudded with Parker's or the dark man's weight thrown against it.

Shioko was in danger. But they were on Kim's turf now. The luger—her weapon was gone. Damn them! They had probably taken it after knocking her out.

She threw open her closet. There, leaning in the corner, stood a long, elegant weapon her grandmother had given to her years ago. According to Grandmother Mitsu and through some reading of her own, Kim had discovered it to be a *naginata*, a weapon of choice among ancient Japanese warrior monks. She had always meant to display the weapon somewhere in her apartment but had never gotten around to it. Now, it just might come in handy.

She stopped, feeling the heft of the weapon as she balanced it in her hands. Sleek and expertly crafted, a sword guard, or *tsuba*, ringed the upper third right below the curved blade, its design that of two intertwined dragons. *Dragons again*, she thought. *Well, this is one dragon that's going to fight on* my *side!*

She listened at the door, now quiet outside. She tried casting a mental scan, something she was just finding out she could do—the hallway seemed to be empty. Unlocking it, she flung open the door and stepped back. Nothing. Both men were no longer in the living room. Joe still knelt on the floor, straining at his restraints—*Go, Kim, damnit! He's with your little girl!*

I heard that! Kim thought, with an unexpected exhilaration.

THE SIXTH PRECEPT

I heard his thoughts! Her ancestor had told her that she would help her to have access to those parts of her power she hadn't been able to use. No time to ponder that miracle now—she ran out into the hall and stopped at Shioko's room. Her back to the wall, standing beside the doorway, she held the *naginata* in both hands, trying to calm her rapidly escalating heartbeat. She closed her eyes and…

There! She could see within the bedroom; that 'force' again, blossoming within her like a hot flash; the ability to use it was ubiquitous, like breathing or blinking your eyes. She only had to will it. The scene coalesced in her mind's eye—an image quivery and indistinct revealed as if Kim were looking at it through a smoky mist.

Parker stood over the sleeping child, pointing his gun at the girl's head. The one who called himself a reincarnated soul was looking at the doorway as if wanting Kim to enter, to watch him perform his heinous act of murder.

There was no trace of the dark man, as if he had simply fled.

How do I make this work? she asked herself frantically. *This power that I have, how can I use it?*

Kim didn't care about herself but Shioko had to be safe.

"Parker," she called out, resorting to her own negotiating tactics, the ones that had served her so well in the past. "Let Shioko go. This is between you and me."

"Ah, perhaps," came the gloating reply. "My so-called associate has left, it's true. So much for loyalty and courage. He fears his masters more than he lets on. If they discover he had the vaunted Yomitsu at his fingertips…" A slight pause as if Parker had just realized something. "Well," he said. "I wonder how you revived from the sedative so quickly?"

"Look," Kim said, gripping the *naginata* until her knuckles turned white. "We need to talk. You obviously have information about what's been happening to me. About Shioko. Information I need to know. Can we make a deal?"

Parker laughed. It sounded like chalk squeaking on a chalkboard. "I tried offering you a full partnership once. You refused. So here is the deal—I will kill the little one here and then you. Agreed? Ko's the key, the one who will complete the circle. I will put a stop to that. I—"

Kim didn't wait for Parker's tirade to end. Through the wall, she mind-cast an esper tether. She grasped one of the lion-dog statues with unseen fingers—just like the book she had practiced with. The statue sprang off the table as if it had a life of its own, crashing into the wall on the opposite side of the room.

She burst into the room, hurling the *naginata* like a javelin at the startled and distracted Parker. At the same time, her mind once again found that power within her. Backed by fear and desperation, Kim put every force of her emotions into that telekinetic force.

Parker jerked as if slapped, his gun hand arcing toward the ceiling. The *naginata*, clumsily angled in mid-flight, hit him broad-edged in the face, snapping his head back. Parker fell back against the wall as Kim telekinesed another invisible punch.

Parker dropped his gun. Holding his hands to his head, he uttered a scream of his own and fell to the floor.

Kim bent over and grasped the *naginata*, never taking her eyes off of the body lying in front of her. He lay still. A thin line of blood trickled from one ear. His eyes were wide and staring. Kim knelt down and felt for a pulse. He was dead.

"Damn you," Kim whispered between clenched teeth. "Don't leave me not knowing." Tentatively she reached out with her mind, probing, trying to make some kind of contact.

She felt smooth tendrils of thought uncoil from her own mind, searching, cast out like a psychic net.

Nothing. Parker, the Eminent Lord reborn, was gone.

She looked at Shioko, miraculously still sleeping. Suddenly the child opened her eyes and sat up. She looked curiously at Kim, fully awake, it seemed, smiled, and said, "Hello, *Oneesan*. I have so much to tell you!"

Kim stared. Shioko had never spoken a complete sentence in English before despite Kim's tutoring. Kim felt the hairs on the back of her neck tingle. "Shioko?" she asked.

Shioko cocked her head to one side as if listening to some inner voice. "I can talk to you, *Oneesan*. And I can understand. It was the Eminent Lord's gift to me. Is that not wonderful?"

"I'm sorry, Lieuten…Kim. I was careless. It could have cost you and your girl your lives. There's no excuse for that."

Kim stood at her apartment door talking with Joe Martin. The ex-marine could barely meet her eyes. His face reflected anger and self-reproach.

"It wasn't your fault, Joe," Kim replied honestly. "None of us knew there was some scumbag stalking me and watching my place."

"I wasn't paying attention. They must have known who I was. They waited until I rang the buzzer and forced their way in. Any idea who they were?"

"No." Kim looked away. "Not really."

The police and forensics staff had left and the body of the 'stalker' who had invaded Kim's apartment had been taken away to be identified and autopsied. Kim and Joe had been interviewed by the investigating officer and a description of the dark man had been given.

The autopsy would reveal, Kim was sure, that a cerebral embolism had been the cause of death. With a police officer's experience to fall back on, she had given some pretty convincing details on how that had happened, ones she thought would not be questioned. An APB would be put out on the dark man.

Somehow, though, Kim suspected he wouldn't be found.

"Besides," she continued, smiling at Joe, "if you hadn't knocked my lamp over, that maniac may have shot me." *And I heard your thoughts! That's some kind of milestone.*

"Yeah, well, I owe you for a new lamp anyway."

Kim laughed and shook Joe's large hand. "Thanks but this book you brought me will make up for it. Go home and forget about it."

The girl seemed fine, had, in fact, hardly stopped talking, now that she could.

"So you are not my mistress Mitsu-san?" Shioko asked, her eyes wide with innocence. "But you look just like her; you seem just like her."

How do I answer that? Yes, I'm the reincarnation of your mistress? That I am her *in a future life? Better not to say too much yet.* "No, honey, I'm not although I think we might be distantly related. You said you had so much to tell me. What do you want to talk about?"

A shy smile crept over the young girl's face, suddenly full of excitement and anticipation. "Everything," she said. "I want to tell you everything."

"Well, young lady." Kim smiled. "Maybe you can start by explaining what you meant by the Eminent Lord's gift to you.'"

Shioko's face fell. She looked down at her hands. "Oh," she said. "That."

THE SIXTH PRECEPT

Kim took both of the girl's hands in hers. "You don't have to, honey," she said softly. "There...there might be another way."

Kim settled back into the couch. *Well,* she thought, letting out a long breath. *This should be interesting.* And, like the figure of her ancestor had suggested, she touched Shioko with her mind.

PART FOUR

Circle of Souls

CHAPTER 16

Somewhere between Philadelphia and Pittsburgh, Pennsylvania, 2010 C. E.

The young woman stood astride a motorcycle on the side of the road, her sloe eyes staring thoughtfully towards the horizon. Someone driving by might have mistaken her for a photographer's model getting ready for a shoot or some young Goth chick pondering the mysteries of life.

The black jeans, boots and T-shirt she wore added to that mystique. Her short dark hair fit her sharp-featured face like a cap, cut in bangs just above her arched, thin eyebrows. Slim yet athletic-looking, she seemed caught between daydreams, as if not quite in the moment.

The bike was an old Vincent Black Shadow, a real collector's item, she had been told, in almost mint condition. It had taken a little effort to buy it off of its reluctant owner but her rationale was she would put the motorcycle to much better use.

And there was the look she had adopted. Her friend, the one with her now, had described it—the mysterious woman in black. Why not? She had assumed several personas in her short life. Why not one more?

She had never ridden before this afternoon but she was good at picking up on new things and the situation demanded a speedy response. A backpack tied to the rear of the bike held her old clothes and some souvenirs of her previous life. She didn't want to leave everything behind.

The same with her male companion, leaning against an old Harley. Older, duskier-skinned and dressed similarly, he had lived previously and longer in this world they had returned to. He seemed more comfortable, almost eager to refamiliarize himself with his original life.

They were about two hundred miles from the city on a quiet backcountry road, devoid of traffic. The sky was a deep blue, the air sweet-smelling and calm. Wooded groves on either side of the road whispered of quiet refuge and safe harbor. She could hear birds, the buzzing of insects. From a distant farm, the faint odors of hay and manure drifted on the breeze.

But despite the urge for some peace in her life, some end to this 'destiny' the young woman found herself following, she had to get to the city. And soon.

"Did we have to arrive so far away from the Nexus Point?" she questioned, a little irritation starting to show.

"Couldn't be helped," her companion answered, running a hand over his shaven head. "Remember? It would have been too dangerous to arrive anywhere near there at this time. Paradoxes and interdimensional glitches and all that. We have to get there by so-called normal means and as inconspicuously as possible. That's why we had to get these clothes first and then the bikes, not to mention directions to where we're going. Plus you know how unreliable the method we used to get here is. It's a wonder we were able to figure out how to ride the time streams at all!"

"I know." She sighed and put on her helmet. The consensus was this was the best they could do under the circumstances. "I'm just glad we're together. I'm going to need your help."

A laugh. Despite being a few years older, her companion

still looked boyishly youthful. "You didn't need our help at the Pavilion of Black Dragons all those years ago."

"Years?"

"Relatively speaking, of course."

The woman smiled. She seemed to come back into herself, her manner relaxing just a little. "Yes, that was my time, wasn't it, even though I was scared to death!"

"It's still your time. Look at all we accomplished—you and me and Midori and Hiroshi. You've made all of us proud. Now, let's go. We've got to be in the city before sunset."

Midori and Hiroshi, she thought sadly. *I just saw them yesterday but today they and everyone else we've known and loved has been dead for five hundred years.* "It'll be great to see everyone again although…I'm afraid. It's been so long." She paused, with a rueful grin. "Relatively speaking, that is."

"No need for fear. You know pretty much how this turns out."

"If we're lucky. If the timelines run true-to-course. If there are no unexpected variables popping up. If, if if…" The woman took a deep breath, donned her helmet, kick-started the Vincent and cruised on down the road.

CHAPTER 17

There was a moment when he thought he would fall.
He could imagine it as clearly as if a video was running in his head—his body twisting and tumbling from the skyscraper's parapet; his screams barely audible over the frenetic noises of the city; his arms flailing, trying to find purchase where there was none; his fragile life shattered on the pavement below.

But that other part of him, the dominant half of the duality that empowered this shared body, recovered in time as always, balancing on the building's edge as easily as a cat.

But who was he? He wasn't this other, he knew that—this powerful, agile entity. This persona that he shared minds with wasn't him (here, wherever here was, somebody else was driving—he was only a reluctant passenger).

Yet, in some way, some distant, almost alien fashion, he knew this *was* his true self.

Below and around him, the city sprawled, its millions of lights glittering in the dark, its sleek, modern superstructure vaulting into the night sky. This was the *other's* turf, his hunting ground, and yet he felt its pull also, it being so much like his own home. A jungle constructed of concrete, steel and glass, it called out to him, beckoning him with a dark, seductive voice.

Against all reason (*his* reason) he stepped off the parapet into the thin night air. Cold wind shot past him as he flipped over and plummeted headfirst toward the street dozens of stories below. His cape streamed out behind him like a giant wing; his outstretched, gloved hands positioned him into a diving stance. The illuminated windows of the skyscraper beside him raced past and blended into one continuous ribbon of light; the ground rushed up hungrily to meet him.

No! he wanted to scream (if only he could!). *What are you doing?!* But that other part barely held in check an exhilaration, a burning of the blood and spirit that was almost intoxicating. He was flying! Flying!

Suddenly his arm shot out, whipping a wire-thin rope towards the side of the building opposite him. Somehow, the grappling mechanism on the tip of the rope caught and he swung smoothly towards another ledge, several stories below the parapet.

No, not toward the ledge—toward one of the windows above it. His hard, muscular body crashed through the glass like a battering ram, catching the occupants of the office inside completely by surprise.

It took him only a heartbeat to analyze the situation— three men, one with a drawn gun, held a fourth prisoner. The victim lay in a corner of the room, his face bloody, his clothes ripped and disheveled. The two men without visible weapons had been ransacking the office. Papers, CDs, flash drives and file folders were strewn everywhere; desk drawers had been pulled out and overturned.

His mind ticked off the visible facts, coolly, calmly, deductively, in the blink of an eye. Robbery of some type, that was certain. But he could tell that the three were thugs, hired muscle paid to do somebody's dirty work. The *other*, with him in mental tow, had spotted them from his high vantage point on the opposite building, like a raptor honing in on his prey.

THE SIXTH PRECEPT

It all happened so fast then as everything changed. He became integrated with the powerful body he inhabited—a fighting machine, arms and legs moving in a deadly, efficient blur. Before the thug with the gun could blink, he had grasped his wrist and broken it, the gun clattering to the floor. As the thug sank to his knees howling in pain, he whirled on the other two. Both had their own weapons revealed now, one a knife, the other a taser. Moving like the wind, he kicked the closest in the chest, the taser sparking harmlessly toward the ceiling. With a cry of pain, the man fell into his comrade and both hit the floor like so many battered bowling pins. He was on them both in an instant. When he was done, the three were lying unconscious on the floor.

Once more, emotions and feelings he had never experienced surged through him. The thrill of the chase, the excitement and satisfaction of the 'kill', burned in him with an almost sexual ferocity.

But control was utmost in his mind and body. He was in complete control.

He knelt at the victim's side to make sure he was all right. The man said something, thanked him, called him a name… something. He nodded and brought his head up. Footsteps outside. Security probably. The alarm had gone off as soon as he had broken into the room. The police wouldn't be far behind. He could hear the sirens in the distance.

He stood and glanced quickly around the room until his gaze became anchored by his reflection in a wall mirror. Masked, darkly uniformed, an avenging hero stared back at him. And it *was* him now. Not the *other*. He controlled this body. He was in charge, just as he was supposed to be. He *was* the *other* now, this champion, this vigilante.

He *was* ArcNight.

He whirled, ran toward the window and slipped through its broken casement, cape spread, like a true creature of the night. And, as he fell plummeting, whisking his service rope out to the nearest safe berth, an image suddenly formed in his mind, striking, almost taking his breath away. Not his, he knew that. This was a memory, a part of the other one's life outside of this—a woman's face, strong, mature, beautiful, framed by short black hair. A fierce and proud intelligence sparkled from those green, Asian eyes. *Who?* He wondered as he swung to a secure landing. *Who is she?*

Wayne Brewster's eyes snapped open. He lay on his back, breathing heavily. His hands gripped the sheet on either side of him, clawing. He let out a ragged sigh as he closed his eyes again, relieved by the knowledge that he had been dreaming. Again. *At least I didn't jump out of bed this time,* he thought. *Of course, that would be a little safer than leaping out of a window!*

Slowly, Brewster raised himself up and sat on the edge of the bed. He rubbed his eyes as he tried to still the hammering of his heart. *ArcNight,* he thought. *It's always ArcNight.*

He got up on shaky legs to get a drink of water. Anything to calm himself down. He was sick to death of these dreams!

But he knew as he stumbled to the kitchen that they didn't really seem like dreams at all. They seemed real. And they were always the same. Oh, the circumstances were different each time—sometimes he'd be clambering over rooftops in pursuit of some criminals; other times he'd be swinging through the city's steel jungle on a mercy mission; and then, often as not, he'd be fighting for his life against some fantastic super-villain.

But he experienced those dreams through the same

viewpoint, no matter what was happening in that weird, subconscious landscape. Brewster was always a comic-book superhero in his nocturnal visions—ArcNight, denizen of the dark, defender of the helpless, dispenser of rough justice—a moody avenger indeed.

He made a sudden detour and fumbled for the latch on his balcony doors. Stepping outside, he let the warm night air wash over him. Ordinarily, though he preferred the penthouse view, he kept such viewing at a safe distance a few feet back from the edge. Tonight he leaned out over the railing, twelve stories up, almost eager to experience the dizzying vantage point his high perch provided him.

Why is this happening? he thought for the thousandth time. *These dreams…they started the night of that violent storm those few months ago.* He stared out at the city, much like he had in his dreams. *That flash of lightning, the pain in my head, the…the vision I saw. Ever since then…*

Brewster didn't know how much time had passed before he realized he was standing on the railing, balancing precariously twenty stories up without a net, his fists clenched at his sides. *ArcNight,* he thought again as he gingerly let himself back down onto the balcony. *And that woman's face. It belongs to Lieutenant Yoshima.*

CHAPTER 18

"S o, tell me again why you're going to this library?" Ken Yoshima asked, his pinched face set with disapproval.

Kim sighed. "Lazo prefers '*Old Books and Research Haven*'."

"Oh, I beg your pardon. Don't want to offend Lazo."

Kim and her brother stood in the living room of Ken and his wife's upper middle-class home. Designed to reflect an 'adventure theme', the décor showed off Ken's love of travel and exotic places. But Kim had always thought the leopard skin rug, the hanging displays of African spears and various animal heads, the bamboo-style furniture and assorted exotic sculpture and pottery, were so sterile. The house seemed more like a museum set piece, not lived in at all.

Kim felt the tension between her and her brother, palpable as a stone wall even after all these years. Her new mental powers didn't help in this case as they picked up on and amplified the edgier nuances of their emotions, emotions that had been at odds for a very long time. But it didn't take a psychic to see Ken's wife, Marjorie, hadn't even made an appearance.

Kim and Marjorie had never hit it off. Ken's wife's not-so-subtle pushing of Ken to succeed in the modern world at all costs, her adherence to all things superficial and materialistic, had caused a decades-old rift between the two women.

Old wounds never heal, Kim thought sadly, remembering the

sibling rivalry and squabbling over the years, Ken's modern outlook vs. Kim's reverence for the past, the disagreements and pain that had finally resulted in the present situation—a situation that probably made it easier to lie to her brother. "Yes, well, I'm going to drop Shioko and Bobby off at Lazo's for about an hour or so while I go to this get-together," she replied, as patiently as she could knowing full well that's not what she intended on doing. She and the Sibuloviches were, in reality, going to conduct their scheduled planning session, a briefing on what to do about Shioko and the other strange things that had been happening to Kim. Kim was going to tell them everything. "Some of my colleagues on the force are meeting at Piper's Pub for a drink. I haven't seen them for a while since I've been on leave."

She paused, waiting. And then, she threw in a nugget of the truth, "Bobby's been to Lazo's before—I think he and Shioko will be kept pretty occupied by all the old books, videos and maps and the DVD library. Lazo's got a whole classic kid's section there. No video games, though, except for educational ones. Plus I thought Bobby and Shioko might get along; he's only a couple of years older. He doesn't have a whole lot of friends, you know."

Ken stood with his arms crossed at his chest, dressed in a blue silk sports jacket and matching shirt and pants, a little older with a little more gray showing than his sister. "And I suppose that's Margaret's and my fault?"

"I didn't say that, although, let's face it, you and Margie are always jetting off somewhere, yes? It's a wonder Bobby doesn't call Raoul and Stephanie his parents!"

"Damnit, Kim! That's not fair."

"It's not fair to Bobby either."

"And what would you know about parenting, hmmm?"

THE SIXTH PRECEPT

Oh, we can cut deep, can't we? Kim glanced down at the floor, collecting herself. "Look, Ken, I'm…I'm sorry," she finally said. "Let's not start, all right? We always seem to end up shouting at each other. You need someone to watch Bobby for the next couple of days besides the housekeeper and the gardener while you're out of town. I'm glad to do it. You know that."

Ken looked away and nodded. "Yes, Kim, and we appreciate it. Bobby loves it when you're around, I don't deny it, and you take good care of him. But this young girl you're trying to gain guardianship of. It all seems so sudden and…mysterious."

Distasteful, you mean. Not something someone with your social status would approve of. Kim snorted. "What? Do you think she'll be a bad influence on Bobby? Please."

"Why is she sitting outside in the car, then?" Ken's features remained like a mask, rigid, only his eyes giving any emotion away.

Kim took a deep breath. "She's very shy, Ken. Backwards and possibly has been abused. I thought it better—"

"Hi, Aunt Kim!" Kim's ten-year old nephew ran into the living room, his backpack slapping against his lanky, baggy-jeaned clad frame. His face split into a large grin beneath a short cut of fine, black hair.

Yes! Thank you, Bobby! "Hey, Kiddo. Are you ready?"

"Yeah! Let's go! Oh, I mean…sorry, Dad."

"It's OK, son." Ken leaned down and hugged Bobby awkwardly, the ten-year old returning the stiff embrace. "Have fun and be careful."

"You too. See you on Friday, I guess."

If you're lucky, Kim thought glumly. *Why did you even have a child, Ken, when you're rarely even home?*

"Have a safe trip and call me when you get back, OK?" Kim opened the front door as Bobby launched himself outside like a tiny, human rocket. She paused for a moment—"And tell Margie hello for me."

"Kim…"

Kim turned back and blinked in surprise. Her brother's usual stern, Type A façade had dropped. His face looked sad, almost pained. And then, it became a mask again. "Yes, talk to you later. Thanks again."

"Right. Bye." *Damn it, Ken, just when I think there's hope for you…you're as bad as Mother and Father sometimes!*

Kim found Bobby standing at the side of her car, looking curiously at Shioko seated in the front passenger side. Stephanie Delacruz, the Yoshimas' housekeeper, and their chauffeur Raoul's wife, got up from a bench in the front garden where she had been keeping an eye on the car at the lieutenant's request. "Thanks, Stephanie," Kim said with a smile.

"You're welcome, ma'am," Stephanie replied. "She was fine, just looking around. She's very pretty."

Kim walked over to Bobby's side. "Well, Bobby, what are you waiting for? Get on in!"

Behind the wheel, Kim eased out of the long driveway and gated front entrance. "Bobby, this is Shioko."

"Hi."

"Hi, Bobby."

"Ready for some sushi tonight, guys?"

"No! Gross!" Bobby's western eyes, a legacy from his non-Asian mother, rolled. "How about some pizza, Aunt Kim? Please?"

Yoshima laughed. "Oh, all right. You have your stuff, kiddo?"

"Yeah. I just packed a few clothes and some of my comic books."

"Got your cell phone? Ok, but you only use that in an

emergency, right? No texting, no games, no internet for the next couple of days. We talked about that."

"Yes, Aunt Kim."

"Do you like to read?" Shioko abruptly asked.

"Yeah!" Bobby answered. "I read a lot of comic books. *ArcNight*'s my favorite! He's awesome. He wears a black outfit and cape with a cowl that covers his entire face. He knows karate and gymnastics and wears a belt that holds all kinds of weapons and stuff. Who's your favorite?"

Shioko thought a moment and then said, "The Ebon Warrior!"

Kim pulled out onto the main road, merging into traffic. *The Ebon Warrior?* she thought. *Where did she get* that *from?* Kim tamped down the sudden frustration she felt—her attempt to 'read' Shioko's mind after Parker and the Dark Man had invaded their apartment hadn't been entirely successful. Despite "wanting to tell Kim everything," the young girl's natural reluctance was strong; Kim didn't want to break those mental walls for fear of hurting Shioko. And, as a result, hadn't found out anything new about her young charge and the Eminent Lord.

Still, she felt an itching at the back of her mind. Somewhere along the line, like the Yomitsu, the Eminent Lord and the Spirit Winds, she had heard of the Ebon Warrior before.

"Yeah?" Bobby asked. "Cool name. I never heard of him. Is he on the Web? What are his powers?"

Kim shook her head and laughed again in spite of herself. Life had certainly taken some unexpected turns for her lately. Her grandmother had always talked about *karma* and how there was no escaping it. Well, for right now, despite everything, that was OK with her.

Bobby and Shioko became engaged in animated

conversation. *Great. Looks like they get along.* It would be nice to have him stay over. For all three of them.

Still, Kim had allowed some other thoughts to take up residence in her mind—she had decided to follow Lazo's example and his periodic advice and at least think about opening up her own investigative agency. She had toyed with the idea for years but with her newfound psi powers as an extra tool, she had a feeling she could take crime-busting to a whole new level and really make a difference. The thought of the sign on her door reading 'Kim Yoshima, Psychic P.I.' made her eyes roll but stranger things had happened to her lately. The concept and the risk were worth taking, though, at least until she could figure out some other use for these abilities. At present, being a cop and a detective were what she knew best.

The drive to Lazo's was relatively uneventful. Shioko and Bobby did seem to hit it off, talking like old friends. In twenty minutes, Kim pulled into the parking garage above Lazo's haven.

She felt a momentary twinge of apprehension as she drove through the neighborhood—the memory of what she had gone through here, the assault by that mysterious creature, that shadow-tracker, was still fresh in her mind, despite the fact that it had happened almost four weeks ago. Plus, the confrontation with the three men in the nearby warehouse was still bothering her.

It was about time she started connecting the dots.

The electronic door of the lot closed behind them as Joe Martin came out to greet them. "Hello, Kim," he said, brandishing a cell phone, a gun holstered at his belt.

"Hi, Joe," Kim said, leaning out the window. "I wanted to thank you again for your help."

'Yes, ma'am." Joe smiled. "You handled yourself pretty well.

I should be thanking you. Any news?" He meant the 'stalker'.

"Nothing yet. Except for running into a lot of dead ends."

Joe nodded knowingly and looked into the car. "Hi there, kids," he said with a wave. "Park anywhere, Kim. Mr. Sibulovich has only got two other guests right now."

"Thanks." Kim parked her car in the same row as the other visitors' vehicles and she, Shioko and Bobby got out.

"Wait'll you see this!" Bobby said. "It's cool! It's like going into the Arc Cave!"

"Is that where ArcNight lives?" Shioko asked, as the threesome boarded the elevator.

"Yeah. It's got all these rooms and laboratories and computers and everything."

The elevator bumped to a halt and the threesome exited into the small, tastefully decorated foyer. Both children oohed and ahhed at the slick, modern décor. Kim and her charges stood in front of the security camera located above the entrance door.

"Hi, Kim," a familiar deep voice sounded from the intercom. "Hey, Bobby and Shioko. Welcome!"

CHAPTER 19

Brewster knew he could get the information he needed on his own PC or at a regular library. They all had microfiche and other assorted reference materials as well as Internet access. But the place he sat in now had sounded so intriguing, he thought he'd give it a try. Besides, the underground, hidden aspect of it appealed to him on a certain level. It was almost like being away from the world completely, in a unique and specially equipped oasis.

So, he had set up an appointment on his day off. *An old books and research haven*, he mused. *By appointment only. I like the sound of that.*

The medium-sized reading room he sat in was decorated like an English-style drawing room—very comfortable with high-backed cushioned chairs, a claw-footed oaken table, side couch, photograph-laden mantle, wall to wall Indian carpet and, of course, several floor-to-ceiling bookcases. What looked to be a Turner landscape graced the far wall while various smaller prints and watercolors were hung throughout the rest of the room. A couple of Victorian-style terrariums were strategically placed on either side of the floor. The temperature was mid-range, not too cool and not too warm, obviously climate-controlled.

Very stylish. And high-tech. A PC and printer sat incongruously on the table while a security cam watched his every move from above the door. He grinned at the memory of his arrival here and was surprised he didn't have to give some kind of password to get in. At least he hadn't been frisked.

The 'managers' of this facility, a Mr. And Mrs. (or Doctor, as he had discovered) Sibulovich, had been pleasant and helpful and there *was* quite a bit of research material stored here. If he couldn't find out anything about his dreams in this place, that kind of data probably didn't exist. If that was the case he might have to seek some sort of therapy after all. Brewster was reluctant to do that. *I'm not crazy!* But he was beginning to get concerned.

He turned his attention back to the old, leather-bound volume sitting on the bookstand in front of him—*Dreams and the Unmapped Territories of the Mental Universe* by someone named Dr. Lilith Cardazio. Here, amidst the large, elaborately illustrated pages, was a description of something resembling his problem—*In rare cases*, the passage began, *the individuals involved will experience, not so much a true dream state, but more an alternate reality, one in which the 'dreamer' inhabits the guise of another, ostensibly real person. This person will engage in his or her day-to-day activities in this reality with the dreamer simply tagging along for the ride, observing through that person's eyes. This type of lucidity can be disorienting and frightening. The origin of this state is, as yet, unknown, but it has been posited that perhaps, in unique individuals or those who have been exposed to some traumatic mental stimuli, there exists a connection or thread to, in fact, another point in the mental universe, one in which the dreamer is actually connected to another, separate entity's mind by way of some telepathic interdimensionality. This has lately been credited as explanations for flashes of déjà vu or sensing fleeting glimpses of a parallel world.*

So, according to this, Brewster thought, *somewhere, there actually is a comic book hero called ArcNight and I'm seeing everything he does because we're mentally connected in some way.* He shook his head, trying to suppress a laugh. *It sounds crazy but that's what I feel like! Maybe I do need to see a shrink! I mean, just because my name's the same as this ArcNight's secret identity…*

He remembered that night, three months ago (*how could I not?*). The thunder had awakened him as, he was sure, it had awakened everyone in the city. It was a very loud, very rainy storm. He jumped up to close his window and that's when it happened.

A flash of lightning lit up the roof of the building next to his. There seemed to be a ripple, a shimmering in the air above. He thought he saw something then, as if through some cosmic viewfinder—a man in a (costume?) was running across the roof. Despite the wind and rain, Brewster leaned out of his bedroom window to get a better look.

Lightning flashed again but brighter than anything he had ever seen, almost as if a small sun had crashed to earth. This time he felt a wave of heat encircle his body. His skin tingled, the hair on his arms stood at attention. A halo of sparks danced around his outstretched hands. He saw the figure just vanish. Brewster fell back into his room, gasping for air, his head feeling like it was on fire.

It took him a minute or two to recover. He sat down on the edge of his bed. He was trembling and out of breath but otherwise OK. Two nights later, he had the first dream.

A slight murmuring of voices sounded from the front room of the library. He glanced back absently through the interconnecting archway. Mr. Sibulovich stood greeting three more 'guests' as he called them—a woman and two children. Brewster hoped the children were well-behaved and went back to his reading. He paused and turned to look again at the woman and blinked in surprise. *It's her. It's Kim Yoshima.*

CHAPTER 20

She welcomed the darkness. It hid her rage. The silence of the underground tunnel helped her concentrate—the steady drip, drip, drip of the upper sewage pipes were like a timer, ticking off the seconds until she would explode into action. The air, warm and dank, settled over her like a blanket, wrapping her hatred in a tidy package, waiting to be opened by the one she hunted.

She's here, the shadow-tracker realized, ignoring the sweat that trickled down her back. *She's returned to where she fought my huntmate. Stupid cow! How appropriate then that this is the place where she'll also meet her death.*

The shadow-tracker knelt at the bottom of the ladder that led upward to a street level manhole. Not that long ago, she had huddled furtively in this very spot. Her nostrils quivered, her whole body tensed with pent up energy. Her clawed hands grasped the ladder so tightly, her knuckles turned white against her copper-colored skin.

She growled softly, closing her eyes as she remembered.

If her masters knew she was here, her life would be forfeit. But she couldn't wait any longer.

Her eyes followed a roach as it scuttled in front of her. She knelt immobile, like a statue. Nothing would distract her from her goal. She had crossed the line and there was no turning back.

She had left the secret confines of the *Totou* on her own to come here, staging her own watch, hoping her target would surface again. None of the other *Totou* agents were stationed here now. Only she and she alone would give her masters what they had wanted for so long. She would do what her huntmate could not.

And all she need do was wait a little longer.

And her patience had paid off sooner than she had expected. The Yomitsu had indeed arrived only a short time ago. She could smell her, the anticipated though hated scent settling deep in her lungs.

The fire within her was so strong, the seeking of vengeance so primary, she put all other thoughts aside. She bared her fangs. In her mind, she could already taste the Yomitsu's blood, feel the Great Enemy's flesh shredding beneath her claws.

I'll stick to the plan, she thought. *I don't care what happens to me as long as she dies!*

She moved then. If anyone could have seen within the murky darkness, they would have sworn the shadows of the sewer system had come to life, that part of the wall had flickered into motion. The shadow-tracker reached into the shoulder bag lying at her feet and pulled out a pair of loose-fitting pants, an oversized T-shirt and tennis shoes, ball cap, sunglasses and hoody. She, like all of her kind, could hide in broad daylight, bred and trained to blend in, no matter what the environment. She had to get into the building, whatever it was, where her target had entered. And what better way than as one of the Yomitsu's own kind? Disguise and deception were tools at her disposal. The shadow-trackers that had come before her had used them to brilliant advantage over the centuries. So would she.

As she went to work, she spoke aloud to the one she served,

softly, slowly, in a melody of whispering song. "Eminent Lord," she crooned, as she pulled the clothes on over her jumpsuit. "Guide me now. Deliver the Great Enemy into my hands!"

CHAPTER 21

"Hi, Bobby. Hi, Shioko. Nice to see you again."

At a chorus of "hellos" from the children, Jenny Sibulovich smiled and shot a mischievous glance at Kim Yoshima. The laugh lines at the corners of her eyes crinkled her freckled face. "Hi, Kim," she said, brushing back a lock of red hair from her forehead. Slight and fair-skinned, the Scottish-American Jenny seemed the yin to Lazo's bulky, dark-complexion, Southern European yang. "Now think about what you'd like to do tonight," she said to the young twosome, her eyes twinkling. "We've got a lot of interesting stuff here."

As Bobby led Shioko off into the main reading room, showing her the sights of the underground haven, Jenny said, "Shioko's English is so much better. And she seems more outgoing. You've done wonders with her in such a short time."

A nod. "She actually is very intelligent but it's not all my doing. There's a lot more I need to talk to you and Lazo about."

"We're ready to listen." Jenny nodded and turned her motherly attention towards the young twosome as they reappeared. "Hey, you two, how about our animation section? We have a lot of old books on cartoons and movies as well as a pretty big animation cell and DVR collection. Not to mention some cookies and juice."

Both Bobby and Shioko sang out a resounding "Yes!" as

Jenny turned to lead them both to another section of the facility. "Talk to you in a minute!" she called over her shoulder.

"You look worried, big guy," Kim said, as Lazo exited his office. "I just want to talk."

"It's what you want to talk about that has me worried. I know you, Kim. Something's up and it's more than just this stalker incident. Let's go into our conference room. I've got a couple of other visitors here tonight. We'll have some privacy there."

As she and Lazo walked down the hall, Kim sensed rather than heard Shioko's gleeful appreciation of something Jenny was showing her. And, like a fly buzzing at the periphery of her mental vision, she picked up on Bobby's curiosity of the girl and something else—one of the other visitor's mental auras seemed very interesting.

She stopped midway to the door as Lazo entered his conference room, and strode toward one of the reading rooms. There it was again, something familiar.

He was standing up at one of the desks, a puzzled expression on his face. He stared right at Kim.

It's him, she thought, her mind suddenly awhirl. "Sir," she said, stopping at the room's entrance. "Excuse me."

The man's expression changed to one of surprise. "Lieutenant Yoshima?"

A feeling of power radiated strongly from this man; Kim's newfound senses were picking up on *something*—he definitely possessed an inner strength but it lay beneath, smoldering, as if he didn't know himself what he could do.

Despite the warnings going off in her mind, her body seemed to act on its own volition as she took a step into the room. "Yes. And you're the man at Lily's, the one who saved the hostages."

THE SIXTH PRECEPT

A tentative nod. "Yes. My name's Wayne Brewster. Am I in trouble?"

Kim laughed. "Are you kidding? We'd like to pin a medal on you!" *Is he blushing?* she thought. *Interesting.*

Brewster waved a dismissive hand. "I was just in the right place at the right time. Glad I could help."

Modest too. "I have something I have to do now. Are you planning on staying here a little longer? I'd like to thank you. Perhaps when I get back, we could talk, yes?"

"Yes." No hesitation now. "Absolutely. I'll be here."

"Good." Kim smiled and turned back to Lazo who had come looking for her.

"There you are!" he said. "I turned around and you were gone."

"Sorry, Laz. I got a little distracted."

Lazo's bushy eyebrows rose up a notch. "Hmmm. So I see."

Jenny joined them as they entered the conference room, Lazo shutting the door behind them. The walls of the small room were hung with old photos of Lazo and Jenny. Many showed the Sibuloviches in their early years—Lazo as a police officer and Jenny as a student teacher.

"These take me back," Kim said, as she perused the pictures. "Hey, is that me?"

"Yep," Lazo said with a grin. "A long time ago."

"I was a rookie then. Look at that hair!"

"Kim?" Jenny sat down at the circular table. "What did you want to talk to us about?"

Kim sighed and sat down. Leave it to the ever-sensible Jenny to get right to it. Kim had rehearsed in her mind what she would say to her friends. Even friendship had its boundaries. Would she be going too far in telling them? Would they even believe her? *Well,* Kim thought, tossing out her mental script. *A picture, as they say, is worth a thousand words.*

Focusing her thoughts like invisible fingers on one of the books on the small corner shelf, Kim lifted it slowly into the air

"OK, Kim. We'll keep this among ourselves for the time being but this is huge. Really huge." Lazo's brows furrowed in concern, making him look ridiculously like a worried bear. Kim had never seen him so dumbfounded.

"We should study this…this power of yours," Jenny added, an excited light burning in her eyes. She devoured Kim with a fierce, intelligent look. "As well as this time anomaly you spoke of."

"Well," Kim began. "I'm not sure how much of *that* is true. This creep, Parker, could have been telling me anything."

"True, but we should at least pay a visit to the *Box Factory* and determine the validity of his statements."

Kim smiled. "I agree. But first—"

Jenny became animated, her eyes lighting up with excitement. "This could be a major scientific discovery, if it's true. Do you realize—"

"Easy, Jen," Lazo said, grasping his wife's hand. "I know that look."

"Sorry, Kim," Jenny replied, suddenly looking sheepish. "It's just that this is so…so incredible! Think of the possibilities."

"I know," Kim said softly. "But there's more you need to know and you're probably going to think I've lost it."

"After what we've just seen, I don't think there'll be a problem," Lazo cracked.

"OK," Kim said, taking a deep breath. "Let me tell you what really happened the night I found Shioko and what's happened after that. And, I swear to you, I'm not making any of this up."

"And you say this creature is called a shadow-tracker?" Lazo asked. It had taken Kim over a half an hour to tell her friends about the incredible events of the past two weeks. She hadn't realized how much of a burden it had been to keep it all to herself. Reluctance had turned to relief. Now, if only her friends wouldn't commit her.

Lazo's expression had gone from incredulous to thoughtful. "And you never did find out this dog-man's origin, huh? Or how it was related to this ancient Japanese warlord?"

Kim shook her head. "Not really. The creature's amulet definitely was inscribed with the same symbol I saw in the reference book about Omori. And I think my up-to-then-unknown psychic powers may have helped me stop that thing."

"Pre-emergent hunches? Could be."

"Plus, it's very strange, but I felt as if I knew that thing, as if I had seen if before."

"Some type of ancient archetypal connection perhaps," Jenny mused.

Kim nodded. "Maybe, but this Parker freak said a couple of strange things to me also. Something about my ancestor, the *shirabyoshi*, and the samurai I encountered being the…the Eminent Lord. Then there was the other one, the dark Asian who was with Parker, the one who smoked clove cigarettes. No one's been able to get a trace on him yet.

"And, during the attack by the shadow-tracker, it called me 'the Great Enemy' which is what the vision of the samurai mentioned too. I don't know. There's something really… monumental happening here. None of this is random. There seems to be some connecting thread running through these incidents. And I think Shioko has a part in this too. If only I can get her to talk about her past. I tried peering into her mind but some part of her is still reluctant, still afraid. I didn't find out a whole lot more than what I already knew except that in some way, and for some unfathomable reason, this Eminent Lord has enabled her to speak English and understand modern concepts."

"That is so incredible!" Jenny exclaimed.

"I know, I know. I don't expect you to—"

"What do you want us to do?" Jenny gently asked. "Kim, we'll help any way we can."

Kim shook her head, her eyes stinging with sudden tears. "I must say you two are taking this pretty calmly, yes? I've certainly questioned my own mental state recently!"

Jenny took Kim's hand. "You're our friend, Kim, and we want to help, plus, like Lazo said—we just saw a demonstration of these…your telekinetic powers. My god! That's something that doesn't happen every day."

"Exactly." Lazo shrugged. "So what's not to believe?"

"Thank you. I owe you guys. Big time." Kim stood up and started pacing, tapping her lower lip. "If you can just help me check your archives to see if you can find something like this happening before. Let's see if we can discover anything unusual that may have occurred during the Muramachi period in Japanese history, particularly concerning this Eminent Lord. See if there's any mention of shadow-trackers or any such creatures."

"No problem," Lazo said. "Research is my life! I knew there was a reason I set this place up."

"Thanks, Laz. Jenny, for right now, can you just spend some time with Shioko? Even though I'm supposed to be the mind reader, maybe you can get something out of her that I couldn't."

"Of course." Jenny rose from her seat and embraced Kim. "We'll work this out," she whispered. "I'm glad you told us."

Showed you, you mean, Kim thought. *If I hadn't levitated that book, would you have believed me?*

As Jenny exited the room, Lazo squeezed Kim's arm. "Always knew you were somethin' special. And I'm glad you told us too but if you start flyin' or breathin' fire…"

"I'll call 911. It's a deal. Thanks."

"And I'm way ahead of you. After you got out of the hospital, I started lookin' for obscure references during the time period of Omori Kadonomaro."

Kim snorted. "Still a cop at heart. And?"

"Omori was allied with a group of Buddhist warrior monks." He chuckled at Kim's look. "The *sohei*, the monks were called, would lend their fighting skill to whatever warlord seemed to match their own interests. Doesn't sound very religious, does it?"

"Hmmm, I don't know about that," Kim murmured, thinking of the *naginata*. "Remember the Crusades?"

"Well, let me just give you this other little tidbit to simmer in that lovely mind of yours while you're ponderin' Mr. Beef Cake over there. Oh yes, I noticed."

"Hey. Laz—"

"OK. Are you sittin' down? Omori's informal title was—"

"The Eminent Lord. I sensed that but was afraid to admit it."

"Right. Now there's a connectin' thread for you!"

"I'm getting a headache trying to put this all together."

"Also, there's this, for what it's worth. Still no clarification on your ancestor but some of the really old texts I perused mentioned entities called the 'Sleepers' and someone known as the 'Luminous One' helpin' out in the battle with Omori. And there was also a brief reference to the 'Ebon Warrior'. Pretty mysterious, huh?"

The Ebon Warrior? That's the name Shioko mentioned to Bobby!

"Kim? You look like you've seen the proverbial ghost. You OK?"

The phone in the conference room rang. As Lazo went to answer it, Kim closed her eyes, trying to make some sense of what Lazo and her ancestor and Parker had told her. All that information was like a giant puzzle scattered all over the ground; she had only to figure out how the pieces fit together.

Omori is the Eminent Lord, she reflected, going into deductive mode. *Shioko knew about the Ebon Warrior. Yoshima Mitsu said Shioko would help defeat the Eminent Lord aka Omori. Could Shioko be the Luminous One? But, then, who is Ko the Little?*

Kim sat down, an overwhelming feeling of astonishment and disbelief enveloping her. *The samisen I found—so perfect and out-of-time, a 'failed test' as Parker described it—and the supposed temporal anomaly at the Box Factory Parker mentioned. The Eminent Lord said I would send Shioko back into the 'Void'.*

She looked down at her hands. They were shaking. She felt a little light-headed. *If Shioko is truly from the past, then she traveled forward in time somehow and will, eventually, travel back to help defeat the Eminent Lord—which would make her Ko the Little. So the Void must be a reference to time travel. That sound and bright light at the warehouse after I shot the shadow-tracker might be some indication of that. Would being snatched back through time explain the shadow-tracker's mysterious disappearance?*

Kim looked back out into the hallway. Jenny had left the door open and Kim could see Wayne Brewster poring over some old tome. *There's something about him too. He's certainly good-looking, but there's something else.*

"Kim," Lazo said, as he hung up the phone, an all-business expression etched upon his face. "That was Joe. I've got to supervise a delivery. Should just take a few minutes. Hey, you all right? You look a little pale."

Kim forced her thoughts back to her real-time situation. "I'm fine. Just tired. What's up?"

"No big deal," Lazo replied. "We've contracted an electrician from a different company then we usually use to redo some of the old wiring here, and to set up some more network connections. We're gonna get a couple more PCs with Internet access. Joe usually handles that kind of thing but I have to sign some papers."

"OK. So, what's going on? You have that look on your face."

"Well, we've used these guys before and I think they may be rippin' us off. They're good and, yeah, I can afford it, but I think they're jackin' up the price."

Kim chuckled. "Ripping off an ex-cop. Imagine! Want me to come up with you and act official? Put the fear of God in them?"

Lazo gave her a sly look. "Not unless you can read minds and tell me what this thing's gonna cost us."

Kim smiled.

CHAPTER 22

There! A vehicle approached the building, a van, scripted company lettering adorning its white-paneled sides. *An electrician,* the shadow-tracker observed, as she watched the van from her hiding place. *Perfect.*

She had walked the perimeter of the structure twice, ambling aimlessly like any other street person. The baggy pants, hoody, ball cap and sunglasses she wore as a disguise hid her true features from any passersby. This area seemed primarily deserted, the modern building where the Yomitsu had entered possibly serving as some flagship for further urban renewal. Thus far the shadow-tracker had encountered no one who had taken a second glance at her. Even the one or two small groups of young men who had stared suspiciously at her had let her go on her way unmolested. Luckily for them.

All in all, just another day in the 'hood'. Which was just what the shadow-tracker wanted.

She had looked for weaknesses in the fenced-in enclosure, any type of access that could be gained to the interior of the building. There were no windows on the building itself and only a couple of doors were visible, one being a possible emergency exit and the other a wider garage door, possibly serving as a main entrance for vehicle parking. The whole structure looked solid as a rock. The security fence encircled the lot. An automated gated entrance to the main garage was visible while another similar exit had been set up outside the emergency door. She could jump the fence, she knew, but this mission of hers required a certain amount of stealth. She must catch the Yomitsu and whoever else was inside by surprise.

The approaching van was definitely headed her way. She ducked behind a concrete abutment and quickly peeled off her disguise. As the van passed her, she slid into its wake, moving swiftly. Grasping the back door handle, she maneuvered her feet onto the bumper.

The van drove down a below-street-level driveway to the rear of the building. There, she saw what appeared to be a service entrance.

The driver stopped at another gate. In one swift, liquid movement, the shadow-tracker dropped to the ground and slid under the van. She braced her hands and feet against the vehicle's frame and lifted herself off the ground, barely shaking the van as her sinewy body squeezed and molded itself into the tiny space. Holding her breath against the exhaust, the shadow-tracker heard the whir of cameras and a voice emanating from a speaker. The driver answered, there was a click of a card key being accessed, the gate opened and the van entered the enclosure.

Thank the Eminent Lord. He is *guiding my hand.*

The outside luminance changed as the van entered the enclosure and artificial light took over. There was a rush of air-conditioned air, a smell of newness, of sterility in complete contrast to the raw, pungent brew of the outside environment. The garage door closed behind her.

She was in.

The shadow-tracker waited, muscles tensed, barely breathing. She heard the driver of the van get out and footsteps approach. There was a conversation—the driver and at least two others. The van door opened and, after a few moments, closed again as the speakers' footsteps moved away from the van.

She dropped to the concrete floor, rolled away from the van opposite the driver's side, and sprinted for the opposing wall. She found herself in a small materials receiving area, a series of ceiling-high shelves of supplies directly in front of her. She ducked between two rows of shelves and peered back the way she had come.

The van blocked most of her view but there was an elevated, glass-enclosed office visible above the vehicle's rooftop where the driver and the other two had gone. She could see the three talking, calling some data up on a computer screen, and exchanging papers. She slowly let out the breath she had been holding. No one had seen her. Though there were security cameras situated throughout the small room, no one seemed to have been paying attention at this moment.

That was their first mistake. But she had to act quickly. The cameras would not be left unattended for long. There were two doors that she could discern—one next to the office, the other to her right.

The threesome in the office were talking, their heads slightly averted. Clinging to whatever meager shadows she could find, the shadow-tracker bolted for the closest door. Moving swiftly, she turned the handle. The door was unlocked. It opened outward and she darted inside.

As the door closed behind her, she heard a distant voice, "Hey! What was that?" She had been spotted or, at least, her movements had been detected. The three men outside would check the security film and see that their facility had been breached although her form would only show as shadowy and indistinct—another inbred ability her masters had given her kind.

Still, she was out of time and couldn't go back. She had to trust her instincts now. She knelt in a short corridor, its newly-painted confines filled with other human smells. This was traversed regularly, possibly the entrance from the receiving area to the main part of the complex.

Good. She had chosen correctly. She would find the Yomitsu within.

A door loomed up ahead, with another security cam positioned above it. She crawled up one of the walls and scuttled sideways like a spider, the pads of her hands and feet gripping the wall's smooth surface like Velcro. She moved to the ceiling, hanging upside down to avoid the camera's eye. She ripped the camera from its perch and flung it to the floor. There was a sound behind her—the door she had just come through was opening.

She flipped and dropped to the floor, grabbed the handle of the door in front of her and pushed. On the other side lay a much smaller storage area with an open door leading to another, longer hallway to her left. Quickly she pulled a heavy metal desk in front of the door she had just come through, blocking its passage.

She sprinted down the hallway, not caring if she was picked up by security now or not. Up ahead, yet another door. *Here,* she thought, knowing she still had the element of surprise. *Now. This is where it ends.*

CHAPTER 23

Kim knew there was something wrong even before Lazo called in. She had stayed in the main reading room to wait until her friend had settled matters with the electrician. Which gave her a chance to continue her conversation with Brewster.

As she approached Brewster, she noticed for the first time the other 'guest' of Lazo's studying in an adjacent room. A young African American sat quietly, dreadlocks, wearing glasses, baggy T-shirt, jeans and sandals. Even though he was listening to his iPod, he looked up from his book as if sensing Kim was looking at him, nodded, smiled, and went back to his reading.

Kim took a deep breath. "Come here often?" she joked inanely, as she smiled down on Brewster.

"No," Brewster answered seriously. "First time, although part of the reason I'm here is you, as it turns out. Or, rather, a dream of you."

Kim's eyes widened. "A dream? Well now—"

Brewster held up his hand. A sheepish look crossed his face. "No, no. Nothing like that, I promise I'm not trying to hit on you. Ummm, it's a long story."

Aren't they all? She sat down at Brewster's table. She suddenly felt fidgety, as if expectant, waiting for something to happen. "I'm listening."

Brewster took a deep breath, his chiseled features troubled. "You're going to think I'm crazy. But that's why I'm here— I'm trying to research the type of dreams I've been having. They're sort of comic book scenarios and ArcNight is a regular participant in them."

"ArcNight? You mean the super hero? My nephew is a big fan."

"Yes." He paused. "I become him, in my dreams. And I learn from him—the way I fought the gunman at Lilly's. I never did anything like that. Ever. No training whatsoever or knowledge. I just knew. It's because of the dreams. I just know it! And you've been there too—in those same dreams."

I can't believe he's telling me this. "You said that before. But I'm no comic book hero. Why would I be in your dreams?"

"I think it has something to do with the ArcNight character," Brewster replied cautiously. "It's not you per se but an alternate you in that world."

What—" She turned away, the now-familiar tingling sensation dancing across the top of her head. It gripped her hard, with a distinct urgency. There was someone—

(*a dark figure raced down the hallway just outside the reading rooms, monstrous, alien*)

At that moment Lazo's voice sounded over the intercom system in his office. It had only been a few minutes since he had left to check on the electrician.

"Jenny! Kim!" He almost shouted. "We think someone's gotten into the building. He'll be coming in through the back door of my office. Get everyone into the elevator and out of there fast!"

But she knew already. That mental klaxon screamed in her mind. A warning, it was a warning. And there was something else...

198

THE SIXTH PRECEPT

(...*lean and powerful, running upright, eyes glowing yellow, fangs bared*)

"What is it?" Brewster asked, leaning forward. "What's wrong?"

"Please, Mr. Brewster." Kim rose to her feet, running her hand through her hair. "No questions. Just leave now. There appears to be an unauthorized intruder on the premises." *It's something familiar. It's—*

(*a clawed hand reached out for the doorknob*)

"What about the children?"

"The children are down the hall," Kim answered, approving of Brewster's concern. "Second door on the right. Can you see that they and Jenny and the other man here get to the elevator safely?"

"Of...Of course. But what about you?"

Kim pulled her gun from her purse. "Never mind about me. Just help Jenny and the kids. Go quickly, please."

Brewster nodded, his features a mix of confusion, apprehension and curiosity, and then darted off down the hall.

Good man, she thought. *His first thought was for the kids.* Kim ran to Lazo's office but she was too late. The door behind his desk was opening. She reached back to close the office's outer door.

(*not human*)

Something exploded into the room—a flash of rigid muscle and sinew, short fur and pale yellow eyes.

Kim backpedaled, her gun held in front of her, as that something leaped over Lazo's desk and came directly at her. *No,* she thought, her mind afire. *Not another one!*

The creature stopped only a few feet away from Kim, its body wound tight, a distinct smell of sweat and something else (*a feralness, pheromones*) emanating from it. Its eyes pierced Kim with a death-like gaze.

This one was female, its small breasts evident through the skin-tight jumpsuit it wore, its features somehow softer than the other one Kim had encountered. It didn't seem to care that Kim pointed a gun at it. It oozed confidence and strength. It looked at Kim with a malicious grin, fangs glinting in the light.

And it was a very shaky gun the lieutenant held. Kim backed up another step, suddenly unable to pull the trigger. This thing, it was like the other that had attacked her—again, she knew it. She knew it long ago as Yoshima Mitsu. Again an unreasoning fear enveloped her like a shroud.

Time seemed to have stopped. The creature and Kim faced each other. The creature cocked its head to one side as if studying its prey. "Yomitsu," it mouthed in a high-pitched whisper, phrasing the word in a sing-song cadence.

"Who...who are you?"

The feral grin widened. "I am the one honored to face the Great Enemy at last. Praise be to the Eminent Lord."

There are no differences; only perceptions. A chill went up Kim's spine. *What in God's name?* For a moment, the creature blinked, eyeing Kim strangely.

Oneesan!

Shioko! Kim could hear the girl—in her mind! *Oh, sweetie—*

Oneesan, it's a shadow-tracker! You said I would be safe. Oneesan—

Shioko was suddenly gone. Her mental presence disappeared as if she had just evaporated into thin air. The creature shook its head, as if ridding it of some unwanted thought.

The she-beast charged. Kim froze, the fear turning her immobile. At the last second, she screamed telepathically, just like she had done with Parker, the cry reverberating throughout her mind. It shook away the fear. And hit the creature. For a moment, the she-beast seemed confused, hesitant as it slowed down, just a little—long enough for Kim to move, trying to jump out of its way.

The creature slammed into Kim with its shoulder, knocking Kim flat. She hit the floor hard. Gasping, she brought her luger up but the creature kicked it out of her hand. Kim scrambled backwards, scuttling like a crab. *No, no, no!* she thought, trying to catch her breath. *Not again!*

The creature shook its head, as if stunned. But she leered at Kim, extending her claws.

Behind the creature and out in the hallway, the elevator door opened. One of Lazo's security guards emerged, gun drawn. "No!" Kim cried. "Watch out!"

The creature whirled and moved like—*Some kind of athlete,* Kim thought, leaping to her feet. *Martial arts style…a ninja.*

The creature was on the guard in a heartbeat, slashing at his gun arm and knocking him back into the elevator. He fell onto his back, his body blocking the elevator door from closing. *NO!* Kim thought-cried again, aiming that mental force straight at the creature. The she-beast stopped its lethal blow, stumbling back away from the trapped and wounded guard.

A mental barrier. Something. Kim focused on the creature, enveloping it in a steely psychic grip. The creature stiffened, caught in Kim's telekinetic noose. The she-beast's eyes bulged, its muscles tensed. Kim struggled to maintain her hold but the creature wasn't wounded like the first one had been. This one was strong, both mentally and physically, and Kim was frightened, confused, not really knowing what she was doing.

The creature's arms flailed the air around its head, its mouth opened in a silent scream. Kim gasped, her knees buckling and her head arching backwards as if she had been slapped. The creature had broken free and, with a howl of rage, rushed at her again.

Another figure dove out of the side hallway. Wayne Brewster body-blocked the creature below the knees, flipping it sideways on to the floor. The she-beast rolled expertly and landed on its feet, surprised but ready to face its new adversary.

Brewster knelt against the wall, holding his shoulder with one hand, his eyes wide and staring. At that moment, Lazo and Joe burst through Lazo's office door.

Kim scrambled for her gun as the creature moved toward the elevator, growling, Kim realized, in anger and frustration. The creature knew it was outnumbered now and would try to escape. Kim, Lazo and Joe raised their guns but the creature grasped the fallen security guard by the collar and pulled him up and in front of it, using him as a shield. Its clawed hand reached out to the elevator controls.

Stop! Stop it! Kim aimed another beam of mental force as the elevator door closed. Kim probed, trying to sense the she-beast through the inches of steel and concrete. *It's there, right there. I can feel it but I can't…Damn it!*

"It's got Bill," Joe said, his face reflecting the fear and disbelief they all felt. His gun hand was shaking. "It'll force him to let it out. There's only the two of us working today. There's no one else. What the hell *was* that?"

"Joe, Kim, get to the lower emergency exit," Lazo said. "See if you can head it off up at street level. I'll wait for the elevator. I've already called the police. They should be here soon."

"Too late," Kim said, her shoulders slumping. "It's gone. It moves too fast. But I think…I think I know where it's going." She sent out another thin thread of mental energy, forcing herself to be calm, taking her time. This time it was successful as her thoughts wound their way to the upper level of the haven. An image formed in her mind's eye—Bill, the security guard, lay in a pool of blood in the parking garage; the garage door was open. The electrician and his truck were nowhere in sight, apparently not wanting to stick around for any trouble.

And the creature was gone. Yet Kim could sense it, faintly, as if she had attached some kind of mental tracer on it.

"Damn!" Kim pounded her fist against the wall. "Bill's down!" With a much stronger curse of his own, Lazo brushed by Kim, heading back toward his office. "I guess I'll call the ambulance then." He paused, leaning in close to the lieutenant. "We need to talk…again."

Kim nodded. Joe looked bleak as he waited for the elevator to return.

The image refocused in Kim's mind, sprang nearer as if in close-up. Bill moved; a groan escaped his lips. Kim felt dizzy, both with the effort to 'see' into the garage above them and with the relief suddenly flooding her body. "Bill's still alive!" she cried, turning towards Lazo's retreating back.

The big man frowned. "How do you—?" and then, with a knowing look, rushed into his office.

"Are you sure, ma'am, er, Kim?" Joe asked hopefully.

"Yes. Here's the elevator. Get to him quickly." Kim turned to Brewster who was just now getting to his feet. "Are you all right?" she asked.

He nodded, his face ashen. "What was it?"

Kim shook her head. "I wish I knew." She looked up at Brewster. "You saved my life. Thank you. Where did you learn that move? Did you play football?"

Brewster shrugged, grimacing in pain as he rubbed his shoulder. He smiled sheepishly. "No. From my dreams. It's like I told you—it's one of the stunts ArcNight performs."

His dreams again. "The children?" Kim turned back down the hall.

Brewster paused. "They're…they're OK," He said as

he walked with her. "The other man here, the young black gentleman, got to them before me and hustled them into another room with a more secure lock. There was no time to get to the elevator. Jenny assured me…I just felt like I needed to help you out here despite—"

"And I owe you one. We need to get your shoulder looked at first off."

"It's OK. But…but your little girl…"

Kim's heart caught in her throat. "Shioko? I thought you said—"

Brewster nodded. "I know. I'm sorry. She collapsed. Jenny had to carry her. Went into some kind of, I don't know, trance or coma or something."

No, no. That's why I can't sense her. Kim broke into a run, leaving an injured and confused Wayne Brewster in her wake.

CHAPTER 24

Brewster grimaced at the pain in his shoulder as he jogged down the hall after Kim Yoshima. What the hell had he been thinking? That creature was something out of a nightmare! And he had blindly gone after it with no thought at all to what he was doing. He had just…reacted.

Was he starting to imagine he really was some kind of super hero?

And yet, he had tipped the balance, it seemed. Despite the situation, he felt a little thrill at that. Though he was in good shape and worked out regularly, he had never thought of himself as heroic or macho. He was a computer analyst, living alone. He had very few friends and no one special shared his life at present. His existence had never been very exciting. In fact, he avoided confrontations at all costs. And yet, as the old saying went, he had risen to the occasion.

Or was he just trying to impress Kim Yoshima?

The moment he had seen her walk into the reading room, he felt like he knew her. It was her face he had seen in his dreams. Was that a coincidence? Why were they meeting here now? Whatever had suddenly brought them together, he felt an almost irrational eagerness to get close to her. Maybe she could shed some light on these dreams he had been having.

Now's not the time, he thought with a shake of his head. *My god, what's happening here?*

As he followed Kim toward a back room of the research haven, the first vestiges of real fear began to worm their way into his mind.

What kind of bizarre, frightening situation had he walked into?

Jenny Sibulovich unlocked the door and let Brewster and Kim inside. The room was a small storage area filled with stocked bookshelves, lined mostly with magazine slip cases. "Aunt Kim!" Bobby, the young boy who had accompanied Kim, ran to his aunt, fear and confusion warring on his young face. "What's goin' on? Somethin's happened to Shioko!"

"It's OK, it's OK," Kim said reassuringly, though she didn't seem to completely believe it herself. "Let's take a look at her."

"She seems to have gone into some kind of fugue state or trance," Jenny said as she led Brewster and Kim to a far corner of the room. "It happened just after we locked ourselves in here." She shot a concerned glance at Kim. "Is—?"

"Lazo's OK," Kim answered Jenny's unspoken question. "He's calling an ambulance for Bill, who was injured."

What they found wasn't what Brewster had expected. The young girl, Shioko, sat on the floor in a corner of the room. She seemed alert, but her eyes were cloudy, her expression almost eerily adult. She looked up as he, Bobby, and the two women approached. Kim turned to Jenny. "Jenny, please, take Bobby out front. It's OK, Bobby. We'll be out in a minute. Shioko's going to be OK."

"OK, Aunt Kim. I'm not scared!"

Jenny nodded, not asking any questions, as she led Bobby out of the room. Brewster hesitated and then began to follow them. "No," Kim said, placing her hand on his arm. "Stay, please. I'll need someone to keep an eye on us." She looked at him strangely. "Will you stay? I know none of this makes any sense and you don't know me at all. You don't have to."

But I do know you, somehow. Brewster shook his head, the throbbing in his shoulder starting to subside. "I'll stay. What do you want me to do?"

"Thank you." Kim looked back at the front of the room. "Please close the door and just watch us. I'm going to try and… contact Shioko and will be in a similar state as she is right now. Make sure…I don't know. Just watch us. This is pretty new to me too. If it looks like I'm, well, losing consciousness or something, shake me or slap me out of it." She smiled crookedly. "Not that I'm into that sort of thing, mind you."

Brewster smiled back. "Me neither. But I'll make an exception in this case."

He closed the storage room door and watched Kim kneel down in front of Shioko. The woman and the girl looked at each other, eyes unblinking. As if turned to stone, they became completely immobile as if catatonic. *What are they doing?* Brewster wondered. *It's as if they're communicating with each other somehow.*

He took a deep breath, sat down on a nearby step stool and began to wait. A second later, he realized his palms were sweating.

CHAPTER 25

Curse that bitch's spawn! The Void take her! The shadow-tracker slid down the ladder onto the sewer system gangway beneath the city streets. Her hackles quivered, her heart hammered in her chest, her feet skimmed the wet surface of the slick, concrete floor. *If the others hadn't interfered, I would have...I would have...*

The blood lust ran in her. Seething with anger and disappointment, she struck out at the pipes overhead, tearing two from their concrete moorings. As steam blasted into the narrow passageway from the rent metal, she threw what remained of the pipes against the wall.

She ran through the passageway into the sanitation system's central processing area. Here on the catwalk above the darkened collecting tanks she grasped the railing and threw her head back, releasing her frustration and anger in a screaming howl. She fell to her knees on the metal catwalk, breathing heavily. *I don't care if they hear me,* she thought, more rage welling up within her. *I don't—*

A noise whispered up ahead of her. Another sound... *closer...the smell of—*

Something sharp pierced her neck. She whirled, her hand clawing at the protruding dart. A stark numbness enveloped her; her vision swam; her legs buckled.

Falling to her knees, she struggled to remain conscious. Her blood felt like fire burning through her veins. Strong clawed hands grasped her hair and jerked her head up.

Dimly she sensed two, maybe three of her fellow shadow-trackers gathered around her, their eyes filled with doubt and betrayal, their lips drawn back in quivering snarls. Another figure faced her, a dart gun held in his black-gloved hand.

Her eyes widened. "Ma…Master," she slurred. "What…?"

The hand holding the gun slammed the weapon across her jaw. Her head went slack, blood and spit drooling down her chin as pain lanced the side of her face. Again her head was yanked up by her hair from behind.

The figure in front of her stood like a statue, his Asian eyes like points of green and blue flame. He stared at her, a barely controlled anger of his own registering in the tightness of his human features. His hair was long and black as night. He wore a knee-length dark coat, open over a jumpsuit much like those worn by the shadow-trackers. But, unlike those who served him, black tennis shoes covered his feet.

"You screwed up," he whispered in a voice she knew well. "Killing the Yomitsu isn't in your job description, only finding her. My superiors won't be pleased with either of us."

His face became blurred, twisting in on itself. The shadow-tracker tried to concentrate on his image, to anchor herself to this reality, no matter how painful.

"It's the masters' job to finish her," the figure continued, scowling. "Don't you remember? Everything has its hierarchy in our world; everyone has their duty; everything has to be perfectly laid out and triple-checked. It's like belonging to a union. You know? Everybody's got their job to do. If we just go running off half-cocked, the system doesn't work. Chaos takes over."

THE SIXTH PRECEPT

She saw him clearly now. Her handler—he was one of the *Totou's* young ones, ambitious and anxious for control. He would make an example of her now to further his rise to power within the *Totou* and to cover up his own mistakes, she was certain. A smell of cloves drifted around him. She remembered he smoked that type of cigarette.

He frowned. "All the signs have to be there as well, all the portents. It's not just politics, you see. Or careful planning. I'm surprised you didn't think of that. We can't just go rushing in any time of day without the moon and stars being in the correct position; without the magic talismans we employ; without what some would call our smoke and mirrors! The Yomitsu and Ko will always win then." He looked at her strangely as if she had just dropped to Earth from outer space. "I really thought, after your huntmate had been killed and we had our little talk, that you would abide by the rules. Even I abide by the rules."

Perhaps it was the drug affecting her; maybe it was the culmination of her frustration that caused her to dare to speak out. "Until you are powerful enough to make them yourself," she croaked. "I've heard the whisperings—that you've already tried to capture the Yomitsu yourself. That you failed in that attempt. That you have been placed under watch. If you fail again—"

"Ah. Resistance and arrogance. And a belief in unfounded rumors." A sigh with a spark of anger flashing in his eyes. "I should have kept a closer watch on you. I should be proud that you would attain such a level of independence and insight but, instead, I'm very disappointed. Such defiance is not what I had hoped for."

The shadow-tracker fought to stay awake. She remembered her training, the constant hammering of knowledge and rules and regulations into her and her huntmate's brains. As long as she could remember, their minds and bodies had been bombarded to the breaking point—to hunt, to hide, to obey, to live for the very moment she had so carelessly thrown away. To veer off of that path meant certain failure.

Just as she had failed.

She saw how it used to be, as real in her memory as the pain she now felt—she and her huntmate coupling in frantic urgency, their desperate longing to live a different type of life—just to experience something else that was not so regimented, so unfeeling, so unreal. Trying to steal those moments away from their seemingly eternal quest.

The other shadow-trackers hadn't acted like that. Why had the two of them been so different? Been more…human?

"We tried to show the two of you the way but you just didn't get it. The Founder was right. Those writings of his that have survived all warn of the dangers of dropping human DNA into the mix."

The Founder. The one who, so long ago, had created the first shadow-trackers and formed the beginnings of the group that would eventually become the *Totou*—he who had been an ally of the Eminent Lord himself. *Human DNA?*

The young master nodded. "Well, making you a little less the beast was my idea and now I'll have to pay for it. It looked like you were going to be OK there for a while but you were an experiment, after all. And, eventually, experiments fail." The master pressed his face close, his eyes gleaming. "So, no more talks. You'll just have to be taught a lesson now, won't you?"

An experiment? The shadow-tracker felt herself lifted and draped over the shoulders of one of the other trackers. Her body bounced along as the one who carried her descended into the processing area along with the others.

THE SIXTH PRECEPT

Experiment?

She started blacking out, her mind crying in terror. She would be punished. She would never exact her revenge. She would be stopped from fulfilling what she suddenly realized was her destiny.

I am one of the Totou no longer. But I must pretend and play my part until I can escape and kill the Yomitsu.

CHAPTER 26

I thought Omori and his evil couldn't touch Shioko in this future time," Yoshima Mitsu said. "I thought my gift would enable me to make her safe. I was so wrong. I have failed."

Kim Yoshima found herself back in another psychic/virtual landscape—a reflection of dreams with just a glimmering of reality.

Or is it the other way around?

She stood once again with the figure of her ancestor, this time on a brilliantly sun-washed tropical beach. A magnificent blue ocean washed in through a rocky cove, the waves crashing against the shoreline; a jungle of palms and lush vegetation stood green and tall at their backs. A warm wind blew in off of the sea, carrying with it the scent of mystery and the unknown.

"You haven't failed and I can think of worse places to hide," Kim said, as she relished the velvety sea air on her face. Yet she knew full well such perfection didn't exist in the real world, only in this 'ambient-milieu'. "But why? Why would Shioko, or her consciousness, take off like this?"

"She's afraid," Mitsu answered. Her ancestor was dressed differently this time, wearing only a simple cotton *kimono*, her hair loose and flowing around her shoulders. Her feet were bare, her face devoid of makeup. "Shioko's fear is overpowering her. The sight of the shadow-tracker was too unnerving."

"But how did she see it?" Kim asked, perplexed. "She was in another part of the building."

"Through you," came the answer. Mitsu's eyes bored into Kim's. Her ancestor's face, even in this perfect world, showed its age now—the lines around those green orbs, the gray streaking her dark hair. "Through us. You inadvertently projected what you saw to her mind. You and she are connected, like she and I were so long ago, as teacher and student, siblings, even mother and daughter."

Then why can't I get through to her? "That's how I know the shadow-trackers. I've seen them before. As you…"

As if in response to the observation, Kim saw a dolphin breach the surface of the water just offshore, leaping high into the air. As the black and gray sea-going mammal arced back down into the waves, one dark fin after another appeared at the water's surface until a pod of the ever-grinning animals frolicked in the surf.

At that moment, the sand underneath Kim's feet shifted. The entire landscape suddenly wavered like a heat mirage. Kim stumbled backwards as Mitsu held out her hand to steady her. "Shioko must be found before she withdraws completely and her mind collapses," Mitsu said. "She is the key to stability in this level of the milieu. You must hurry! I cannot go beyond this point—I can only help you so much. As I have told you, there are imperatives even in this astral domain that cannot be denied. But the dolphins will guide you—they are avatars of Shioko's subconscious mind—parts of her secret self made incarnate. They know where she is."

Kim grasped Mitsu's hand. "Listen, Mitsu, I…there's so much I need to know. So many questions I want to ask you."

"In time…" Then the figure of her ancestor was suddenly gone, vanished like smoke in the wind.

THE SIXTH PRECEPT

OK, Kim thought, staring at her empty hand. *I get it. Let's get a move on, shall we, Yoshima?* She raced to the edge of the surf, waded in, took a deep breath, and dove into the sea. It was only then that she realized she was completely naked.

CHAPTER 27

If spotted from above, the Vincent Black Shadow and the Harley Davidson might have seemed mere blurs as they skimmed over the tree-shrouded back roads. Birds winging skyward would have called out to a couple of shimmering shadows, black and gleaming silver ground-demons that flitted by in bursts of speed and wavering heat.

Under the Vincent rider's helmet, the young, black-clad woman hunched over her metal steed, her eyes flashing points of green.

"There's an old saying," her comrade began, shouting above the roar of the engines.

"Don't start. Please."

"No ancient philosophy, I promise. Just loosen up a little. Everything's going to be OK."

Despite the wind and clamor of the engines, the woman's sigh was inescapable. "So you keep saying. But things can change. Events are not immutable. You should know that by now, even with all of your conditioning!"

"Yes," came the shouted reply. "But there's such a thing as faith too. I've come to believe in that concept, despite my upbringing."

The young woman smiled in spite of herself as the countryside rolled by—a hazy mixture of trees, farmland and small towns. It was a beautiful day. So why was she afraid? And was it fear she truly felt? *Yes.* And what was it she feared? A number of things, she realized, not the least of which was finding herself in this different land after so many years. This different time.

"I just want to get there!"

"You haven't eaten today. You need to be strong."

"OK. OK. Stop acting like my mother!" She frowned then at the thought. Her real mother had been dead for centuries. She hadn't seen the woman who birthed her since she had been sold into service by her father. Oh, she had toyed with the idea of finding her after she had returned to the past. But, somehow, that hadn't worked out.

The woman who had employed her as a young girl had, surprisingly, been like an older sister in the truest sense. Mitsu had sacrificed everything to save her; and then, in this future time, *Oneesan* had taught her to laugh and to have courage, to live her life to help others and serve in another way. She missed them both but which was her *real* mother?

As if on cue, a sign advertising a restaurant popped up at the side of the road. "See? It's fate!" her friend shouted. "We have to stop. Only a couple of more miles. When was the last time you had a cheeseburger, huh?"

The woman smiled again, "Well, I don't think I've *ever* had one." Come to think of it, her stomach *was* growling. The food wouldn't be what she had been used to but…"OK, maybe you're right. Let's eat! But, if I remember right, this area has these salads with grilled chicken and, uh, French fries, I think."

She laughed out loud, letting the wind carry the sound into the sky. This was, after all, another adventure. But an important one. Her life would come full circle and she prayed that coming here would not turn out to be the biggest mistake she could have made.

CHAPTER 28

Brewster found himself staring at Kim and Shioko. Both the woman and the girl were beautiful; Shioko radiated a pure, untainted childhood glow; Kim a striking, ageless maturity and strength.

But there was more to his fascination than mere physicality. There was an aura about the two of them—something powerfully mental. He felt a tangible 'presence' in the air as if they were locked into some kind of dreamscape only they could enter.

And that was the question—what *was* going on here? What were the two of them really doing? Brewster was doing just what Kim had asked him to do—watching for any types of problems. As if he even knew what to look for and yet, a part of him felt as if he did, as if he knew exactly what to do. He felt like a character in a movie. With what he had experienced this afternoon and now this—that didn't happen in real life, did it?

No, he thought. *But it has happened in my dreams.*

At a sound behind him, he turned towards the now opened door. The young man who had helped Jenny and the children stood there, looking concerned; worry and some other unreadable emotion were written on his dark brown face. There was something clutched in his right hand—no doubt some kind of smart phone. "I'm sorry to intrude," he said in a low, soft voice. "Is everything OK?"

Brewster let out a long breath. "Honestly? I really don't know but thanks for your help earlier."

The man approached him looking at him curiously. "I saw that…that creature," the man said, his eyes suddenly shifting to Kim and Shioko. "Right before it escaped into the elevator."

Brewster shook his head. "There was someone injured. The ambulance—"

"It's here now. Mr. Sibulovich is with the crew and talking to the police. His wife is with the young boy who seems to be OK." His gaze strayed again to Kim and Shioko.

"I'm not exactly sure what's going on here," Brewster confessed again. "I'm not involved in any of this. I just sort of got caught up in it. You know, wrong place at the wrong time."

The man speared him with a knowing glance. "Mmm, I don't think so," he said mysteriously. "I think you're exactly where you should be." He took a tentative step toward the two women.

Brewster blocked his path, holding his hand out in front of him. "I don't think you should interfere here. I don't think that would be appropriate."

The man turned his gaze back to Brewster. "I'm…I'm sorry. I don't mean any intrusion or harm. It's just that if this is what I think it is…well, we've been waiting and hoping a long time for this."

"We?"

"Yes. My name is Jackson Yamaguchi and I belong to a group. The other side of the coin, as it were." The man folded his arms over his chest, his head slightly down as he looked at Brewster over his glasses. Brewster felt a sudden charge in the air, like an oncoming summer storm.

"My group is called the *Shuugouteki*, the Collective,"

THE SIXTH PRECEPT

Yamaguchi continued. "We've been expecting this…this type of incident. At least I think this is what we've been expecting. Actually, the *Shuugouteki's* been hoping for something like this for hundreds of years." The man shook his head as if not quite believing what he was about to say. "The shadow-tracker. I never thought I'd ever see one. Sometimes, even though you're conditioned with this eventuality from birth, when you live every single day with such arcane knowledge as I possess, you really never believe it'll happen in your lifetime. For most of us, it never has."

"What are you talking about?" A sudden chill ran up Brewster's spine. Shadow-tracker. Was that what that creature was called? It was then he noticed the tattoo on the man's neck as he tossed his dreadlocks over his right shoulder — some kind of Japanese symbol.

"The legends, of course." Yamaguchi gestured toward Kim and Shioko. "The ancient prophecies, the old histories, the very reason for the *Shuugouteki's* existence. And them. They're the stuff of myth, you know. She's the Yomitsu, isn't she? And the girl is Ko. Ko the Little."

CHAPTER 29

The ocean surrounded her in a warm embrace. If the sea was the mother of all life, then, as one of her children, Kim felt the love that emanated around her like a physical presence. It was strong, primal and yet not quite real.

And, just as imaginary, she swam as if she'd been born to it—swift and strong and easy, impossibly breathing the water in openly through her nose and mouth. Her legs and arms moved so naturally through the depths—gliding and plying its warm waters like a seal while her lungs and body acclimated instantly to the ever-changing pressure.

Sunlight lanced into the deep from above, illuminating schools of fish, angled rock formations, and undulating undersea vegetation. Rainbow arcs of color weaved around and through brilliant gardens of anemones, forests of tube-vents, and sculpted coral.

It's beautiful. So beautiful. But—

But, of course, this really wasn't the ocean but a mental facsimile more like something out of a Disney movie. Everything was a little too serene and perfect, a little too animated and brightly hued…except for the occasional dark flickering around the edges that she assumed signaled Shioko's psychic distress.

Hang on, baby. I'm coming.

The dolphins surrounded her in a protective formation.

Their lean and powerful bodies cut through the ocean depths like knives, their flukes and tail fins propelling them forward. The pod leader darted past Kim and the others and then doubled back, twisting and tumbling, his squealing chitterings sounding in her head. He cruised briefly alongside Kim and looked at her, a strong intelligence sparkling behind those eyes. He nudged her gently in the shoulder with his nose and fell back into place behind her.

Finally they stopped and floated in front of a large, sheer rock wall. What looked to be a cave situated farther down toward the base of the cliff, yawned open. The dolphins trilled one last time and swam off.

That's where Shioko is, she reasoned, dropping down towards the cave. *You're on your own from here, Yoshima.*

Once more she found herself mouthing a silent prayer to her grandmother's gods and slid into the cave opening.

The entrance was dark and foreboding; a green phosphorescence clung to its walls, giving it a gooey, ghostly light. Kim entered warily, feeling something tugging and grasping at her, trying to keep her from getting inside. As if working her way through a block of Jell-O, she slowly pushed through into the rocky opening beyond. *Shioko,* she thought-sent, swimming freely now. *Baby, are you there? It's me, Kim… Oneesan. Where are you, honey?*

Mitsu-san… A voice in the ambient-milieu, faded and garbled.

Kim swam as fast as she could, squeezing through rock columns, sidestepping baleful-looking octopi and distant cruising sharks, winding her serpentine way into the heart of the rock wall.

At last the twisting corridor she traveled came to a dead-end. There was no way to go but up. And so she did, shooting upwards through a short vertical shaft to break the surface of an undersea pool. She was in a wide, high cavern, dry and warm and illuminated like the morning sun. Multi-colored, man-high stalagmites vaulted toward the cave's roof. Stalactites, coiling and sharp, hung from that same roof, they and the stalagmites looking like a mouthful of giant, deadly fangs.

She crawled out of the pool, realizing with a start that this persona she occupied in this astral plane was completely dry and was no longer naked but, instead, was now clothed in shorts, hiking boots and socks, and a flannel shirt.

This level of the milieu allows the users' thoughts to become real to them, she thought, noting with some other part of her mind that she hadn't worn this type of outfit since college. *There's a bit of my influence here as well as Shioko's. It's like an ongoing mental construct.*

Oneesan…

Rounding a huge stalagmite, Kim saw her. Shioko lay in an almost-fetal position on the hard, rocky floor. Her eyes were wide and full of fear, her small body shook under the light dress she wore.

"*Oneesan!*" she cried aloud. "Go back! It's here! It's here!"

"Oh, honey." Kim ran towards Shioko, her heart catching in her throat. The young girl was terrified. "What's wrong?" She reached out for Shioko.

"It's here! It's here!" Shioko cried again, struggling to her knees. "Oh, *Oneesan*. Mitsu-san said the shadow-trackers would never find me in this future place. She said…she said I would be safe!"

Kim reached out to Shioko, mentally probing. "OK, honey. Everything's all right." She felt her psychic energy flowing into Shioko.

The child lay back down, her shivering noticeably lessened, her eyes growing clearer.

"All right, baby," Kim said, putting all the reassurance she could muster into her thoughts. "Let me see, OK? Don't be afraid. I won't let anyone or anything hurt you. Open your mind up to me. Like you did before only all the way this time. Show me where you came from, your past, your home. Show me the shadow-tracker and why you fear it. Show me the Eminent Lord. Don't hold back. Show me everything."

Kim felt Shioko do as she was told, her mind becoming a secondary entry point, another deeper pathway through the mental universe she had come to know as the ambient-milieu.

And it was there that Kim sensed something else— something frightening and evil. Something that should have been dead but instead was here with Shioko—hiding within this secretive part of her.

She directed her will to follow that evil, anger and disgust driving her.

CHAPTER 30

The shadow-tracker bolted upright, a leg shackle binding her to the hard, concrete floor and digging into her flesh.

Her head swam. She groaned against the muzzle clamped over her jaws; her arms strained within the captive strait jacket. A prisoner, she was a prisoner. Weak and dizzy, she crumpled back onto the floor.

"I know. I take full responsibility," a silky voice crooned out of the semi-darkness of her cramped, dirty cell. It sounded far away but through her blurring vision she saw a figure, a shadow standing in a corner and talking on a cell phone.

Her handler. The young master. It had to be.

"Yes," the voice continued. "I know we have quite an investment in her. I promise you we won't lose her like we did her huntmate."

Investment. Another unnatural word. She struggled in vain, her throat constricting with the need to vent her frustration. That's all she and her huntmate had been, she realized—something to further the *Totou's* cause, mere tools to be used and then discarded. That knowledge, that betrayal, overwhelmed her.

"We'll take the reconditioning slowly," the master continued, stepping closer, his eyes darkened pinpricks. "We don't want to damage her. She can still be of use and, in the end, she'll be one of us. Something she and her mate never truly were."

One of us? What does he mean? She struggled to her knees, her eyes never leaving the man standing in front of her.

"No. We gave them a little too much individuality, a little too much humanity. We...I thought that would make them more intuitive trackers, able to make better decisions in the field, more equipped to deal with certain types of situations. That was my mistake. I take full responsibility." He paused, frowning. "Yes. I'm going to correct that. Immediately. Yes, I'll keep you informed." Another pause as he turned away. "I...I know. I realize I've made mistakes. But I won't fail this time. I appreciate the second chance. Yes, yes. Understood."

What were they talking about? What about the Yomitsu? Shouldn't that be the *Totou's* main concern? What were they doing wasting time on her? She struggled, her frustration and anger mounting.

That's when she remembered the other word the young master had mentioned. It came back to her in all of its terrifying mystery. *Experiment. He said we were an experiment.*

She and her huntmate had been made more intuitive, the young master had said. More human. Perhaps the *Totou had* succeeded after all. She trembled. A shiver of fear ran through her at the jump in perception she felt within, at the idea she had never considered before. Perhaps there was another reason besides politics and tradition that was delaying the *Totou's* hunt for the Yomitsu.

Once the Yomitsu was killed and prevented from bringing down the Eminent Lord, what would happen to the *Totou*? What would happen to its masters and the shadow-trackers? Perhaps the Masters had thought they would never find the Yomitsu and had been shocked to face the reality of her being here. The *Totou's* only purpose gone, what would become of all of them? Hunting the Yomitsu and Ko were the only things they knew.

THE SIXTH PRECEPT

She growled, struggling again at her restraints. *More lies and secrets!* Her whole life had been built upon such a travesty.

No more, she thought, slavering beneath the muzzle, her eyes narrowed with hate. *I will escape this prison. And when I do, I will make my masters pay.*

CHAPTER 31

All I wanted to do was to conduct some dream research here. I never expected any of this."

Wayne Brewster stood next to Lazo Sibulovich, both men looking at the comatose-like figures of Kim and Shioko.

"Believe me, you're not the only one. How long have they been like that?" Sibulovich asked, never taking his eyes off the two women.

"About half an hour."

Sibulovich nodded. "Thanks for your help. If anything happened to Jenny or any of us…" Sibulovich looked down for a moment, his attention suddenly elsewhere.

Family and friends. Yes, it would be hard to have those close to you trapped in a situation like this and be helpless to do anything about it. Brewster understood that and sympathized—to an extent. He didn't have many friends and didn't really keep in touch with those members of his family that he did care about. He had always been a loner, quiet, reserved, not one prone to developing and maintaining many relationships. It was just the way he was and he had always been satisfied with that.

Yet he knew now—there was this nagging feeling in the back of his mind—he wanted to help these people. More than anything, he wanted to help. Especially *her*. Kim. He especially wanted to help *her*.

"What did you tell the police?" he asked.

Sibulovich came back into himself, taking a deep breath. "I left you and Kim and Shioko out of it. They don't know you had any involvement. Joe's riding in the ambulance with Bill. I told my boys in blue the truth, or at least part of it—that it was some kind of animal that got in and attacked us. They've taken our surveillance tapes but I doubt they'll find anything. Whatever that creature was, it doesn't show up clearly on video."

"Won't they question that?"

"Possibly. But it won't be the first unexplained thing they've seen." Sibulovich shrugged. "We were goin' to talk about what action we'd take tonight. It looks like that decision was made for us. Kim didn't want to involve the law in on this yet until we had a better idea of what we were up against. It's pretty damn unbelievable, you know."

Brewster glanced towards the door to the storage room, suddenly feeling a little like a voyeur—the two women were so still and unmoving, almost like wax figures. It was a little unnerving. He felt as if he was spying on some extremely intimate moment between the two.

His averting gaze found Yamaguchi, standing in the open doorway, texting on his phone. Was he contacting this Collective of his?

Brewster shook his head. He recalled again the offensive move he had put on the creature and his earlier thoughts about another mind assisting him. Was he getting some of this knowledge, this bravado, this instinct, from his dreams? From that 'mental universe' he had read about? Why would he even consider such a fantastic theory? And yet, he had acted and thought in a manner atypical of his usual mild-mannered, cautious self. There was a certain amount of fear and confusion in realizing that, but a kind of anticipatory rush coursed through him as well. He found he had been thrilled to join the fight.

"What about him?" Lazo asked, jerking his head towards Yamaguchi.

"I'm not sure. He said he'd like to talk to all of us whenever Kim comes back from wherever she's gone. She and Shioko are engaged in some kind of mental union or something of that nature." Brewster looked pointedly at Sibulovich. "He… Yamaguchi wasn't very forthcoming on many details but he seems to have some knowledge of what's happening. He rattled off some terms about some ancient Japanese warlord and had a name for the monster that attacked us."

"Was this monster called a shadow-tracker?"

Brewster nodded, frowning. It appeared Yamaguchi wasn't the only one with information. And yet, a million new thoughts and ideas suddenly skidded and crashed inside his brain. A sudden confidence welled up inside him. He felt the expectation of joining the good fight. He had to struggle to suppress a smile—it was so cliched but he suddenly couldn't wait to see what would happen next.

CHAPTER 32

Kim Yoshima stepped into white light. A soft, lambent cocoon surrounded her with no beginning and no end. She stood on a flickering, pure-white surface with the 'sky' and 'horizon' above and around her shimmering like the soft-edged remnants of cloudstuff.

Through the tear-soaked eyes of Shioko, she had peered into the child's ancient past; had seen the young girl's previous life, indentured to a *shirabyoshi* in medieval Japan.

The *shirabyoshi* faced Shioko, kneeling in a muddy street all those centuries ago. Despite the plainness of the older woman's clothes and appearance, a familiar beauty and determination pierced the veil of time that separated Kim from that moment so long ago.

Not just any *shirabyoshi*, she had realized then with a start. Her resolve to use her esper powers to the fullest almost crumbled in light of what she had discovered. The pre-geisha courtesan Shioko had served had been Yoshima Mitsu, Kim's distant ancestor.

"I have seen what will happen," Mitsu had said in a clear, low voice, a husky sensuality edging it. "Or, at least, the fringes of it. I cannot protect you here when the purges begin, not for long. No matter where or how you'll hide, Omori or one of his monks will find you out. He will unleash his shadow-trackers to scour the villages and the surrounding countryside in his mad bid for power. The shadow-trackers are homunculi, creatures between, forged into being by Omori's alliance with those of the Left Hand Path."

Images of Odawara, Japan, early 16th century, rushed out of the past. The jarring emotions of battle-hardened *daimyos* during the Epoch of a Warring Country melded with those of a woman—a woman who had Kim's face. And, above it all, there remained a little girl who loved them both. All those sights, sounds and feelings penetrated Kim's mind to be etched there forever.

Shioko had revealed to her the 'One Who Knows' and how she had foreseen danger and helped send her attendant ahead into the future.

By way of the temporal displacement tremors—the Spirit Winds. The same force that had brought the samisen *to the future, the forces epicentered in the Horowitz Box Factory.*

Kim looked away, her head spinning. And the shadow-trackers—what about them?

THE SIXTH PRECEPT

Yoshima Mitsu closed her eyes and concentrated. Her thoughts coalesced into a single thread of energy, sending a thin tendril of vision into the mind of her young charge, once again transmitted across the timeline.

(*an image of a man-beast, lean and powerful, running upright, eyes glowing yellow, fangs bared*)

"You're her—Yoshima Mitsu. Just like I said. That bitch, the Yomitsu, along with her little girl-child, Ko, have come back to defeat me a second time."

A voice, croaking and weak. Kim saw something huddled in a 'corner' of the milky landscape, in effect, a remote, hidden corner of the ambient-milieu. So remote that this puddle of virtual flesh that had just spoken had remained undetected. Until now.

Kim approached a damaged mental persona—a skeletal figure, naked and bloody, its eyes rheumy and staring out of a pain-ravaged face. It was so weak it could barely raise its head.

"We meet again, Ghost," it rasped. "Unfortunate it's not under better circumstances, namely me sticking a knife in your gut."

Parker, the Eminent Lord. Or what was left of him.

Kim had thought there wasn't much more that could surprise her on this magical road she had been traveling since first being attacked by the shadow-tracker. But this did.

Anger and revulsion flared within her. It was all she could do to look at this putrid excuse for a human being. "You're alive," she said aloud, her voice shaking. "How? How did you get…here?"

Parker laughed, spitting up blood and mucus. "Surprised, are you?" he said, between hacking coughs. "Well, not any more than I am. Somehow, before my body died, a part of my mind managed to drag its way here, to wherever here is."

Kim lashed out, her control dropping just for a moment. She grasped the pitiful body of Parker in a telekinetic grip, lifting him off the floor. He hung there in front of her, slack and weak, a gross and deformed approximation of anything sentient. "Talk, you shit," she hissed. "What's going on? If you've harmed Shioko…"

A gurgling laugh. "Observe, Ghost. I couldn't harm a beetle. It's your precious Shioko who's harming *me*!"

Kim let him down slowly, checking her anger. She needed answers. This creature, however vile and hideous, might be able to provide them.

She realized she could make him comfortable. She could encase him in a variation of the psi force filter she had attempted to trap the shadow-tracker in when she attacked them in Lazo's haven, one that would ease his pain and allow him to be more lucid. The knowledge of such a 'force field' was there, right there in her mind, suddenly so easy to access.

"Ahhhh. That's better." Parker leaned back as if on an invisible pillow, his features relaxing a little. "I suppose I should thank you for that. It's all this white light, all this goodness that's filtering in from Shioko that's killing me, you know. I must have an aversion to it." He looked up at her sharply. "She's been sucking me dry. Subconsciously, her mind is taking what it needs from me—understanding of the language and the time period she's in now. Ironic, is it not?"

So that's how she did it! "Yes, but enough about you. I need answers. Tell me. Now."

Parker sighed. "Yes, well, if I don't, I imagine you'll just get what you want to know out of me anyway." He eyed her studiously. "You've grown stronger and more confident since last we met."

"And you, obviously, have not."

"Yes. So it seems." Another cough. "I thought, after being sucked into this part of the milieu, I could regroup, get stronger, but…So, shall I start at the beginning?"

Kim nodded.

Parker's face twisted into a skull-like grin. "Well! Once upon a time, there was this warlord—the *daimyo* Omori. He was me. I was Kadonomaro so very long ago in medieval Japan. What you see before you is what's left of the reincarnated soul of that warlord." He paused, as if waiting for Kim to say something.

Which she did. "The Eminent Lord. I know. You've said as much before."

"So! That knowledge enabled me to see everything clearly. It made me understand why I had wanted to kill, why I had these ravenous, murderous cravings and desires in what had become my new life as a twenty-first century man. Power, you know, power is the great aphrodisiac."

He started to giggle. "Somehow that knowledge was a vindication for everything I had done in my present life. I knew then I had a purpose, a destiny that stretched back centuries." A sigh. "Which you and your friends promptly squashed."

Kim knelt at Parker's side, her eyes never leaving that pitiful face. "Go on," she whispered.

"I sensed something else when first we met. I could see your past as well as my own. You're an old soul too, you know. You're my nemesis, Yoshima Mitsu, your ancestral self come back to haunt me.

"Maybe you can't see the whole picture yet," Parker

continued. "The forest for the trees thing. But I can. Perhaps it's the dying. Oh, yes. I am dying in here. Now that that's happening, maybe I'm being allowed a little insight.

"We were adversaries back in Odawara. You and me and Ko. You know who Ko is now, don't you?"

She did know. Like a shot, that piece of the puzzle fell into place. Shioko. Just like the word, Yomitsu, had been garbled over the centuries into a combination of two names, two people, so had Ko become a shorthand form of Shioko. But Shioko wasn't an old soul.

"Shioko is the child in the prophecy," Kim said. "The real deal. The one that would bring you down. She really is from the past."

Parker made another sound like a laugh. "And bring me down she did...with your help."

Kim nodded. "Yoshima Mitsu's psychic powers zeroed in on the displacement tremors and their purpose and she sent Shioko here, into the future, to save her from your purges."

"Yes! Curse her!"

"And then, somehow, Shioko goes back into the past to confront you."

"Ko, the Little. You will send her back into the Void to deal with me."

The Void—the timelines. Kim shook her head. "No, I don't think I would do that."

"You're the Great Enemy. I'm the Eminent Lord. It's already happened, long, long ago. Unless—"

"The shadow-trackers—"

"And my other, uh, colleagues. You've met one already— in your apartment, the man with the dart gun. And there are more—members of the *Totou*. They can still stop you, you know. The future can have many endings. Like branches on a tree. A decision here, another there. Anything can happen. There's a probability it won't end up like this, that this situation here and now could be reversed and you could end up lying here like a diseased pile of dung instead of me."

Even in this virtual world Kim found she still acted out familiar mannerisms. She tapped her lower lip with her finger. "The shadow-trackers were your servants back in medieval Japan."

"Yes. Under the ultimate control of my breeder. A very special man."

"And this 'special man' set up this breeding program. But magic played a part in all of this too, yes?"

A weak shrug. "I was known at the time to dabble in things supernatural. At that time, like everywhere in the world, magic and the followers of the Left Hand Path had a little more of a foothold, a little more basis in so-called reality. The breeding is another story."

"But the shadow-trackers are here, in our time. Looking for me and Shioko." She felt Parker weaken further, his fragile state slipping. Despite her efforts to sustain him, he was going fast. There wasn't much time left. "Not because they've also been traveling through time but...but—"

A twisted determination. Madness. A relentless lust for power and revenge. A goal so insanely strong and focused that it would endure for centuries through countless generations. The scope of the emotions, motivations and patience involved hit Kim like a hammer. "After you were defeated, some of your people and their shadow-trackers escaped. Somehow they had discovered Shioko had been sent somewhere and sometime into the future and would eventually return to fulfill the prophecy; that the one who would help her would be a descendant of Mitsu herself.

"The *Totou* continued to breed and refine their shadow-trackers, hiding and existing in secret all this time, and, throughout the centuries and all over the world, hunted for me and Shioko—Shioko as her true self and me in whatever form I would take in a future incarnation. The *Totou*, an obsessed cabal…its members intended to stop me from possibly sending Shioko back into the past to help defeat their master."

Parker weakly waved a cadaverous hand. "As you say," he croaked. "Power, opportunity and imagination can work miracles, can they not?"

"But how?" How had the shadow-trackers found her, after all these centuries? What methods had they and the ones who controlled them employed to track her down? It had taken them over four hundred years to find her but they had finally done it.

She felt it then—a memory washing over her.

(*clawed hands and gleaming fangs tore at her, beat her, made her tell the ones who controlled them what she, what Mitsu, had done to save Shioko; they took pieces of her flesh and cups of her blood to supply their men-beasts and she-creatures with the spoor they would use to hunt for her over the next four centuries*)

Kim shook herself, feeling a coldness out of the grave. *Mitsu. My ancestor. They found her eventually, knowing she had an attendant child of the right age and tortured her into telling them what had happened to…to Shioko. They had some knowledge of biology, chemistry and genetics—they took a sample of her body fluids, her DNA, to mix into their future shadow-trackers so they could continue the hunt for the Great Enemy and Ko the Little—me and Shioko. My God.*

She looked at Parker. "All this?" she asked incredulously. "All this just so you could have a little bit of power?"

Parker looked just as surprised. "A little bit of power?" he whispered, his life-force almost gone now. "You underestimate me, Yoshima Mitsu, vaunted enemy. You think this is the last you'll ever see of me? Think again. Surely you know every warlord has an escape hole, a Plan B."

He sneered one last time and spoke, this time in ancient Japanese, "It is not yet over, Ghost. I will come back again, and again, and again—"

And then what was left of Parker's astral entity crumbled into dust and blew away.

CHAPTER 33

They're back! Brewster thought, snapping to attention.

He moved toward Kim Yoshima and Shioko as the two suddenly came out of their 'trance', Sibulovich at his side. The young Japanese and the beautiful Asian-American both gasped for breath and fell shakily into each other's arms.

Brewster hesitated as Sibulovich reached the twosome first, kneeling in front of them. "Kim, Shioko," the big man said softly. "Are you OK?"

Kim turned what Brewster perceived as very, very tired eyes toward her friend. Her face was slicked with sweat. "Yes," she whispered. She nuzzled the young girl huddling in her embrace. "Shioko, baby," she said, her voice stronger now. "Sweetie, are you all right?"

The little girl smiled wanly, fatigue and exhaustion evident in her small frame. Brewster could see her holding onto Kim as if her life depended on it. "Yes, *Oneesan*," she answered, a hint of uncertainty edging her little-girl voice. "Thank you. I…I was so scared. The shadow-tracker—"

"It can't hurt you now," Kim said, running her hand through Shioko's hair. "It's gone. You're safe." *There's a real bond between these two*, Brewster thought. *Evidently, Kim risked more than just her life to save her.*

Sibulovich glanced at Brewster. "Give me a hand."

Brewster and the big man helped the two women to their feet.

"Thanks." Kim looked at both men. "I guess some explanations are in order," she said with a grim smile. "Especially for you, Mr. Brewster. You've become involved in this fantastic situation, whether you want to be or not. But there's still time. You can just walk away; you both can just walk away—"

"No!" Brewster surprised himself with the vehemence of his reply. He realized that he wanted to find out what was going on more than anything. He stood here in an underground library, in a small storage room lined with shelves and boxes, and discovered in this completely nondescript, out-of-the-way place that looking into Kim Yoshima's eyes was an experience he didn't want to end. No matter what. "I want...I *need* to help."

"And you know I'm in," Lazo said. "Nobody messes with my family and friends, whether I'm retired or not!"

A nod, though a reluctant affirmation, Brewster sensed. Kim took a deep breath, a flicker of a smile creasing her face. Her emerald eyes appraised both men. "How are Bobby and Jenny? And Joe and Bill?"

"Everyone seems to be fine," Brewster replied. "Bill's on his way to the hospital with Joe. Jenny's got Bobby calmed down. Plus we owe some thanks to this gentleman here, Jackson Yamaguchi."

But Kim had already turned her gaze towards the young man who had moved into the room, almost as if she had sensed his presence. Those same green eyes focused now, suspicion burning brightly.

"Umm, Ms. Kim Yoshima," Yamaguchi said, clasping his hands behind his back. He looked for all the world to Brewster like an ordinary twenty-something, a little on the nerdy side—

slacker, gen…well, whatever letter or terminology was for his demographic these days. "*Konichiwa*. Very good to meet you. Honored, in fact, if you are who I think you are."

"And that would be?"

Yamaguchi cleared his throat. "The Yomitsu, of course."

Kim nodded. "Of course. And what do you know about all of this?"

Kim moved to Brewster's side. He smelled her perfume, faint yet alluring. Despite her own apparent weariness, strength and determination radiated from her in waves. He caught himself struggling to keep from staring at her.

"You may have helped us," Brewster suddenly blurted out, "but you may also have some kind of secret agenda. We need to know how you fit in here. I won't let you hurt these people."

"Us," Kim said, glancing sideways at Brewster. "You'll have both of us to contend with."

"Make that three," Sibulovich said, holding onto Shioko's hand. "I don't know what's going on here, but I'll be damned if I'm going to just sit by and do nothing!"

Brewster suppressed a grin, his chest swelling with an unfamiliar emotion. He found that he liked the big 'librarian'. And for the first time in his life, he felt a part of something larger than himself even though he wasn't absolutely sure what that was. Even so, it was not a bad feeling.

Yamaguchi backed up a step, his eyes wide. "Absolutely!" he said, holding his hands out in front of him—one held his smart phone. "I'm on your side, believe me. It seems you're in a little bit of trouble here, trouble that I'd like to investigate as much as you. There are others like me, other members of my group, that can help as well."

"I'm more in the dark than anyone," Brewster said. "But I get the sense we don't have a lot of time here."

"I'll tell you everything I know," Yamaguchi said. Brewster felt the young man's sincerity, his almost reverential manner. He could see by Kim's expression she felt the same way.

"Yes," she said. "I think we have to act quickly too."

"Especially now that the law is involved," Lazo said.

"Yes. Yes," Yamaguchi interjected. "We can't have the police in on this yet. Just let me explain."

Kim Yoshima nodded, glancing at her companions. "OK. But I need to get Shioko cleaned up and settled first."

"I'll see if I can get the police to ease off," Lazo said. "Those guys still owe me a favor or two."

"Fine," Brewster said as if he knew just what he was doing. "We'll meet in your conference room?"

At a nod from everyone, Brewster experienced another feeling. This one was more from the Wayne Brewster he had been all of his life, not this new action-oriented persona that seemed to be taking over—a feeling he might be getting into something way over his head.

CHAPTER 34

She awoke to the sounds of gunfire and some kind of animal sounds. Roaring? Chuffing? Groggily, the shadow-tracker tried to shake off the effects of the drugs that she had been given. In the hallway outside her cell, the noises of a furious struggle had erupted.

Her mind pushed upward through a fog of pain and confusion. She had been beaten, pricked with needles and probed. She moaned softly through the muzzle covering her nose and mouth. Her masters—those she had served so faithfully—had done things to her, things that were supposed to break her, mold her to their will.

There were more sounds—explosions, a loud hissing like fire or gas being expelled. Pounding, scraping noises. Screams, the growls of her fellow shadow-trackers, orders being barked. She shook her head, trying to regain at least a semblance of control over her senses. She smelled something akin to burning rubber.

Suddenly the door to her cell lit up, as if being illuminated from the outside by a great light. There was a spitting and melting sound. The door buckled and fell inward, a steaming, hot mass of twisted metal. She backed up frantically into the corner of her cell, pushing at the confining boundaries of the straitjacket. The hackles on her back quivered.

What in the name of the Eminent Lord is happening?

Through the smoke and burning, another smell assaulted her senses—strange, feral. An animal squeezed itself into her cell. Her eyes widened, her brain trying to make sense of what she was seeing. Oh yes, there were those in the *Totou* who considered the shadow-trackers monsters—abominations unnaturally created though employed for a useful purpose. But this...

It *was* an animal—not one she knew in the world outside but a beast right out of myth and legend. Despite the closed, restricted confines of the *Totou*, she was still able to recognize this fantastic living thing.

A *kirin* stood in front of her, its long-haired pelt glimmering in rainbow colors. About the size of a horse, the creature was impressive—like in the stories the shadow-tracker had heard, the *kirin* had the body and head of a deer (with a single horn sprouting from its brow), the hooves and mane of a horse and the tail of an ox, which whipped back through the broken doorway and out into the smoking corridor. The light, the broken, melted door—it was said the *kirin* could call down lightning to attack its enemies. Was it so? Is that how this beast had gained entrance to the shadow-tracker's cell?

The shadow-tracker froze, transfixed by the *kirin's* gaze. A benevolent intelligence shone from those limpid eyes—though slightly skewed and touched with a hint of unpredictability.

And then the kirin opened its mouth and began to sing. Like soft music, the cry of the *kirin* was lilting and peaceful. The shadow-tracker never knew the one who birthed her, pups being taken to begin their training right from the womb. But this sound, the presence of this beautiful animal seemed... motherly to her.

The kirin took a few steps toward her and bent its head, its horn touching the chain that held the shadow-tracker. *It's going to free me!* she thought with a thrill. *It's going to free me!*

At that moment there was a snicking sound from behind. A dart flew from the corridor and imbedded itself in the *kirin's* neck. The *kirin* turned, warbling in pain and confusion. Flickering light suddenly appeared around it, coalescing into sharp, jagged flashes. It was forming lightning! The tales were true! Another dart found its mark in the creature's thigh. The kirin turned back to the shadow-tracker, the lightning gone, the animal's expression angry, its eyes filled with pain. It tottered on weakened legs and crumpled heavily to the floor, the sedative darts rendering it unconscious.

The shadow-tracker's handler, accompanied by three of his followers, rushed into the room, crying, "I want this thing alive!"

No! the shadow tracker thought, an emotion unknown to her taking control. *Don't harm it!*

"Get it in another cell quickly!" the young master ordered. As the *kirin* was roughly heaved onto a large cart, the master threw a furious, harried gaze at the shadow-tracker, the dart gun he held trembling in his hand. "Don't worry," he hissed. "We'll fix your freaking door in due time. Can't have any bad *feng shui,* can we?" And then he strode out, leaving the shadow-tracker trembling and shaking her head.

The *kirin*…where had it come from? Was its appearance part of the *Totou's* great plan? It must have had some power to have apparently taken the *Totou* by surprise.

Something the *Totou* hadn't expected then?

Her mind tried to break through the chemical murk that had been enveloping her. She looked at the hot, smoking, jagged edges of the fallen door. It lay close and those same edges might be the key to her escape. Her leg shackle's chain might be long enough to allow her to reach it. If she could cut herself loose from the strait jacket before anyone returned, if she could free her arms and face, there might be a way to get out of the shackle. Everyone seemed to be occupied with this kirin at the moment. She might have a chance if she acted immediately.

Filled with purpose, she began to move toward the door.

CHAPTER 35

I find it interestin' you just happened to be here when that monster attacked us."

Lazo was angry and suspicious, Kim knew, despite the strange young man's assistance. But she could sense Yamaguchi's sincerity and openness. He looked determined to help. As far as him just being here…

"I know. I know," Yamaguchi said with a shrug. "But I don't think that was an accident. I'm *supposed* to be here!"

"Enough of this mumbo-jumbo and pre-destination crap!" Lazo exclaimed. "Whatever happened to free will?"

Kim, Lazo, Jenny, Brewster and Yamaguchi sat around the table in the conference room. Shioko and Bobby lay sleeping on a couch in the far corner of the room. Kim had gently massaged the area of their brains that brought on sleep, wanting them to rest and not have to dwell on what had happened. She wished she could get a few winks herself.

"Let's hear him out, Laz," Kim said softly. "I'm just as interested as you are."

"OK!" Yamaguchi bowed his head for a second and then began talking. "The shadow-trackers are servants of the *Totou*—"

"Which means 'cabal' in Japanese," Kim gently interrupted.

"Yes. The *Totou*, in turn, was formed by followers,

specifically a man known as the 'Founder', of the *daimyo*, Omori Kadonamaro. The *Totou* has been around for almost five hundred years. Most of that time has been spent breeding shadow-trackers, recruiting new members, causing infinite trouble, and hunting the Yomitsu and Ko the Little, respectively Ms. Yoshima and Shioko."

"Come on!" Lazo snorted. "How can that be? Breeding those monsters?"

"A form of genetics, Laz," Kim said. "DNA implants of some kind. Taken from my ancestor and inbred into the gene pool."

Lazo stared at Kim. "You know this? You're tryin' to tell us the ancient Japanese were involved in genetic engineering? How's that possible?"

Kim shrugged. "I've figured some of it out but some of the details are a little foggy, I admit." She paused then added, "I can tell you that I have a source that corroborates the genetic angle. This *Totou* has been able to breed these shadow-trackers."

"And we're talking time-travel as well?" Brewster asked. "Is this even a possibility?" He looked grim and very intent on the conversation. He was, Kim noted with some satisfaction, taking this very seriously indeed.

"We think so, yes," Yamaguchi said. "The idea of time travel does fit into the whole mythos of the Yomitsu and Ko."

"And who's 'we'?" Kim asked.

Yamaguchi took a deep breath. "I belong to a rival sect of the *Totou* called the *Shuugouteki*. The Collective was formed shortly after the Cabal by some of the followers of Princess Midori and Chancellor Hiroshi."

"Who?" Brewster asked.

Yamaguchi nodded. "There's not much written about their rule. They pretty much worked behind the scenes during that time. It was an interim period in Odawaran history after Omori had been defeated. Midori and Hiroshi were part of the coalition that brought down his rule. Suffice to say the *Shuugouteki* was created to challenge the *Totou* and stop their ultimate mission, which is to kill both the Yomitsu and Ko to prevent them from returning to the past to stop Omori. Both groups have fought and hounded each other for centuries, always in the fringes of society, hiding in plain sight, as it were."

"And how did you get involved in all of this?" Brewster asked.

"I'm...I'm a direct descendant of Midori and Hiroshi. The *Shuugouteki* is made up of many races and nationalities. My grandmother was Japanese, my great-grandfather was Congolese—he actually was supposed to have met one of the Yomitsu's ancestors. The story in my family is that he met the young girl who we know as She-Who-Comes-Before and gave her something that would help her descendant—you, Ms. Yoshima. Both my parents initiated me into the group. I've spent my whole life waiting for this moment. I can show you our web site on my phone—it's blocked except for anyone who's in the *Shuugouteki*. And if anyone does hack in, it will appear as just the site for a boring fraternal order."

"That's OK," Lazo said, rolling his eyes. "We can get the history lesson and family tree later. What do we need to do? I'm for callin' the authorities right now. This is gettin' way too big and strange."

"It'll get even stranger," Kim said. "We need to check out the *Horowitz Box Factory*. That's where this time anomaly is supposed to be. That's where Parker hinted we might find his 'associates', who, I'll bet, after having heard Jackson's story, are members of the *Totou*."

"I want to go with you." Jenny Sibulovich looked first at

Kim and then turned her determined gaze to her husband.

"Whoa, hon, no way." Lazo shook his head, an equally determined set to his jaw.

Kim sighed. She hated to take sides when it came to her friends. "Lazo's right, Jen. This isn't something that happens every day. It's definitely going to be dangerous."

Jenny rose from her seat, her eyes afire. "If even half of this is true, if this so-called anomaly does exist, it would be a cosmologist's dream. Don't you see? It's something I've only conjured up in theories and models, something that's only in science fiction novels. I can help you with this!"

"I'm sorry, hon," Lazo replied. "But you'd also just get in the way."

"I know how you feel, Jen," Kim said. "But this isn't the time to be exploring. I hate to say it but Lazo's right. When this is over, if there's any chance of going back and studying this phenomenon, then I'll be right there with you. But not now. Someone has to hold down the fort here."

Jenny stared defiantly at Kim and then swung that gaze back to her husband. Finally, with a sigh, she hung her head, the disappointment evident in every line and muscle of her slim body. She faced the group again, determination transformed into resignation. "OK. I guess I understand. But, at least, let me help you with any information on temporal physics. You're not going to know what you'll be facing there but some basic facts may help you. It's all theoretical, of course, and a lot of my theorems are outside the mainstream but—"

"We can use all the information we can get," Kim said with a smile. "And you're the expert."

"And I want descriptions when you get back! Any chance you can at least take some pictures?"

"Hold on, everyone!" The big man frowned. "I don't like

this," he said, addressing Kim and his wife. "This is risky—the *Box Factory* is a known hangout for street people and gangbangers. And we're still not positive about any of this. We should call the police or the freakin' National Guard, for that matter."

"No!" Kim said. "This is our...my fight. Everything that's happened in the last few weeks is connected to me somehow. I know it! It bears out the idea that I'm the Yomitsu and Shioko is Ko the Little. As crazy as it sounds, we've got to follow this through first. We've got to find out all the information we can before we bring in any outside help. That could scare the *Totou* off. If they've remained hidden all these years, they must know how to disappear."

"I agree," Yamaguchi said. "Even for the *Shuugouteki*. I have to have absolute confirmation before I start sounding any alarms. We've confronted the *Totou* so many times before but we've also had a lot of false leads throughout our history. Plus I, too, can speak Japanese. It might come in handy."

"Then," Brewster said, standing up. "What are we sitting around talking for?"

Forty minutes later, Kim, Wayne Brewster and Yamaguchi stood in the shadows outside a deserted carcass of a multi-building structure—the *Horowitz Box Factory*.

It turned out that Jackson Yamaguchi owned a firearm. A Glock 21 had been hidden in his backpack. "Don't worry," he said, as he retrieved the weapon and put it in his pocket. "I'm trained and registered. All *Shuugouteki* members are."

"Good," Kim said with a wink. "Else I'd have to bust you."

Lazo had given Brewster a loaded service revolver from

his collection. "Ever fire one of these before?" the big man had asked him.

"In a way," Brewster had answered cryptically, handling the gun like an expert. "But do you think this is really necessary?"

"You saw the shadow-tracker, yes?" Kim asked.

Brewster, nodded and placed the gun in his belt. "All right," Brewster said, "I won't even pretend to understand all of this but what do we do? Right now, what's our next move? Are we actually going to infiltrate this complex?" Despite his uncertainty, he carried himself with a degree of bravery and the definite air of a fighter.

Against all logic, Kim found herself drawn to the charismatic aura radiating from him. "Uh, well," she answered, mentally shaking herself. What was it about this guy? "If it were up to me, you wouldn't even be here. Like Jenny—you should take your own advice. It's too dangerous! That's why I refused to bring Shioko with us."

"But she's Ko," Yamaguchi said. "She *has* to be a part of this."

"And she will," Kim replied. "If it's her part to play, but I won't deliberately put her in any danger. Not yet. She'll stay with Jenny and Bobby until we get back."

"And I feel like I have to be here," Brewster said. "Especially since you've explained the situation. I don't know why but I want, I need, to be a part of this."

I know, your dreams again. Kim sighed in reluctant agreement. "All right, and I appreciate the help but you'll do what I say. Agreed?" Kim turned and walked back to the mini-van parked a few yards away. "Laz," she said to the driver. "Look, no need to wait around. Just cruise back here in a couple of hours and if we're not here, come back in a couple more. I'll call you on your cell phone if anything comes up. If it's a real emergency,

I'll contact you psychically. I think I can do that now. I can be both transmitter and receiver."

"Kim—"

"We're not sure what we're going to find in there. I want to do this my way. Yes? Anyway, you think anyone would believe us? Besides, someone should keep an eye on Jenny and the others."

"Exactly. You *don't* know what you'll find in there! And all that's happened—you levitating a book for God's sake, and this guy being a member of this secret group and all this incredible stuff I'm now privy to—it's all so freakin' unbelievable. At least let me—"

"Please, Laz. I know this is crazy. I can barely believe it myself. But I'll alert you if something comes up. Just give us a couple of hours, big guy. OK?"

"Damn you, Kim! All…all right," he said slowly. "But I'll be back every *hour*."

Kim waved as Lazo reluctantly drove off. Mustering her thoughts, she carefully scanned the surrounding perimeter (the wasted shell of Parker had been right—she was better and stronger at this now). There seemed to be no one else in the immediate vicinity—to her left a couple of blocks away, a few homeless people gathered around a trash fire; closer, but still about a block and a half distant, some teenagers were drinking and toking up; in the opposite direction on her right, at about the same distance, a hidden couple shuddered in the final throes of drunken passion. It was early evening on a weeknight and not many people were out and about in the Strip District, especially here, an area which consisted of a number of abandoned buildings, overgrown empty lots and forgotten storefronts.

The *Box Factory* stood in front of her, its jumbled back to the river. Like a rejected lover come back to haunt her, it seemed to call out, beckoning. There was a strange sense of familiarity and dread clinging about the place. She felt a chill run up her spine.

Without a second thought, she flung a psychic barrier, like the one she had used against the shadow-tracker, around Brewster and Yamaguchi.

Brewster gave Kim an odd look and started walking toward her. He abruptly hit the barrier. "Kim!" he cried out, his voice muted by the mental force shield. "What's happened? Is…is this your doing?"

Both Yamaguchi and Brewster were pushing against their unseen prison. Yamaguchi called out now, his own voice pleading. "Ms. Yoshima! Don't do this. You're going to need help. I can help you. I've been trained for this!"

"No," Kim said. "I won't have you risking your lives. I should be able to check this out myself."

But Yamaguchi wouldn't be deterred. "I know you feel empowered with these new abilities of yours but I've dealt with the *Totou* and have seen what their agents are capable of. This temporal distortion is something the *Shuugouteki* hadn't known about—the Void has always been something rather fuzzy in our mythology. If they're attempting something beyond our understanding, then you won't be able to face them alone, no matter how strong you are."

Kim picked up on a sudden, intense burst of mental energy from Brewster. Brewster stared at her, a dark look on his face. He was trying to aim his thoughts at her, she realized, hoping she would read them. *Do what you have to,* the words formed in her mind. *But don't try to be a hero. At least not by yourself. We're part of this too, no matter what you may think.* He placed his hand on the gun Lazo had loaned him. It was obvious Brewster would attempt to shoot his way out of the barrier if he thought he had to.

No sense in getting angry yet. Waste of energy. Kim nodded at Brewster and released the psi barrier. "All right, then," she said. "Let's go." Then she turned and started walking towards the *Box Factory*.

After a few steps, Kim shot a quizzical look at Yamaguchi. "So, what's your story?" she asked, curiosity getting the better of her. There was so little they knew about this young man.

Yamaguchi nodded vigorously, his dreadlocks bobbing about his shoulders. "Well, my life *has* been a little different."

"Yes?"

"I was home-schooled by my parents and attended a unique type of high school sponsored by the *Shuugouteki*." Yamaguchi's face took on a very serious appearance. "All very secret, of course."

"Of course."

"Eventually I got a series of jobs—menial ones—ones you can lose yourself in and quit easily yet still be a part of society at large. The *Shuugouteki* supplies us with most of what we need. They've attained a certain amount of financial strength and expertise over the centuries."

"But they haven't come out yet," Kim said. "Fiscally speaking, that is."

"Look." Yamaguchi seemed to bristle at Kim's teasing and her questioning looks. "I've not been brainwashed, if that's what you're thinking. It's important work the *Shuugouteki* are doing. I've been raised to be a part of that work and I'm proud of it. It's my *karma*."

Karma again. Kim nodded. "And I'm grateful for your help. No offense intended. It's just that any information that can help us needs to be shared. We've never heard of the *Shouugateki*, after all."

A reluctant nod. "Agreed."

"OK, here we are."

They were only a few feet away from the door to the interior of the factory. "All right," she said. "I'll try to scan the interior of the buildings first. If I can figure it out, I should be able to mentally sweep the entire complex."

Kim closed her eyes and sent out what she had dubbed a 'psychic search net'. Again, she found it easier now to enter the ambient-milieu, at least this particular level, and to control its ebb and flow. It was almost as if her line of sight had become a thin beam of light, shooting out from her mind to pierce the surrounding air, to break a slim, tenuous surface of a hidden world, co-existing next to hers but unseen, invisible.

There she could soar within the milieu, aware of all that transpired around her in flashes of images and sound. She could see and feel the surfaces and empty places within the abandoned buildings as if she walked its floors in the flesh. Her far-seeing mind's eye performed like a floating camera as it winged its way down musty corridors and vacant, trash-filled rooms. She blinked as a number of voices and thoughts merged in her mind. A picture of two elaborately furnished, well-lit, high-ceilinged chambers came into view. There were people there and…and—

More shadow-trackers, she thought, her skin crawling. *And what is all that equipment? Wait! I sense some others…prisoners. There is someone being held prisoner.*

And then…everything stopped.

Kim shook her head. The sights, sounds and smells of the interior of the *Horowitz Box Factory* wavered and swirled like a pool of multi-colored tie-dye and vanished. She put her hands to her temples.

What happened? What just happened?

THE SIXTH PRECEPT

The information Jenny had shared with her leaped into her mind—*Some kind of temporal energy field?* Kim wondered.

Kim felt a chilly flash of deja-vu. It was then that she saw it, not as evident as when she and Parker had met out in the parking lot, but it was there—a slight bluish aura surrounding the complex—an inter-dimensional iridescence.

"OK," she said, pulling her gun. "Let's go!"

CHAPTER 36

I am free!

Almost. The shadow-tracker had cut the restraining straitjacket with the still-hot ragged edges of the door that had fallen into her cell. Rubbing her upper body against the metal to engage the makeshift blades had sustained her some painful cuts and burns.

No matter. Pain, regardless of the degree, was meaningless to her now. It was revenge that she desired. And not necessarily against the Yomitsu.

She and the others of her kind had been lied to. She knew that now and bristled at the thought. The shadow-trackers had been created and manipulated throughout the centuries as pawns to the Masters. They were slaves, obeying rules that changed constantly for convenience sake and insane whim. Nothing more. They weren't even given names, only some type of designation known only to her handlers.

When they were no longer of use, what would become of them?

The reference by her handler to this 'experiment' had solidified those doubts in her mind. What was she really? What had her huntmate been? They could think and feel! Why bring them into the world at all only to throw everything that they had been given back in their faces? She felt as if all that she had lived for and known had been turned upside-down.

Her body ached with the desire to be free. She would make the young master tell her of this 'experiment'. Perhaps she would even allow him to beg for mercy before she killed him.

She shook free of the jacket, throwing it against the far wall. Stretching her arms and flexing her stiffened fingers, she then ripped the muzzle from her jaws. Taking a deep breath, she yanked at the chain that held her by the ankle to the wall. Growling and snapping her jaws, she pulled hard, her muscles bulging.

Snarling in frustration, she stopped and listened. Sounds of confusion still reached her ears but her handler would not leave her unattended for long. Someone would return to make sure she was still in their power. She had to act quickly.

Time was running out, regardless. She and the others of her kind had been bred with many built-in organic defenses— extraordinary speed and strength, meta senses of smell, hearing and sight, their bodies designed to be supple yet strong. She concentrated, working the muscles of her foot and ankle so they became softer, more pliable. Just like she had been able to squeeze her body into the narrow confines of the van's undercarriage to gain access to the library, she worked the flesh and bone of her foot to the point that it became thinner and softer.

Gritting her teeth, she pulled hard.

CHAPTER 37

Kim and her companions entered the main *Box Factory* building. Dirty and cavernous, the run-down complex seemed to beckon her, to call to her from some distant time and place. Something dangerously different hung thickly in the air. She felt a chill as she looked around.

Graffiti covered the dirty walls; trash, broken glass and dust lay thick throughout; a smell of disuse and decay surrounded them. She felt as though she had been swallowed up and was in the belly of some dark and insidious beast. The walls and ceilings seemed to glow dully with menacing power. She knew that if it weren't for her psi abilities, she would never have had such powerful feelings. The muted light and dilapidated surroundings seemed to tighten around her like a noose.

Shaking off her unease, Kim ran the ambient-milieu again, pushing through whatever interference had stopped her a moment earlier. It had caught her by surprise then; perhaps that was why it had been able to block her esper abilities. She had been concentrating too much; before, when she was using her newfound abilities, she had acted subconsciously; she hadn't known what she was doing or that certain things just couldn't be done, and so, she had done them. She broke down the barrier easily now and spied further into the factory.

(Chaos, confusion. Several armed men were milling about ahead;

they seemed anxious as if trying to ward off some kind of attack; smoke filled the hallways; somewhere, once again, there existed a room filled with elaborate machinery and equipment; there was—

—an explosion)

Kim felt a jarring rumble through the floor. Dust fell from the ceiling. The room itself felt like it was spinning.

"What's that?" Yamaguchi whispered. Fear and uncertainty were evident in every motion of his body. As they were with Brewster, although a little more controlled. In fact, Kim was beginning to feel a little nervous herself.

"Perhaps we shouldn't be going in here by ourselves after all," she said.

It was then that she sensed the shadow-trackers.

There were a dozen of them, just like the ones Kim had encountered before but they were different somehow—more brutal-seeming, bestial and primitive. They loped and crawled out of the dark corners, facing Kim, Yamaguchi and Brewster, snarling and howling like a wolf pack from Hell. These were naked, radiating a primal ferocity, their eyes flashing, fangs bared.

Homunculi, she thought, her hands suddenly trembling. *Monsters of the Left Hand Path.* Kim felt that fear again, some kind of reincarnated memory from her past life. But it was real enough no matter where it came from. She fought a wrenching desire to turn and run.

No, she thought, (*the shadow-trackers attacking her ancestor, the* shirabyoshi, *hurting her*) *Not this time.*

The shadow-trackers stopped, nostrils flaring, their yellow eyes focusing on where Kim and her comrades stood.

"My god," Yamaguchi whispered, his voice tremulous as he drew his gun. "It's one thing to read about this but I never realized...I never really knew..."

THE SIXTH PRECEPT

"Kim," Brewster said, holding his own weapon. "Can your powers handle all of these things? I'm not sure we can outrun them."

"I don't know," she replied, raising her gun. "But I don't have the time to find out. Start backing up slowly and when I say fire—"

A chorus of whispers echoed throughout the sepulchral interior of the building. The dog-creatures began to call out a name, to recite a mantra full of wonder and murderous desire, a chanting from out of some sick nightmare—"The Yomitsu, the Yomitsu, the Yomitsu, the Yomitsu…"

It's me they want, she said. *Even after all these centuries. Especially after all this time!*

They charged, moving like wraiths, their bodies fluid and serpentine. Kim gritted her teeth, aimed her gun, and cried, "Fire!"

Yamaguchi and Brewster, despite radiating fear and disbelief, stood on either side of her, adding their firepower to hers.

The lead creatures fell, their bodies gushing blood as the bullets ripped into them. Their snarling and spitting comrades leaped over them, reaching out for Kim and her companions as if they had no concern for their own lives.

There was another distant explosion.

(*In another part of the factory—a monster out of legend; a demon beast…somewhere up ahead attacking armed men*)

Kim blinked, her knees suddenly weak as she lost focus. Her vision swam; her body was buffeted and spun wildly about by some spectral force.

(*She stood on a stone stairway. A blue sky and distant mountains met her surprised gaze. She turned back toward the castle tower that loomed above her and, still holding her gun outstretched in front of her, looked down to see two strangely dressed men staring back at her*)

And then, she was back. The shadow-trackers were gone. "What?" Kim looked toward an equally stunned Brewster and Yamaguchi, steadying herself against a pillar several feet from where she had stood.

"What...what happened to you?" Yamaguchi asked. He looked around, wild-eyed. Brewster seemed equally puzzled.

"Kim," Brewster said, walking toward her. "I know it sounds crazy but you, your body, seemed to flicker or something. One minute you were right beside us and now—"

The Spirit Winds. "I think something happened. Something to do with those so-called temporal displacement tremors. I was actually...I was sent back into the past. Only for a moment... I'm sure of it!"

"It's happening," Yamaguchi said, licking his lips. "It's starting to happen. The *Totou* has somehow harnessed the power of time travel. It's how you and Ko will get back to Omori's time. That has to be how the ancient prophecy will be fulfilled!" Yamaguchi held his gun tightly, looking more and more frightened. "The Prophecy of the One Child!"

Kim shook her head, trying to throw off the sudden dizziness encompassing her. Somehow, what Yamaguchi said made sense. "What happened to the shadow-trackers?"

"They ran off," Yamaguchi said, licking his lips. "They stopped after you vanished and seemed to be listening and then—"

"It was almost as if they were afraid," Brewster said. "As if...as if they were running from something."

"Yes," Kim said, remembering the monster she had seen in her mind's eye. *I should have listened to Lazo.* "There's something else in this factory, something that's loose and out of control.

We've got to get back and get some help. I don't think we can handle the situation here ourselves."

"Yes!" Yamaguchi agreed, as they started running back the way they had come. "Yes! Good idea. I have a cell phone. Let me call my colleagues with the *Shuugouteki*. I think now would be a good time."

"Didn't you text them before?" Brewster asked.

"Yes, but just to say I was following up on a lead. I didn't want to pass on any details before I was sure." Yamaguchi pulled a tiny cell phone from his shirt pocket and punched a button. "Nothing!" he cried, shaking his phone. "No service! It must be this damn building."

"Let me try." Kim stopped and pulled out her own cell. "I'll call Lazo." Her scalp began to tingle.

(*Something crawling out of the shadows—reptilian, gigantic*)

She turned and saw the monster enter the hallway from a side corridor. Instinctively, her mind reached out.

The beast hissed and backed up, its slanted, blue eyes ablaze. Long and serpentine, and covered in shiny blue-green scales, it walked on four short legs, its belly dragging on the floor as powerful muscles rippled beneath its skin. A whip-like tail curled and undulated behind it. Smoke drifted from its whiskered nostrils. Great curved horns sprouted from the top of its head.

"My god," Yamaguchi whispered. "It's a dragon. A fucking dragon as big as a fucking truck!"

Yes, Kim thought. *A Japanese dragon.*

Yamaguchi's fear was as palpable as the floor underneath Kim's feet. His legs seemed to fail him as his whole body began to tremble. Kim realized she didn't feel so courageous herself. But something took hold of her then, something that surged through her like fire.

"Wayne," she said, her resolve hardening. "Help get Jackson out of here. I think I can slow this thing down."

Brewster supported an evidently weakened Yamaguchi. "Kim, you can't—"

The dragon roared, tongues of flame licking from its mouth. It moved forward, the claws on its feet grating against the concrete floor.

Kim concentrated and sent another wave of mental energy straight toward the monster. The dragon stopped, as if hitting an invisible wall. It roared again and pushed on through the mental barrier Kim had thrown up.

"Go!" Kim shouted.

"I'm not leaving you!" Brewster replied, grasping Kim's arm.

"Listen to me!" Kim gritted her teeth. The dragon's roaring was as loud as a wind tunnel. The very air around her seemed to shimmer and fold. "I think the *Totou* discovered the temporal anomaly here. They were trying to control time travel for some insane reason but something went wrong— everything's become unstable. Things are breaking through different timelines."

"A dragon?" Brewster yelled back. "How is something mythical like that here? It's not real. Where is it coming from?"

Kim shook her head. "I don't know but it obviously *is* real."

"Another reality!" Brewster cried. "Just like my dreams and ArcNight. It's how I saw him that night on the roof. It's not just the timelines that are unstable."

"Other dimensions!" Yamaguchi shouted, suddenly animated. "They've tapped into alternate realities!"

"My god. As if we don't have enough to worry about." Kim felt her psi barrier begin to weaken as her mind turned upside down at that thought. The dragon opened its mouth. A spark lit up from within its giant maw.

It came to her then, a buzzing sensation through the floor that jolted her through the soles of her shoes. A slight reverberation in the milieu, a tingling in her mind.

And then they *all* felt it—a rumbling, rocking sensation as if the floor was buckling and heaving, a strobe-like dancing in the very air about them. Kim and Brewster stumbled, Yamaguchi fell to his knees.

As a churning whirlpool of light and sound enveloped Kim like a tight fist, she fought to exert some kind of control. She flailed about like a leaf in a storm. Her mind cried out in terror and panic. And then, from somewhere far away, she heard—
The end is the beginning; the beginning has no end.

She spun around and around like a top out of control. *Those words,* she thought numbly. *Yira's again!*

And then she and the others were gone.

PART FIVE

The Road Not Taken

CHAPTER 38

Odawara, Japan—1520, C.E.

This had happened to her before, this temporal displacement. She had been in one place and time and, then, just like that, had found herself transported to another.

At least, that's what she thought this was. But she didn't remember the shift from one time period to another then as being like it was now. Then, it had seemed instantaneous, giddily quick and dirty. She felt like she had blacked out for a minute and had been disoriented when she came to. That was when she had seen who she presumed were ancient Japanese, standing in a medieval castle within some kind of open-aired structure. They had looked as surprised as she had felt. It had all happened so quickly.

But now she seemed to be falling through a grayish murk. A thick, pea soup of temporal energy and blinding flashes of light whirled her around in a fantastic carousel of alternating heat and cold, of screeching noise and eerie silence. Was this awareness occurring because she was so much more cognizant of, and attuned to, her psi powers? Because she was now allowed access to other variants of the ambient-milieu like the one where her ancestor dwelled?

Whatever the reason, it didn't matter. She felt disembodied, her mind reaching out to see something, anything familiar;

to latch onto some corporeal anchor so she could stop this headlong plunge into oblivion.

Brewster was with her, clutching her hand. His mind was filled with surprise and confusion and an increasing desire to protect her.

And Yamaguchi, he was with them too, also struggling to stop their downward (or was it upward?) spiral. His mind seemed almost paralyzed with fear but a scientific curiosity and a mounting excitement were present as well.

And then she twisted around, as if a huge wind had scooped her up, squeezing and ripping her from Brewster's grip. She saw a bright light up ahead and hit something…

…hard.

Kim Yoshima clawed her way back to consciousness, her mind pushing aside the darkness that had overtaken her. She groaned. Her body felt bruised in a thousand places. Her head ached.

She lay still, flat on her back, breathing in a warm, dusty air that was tainted with tinges of spoiled food, smoke and blood. She opened her eyes, blinking in the light. Above her towered the remnants of a building—broken boards, splintered plaster and torn shingling loomed like a giant, battered scarecrow. A heavy silence hung thickly in the air.

Kim pushed herself up on her elbows, her head spinning. More burned-out buildings spread out before her in what used to be some kind of neighborhood—now a ruined and blasted muddle. A thin pall of smoke hung in the distant sky. *There has been a war here.*

She struggled to her knees and put her hand to her aching

head. Blood came away on her fingers. *I must have hit something when I—*

She sensed them before any noise forewarned her. Several people coming her way. She looked around. Where was Brewster? And Yamaguchi?

And my gun? Where's my gun? No time. She picked herself up from the rubble and shakily hid within the still-standing skeleton of the building.

She peered through a hole in the wall. Five figures strode into view as they rounded a curve in the debris-strewn roadway. Four were the *sohei*, the warrior monks of medieval Japan, although not all wore the head/face turbans her research had revealed to her. Two went bare-headed, their bald pates distinctive against their fighting garb. Three carried a body wrapped in a white shroud while the fourth held a blazing torch.

The fifth was on horseback, seemingly the leader of the group, his horse dressed in what appeared to be some type of military regalia. Kim's eyes widened. Tall, thin, dressed in a black, belted robe; long, dark, braided hair; those green and blue eyes set in a cruel, angular face...she had seen this one before.

The first tremor in the Box Factory, she thought, once again remembering. *When Wayne and Jackson and I were shooting at the shadow-trackers—this man was one of those who was standing at that castle when I got...displaced. I saw him. Somehow I've come back to this same place and time.*

But it was more than that. She closed her eyes as another shock of recognition slammed into her. *It's him,* she thought, incredulous. *The one who invaded my apartment with Parker, who shot me with the dart and who was in the warehouse when I found Shioko. It's the same man! How in heaven can that be?*

The horseman pointed to a pile of debris and barked a series of commands to the monks. The monks unceremoniously threw the shroud-wrapped body on top of the pile. The torch-holder set the tip of the brazier to the end of the corpse. Flames licked the shroud.

More commands. Kim zoned in on the horseman, trying to cut through the particular ancient dialect he spoke. "Return to the pavilion," she roughly translated the leader's spoken words. "The bitch no longer concerns us."

Another old soul? Kim wondered. *Is he the ancestor of the... the shadow-tracker's handler, or is he the handler himself sent back in time like me?*

At that moment, as the monks turned and started walking back the way they had come, the horseman turned his green-eyed gaze in Kim's direction. A look of puzzlement crossed his features. He stared intently at Kim's hiding place.

Does he know I'm here? How could he? She mustered a thin mental beam and directed it at the horseman as her strength started to return. The leader of the monks blinked as if waking from a dream, looked around, and directed his horse to follow the *sohei*.

Kim debated scanning the horseman's mind but decided against it. She had to be careful. As unbelievable as it seemed, there was no doubt in her own mind that she had arrived somewhere in the past—Japan's past. *From Pittsburgh to Japan,* she thought ruefully. *Gives the concept of a sister-city a whole new turn.* She had to gather her wits, make a plan.

How much time would she have in this era? If her theory was correct, her arrival here had been an unintentional manipulation of the time streams by the members of the *Totou* and not a natural occurrence. She and Wayne and Yamaguchi had been flung back into Japan's medieval past but would another temporal displacement tremor necessarily pull them back to their own time and place? Parker had mentioned "aftershocks." And what had happened to the dragon?

Whatever the case, she would have to work fast.

She got to her feet, a sudden fatigue gripping her. She had been through a lot today and she wasn't getting any younger. She remembered herself twenty years ago—ready to take on all comers; to do whatever it took to reach her goals. If only she could tap into that energy again. God knows she needed it.

The sun shone low in what Kim presumed was the eastern sky—*mid-morning perhaps*. Yet when she had been pulled out of the *Box Factory* into this time and place, it had been early evening in Pittsburgh. It looked like the day was going to get a lot longer. Would she experience something like jet lag—time lag perhaps?

She hurried to the rapidly growing makeshift funeral pyre. Focusing her thoughts, concentrating and utilizing the knowledge released within her by her ancestor's spirit, she modified her telekinetic ability to stop the fire from spreading to the rest of the body. Slowly, carefully, with mental fingers, she unwrapped the shroud from the corpse's head.

Kim's own face stared back at her.

She stepped back in shock, inadvertently allowing the fire to rage again. That face, untouched by the rips and tears and horrible gouges Kim sensed lay beneath the rest of the shroud, was Yoshima Mitsu, her *shirabyoshi* ancestor.

Herself.

She fell to her knees and let the fire finish its work, allowing her ancestor a semblance of an honorable cremation. She cradled her head in her hands. *That vision I saw when I found Parker in Shioko's Dreamspace. The shadow-trackers didn't just torture Mitsu, they killed her.* She looked back at the flames consuming the *shirabyoshi*, wiping the tears from her eyes. *But how?* she wondered. *The information from my research stated Mitsu helped defeat Omori Kadonomaro. How can she do that if she's dead?*

She hugged herself, trying to shake off the dread that had fallen over her, and then concentrated on entering the ambient-milieu. Yamaguchi's neural signature, an odd mental burping, was somewhere here, but distant and weak. *He may be unconscious. But at least he's alive.*

And then Brewster…there! She recognized him immediately, also far away but here in this time and place as well. *We were separated physically,* she mused. *The force of the tremor tore us apart.*

Brewster! she cried into the milieu, hoping he would be able to receive her thoughts. *It's Kim Yoshima! Can you hear me? Just think your response!* She paused, listening, fervently hoping Brewster would respond as, behind her, the flames crackled and consumed the woman she once was.

CHAPTER 39

Wayne Brewster was still falling.

But this wasn't any dream he was having. This was real!

He had been spit out from whatever wild, unnatural vortex had sucked him and Kim and Yamaguchi up like some cosmic blender. Bright sunlight blinded him; warm air embraced him; from somewhere up above, through frantic, blinking eyes, he caught a glimpse of blue sky.

He reached out wildly, his flailing hands trying to arrest his rapid descent. Something flashed by him—a roof, a gutter. He stretched and grabbed it, grunting in pain and shock as his body abruptly slammed against the side of a building. He hung like a marionette dangling on its strings. His heart beat hard against his chest as he gasped for breath.

Some instinct, some presence of mind took over. He hoisted himself up onto the roof, his aching muscles acting as if they had a will of their own. Kneeling there, catching his breath, he surveyed his surroundings, his mind trying to process what had happened to him. *Where am I? What is this place?*

The building he knelt on seemed to be some kind of temple. It rose five stories high, constructed, from what he could discern, in an Asian style. Japanese? He didn't know that much about architecture but, with its pointed, upsweeping series of gabled roofs, and elegant, ethereal overall style, the temple seemed an example of that country's design. It was situated on a small hill in the middle of what looked to be a city business district. A finely manicured garden complete with a central pond lay below him at the front of the temple. Below and beyond and around it sprawled a grid of busy streets, yet not a contemporary scene, it seemed. It had an air, a feeling, of being in the past. Could this be a poor Chinatown instead? No, no, the people he saw were dressed in what he thought of as ancient Japanese clothing—he actually recognized the attire from the Hong Kong action flicks and 'samurai cinema' movies and tapes he had watched as a kid. Some kind of massive historical reenactment? A movie set perhaps?

No. None of those either. The sounds, the smells, the peculiar lilt to the people's speech. This scene with its shops and houses built so closely together, its outdoor vendors, the lettered signs written in a distinctive Asian script, the dirt and cobblestoned streets, seemed all too real.

There was something else as well…the air seemed pure, almost sweet. He breathed in a mostly clean, heady mix; not the polluted atmosphere he was so used to. Where on earth would the air be so fresh?

He closed his eyes, leaning back against the heavily tiled roof. Kim had told him the *Totou* was trying to travel through time. She had actually done that herself, she said, albeit briefly.

Despite everything that had happened to him, he found that hard to believe.

And yet…*Could I be in medieval Japan?* he asked himself, incredible as it sounded. *Have I gone back in time?*

He looked down, aware that his fear of heights was no longer bothering him at all. Radiating outward from where he perched, more streets and buildings formed a spider web of city blocks, the gabled rooftops undulating towards a great, surrounding wall in the distance. And near that…*A castle,* he thought, staring at the huge, multi-tiered structure. *Kim would know.*

He blinked. Where *were* Kim and Yamaguchi? And that dragon! Even his dreams weren't this crazy!.

Damn it! he thought. *Now what?* His hand went instinctively to his belt, groping for his service rope. *No, no!* he thought, shaking his head. *That's ArcNight, not me!* And the gun given to him by Sibulovich was gone, torn from his grasp as he tumbled through time.

Still…

Slowly at first, then more quickly and nimbly, he made his way around to the side of the roof. His feet seemed to pick out safe toeholds of their own accord, as if he had done this type of acrobatic stunt all of his life. Carvings of fantastic beasts and warriors adorned the edges of the roof. Brewster crouched within the shadows of a winged creature, its mouth open in a silent, toothy roar as he surveyed the area at the rear of the structure.

A grassy knoll with a path leading to street level lay below, deserted, at least at the moment. More gardens dotted the hillside. Taking a deep breath, Brewster swung over the edge of the building and dropped to the balcony of the topmost level below the roof. Making sure no one had seen him, he slipped over a wooden railing, crawled out to the edge of the upper level roof and clambered down the succeeding levels of the five-story temple.

Like a spider, he shimmied to the ground, dropping the last short distance to land lightly on his feet. *I'm not afraid,* he thought in wonder. *Fantastic! But on the other hand, what do I do now?*

That question was answered for him as the sound of voices

caused him to whirl around. What appeared to be two well-dressed noble types had exited the back entrance of the temple. They were engaged in conversation and hadn't yet noticed Brewster.

Looking around wildly, Brewster ran for the edge of the garden. He ducked behind a small grove of ginkgo trees, sequestering himself among their tangled shade. Holding his breath, he decided to wait until the two had passed.

When the two men neared the trees, they stopped, talking pleasantly. These two didn't seem to be dressed as priests and he wondered if they might have come to worship or were patrons of the temple.

After a few moments, both men bowed to each other and one walked off. The other, the taller and broader of the two, clasped his hands behind his back and turned towards the garden. He began to walk straight toward the ginkgo grove.

Again, some silent urging caused Brewster to act. He reached out and grabbed the man by the front of his black *kimono* and pulled. The man's head connected with the open palm of Brewster's other hand; he grunted and fell to the ground.

Gritting his teeth, Brewster knelt down by the unconscious man. He began to undress him. *I have to do this,* he thought distastefully, feeling sorry for the man. *I have to survive.*

The clothes weren't a bad fit, his muscular frame being pretty close to that of the unconscious man who seemed quite large for an ancient Japanese. The black baggy pants were a little tight around the waist yet comfortable enough. The short, waist-length *kimono* with an interesting ninja-like hood and black short-jacket, fit well. There was a pocket in the jacket where Brewster put his wallet and phone. He hoped he would still need them eventually.

THE SIXTH PRECEPT

As he pulled the two-toed socks and knee-length two-toed boots over his own feet, he realized he still had a problem. He didn't need to use the man's belt, or *obi*, Brewster remembered it was called, because the pants fit so snugly. Brewster removed the *obi*, wrapped it around the lower part of his face and then tucked the rest under the *kimono's* hood. With this impromptu face-wrap and hood covering most of his decidedly non-Asian features, no one might look at him too closely and see that he wasn't Japanese.

He arranged his 'victim' into a sitting position against one of the trees, the man now clothed in nothing but a loincloth.

At that moment, his head tingled as if on fire. He placed his fingers against his temples. *Brewster!* a voice cried in his mind. *It's Kim Yoshima! Can you hear me? Just think your response!*

Brewster smiled and then concentrated. *Kim. Thank God. I'm…well, I don't know where I am. Can you hear me? I don't know if I'm doing this right.*

Yes. You're OK? Good. Listen, I've got a lot to tell you…

CHAPTER 40

Kim Yoshima watched the fire engulf her *shirabyoshi* ancestor. Yoshima Mitsu deserved a more fitting and honorable last resting place, Kim knew, but there was no time now, only a feeling of desperation. Using her telekinesis, she levitated loose rocks and pieces of burnt timber to bury what was left of the dead woman.

After finishing, Kim sat down at the side of the makeshift grave, her shoulders slumped, sudden despair and grief compounding her weariness. She seemed to be the only person in the world—there was no one else; she sensed no others in this burnt-out shell of a neighborhood. She shivered as fear and a sense of encroaching awe begin to enfold her in insidious tentacles. *I'm in the past,* she marveled incredulously. *I've traveled through time and I've just buried my ancestor.* She centered herself with deep breaths, trying to quell the rising terror. *It's me,* she thought. *It's all come down to me.*

Ever since the first awakenings of her mental abilities, she had asked herself why. Why was this happening to her? Why was there such a connection between Pittsburgh and Odawara? Because they were sister cities? It had to be more than that!

Karma. It always circled back to *karma.* Somehow she had been chosen for this particular part in this particular drama and she had to play the role she had been given. There was much more at stake here than just herself and, she knew, there was no turning back.

Like the *Box Factory*, she, Kim Yoshima, had become a kind of Nexus Point and all these people, all this weirdness and unpredictability, were like satellites orbiting around her, drawn to whatever ending awaited them all. A laugh bubbled up from inside her. *Really? I should help Jenny write her next book!*.

One of those 'satellites' was suddenly uppermost in her mind--she had instructed Brewster to stay put. It would be easier for her to get to him, following his mental signature. Yet she would stick out like a sore thumb with her modern clothes.

Come on, Yoshima, she thought irritably. *Concentrate! Focus!* Maybe if she prayed to her grandmother's *kami* again, they might help instill her with some hope and determination. Encountering her dead ancestor had drained her of both.

It was like seeing herself lying there, burnt and lifeless. And were the histories she had studied wrong? *If Yoshima Mitsu was dead—*

No time for that now. I've got to find Wayne and Jackson! She got up and started walking in Brewster's direction, picking her way through the rubble, once again thinking of the old Japanese *kami*. Parker had said that in this distant time, the world had been more attuned to magic and those old gods were much younger, much more accessible, much more real. Maybe praying to them wasn't such a crazy idea after all.

But she had her own kind of magic, a psychic kind that suddenly stopped her and pulled her back in the direction the dark rider and his monks had taken. *It's there I need to go,* she realized, shocked at the intensity of the calling. She cast out a psychic net, letting it spread outward in a random toss—a trail was there, calling to her to follow it. *That's where all this has to end.* She sensed danger, power and great evil like the roiling of dark thunderheads. She felt a presence there, strong and amoral. *It's where Omori is. I know it now! That's what this has always been about.*

She entered the ambient-milieu. *Brewster!* she called. *Are you there?*

Ye…yes, came the tentative reply.

I can't come to you after all. I have a feeling there's not enough time. We might get sucked back up into another temporal tremor or one of its aftershocks and there's something I have to do. I'm going to try to lay a mental trail for you. Concentrate and try to follow me. Do you understand?

No, I don't. How can I hear your thoughts and you hear mine? I'm not telepathic.

Don't know. It's just the way this 'Gift of the Mind' has empowered me.

All right, whatever, but what's going on?

Everything I've told you, everything that's happened…I think I'm the focus of this whole thing and I have to see it through. I'm just sorry you had to be caught up in this.

Don't worry about me. I'm going through some…some changes myself. In fact, I may end up thanking you before this is all over. I haven't felt this…alive in years. Do you know where Yamaguchi is?

No, but I think he's close to the area I have to get to.

For a moment, Kim thought of Shioko. At least the young girl was safe. But what about her part in this skewed history? What about Ko the Little?

OK. What's done is done. Let's carry on from here, yes? Do you still have your gun?

No, I don't know what happened to it.

Same here. I hope to God no child finds them! OK, I'm opening up a level of the milieu for you so you can follow my mental transmissions.

You can do that? O…OK. Just…just be careful.

You too.

Kim winced at the concern clearly evident in Brewster's thoughts. She felt terrible about leaving him on his own but her senses continued to pull her in the opposite direction. It was a feeling too strong to ignore and, besides, she had a hunch Brewster could take care of himself. Even in the short time she had known him, he had become stronger, more…heroic. Alive, he had said.

We're all going through some kind of metamorphosis. I just hope we live to see how it works out.

That was when she saw the bodies. She smelled them first—the odor of death and decay hung heavily in the air and struck her like a slap in the face. The corpses had all been victims of the attack—men, women, children, even dogs and horses. All were hacked or burnt almost beyond recognition, left out in the open to rot.

Kim gasped and leaned over to throw up. *Why?* she thought, pounding her fist on the ground after she was finished. *How can people do this to other people?* She knelt there, stunned at the results of the brutality in front of her, realizing that, even in her own time, nothing had changed. People still killed, waged war, committed genocide. Was the human race cursed to follow this cruel path forever?

She shook her head and stood. *I can't think about that now. All I know is I have to make a difference here and now.*

She walked past the carnage, tears stinging her eyes, and then, once again projected her farseeing mental net. The rider and his monks were not far ahead, apparently taking their time. Kim could see they were in a less damaged, more populated part of the city. As if looking through a porthole into another era of history, she saw people parting before the rider's party, bowing and muttering obeisance. Fearful looks were cast in his direction. It was obvious the one she was following was not well loved. What did she expect from a servant of Omori Kadonomaro?

She closed her eyes and concentrated. If she could modify her telekinetics to snuff out a fire, perhaps she could use those same powers in a different way to rejuvenate herself. Yes, a flow of energy and strength rushed through her body with a soothing warmth. That was better. She felt refreshed, a little stronger. She picked up the pace. Sensing no one in the immediate area, she started jogging through the ruined neighborhood.

Among the various odors drifting about, she smelled different types of food in that pungent mix and wondered if this had been a market district. A great stone wall, a mortared extension of this *jokamachi*, this fortress-city, loomed over the street like a rocky sentinel. And above that on a large hill, sat Odawara Castle or, in the Japanese tongue — *Odawara-jo*.

A large moat surrounded the structure with a series of walled gates beyond that. The castle itself was enormous with four gabled stories arching into the sky. The succession of pointed roofs and intricate design gave *Odawara-jo* an elegance that Kim knew belied its true protective aspect.

Sections of the wall nearest her had obviously been breached at some point, allowing Omori's soldiers to — she stopped, her inner vision glimpsing armed invaders breaking through the gates, killing and pillaging. Blood soaked into the ground; painted the air with red.

She shook her head. No distractions! She had to keep this fear and uncertainty at bay! She paused again and turned towards one of the buildings to her left. This one was small but less damaged, its plaster-and-wooden shell darkened with soot but otherwise untouched. It looked to have been spared the destruction its neighbors had received. The sign hanging over the door translated into '*Kimonos* and *Obis* for Much Young Women. Many Available Wares'.

With a sudden idea gripping her, Kim walked into the small shop, a clothing store by the look of it. Reams of cloth of different colors and designs lay scattered on the floor as if the occupants had left in a great hurry. A small doorway led to a back room. Within the rear chamber's darkened interior, Kim found piles of women's *kimonos*, pants, *obis* and clogs, and the two-toed socks called *tabi*. A small wooden shelf held several small containers of makeup and face-paint.

She went to the clothes, running her hand over their silky lengths. Kim picked out a *kimono* that looked her size and tried it on. A full-length mirror encased within a bamboo frame leaned in one corner.

Yoshima Mitsu is dead, she thought, looking at her reflection. *But maybe she can still make history.*

CHAPTER 41

The rooftops. That was where he needed to go.

A sudden longing for height gripped Brewster; a compulsion that would allow him to make his way where he could avoid detection and find Kim as quickly as possible.

He darted down the pathway leading from the back of the temple to the town below, surprised at how comfortable he felt. *I'm in ancient Japan,* he thought, almost giddy with that realization. *I should be cringing on the ground, wallowing in terror but I…I'm fine.* If he didn't know better, he would have thought his dreams were controlling his emotions, infusing him with a great sense of wonder and purpose.

But no, this was business as usual for a super hero. Wasn't it? This kind of thing happens all the time to those costumed vigilantes. Right? *No,* he thought, as if trying to convince himself. *I'm not that. I'm just me. I'm Wayne Brewster, that's all!*

He reached street-level and stopped, looking around. *Easy. You're not exactly inconspicuous.* A couple walked past him, regarding him curiously and then moving on. His face-wrap might not be the height of fashion but perhaps the complete blackness of his 'borrowed' outfit had some significance—perhaps they thought him a ninja of some sort? If this town was in thrall to the warlord, Omori, then it was probably host to a variety of strange and dangerous warrior-types.

He jogged over to the nearest small building and deftly scrambled up its wall to the roof, easily finding hand and toe holds in the plaster and wooden walls. He crouched down and surveyed the street below. No one seemed to have seen him. Or maybe they didn't care. Again, this type of thing may happen here all the time. He shrugged and continued on.

He clambered over the angled shingles like a monkey, leaping from building to building with no fear and more than a little exhilaration. He felt free. His body and mind were one as he performed acrobatics he had only, literally, dreamed about. This time he wasn't a mental hitchhiker, riding along in someone else's body in some kind of fantasy world or 'mental universe'. He was accomplishing this with his own strength and will, in a reality he wasn't exactly sure of but one he certainly felt like he belonged to.

From time to time he would stop and study this place he had been so ignobly dropped into, shaking his head in amazement. *Just like ArcNight,* he noted, once again reflecting on the pulp hero's participation in his dreams. *Somehow, I'm acting out one of his adventures.*

For the first time he saw smoke billowing thickly in a far corner of the city. Birds circled overhead as if some great catastrophe had occurred. A battle? As Kim had said, this was a time of great warfare in Japan's history. If he was truly in medieval Odawara, that would account for such a sight.

The mental 'trail' Kim had laid for him was more like a hunch, a feeling rather than anything physical. This direction, where he was headed now—this seemed right even though he was headed directly into that possible war-torn area. *So? It's not like everything else that's happened today has been a walk-in-the-park!*

A cry from below diverted his attention. A small group

of four samurai and what, from Kim's description (turban-wrapped faces and gauntleted chain-mail), could only be two warrior monks, stood in the street. They surrounded a quintet of ordinary-looking citizens—peasants by the look of them—three men, one woman, and a teenage boy—who were exhibiting a great degree of fear and confusion. Other passers-by kept a wide berth, going indoors or retreating back the way they had come.

Keep going. This is none of your concern.

But he stayed where he was, watching as one of the samurai laughingly shoved one of the peasants to the ground. His comrades joined in his mirth; one picked up a nearby jug of water from a seller's bench and dumped its contents over the supine man. More laughing and shouting followed. Brewster couldn't understand what was being said but the actions of those below told him everything.

Bullies, he reasoned. *Possibly drunk. So much for the warrior's credo!* Still he maintained his position, his body taut. The tugging of Kim's mental rope urged him on but he felt another calling at this moment. Almost instinctively he went into defensive mode; his senses engaged just like they had in Lily's Restaurant. *First things first. I have to help these people. If they're being harassed for no reason…*

The samurai who had knocked down the peasant drew his sword. He stood over the quaking man, pressing the blade point under the peasant's chin. He laughed again, yelling something at the fallen man's adult comrades. The two other men bowed fearfully and ran, apparently being allowed to leave. The samurai who had dumped the water tripped one of the peasants and smacked the other's rear with the flat of his own drawn sword as the two made their clumsy escape. The woman, however, was kept from leaving, thrown to the ground by yet a third of the so-called honorable warriors. To Brewster's surprise, the young boy exhibited the only resistance to the ensuing abuse. He pushed against this third samurai who was now advancing on the woman and threw a well-placed kick at the soldier's stomach. But the warrior swatted him aside like a fly.

The samurai leered over the woman, grasping his crotch to the bellowing amusement of his fellows. The woman cried out, her hands folded in front of her, obviously begging for mercy.

The two warrior-monks stood quietly all this time and then turned their backs on the proceedings, apparently giving their silent consent. The streets had become empty, also a sign that these men could have their way and do whatever they wanted with no opposition.

The boy charged the samurai again. This time he wielded a wooden staff that one of the other soldiers had tossed to him. They seemed to be urging the boy to continue his fight, more for the samurais' own amusement than any sense of justice. The boy rammed the end of the staff into the samurai's kidney region. The big soldier, though protected by his armor, still grunted and turned toward the boy. With surprising skill and agility, the boy ducked under the soldier's reaching grasp and swung the staff at the samurai's head. The samurai blocked the staff with his gauntleted forearm and reached for his sword.

That's enough, Brewster thought, admiring the boy's courage and skill with the staff. *Whatever these three have done, if anything, they don't deserve this. I won't stand by and let this happen.* Without a second thought, he leaped from the roof...

...and became that *other* in his dreams; the one he had been denying since he had joined in the fight with the shadow-tracker; a masked and costumed hero that had become a part of him and vice versa. He became ArcNight.

THE SIXTH PRECEPT

He yelled on his way down, causing the samurai holding the sword on the peasant male to look up and inadvertently move his weapon away from the man's throat. Brewster's straightened legs slammed into the warrior's chest and head and sent him crashing to the ground. Brewster rolled to his feet and launched himself toward the warrior standing near the fallen woman, who had now turned away from her and the boy. Again he left his feet in a flying drop-kick that caught the dumbfounded warrior in the midsection, knocking him flat on his back.

Brewster ripped the samurai's sword from the stunned soldier's *obi*. He whirled to face the two remaining soldiers, keeping the warrior-monks in his peripheral vision. "Go!" he yelled to the man and the woman who, not understanding what Brewster said, understood his meaning well enough and scrambled to their feet and raced down an adjoining side-street. The boy hesitated as if he wanted to stay and help but Brewster repeated his shouted command and the boy haltingly ran after the other two.

The two standing samurai advanced, recovering from their surprise at this masked intruder's attack. Brewster had never used a sword before but he stepped forward and parried the first samurai's thrust as if he had been wielding such a weapon all of his life. He dropped to the ground and kicked the warrior's legs out from under him. Vaulting back to his feet, he sidestepped away from the second samurai's lunging attack.

He slammed the weapon's sword-guard across the samurai's jaw, swiveling the warrior around painfully to his right. Using his feet once again, Brewster kicked the stunned warrior in the back and knocked him onto the first samurai, who was starting to get up.

Brewster turned then to face the warrior monks. He jerked

in surprise. The monks were gone. *And I am too*, he thought. He threw the sword down and ran for the opposite building, anxious now to resume his rooftop search for Kim. But one menacing figure and a very long and sharp weapon suddenly blocked his way. One of the monks stood in front of him, his eyes wary but with a hint of something else flashing there. *Curiosity? Respect?*

Brewster crouched back on his heels, fists clenched, hearing the grunts and groans of the recovering samurai behind him. The monk didn't move. Instead, he spoke to Brewster, softly, demanding. Brewster shook his head, not understanding and beginning to get antsy. Something was happening here but he had no time for whatever it was.

The monk stared behind Brewster and barked something to the samurai. He then gestured upward. Brewster looked up and saw the second monk standing on the rooftop, blocking Brewster's path in that direction. The first monk then beckoned to Brewster to follow him and strode off down the main street. Brewster glanced back at the samurai who were shooting him murderous looks but, apparently, were not going to give him any more trouble. It looked like the monks were in charge here.

He watched the monk's retreating back and looked upward at the one on the roof. Brewster could run; there were only the two of them and the bigger, more ungainly samurai would probably not be able to catch him. But the monk walking away was going in the same direction Brewster had been. Why not take advantage of this unexpected escort ? It might be easier than fighting his way through.

Kim's psychic signal was still strong. Brewster shrugged and trotted off after the monk. It was only later that he remembered and realized the significance of the symbol emblazoned on the samurais' armor—a dragon swallowing its tail. But by then it was too late.

CHAPTER 42

Pittsburgh, Pennsylvania, 2010 C.E.

The shadow-tracker felt as if a million bony fingers grasped at her, pulling her with ragged claws.

There had been a moment of disorientation, of flashing lights and a whirling dizziness. Her sense of balance had become skewed. The pain in her foot was the only thing that allowed her to stay focused and aware.

She lay on the floor in what appeared to be a boiler room. The door to the room had been open and she had crawled in and hid behind a floor-to-ceiling utility cage, panting and trying to figure out what had happened. She must have passed out, only for a moment. Her hackles rose stiffly as she looked back over the cage's boxed contents into another, larger, room across the hall.

That chamber was full of people running in every direction and lined with machinery and equipment. Smoke drifted through the hallway while the distant sounds of gunfire reached her ears. She shook her head in confusion. After she had escaped from her imprisonment, pulling her foot out of the shackle, she had tried to find her way through the labyrinthine structure that had become the *Totou's* new base of operations.

Confusion and chaos were erupting everywhere—bodies

lay strewn about, bloodied and burned; men and women ran in confusion and fear; no one seemed to notice her or care if they did; fellow shadow-trackers lay dead and dying; the smell of death was everywhere.

As well as another smell, new and overpowering, fearsome and full of dread. Kirin again? No, something fierce and deadly.

How? How had this happened? The shadow-tracker whined softly. Such concepts were beyond her understanding. She only knew that she was hurt and alone and that the Eminent Lord no longer cared enough to help her. He had certainly not helped her huntmate! How could she ever have had any faith in him? And in the *Totou*?

Several men ran out of the larger room. One barked commands as he and another stood at the entrance while the rest jogged down the hallway. Moans and crying sounded throughout the corridor.

The shadow-tracker gnashed her teeth, her hands tightened on the bars of the cage. The young master, her handler, and one of his minions, stood talking only a few yards from her!

"It's all gone wrong," the master said with a rage-inflected voice. His green and blue eyes flashed. "How could this have happened?"

"I don't know, sir," the other man said with a shaky bow. "Our tests and projections never foresaw—"

"The Void take your tests! Now that monster has been released from the Eminent Lord knows where and all our plans are in ruins! That freaking dragon!"

The shadow-tracker snarled sub-vocally, her eyes blazing with hate. *Dragon. So that is the spoor I sense.*

"Sir, I—"

Her handler continued. "When I discovered the temporal anomaly here, never did I think we might be able to tap into that power. But thanks to the Founder's ancient notes and you and your staff interpreting them as well as you have, we were able to harness that power. And now look what you've done!"

The other man wrung his hands, his eyes darting back and forth. "But it was too soon," he countered. "You forced us to speed the process up! Now we can't control it! The continuum is too unstable. We shouldn't have—"

The master raised a gun and shot the other man, once, twice, three times. The body fell in a jerking, bloody heap on the floor.

The young master stood shaking, dropping the gun to the floor as if it burned him. From his pocket, he took out a pack of cigarettes. Lighting one, he inhaled deeply. He suddenly seemed not to care as he threw the pack away from him. The odor of cloves reached the shadow-tracker. By the Eminent Lord, she hated that smell!

And yet, that odor was like a signal—now was the time. Concentrating on muffling the pain in her foot as much as she could, the shadow-tracker rounded the corner of the utility cage and charged through the boiler room door. She leaped at the hated object of her attack.

Too late she sensed the other two shadow-trackers charging from the room behind the young master. They must have been waiting for their handler, patiently anticipating his next command. Now they rushed to his defense, rocketing toward her to intercept her attack.

But, despite her injury, she was too fast for them. As she slammed into her handler, as she pushed his body into the wall behind him, as her open jaws went for his throat, there was another flash of light.

CHAPTER 43

Odawara, Japan—1520, C.E.

Yes, Kim Yoshima thought approvingly, even as a chill ran up her spine. *This will do.*
Her reflection stared back at her from the bamboo-encased mirror or, rather, the ghost of Yoshima Mitsu did. Kim had dressed in a simple cotton kimono and slippers. All fit her perfectly as if they had been waiting for her. It was almost as if the spirit of Kim's ancestor had been channeled to direct her every move and selection. She had tied her hair into a small topknot and applied a small amount of makeup.

No sense in attracting too much attention to myself,. Oh my, Grandmother Mitsu, if only you could see me now.

She left her other clothes wadded up in a pile in the shop except for her phone and IDs, which she placed in a small shoulder bag. She walked out into the street, moving quickly and purposefully. Her fatigue and depression were gone, replaced by a desire to finish her ancestor's work—to protect Shioko and destroy the menace of the warlord Omori.

But it was more than that—it had become her work now too. There was more going on here than just a warlord's bid for power. Perhaps her whole life had been leading up to this moment. Again her grandmother's voice sounded in her mind, her words of wisdom, her teachings. Kim realized now that there had been a purpose there, a gentle turning. *You knew, Grandmother*, she thought in awe. *Somehow you knew this, or something huge like this, would happen and, in your own way, you were preparing me for it*. She sighed then, a smile creasing her face. *You could have given me a hint though!*

But maybe she had. Again, Kim's thoughts returned to the book written about the philosopher, Yira. Now, she vaguely remembered that Mitsu had sent her a box of books just before she died. That one must have been with that group and Kim had absently put it in with her collection at her office.

If so, perhaps the book was the hint. The *Five Precepts to Enlightenment* that Yira espoused—those were the expressions that kept coming to Kim's mind, as if out of the blue. Yes, she had no doubt that her ancestor, Yoshima Mitsu, was familiar with those credos and maybe that's why Kim remembered them—another blast from her past, so to speak. But the timing of the recollections, they popped into her mind whenever she had been in the middle of her latest cases, whenever she was in doubt or danger.

I'm missing something. No surprise there considering what's been happening. But there's another piece of this puzzle that I need to find a fit for.

She had wandered out of the battle site now, it seemed. This part of Odawara had not been touched by the warfare that had consumed the area she had just exited. Gradually, the desolate, burnt-out neighborhood gave way to undamaged houses and shops; the smells of rotting corpses and human offal segued into that of grilling rice cakes, sweat and fresh garbage.

Brewster, are you there?

Yes. What's going on?

I'm on my way. Judging by the increased intensity of the mental presence I'm picking up on, it shouldn't be too much longer. What about you?

I'm on my way too, in the escort of some warrior-monks. Long story. I'm OK though. So far.

Hmmm. OK. Tell me later but just be careful. If you've got your own personal honor guard, they must think you're pretty special, yes?

I was hoping you might think that too.

Kim smiled. *Just watch your back. We appear to be headed in the same direction so I'll hopefully see you soon.*

Kim! Listen...I...you be careful too. I think we have a lot to talk about.

I will. At that moment, as Kim passed a small teahouse, her mental alarms started buzzing. She stopped and turned towards the house, its upswept corner gables and domed cupola distinctive amid the other shops. A banner extended on a pole above the door proclaimed, 'Teahouse of the Five Flying Storks'.

A crying within the milieu, a distinctly odd but vaguely recognizable mental signature, flared from within.

She entered the tea house and, without a word to the young girl (who possessed the air of the proprietor, Yoshima's senses informed her), and a handful of customers who stared open-mouthed at her passing, strode directly into a rear room. Kim pushed aside a sliding paper door to look inside. There on a thick *tatami* mat, lay Jackson Yamaguchi.

CHAPTER 44

Pittsburgh, Pennsylvania, 2010 C.E.

The Vincent Black Shadow and Harley Davidson roared into the empty street in front of the *Old Books and Research Haven*. The riders screeched the bikes to a halt and, amidst a mini-tornado of dust and gravel, took off their helmets to scan the desolate urban area around them.

There was no one here; no one even visible in the immediate vicinity as if this area of the city had been cleared just for them. Twilight was just coming on, spreading its violet blanket over the North Side; Pittsburgh's twinkling skyline had just begun to light up, the glass-spired towers of the PPG Building glimmering in the distance.

The young woman felt a strange, twisted sense of deja-vu. It was just like she remembered.

A chill enveloped her, shaking her slim body. *How strange,* she thought. *To be here now, in this time and place, after everything that's happened—before anything happened.*

"See?" her companion said, intruding on her reverie. "I told you we'd make it in plenty of time."

She nodded absently, her eyes searching the modern building behind the fence. "Can you get any kind of sense of her?" she asked, hanging her helmet on one of the handlebars.

"I can't make out where she might be in there. I'm not even sure I remember."

"You just sneaked out," came the reply. "That's what you told me. Right past Mrs. Sibulovich and Bobby and the security guard, stealing the card-key in the process. You were worried and afraid. You wanted to find—"

"This is so…so bizarre." She positioned the kickstand down on the road and got off the bike, rubbing her hands through her hair. "I mean, what about paradoxes and all of that? How can I just—?"

"*Did* anything happen? Do you remember any problems?"

She sighed, placing her hands on her hips and looking down at her feet. "No," she said. "Nothing happened. And everything happened."

"Exactly. So don't worry. You know you have to take her to the *Box Factory*. It's part of your history. If you don't, lives will be lost; lives of the people you care about."

"People I haven't seen in twelve years!" She began to walk across the street, slapping her balled-up fists against her thighs. "They left me back there! A little girl of eight! I was supposed to be a hero, a savior, an adult! Ko, the Little for god's sake! I never even had a childhood! I would have been better off as a serving girl all of my life, as Mitsu's attendant. I was so lonely. So afraid. Even with all of you there with me, I just…I…"

She stopped, the tears flowing down her cheeks. She had wanted to stay. She remembered. Her elder sister, her *Oneesan*, had wanted to bring her back but she had wanted to stay. Such a brave, noble little girl! *Why me? Why did it have to be me?*

"We all came together for this one purpose," her companion continued, a sad edge to his voice. "A grand, glorious convergence of minds, hearts and talents. I was trained for it from birth—to study and work constantly, encouraged not to get too close to people, to be alone as much as possible so I wouldn't lose much if this time came. And I'm older. It's been easier for me than you to have been stranded in the past even though that's where you're from. But, regardless, it was meant to be. There's no getting away from it."

"Yes. I know. I'm sorry. I didn't mean—"

"Besides," her companion shrugged, smiling that brilliant smile of his, "after this, it's the Great Unknown. You know what I mean? You can do what you want with the rest of your life. Providing you can go through with this now."

"I'm afraid."

"So am I. But you won't be alone. And you know, we've been over this a thousand times. You have to decide now. You have to finally decide."

She shook her head, more tears welling in her eyes. "You've been like a brother to me, you've helped me through keeping all those events from the past from being recorded so everything could follow its own path; I've cried in your arms with the weight of this damned responsibility; you've protected me; you've helped me through, I don't know, everything!"

He smiled. "And loved every minute of it. I have no regrets. Except…" His eyes took on a sudden faraway look.

Aimi and their son. He too had left a life and loves behind. "Listen, I—"

She saw her then—a little girl exiting the library, looking in her direction. So small, so helpless.

"Go," her companion said.

The young woman walked over to the fence surrounding the building, her hands trembling. *Help me,* she prayed silently, knowing she had made her decision long ago. She reached out, her shaking fingers holding the card-key she had kept all these years, or centuries, or however the hell long it had been!

Swiping the card through the locking mechanism, she walked through the opened gate and bent down next to the girl. The child stared at her with a rapt expression on her face, the same card-key held in her small hand. So young. So innocent once upon a time.

She gently cupped the little girl's face. "Shioko," she whispered. "It's time. It's time to fulfill your destiny. It's time to become me."

CHAPTER 45

Odawara, Japan—1520, C.E.

Wayne Brewster and his guardian monks walked through what Brewster assumed was the center of Odawara— its 'main street'. Shops, inns and teahouses crowded each other for space; vendors hawked food items on every corner; brightly-colored palanquins carried by servants traversed the intersecting avenues like taxis; beggars, dogs and children intermingled with samurai and peasants. A buzzing of conversation and other noises filled the air. Despite the recent battle here and the tyranny of Omori, life seemed to be getting on as usual. Again Brewster thought of the old samurai action movies he had watched growing up.

It was an exotic movie genre not many kids he knew besides himself were into at the time. The Japanese version of 'Cowboys and Indians', the movies took place in that country's medieval past and dramatized scenes just like this. Amazingly, just like this.

Except...*this is real*.

Curious onlookers gathered at a respectful distance from the trio, standing on the occasional wooden sidewalk, gawking. Were they wondering what the monks had dredged up now? Were they asking themselves who this black-clad stranger among them could be? Were they trying to figure out why the monks hadn't killed him like they had so many others?

Brewster wished now that he could not only speak Japanese but could also read minds like Kim Yoshima. So far, Kim's mental trail coincided with the direction the monks were taking him. That was a good thing but he didn't know what the monks were up to. He'd just have to bide his time and make a move when the opportunity presented itself.

He picked out a movement among the crowds of onlookers, more stealthy and deliberate, one that was paralleling him and the monks. There! Brewster saw the boy who had tried to aid him in his fight with the samurai—keeping abreast of him and his guards, watching Brewster intently. He still carried his staff with both hands and moved through the crowd as lithely as a snake.

He has some skill, Brewster thought, considering his situation. *And a certain technique with that staff. Well*, he mused. *Every super hero needs a sidekick. I don't want to put him in danger but maybe there's an advantage here for both of us.*

He gave a brief nod, acknowledging the boy's presence and then moved his right hand at his hip in a slight, outstretched cutting motion, hoping the boy would notice and understand Brewster's attempt to communicate "wait" or "not now." The boy nodded in return and melted away into the crowd.

Good, Brewster thought. *I need to get near where Kim is, at least before I, or we, make a move.* The smells of food grilling surrounded Brewster—Pork? Chicken? Vegetables? His stomach growled as he started to salivate. He hadn't eaten anything since before he had gone to the book haven. Who knew what time it was now? It looked to be mid-morning but that wasn't the case when he got pulled out of his own time and place.

They approached the end of the street. Here, the avenue

veered at a right angle to wind its way through another crowded section of town (which was where Kim's signal was leading) while straight ahead a stone-lined path continued and ended at a gate in the fortress wall.

Beyond that, the path wound its way up the base of an adjoining hill, stone stairways cut into the rock, marked at intervals by small poles with hanging paper lanterns. A few yards higher up, one of those pi-shaped *Torii* gateways he recognized as being a prominent motif in Japanese design, arched over the pathway as it wound its way upwards at a slight angle.

At the hill's wide summit sat Odawara Castle. An imposing structure, now that he could see it so much closer. But what was that near its top? It looked to be some type of open-air shelter, pennants flapping in the wind.

There were two more monks, two samurai, and a fifth figure standing at the wall engaged in an earnest conversation. The fifth man, tall and thin and covered in a belted black robe, turned at their approach and strode forward from the gate, strange, bi-colored eyes flashing beneath long black hair. He stopped within inches of Brewster, studying his face, his brow furrowing in puzzlement.

This is a dangerous man, Brewster realized, meeting that curious gaze. *And different. There's something about him.* One of his guards said something, the man-in-black replying in turn. He then reached up to Brewster's makeshift face-wrap with a claw-like hand. Brewster knocked the hand away, not taking his eyes off the man, not wanting to be touched by him.

Two sharp blades pricked his neck, his guards silently urging him to stand down while the other two monks and samurai approached, weapons at the ready. This man in black was obviously a leader of some sort. Omori? Brewster didn't think so. Yet allied with the warlord? Perhaps. With a silent groan, he remembered now the symbol on the front of the samurai's uniforms. As Kim had described it, it identified these men as Omori's.

Kim's 'signal' was behind and to his right now but Brewster had a feeling this was where she had intended to end up as well. Somehow he had gotten ahead of her. He hoped she wasn't in trouble. He hoped she might be able to help him. Even he, with his newfound abilities and confidence, doubted he could take on these seven at once.

Kim, he thought, trying to project his own thoughts outward. *Kim, can you hear me?*

The man in black reached out again, grabbed Brewster's face-wrap and ripped it off. His green and blue eyes widened, some genetic defect perhaps, some way to further instill fear. "Christ," he said in perfect English. "A freaking white-ass round-eye. How in the hell did you get here?"

CHAPTER 46

Jackson! What in heaven happened to you?"

"Ms…Ms. Yoshima?" Jackson Yahmaguchi lay on the *tatami* mat, his face grimacing in pain. A pair of cotton work pants and a shirt covered his body; a bandage, wet with blood, had been wrapped around his head. Oddly, the tattoo on his neck looked darker, standing out starkly against his dusky skin. "Thank the Yomitsu," he said, and then, looking at her curiously. "Oh, I forgot. That's you."

"Ha…hang on, Jackson," Kim said. A bowl of water and a wash cloth lay on the floor near the bed. Kim wiped Yamaguchi's face and neck, trying to pierce the wall of thoughts and images that had built up within his mind. She gently probed the realm of his conscious thought.

He landed hard like I did, she reasoned, sorting out the jumbled mix of emotions and memories. *But was injured. I don't think any of it's really serious.*

She retrieved a couple pieces of fruit and some rice from another set of bowls sitting on a nearby table, as well as a jug of water.

As Yamaguchi ate and drank, Kim was alerted mentally to someone standing just outside the doorway. She turned to see a young girl dressed in a traditional kimono enter the room, eyes downcast. She was the one Kim had seen in the front room, the one who seemed to be the owner, despite her youth.

She was very pretty. Her dark hair was pulled back into a bun at the base of her neck and, despite very little makeup, her high-cheek boned face shone with a youthful, exotic beauty. For a moment, Kim was reminded of Shioko and her chest tightened at the thought of possibly never seeing her again.

At least Shioko's safe, she thought, mindful of how her present situation must have been much like her ancestor's when Yoshima Mitsu sent Shioko to the future.

"Forgive me, Mistress," the girl said. She spoke in the same ancient form of Japanese that Shioko had used. Kim still had to listen closely to completely understand. "Please follow me. Jackson-san will be safe here."

Kim stared at the girl who had bowed to her and was still standing with head down. "You act as if you expected me," she said, enunciating slowly and clearly.

"Yes, Mistress," the girl replied, her voice a melody of distinct phrasing. "You are expected. Please, come with me."

Expected by who? Should I look into her mind? No, I don't sense any hostility. "What's happened to Jackson?" she demanded, pointing at the young man.

"All will be explained. Jackson-san will be safe here for the moment. I have been caring for him. Please." The girl turned and walked out of the room.

Kim handed Yamaguchi another apple and a bunch of grapes, settled a light esper suggestion over him to calm him and ease his discomfort, and followed the girl.

The girl waited at the back of the teahouse, standing patiently at the rear door at the end of a short hallway. She opened it and went through, Kim right behind her.

She stepped into a surprisingly large, fenced-in courtyard; one that couldn't be seen from the street-side of the teahouse.

THE SIXTH PRECEPT

Within that hidden landscape lay a *rojiniwa*—a tea garden. An elaborately carved bench nestled among a group of miniature Japanese pines; a tiny pond played host to golden koi shimmering beneath a small man-made span known as a moonbridge. The arrangement of stones and raked sand, the placement of the traditional stone lantern and carved lion, the alignment or *feng shui* of plants and sculpture lent an ethereal feel to the courtyard as if Kim had stepped into a world within this already strange time and place. All sounds of the outside had stopped as if blocked by some invisible barrier; here only birds and the rustling of water made any kind of noise.

But it wasn't the sparse, serene beauty of the courtyard that caught Kim's attention. Rather, it was the twelve armored figures that suddenly appeared, each one stepping out from behind a bush or tree as if materializing from within the small space itself.

Each one was dressed in a type of stylized Japanese armor and a horned helmet which completely covered their faces. Their weapons were sheathed and their posture seemed relaxed yet on-guard. Kim glanced quickly at the girl who had led her here. The young woman knelt at her side, hands in her lap, eyes closed and head down.

One of the twelve stepped forward and bowed. The others fell to one knee, holding their swords out in front of them.

Kim felt no danger here. But she was confused. Gently, she directed a mental probing at the man standing in front of her.

Nothing. Empty. His mind was like a blank slate.

Kim looked down at the girl. "Tell me," she said softly.

"They are Sleepers, Mistress," the young girl said, her head still lowered. "They have been waiting for you for many, many passages of years. They have awakened to serve you."

Sleepers? That's the name Lazo found in his research. "I...I don't understand."

The girl then raised her head. Her face glowed, her eyes sparkled, reflecting something akin to awe. "I am their Guardian, Mistress. My name is Midori. I have kept the Sleepers hidden and safe just like my father and our ancestors did before us. It was a duty placed upon my family long, long ago. The Sleepers were enspelled only to be awakened when they were needed at a future time. Never did I think I would be the one to witness this time and to welcome the Luminous One to us."

Kim felt a sudden dizziness. Midori. 'Princess Midori' was someone Yamaguchi had mentioned. And the 'Luminous One' was another term Lazo had uncovered. Was this girl referring to her, Kim Yoshima, as the Luminous One? That might explain why there had been no reference to Yoshima Mitsu in most of the old texts. How many more prophecies did Kim and Shioko figure in anyway? And how many more names did they have? Talk about an identity crisis!

"An ancient *mahoutsukai* predicted long ago that you would come. He was the one who cast the spell on the Sleepers."

Mahoutsukai. Sorcerer.

"He said that you would come during a time of great upheaval; a time of the rise of the forces of the Left Hand Path. The coming of the dark man, Jackson-san, would be the sign that you would arrive next among us."

Kim shook her head in disbelief. She had thought nothing could surprise her anymore. But now—

"We are caught up in something terrible," Midori said, her dark eyes reflecting the light. "And something wonderful. Forgive me for being so bold but I see you are hesitant. How can we turn our backs on this situation before it has come to its dark fruition? All of us have a part to play in this, surely."

Parts again. Destiny. Freaking karma. Like Lazo said—whatever happened to free will? "Damn."

THE SIXTH PRECEPT

"Mistress?"

"Ye...yes," Kim said. "I could definitely use the help. Thank you." *But first I have to reestablish contact with Brewster.*

A cacophony of cries, both from the interior of the teahouse and the street outside, shattered the silence of the garden. A dark, ragged shape suddenly sailed over the garden's wall. A body, torn and broken, landed in a cracked, bloody heap in the sand.

A roar, a cry of something not human, reverberated from the street. It was a sound from hell. *The dragon from the Box Factory*, Kim thought, the hair on the nape of her neck standing on end. *And now this, whatever this is. God help us, could it be happening here too? The breaking through from alternate realities?*

Brewster! Are you there? I had to stop my transmission but I'm back. Be careful. All hell's broken loose here!

Midori trembled at her side. "It would appear, Mistress," she said, rising quickly to her feet, "that you have arrived just in time."

CHAPTER 47

Omori Kadonamoro watched it all from the safety of the upper courtyards encircling the main keep. There, the view of the maze-like outer perimeter of Odawara-jo, its gardens, baileys and multi-leveled fortifications, was unobstructed.

But he still couldn't believe what he was seeing. It was like something from a tale told to frighten children.

The water in the front moat seemed to boil, its surface rippling with bubbling froth. A party of Omori's troops heading over the moat's bridge out of the castle halted, hesitant, glancing nervously at the roiling water while the commanding samurais' horses nickered in fear.

Then the impossible happened.

The water exploded upward as something erupted from the moat. Something blindingly fast. A large group of hideous beings swarmed over the surprised troops like ants—beings with the faces of monkeys, possessing webbed hands and feet and covered in hard, shell-like skin. Several samurai were dragged screaming into the moat, the creatures' hooked claws piercing the soldiers' armor as if it were so much silk. The horses reared, terrified, sending some of their riders crashing onto the bridge.

The samurai bringing up the rear of the procession fled, running back toward the main gate. One riderless horse escaped to the opposite side, its flanks red with bloody gashes, its eyes white with terror.

The creatures finished their grisly work and vanished into the moat's depths, leaving the bridge picked clean of life. The fantastic horror had transpired in only a moment's breath.

Omori stood, transfixed. Slowly, he felt the hair on his arms and on the back of his neck begin to rise.

"*Kappa*," a whispered voice uttered next to Omori, a voice filled with awe and fear.

Omori turned to one of his personal guard, a samurai named Fujiwara, one he knew did not frighten easily. The man was shaking. "What did you say?" the *daimyo* hissed.

Fujiwara bowed to his lord, his voice tremulous. He was a big man, his face and arms covered with scars. "Lord, they were *kappa*, monkey demons. They killed our men. You saw. Never have we faced such an enemy."

Yes, I saw. "See to those samurai who escaped," he said, walking past Fujiwara. "And assemble another contingent immediately with them as the foreguard."

"Lord?"

Omori turned, bluffing past his own fear, hiding the trembling of his hands. "I will see what is truly happening. You, yourself, have brought me the reports—the sightings of creatures straight out of the mythical world plus the whisperings of unrest and fear among the Odawarans. Now we have seen the proof of the first part with our own eyes. The servants of the Left Hand Path walk among us."

And the woman who appeared before me and the witch as if by magic. That is when this all started—this crossing over from the Other Side.

A bow. "Yes, Lord. At once. But the bridge—."

"Pour oil into the moat and set it aflame. And bring the

majo, Eela, to me! We will go into the heart of the city and show these Odawarans that Omori Kadonomaro fears nothing, not even black *kami* incarnate!"

But as Omori walked back into the donjon, his heart thudded in his chest, his breath caught in his throat. *I must not falter*, he thought, seeing once again his men become victims of the *kappa*. Not now…not now. *If I can keep these creatures at bay, the* majo *can get me the weapons from the future I will need to end this once and for all!*

CHAPTER 48

The group of warrior monks and samurai surrounded Brewster like a wall of living armor. The man-in-black stood in front of him, a look Brewster couldn't quite decipher etched on his cruel face. *He spoke English!* Brewster thought in amazement. *And used modern phrasing! Is he from the future too?*

But Brewster pushed those thoughts from his mind. *I have to find Kim. Nothing else matters right now. She's the key, I know it! Without her, there's no hope of resolving this.*

Brewster gritted his teeth. Kim's signal seemed far away, as if she had become distracted. *Or hurt maybe. If anything had happened to her…*

Quickly bending his knees, he pushed hard. Vaulting over the heads of his captors, Brewster somersaulted in mid-air and landed several feet beyond the surprised samurai. He hit the ground running, heading back toward the spot where Kim's mental signal had veered. He had to find her.

Shouts from behind and ahead—a small crowd of townspeople had gathered at the bend in the street; curious onlookers, some of whom had followed Brewster and his captors for several blocks. He almost felt like a celebrity.

Now the crowd moved back, suddenly excited, pointing. Something shot past Brewster's shoulder—the spear-like weapon of one of the monks almost struck him. He ran in a serpentine fashion, dodging back and forth, deliberately heading away from the crowd so as not to get any innocent bystanders injured. Brewster ran faster than he had ever run before, his legs pumping, his lungs straining. Some of the crowd actually seemed to be cheering him on.

A whirring sound…something hard hit his calves, wrapping itself around and biting into his lower legs. He fell and rolled, the breath knocked out of him as he hit the street. Gasping for air he tugged at the weighted chain that had entangled him like a bolo. The man-in-black's warrior attendants sprinted in his direction; they were almost upon him.

More cries sounded from the crowd—this time of shock and terror—as hideous, unearthly creatures dropped out of the sky, monsters from someone's depraved nightmare. Black shapes with wings yet man-like—four avian humanoids screamed downward, their beak-like mouths snapping, their taloned hands grasping. They had human bodies but their hands and feet, their faces, those wings…

Both the samurais and warrior monks chasing Brewster yelled in dismay and fear. The word '*tengu*' kept repeating over and over. Two samurai broke and ran as one of the winged harpy-like monstrosities grasped one by the head in its talons and lifted him screaming and kicking into the air. The man-in-black stood open-mouthed, his eyes widening incredulously. Then he turned and ran, heading back for the castle pathway.

The scene erupted into chaos. It was like something out of a movie. The flying bird-men screeched and buzzed the fleeing men like strafing fighter jets. The crowd scattered and ran. The monks swung their weapons, trying to fight the creatures off. Brewster got a grip on his own fear and amazement and wrestled the chain off of his calves. As he got painfully to his feet, one of the bird-men dove toward him like an obscene, mutated raptor. Its face, oddly human, like an old man's, held two blazing red eyes. This close, Brewster could see it was smaller than he was, almost dwarf-like, but those scrawny, sinewy arms ended in long talons, and he had seen the strength its fellows possessed in picking up one of the samurai.

He swung the weighted chain over his head in a whirling arc. The bird-man backed off, hovering in front of him. Its eyes followed the chain as Brewster whirled it around and around. Then, it spoke, a husky, croaking sound, something in Japanese.

Brewster started to back away, still swinging the chain, when the bird-man plunged toward him like a falcon plummeting toward its prey. Brewster flung the chain at the creature but the bird-man flitted out of its way and rammed Brewster in the chest with its sharp feet. Brewster fell on his back, grunting in pain.

He rolled over backwards and, reaching out, found a loose rock lying on the street. He staggered to his knees, his hand cocked and ready to throw.

The young boy with the staff appeared (*where had he come from?*) and was swinging his weapon at the attacking bird-man. The creature bobbed up and down above him as it dodged the boy's attack. Screeching, the bird-man grasped the staff in both clawed feet and wrenched it free of the boy's grasp. Cracking the staff in two, the creature dropped down to finish his attacker off.

Brewster stood and threw the rock. His aim was true as the rock struck the creature in the head, sending it spinning out-of-control. It hit the ground and lay squawking and fluttering.

"Come on!" Brewster shouted. He ran forward, grabbed the boy by the arm and pulled him along with him as both started running. Brewster looked back once. The bird-men were gone but their bloodied victims lay strewn about the castle gate. He couldn't tell if the man-in-black was among them but one of the monks staggered about as if drunk, his clothes torn and his hands bloody, his face twisted with shock.

As they entered the now deserted street a series of thoughts rang out like bells in his head.

Brewster! Are you there? I had to stop my transmission but I'm back. Be careful. All hell's broken loose here!

Kim! Just show me where you are! He shouted back mentally, relief shuddering through him. *Just show me where you are!*

CHAPTER 49

Behind a psionic curtain, gauzy and wavering, stood a man-like creature—a hulking, brutish beast, like something out of a nightmare.

Kim's mind's eye blazed with images of danger, terror and the impossible—she felt the instability of the metaverse like worn, frayed strands of rope, splitting apart at both ends.

People screamed and ran for their lives; crowds scattered like frightened cattle; blood splattered everywhere.

A sound like thunder; a screeching like nails on glass as dimensional portals were flung open, allowing access to giant spiders; animals with the heads of monkeys, the bodies of badgers and the tails of serpents; giant birds with old men's faces.

The maelstrom of fear and death Kim's senses encountered was all too real. The blood and corpses testified to that; the terrified Odawarans running helplessly in every direction. It was chaos, it was bedlam, it was—

"A giant *oni*!" Midori cried in horror, as she and the Sleepers followed Kim. "A being of the Left Hand Path! How can such a thing be?"

The Left Hand Path, Kim thought. *Alchemy, black magic, Satanism.*

She stood outside of the teahouse, the twelve 'samurai' and Midori crowded around her. Pandemonium reigned just as she had envisioned it. Kim stared in disbelief as a giant monstrosity of a creature stood roaring in the street. Standing upright, easily as tall as a three-story building and heavily muscled, it wore a tiger-skin loin cloth over its dark green skin. The *oni*'s head sprouted two large horns and an even larger, fanged mouth with a crest of stiff, black hair leaping up from its brow to end in a long tail at the middle of its back. Clawed hands flailed the air as it shrieked and roared. The *oni* bent down and plucked an old woman from the fleeing crowd and twisted her head off.

Kim shouted. "Midori, these Sleepers—?"

"They will follow your commands, Mistress! They are skilled warriors and have awakened for you!"

Right. The Luminous One. Kim pointed at who she presumed to be the head Sleeper. "OK! You! Get some of your men to try to help the townspeople. Midori, get back in the teahouse and get Jackson to a safe place."

"Yes," Midori said, turning back inside. "We have an underground shelter."

Like someone else I know, Kim thought. *I hope it's safer than Laz's.*

The *oni* took a step closer, obviously curious about these brightly-outfitted beings who didn't seem to be afraid of him.

It roared and picked up a farmer's wagon, lifted it over its head and threw it straight at Kim.

The wagon fell short of its target, shattering and spilling its contents into the street. Like wooden shrapnel, shards of broken boards exploded into the air. As Kim darted away, dodging and ducking the flying debris, she saw four of the Sleepers directing dozens of still-terrified onlookers into the relative safety of the side streets. The eight others of the strange samurai drew their swords and advanced on the *oni*.

The samurai danced in and out of the *oni*'s reach, jabbing and poking their swords to keep it occupied. The monster roared in frustration as it swatted at them with a giant hand.

Suddenly, a slashing uppercut caught one of the Sleepers on the shoulder, ripping through armor and skin. The samurai went down and rolled onto his knees, blood flowing from the wound. The *oni* loomed over him, readying another blow. The other Sleepers moved forward, swinging their swords and blocking the deadly claws. But a ham-fisted backhanded swipe tumbled four of them jarringly onto their backs.

Yoshima Mitsu! Kim screamed in her mind. *My ancestor, help me!*

Kim entered the milieu and felt her power explode within her. Her mind expanded, her body shot through with a jarring heat. Like the yogic Kundalini serpent, a pressure built up at the base of her spine and rose upward, culminating in a bright lambent explosion within her brain.

A bolt of mental energy erupted from Kim's mind, tracers of psi power shooting off of her fingertips and flashing from her eyes like lightning. Melded into a blazing blue arc, it struck the *oni* in the chest.

The monster howled and stumbled backwards, blue sparks dancing off its body. Kim hit the *oni* with a second blow but, this time, a mental recoil from the force of her energy threw Kim off of her feet and onto her back.

She struggled to her knees, dizzy and weak. She had never generated that much mental energy before. Her head spun, her vision blurred, her body shook, blood ran from her nose down her chin. She looked up.

The *oni*'s thick body swayed, its eyes screwed up in its fearsome head. The unconscious creature began to fall forward like some giant tree that had been hacked from its rooted moorings.

"No!" Kim cried. The wounded Sleeper was trying to pull an unconscious comrade out of the way of the falling monster but his gashed shoulder rendered one arm useless. The unharmed Sleepers were helping their other fallen comrades. *They're going to be crushed or smothered by that thing!* Kim shot her telekinetic force straight at the *oni*. Though weakened, her power caught the beast in mid-drop and slowed it down...just a little. But as sweat popped out on her brow and she clenched her jaw, she realized it was still not enough. She was too shaken to move it. The *oni*'s huge bulk continued its downward plunge.

Two figures dashed from an adjoining alley and ran to the Sleepers, adding their strength to pick the unconscious one up off the ground. One of the figures was dressed in black but he was a familiar figure. Kim held on to the *oni* until Wayne Brewster and the young boy who was with him helped get the Sleepers out of the way. With a grateful sigh, Kim cut off her telekinetic beam and the *oni* crashed face-first to the street, lights out.

*I...can't...stay...awake...*Kim's eyelids fluttered and, just before she too spun into unconsciousness, she saw Brewster running her way.

CHAPTER 50

The shadow-tracker no longer paid attention to the pain—those sensations were far away, stuck in some remote corner of her mind as if they belonged to someone else. The hunger bothered her a little but the deprivation had been going on for so long, she was almost used to it. She knew she would get fed three times a day even if it wasn't much. They had to keep her alive and relatively healthy because they needed her lifeblood, her womb and the cells of her body.

At least, that was what she had been told even if she didn't completely understand it. She was, they whispered, the Source of All Things. She moved restlessly about the pit where they kept her imprisoned, dragging her bad foot which was, in turn, bound once again in an iron shackle. The pit was just that—a large oval depression sunk several feet below floor level in a holding area beneath Odawara Castle. She had water and a privy and *tatami* mats to sleep on but the poison-swathed bamboo spikes surrounding the pit, and the rope netting that covered the opening, kept any thoughts of escape to a minimum.

Oh, she had tried to escape before, several times. Her handler apparently had thought her spirit had been broken and that she wouldn't try anything. Initially, it had been no problem to jump out of the pit. She had even gotten as far as the Eminent Lord's pavilion at the topmost level of the castle before she had been recaptured. That was why her captors had broken her already injured foot and let it heal crookedly. She wouldn't be able to squeeze out of the leg iron with such an injury as she had done before. The poison spikes and net had been added as a final precaution.

She sat down on the hard, packed sand that served as a floor and leaned back against the wall. Her own waste littered the space around her. Closing her eyes, she remembered. How long ago had it been? She had lost all track of time here; even day and night were unknown to her. Flaming torches kept the light at a steady muted state. But she could see again her handler as she leaped toward him in the *Totou*'s quarters, could feel her jaws ready to clamp down on his throat.

The light had blotted out all existence and thrown her far, far away. When her vision had cleared, she looked upon a strange place, remote both in distance and, as she was soon to learn, in another aspect as well. She had traveled back to the land and time of the Eminent Lord himself! The young master and the two other shadow-trackers were also with her, as confused and frightened as she was.

But when the master realized what had happened, he immediately took control. He commanded the other shadow-trackers to overpower her and began to formulate a plan for survival, one which he forced her to listen to over and over.

He was cruel and evil but he was clever and possessed a certain courage. The shadow-tracker gave him that.

The rest of her memories of that time had been a blur of hiding and consolidating power, of lying and bribing the right people, of trying to understand the ways of the time and place they had arrived in, of bullying and killing to make their way. Using fear to achieve his ends was the young master's strong suit.

THE SIXTH PRECEPT

Employing herbs and potions, her handler had kept her drugged most of the time. Eventually, he had come to fit in perfectly with his new surroundings and it seemed that he had special plans for her as well.

And so, once the young master, now known as the Founder (it had been him all along!) had insinuated himself into the graces of the Eminent Lord, the shadow-tracker became the Source of All Things. That was what they called her. She was the carrier of the…DNA? that would be used to breed more shadow-trackers. The master had laughed when he remembered how he had tried to destroy her conditioning in their own time; how he had called her a mistake. How the fates had turned and how useful to his quest for power she would now be!

The other two shadow-trackers had played their part too. They had mated with her, coupling in a frenzy at the master's command to get her with litters. She had howled and struggled but the potions had kept her pliant, unable to stop them.

Her young had been taken from her after their birthing. She growled at the harsh and painful memory. *No matter. I will still escape and kill him. Even now the herbs and potions they give me don't affect me as they once did. I'm getting used to them. I'll keep pretending until the right time; until I can rip his heart out.*

The Eminent Lord too. Could she kill the one she had served all those years? She had seen him once. He had come with the young master, who now called himself Eela, a self-styled witch. They had stood above the pit, looking down on her. She remembered how empty she had felt returning his gaze as he regarded her with cold, uncaring eyes. *It cannot end like this*, she thought, licking her lips. *I will avenge my huntmate. I will get my satisfaction!*

A rattling noise came from the opposite wall of the pit, the sound of a bolt being drawn. A wooden door inset into the wall opened. One of the warlord's soldiers appeared in the doorway, a bucket filled with her so-called food in one hand. The soldier placed the bucket on the sand and retreated back the way he had come, bolting the door behind him.

Even so, they fear me, she thought with grim satisfaction. The disgusted look on the soldier's face told her everything. She got up and went to the bucket, looking at the slop of foul meat and bones, vegetables and milk they provided her for sustenance. *I'll eat their food; I need to get stronger and I'll pretend to obey. But when the times comes...*

Despite everything, she realized her stomach was growling. Snorting at the irony, she bent down to feed.

CHAPTER 51

The shelter beneath the *Teahouse of the Five Flying Storks* was an almost exact replica of the structure's interior above it. A little smaller and not as elaborately furnished, but close enough, at least as much as Brewster had seen of it.

It was certainly a little more crowded. Brewster shared the underground space with Yamaguchi; the young 'Guardian of the Sleepers' named Midori (as in Princess); Hiroshi, the brave young staff-wielder (*would he be the 'Chancellor Hiroshi' Yamaguchi had mentioned?*); the strangely mute samurai warriors Kim had discovered; four frightened customers of Midori's; and, last but not least, Kim Yoshima herself.

Brewster wasn't worried about the others. Hiroshi and young Midori had taken a sudden interest in each other, talking shyly and giving each other wide-eyed looks. It hadn't taken long, even in these circumstances, for them to notice one another. Apparently Hiroshi had been a reluctant slave of Omori's samurai but had finally rebelled against them when Brewster intervened in the recent altercation.

As for Yamaguchi, he seemed to have abruptly started to recover, a sudden excitement and urgency animating him. He was sitting up, eating and asking numerous questions. He was particularly interested in Midori and Hiroshi.

Well, Brewster mused. *I would say strange is the operative word here.* The dozen samurai, or "Sleepers," were stationed around the shelter as if keeping lookout, oddly still and statue-like, their faces hidden by their helmets. The one wounded by the *oni* had also seemed to have gotten better, standing as stoically and quietly as the rest. Without their help against the *oni*, many more lives may have been lost.

And Kim...in a back room beneath the upper rear of the teahouse, Brewster could see the lieutenant's flickering silhouette through the sliding paper door. She had wanted to be alone after he had carried her here and she had regained consciousness from her bout with the *oni*.

The streets outside were quiet—reports coming in from some of Midori's contacts told of a lull in appearances of the fantastic creatures. The populace as a whole was hiding indoors, barricading themselves against the 'supernatural' danger.

Kim wanted her and her companions to rest, to regroup, to develop a definite plan of action. She seemed more determined, yet more sad than Brewster had seen her before.

I need to talk to her.

They had all refreshed themselves and eaten some rice cakes with fish and vegetables. Tea had been served after all of them had slept a little which revived Brewster somewhat and it had certainly felt good to wash up. Yet he was still anxious.

Maybe that antsy feeling that was spreading throughout his body was why he had now screwed up his courage. He could fight flying bird-men and sword-wielding samurai in this new role of his as Hero, but to get close to Kim Yoshima was another matter altogether. He walked over and let himself into the room, sliding the door shut behind him.

Kim knelt in the middle of the candlelit chamber, head bowed, eyes closed, in front of a small fountain. Brewster had been told the fountain was fed by an underground stream and used for meditation purposes. Kim was dressed in a kimono, her feet bare. Incense burned from two clay bowls set in niches in the back wall. A *tatami* mat lay in one corner. Kim opened her eyes and turned towards him.

"I tried to contact her," she said softly. "My ancestor, to find out what to do next, why she didn't tell me she would die and that I would become her." She looked away. "But either I couldn't or she's just not answering me. I don't know why." She hung her head then and laughed softly. "It's crazy, isn't it? Who would have thought something like this could happen?"

That's for damned sure. "Kim," Brewster said. "Are you OK? I'm sorry to disturb you but there's a few things I have to say."

In response, Kim rose, walked over to Brewster and put her arms around his neck. She kissed him—hard. Brewster hesitated in surprise and then returned the kiss, embracing her, his body pressing tightly against hers. She radiated a startling warmth; even through the clothes they wore he could feel it spreading throughout his own trembling body.

He held her tightly, kissing her again and again. He tasted her lips, her tongue, her neck. He smelled her scent, felt the strong curves of her body and its urgent responses to his own. "This is part of what I wanted to talk to you about," he murmured hoarsely between breaths, his heart pounding in his chest.

Kim pulled back at arm's length and looked at him, breathing hard. "Ironically, I can't see the future like my ancestor could," she whispered. "So I don't know if we'll get out of this."

"I know." He took her hands in his and led her gently to the *tatami* mat.

Later, lying in each other's arms, Brewster knew time was dangerously short but he found himself hesitating. He hadn't felt this good in a long while. More than extraordinary events had brought him and Kim together, he knew, and he didn't want this moment to end.

One thing he was certain of, though—they would make it out of here. He would do anything to keep them safe, to keep them together. "Kim," he said, running his hand through her hair. "What's our next move? I wish we could just lie here forever."

Kim put her fingers to his lips. Her green eyes looked into his. "So do I but we've got a date with a very evil man, and I'm going to need your help. If you're willing."

She stood up and walked to her kimono, lying on the floor where she had dropped it. *God, she is amazing!* Brewster watched her lean, firm body cross the floor like a cat. She looked like a woman half her age. He pushed himself up on one elbow, never taking his eyes off of her, his own body starting to stir again. In many ways, they hardly knew each other. And yet he had seen her in his dreams or someone very like her. In that other world, he *did* know her.

Kim put her kimono back on and knelt by his side, her hands resting on her thighs. "We have to get going," she said. "Midori and her Sleepers are going to organize parts of the local populace. Midori's told me her family has been recruiting people and stockpiling supplies and weapons for years in case this day finally came. They're going to serve as a distraction so we can get to Omori. At least, that's the plan I'm going to propose."

"And these creatures? What about them?"

"I'm not sure. Remember the dragon back at the *Box Factory*? The *Totou* were trying to manipulate time and they opened a Pandora's Box instead. That's the only explanation I can think of. They screwed up." Kim sighed. "So there could be god-knows-how-many monsters out of Japanese myth running around out here now and maybe back in our own time as well. That complicates things. With Omori's army and warrior monks and packs of shadow-trackers, we'll need all the help we can get."

"And us? You and me and the others?"

"We're going to make history, at least a little branch of it. And fulfill some old prophecies in the process. We're going to prevent Omori and his monsters from ever hurting Shioko or anyone else again. We're going to put a stop to this time-traveling travesty. If you'll pardon the analogy, we're going straight into the dragon's belly."

She grinned, her eyes twinkling. "Are you game?" and then, more seriously, "You don't have to go if you don't want to. You've already done more than enough. I dragged you into this mess and there's no need to put yourself in any more danger. I mean that, Wayne. Especially now. I won't think any less of you. No one will."

Brewster shook his head. He hadn't done nearly enough in his estimation. He was in this until the end. Super heroes never left a friend in need in any case. There was a Japanese word—he wasn't sure where he'd picked it up but it seemed appropriate now: *giri*—honor, duty, responsibility.

He got to his feet and reached for his clothes. "What are we waiting for?" he said with a smile. "Let's go make history!"

CHAPTER 52

Omori Kadonomaro rode his war-horse through Odawara in a neighborhood known as the China Sect. His personal guard, made up of both *sohei* and samurai retainers, were spread out on foot around him. Fear was clearly etched into the usually inscrutable samurais' faces; even a few of the monks looked jittery. *They have heard it too*, the *daimyo* thought with a shudder. *That monsters and demons and black* kami *attacked the city*.

The streets were eerily quiet. Bloody corpses, both animal and human, many mutilated beyond recognition, lay strewn about like so many broken dolls. Some of the building fronts were damaged, pushed in and splintered as if by a great force. Palanquins and vegetable carts were upended in the street. The sky had become forbiddingly overcast, blotting out the mid-afternoon sun. Omori's men carried torches to light their way in the unnatural darkness.

Omori had always been certain that those who walked the Left Hand Path were waiting, just out of reach, ready to break through the membrane between worlds at any opportunity. Even in his own time, he had experienced things he could not explain. There had been the clothed shadow-tracker who had seemingly appeared out of thin air, the threat of the *shirabyoshi* to return even after death, the attack by the *kappa*, his own incredible plan to bring weapons back from a time far in the future. But monsters and beasts out of legend—it was indeed an old fear of his—to face the demons of the Left Hand Path in this world.

I have to know, he thought, a chill running up his back. *I have to see for myself. If it is true, then the* kami *have turned against me, indeed.*

More likely though, Eela had told him, it was a clever sneak attack by his enemies, disguising themselves as *oni* or *nue* to strike fear into his people's hearts, to break their spirits and be more accessible to defeat. Surely, that had to be the explanation! Yes, yes, that had to be it! The witch had always been right before! Omori couldn't afford to fight the supernatural, something unseen and unexplainable. Not now.

Yet, the witch had fled, refusing to accompany him, muttering about *tengu* and the end of the world. And Omori had seen the *kappa* attack with his own eyes.

He reined in his nervous horse and called his men to a halt. There, on the ground, leading into a small house lay a trail of blood, fresh from the looks of it. The earth here was disturbed, marked by a series of strange gouge marks. Omori dismounted, gave the reins to a guardsman and walked up to the door of the house. A sobbing sounded from within.

Against the protest of his guard, he took a torch from one of his men and kicked open the door, drawing his sword as he entered. An old man lay huddled in a corner, crying. Omori approached the man, who was lying injured, shaking uncontrollably and covered in blood.

Omori knelt at the man's side. "Grandfather," he said, placing his sword at the man's neck. "Tell me what happened here and do not lie to me!"

The old man quaked anew at the sight of the dreaded

daimyo. "Lo…Lord," he croaked, bloody froth bubbling from his mouth. "Please, help…help us. *Kumo…kumo* attacked… abomination…"

Kumo. Giant Spiders. Tales told to frighten children. And yet, what was this strange material wrapped around the old man's leg? Broken strands of a spider's web? Omori shivered, a sudden dread encompassing him. He pressed the blade closer. The old man whimpered as Omori asked softly, "Are you telling me the truth?"

"Yes…truly, I swear! Look…my arm…"

Omori used his sword-point to push aside the tattered, blood-stained remnant of the *kimono* that covered the man's right arm. Only a ragged, gaping socket was revealed, bone, blood and sinew gruesomely visible through the shoulder.

"I hurt so badly. Ahhhhhhhh, mercy, Lord, mercy."

"And you shall have it. The only kind I know how to give." The *daimyo* ran his blade across and through the man's throat. As the old man's death rattle sounded in his ears, Omori walked back outside. He looked up and down the street, ignoring the frightened and confused stares of his men and the skittery shuffling of his mount. *I am frightened too,* he thought. *But they shall never know it!*

He walked to the end of the street, listening. There was something in the air—a smell, strange and foreign; a noise, soft but audible—a lapping, slurping sound.

He knew this neighborhood; he had once lived here. His family, before they had been defeated and driven out by Ujitsuna, had owned some dwellings here, renting them to the refugees, outcasts and no-accounts who made this slum their home. The China Sect was inhabited mostly by Chinese immigrants, those who had fled their own country for reasons known only to them. It was comparable in poverty and neglect to the Gettoo but not quite so harsh. At least that was how he remembered it.

Memories came flooding back to him. He had taken his first woman here. His father, in his infinite cruel wisdom, thought living here for a time would be a learning experience for the young and privileged Omori, would teach him a few of life's hard lessons. And so it had.

The girl was not much older than he was at the time. The group of slum-rats he shared a house with had goaded him on until finally he had forced her onto the dirty *tatami* mats he and the others slept in, ravaging her body and mind. And then he had killed her, strangling her, reveling in her desperate struggle, discovering that he liked it—this control, this power, this snuffing out of a life. The others had been caught off-guard by his sudden brutality and from that point on, he was their leader. It was a lesson in fear and control he would heed the rest of his life.

He smiled grimly as he forced those memories into the back of his mind. Now was not the time to get nostalgic. He turned toward a block of houses to his right, following the singular smell and sounds he had honed in on. Here, the ravaged structures had also fallen victim to fire, their walls and interiors burnt and blackened, smoke still rising in gray, billowing patches. One such dwelling's door was slightly ajar; he pushed it open and stuck his torch within. There was something inside.

Omori gasped. Among the broken and scorched furniture, a naked, skeletal figure, deathly pale and hairless, looked up with bulging eyes from the mangled and half-eaten body of a peasant. Blood and pieces of burnt, dead flesh clung to its bluish lips. Its sex was indeterminate, despite its nakedness. It leered at the *daimyo* and hissed between rotting, blood-stained teeth.

THE SIXTH PRECEPT

A *jikininki*. Omori stepped back in shock and revulsion. A corpse-eating demon right out of the old legends knelt right there, right in front of him. The creature hissed again and bounded off towards the rear of the house.

Fear shot through the Warlord of Odawara. *No,* he thought, gritting his teeth. *This will not happen!* Raising his sword and the torch, Omori bellowed a war cry and shot after the demon. The shouts of his guard faded into the background as he concentrated on navigating through the fallen, charred timbers and cracked flooring.

There! Up ahead, a pale shape darted, flitting out the back door. *Curse this darkness!* Omori thought angrily. But he pressed on, jumping over an overturned table and another desecrated body. If he could defeat such a creature, that act would inspire his men. It would show them that not even those of the Left Hand Path could stand up to the Warlord of Odawara.

Outside the house lay a small fenced-in courtyard, littered with garbage and scarred by fire. The *jikininki* turned to face Omori, crouching low and hissing like a cornered cat. It wasted no time as it charged the warlord.

Omori swung his torch in a backhanded swipe. But the demon ducked under the arcing flame and butted its head into Omori's chest. The warlord grunted and spun sideways as the *jikininki* pivoted back toward the *daimyo*.

Omori managed to keep his balance and once again swung the torch at the corpse-eater. The demon ducked but as it rose to charge again, Omori brought his sword down onto the creature's raised forearm. The *jikininki* howled as its forearm was cleaved from its body, the severed half-limb flying across the yard.

No blood, Omori noted, as he tossed his torch straight up into the air. The spinning flames lit the yard with a flickering light as Omori grasped his sword with both hands and swung at the still-oncoming creature.

The sword struck the *jikininki* with all the strength the warlord could muster behind it. Omori's arms vibrated with the force of the blow, his breath catching in his throat. The blade entered the creature's shoulder, sliced through its chest and ribs and exited its opposite hip. The *jikininki* shrieked a garbled cry as it fell, cut in half, to the ground.

Omori reached up and caught the spinning torch as it descended and held it over the demon, watching both halves of its hideous body convulse as it died. And then Omori looked on in horror and fascination as, like smoke on the wind, the demon withered and fell in upon itself, leaving only a husk of dried skin.

"Lord, are you well? What…what has happened here?"

Omori looked up to see three of his *sohei* approaching him through the rear of the house, staring at the spot where the *jikininki* had just disappeared. "You should have been right behind me!" he cried, advancing on the three. He must not show weakness and indecision at what he had just seen. Not now. "Where were you?"

The foremost *sohei* bowed. "Lord. We—"

Omori ran his blade through the monk's neck as the *sohei* raised himself upright. The monk crumpled to the ground, dropping his torch, his mouth opened in surprise. The other monks looked at their fallen comrade, their eyes wide.

"Did you see it?" demanded Omori. "Did you see the *jikininki*? Did you see what happened?"

"Ye…yes, Lord." one answered. "It was there and then it wasn't."

"So they can be killed. And if they can, the others—the *kappa*, the *tengu*, the *kumo*—they can too. Remember that and never allow me to face such an enemy alone again! You are my personal guards, my retainers. You belong at my side, no matter what the danger!"

Omori marched through the house, anger seething within him. This was the *majo's* fault! Why hadn't Eela foreseen this horror? Why hadn't he warned him of this danger as he had of others so many times before? Instead, at the first sign of a real, significant threat, he had brushed it off. Omori would demand a reckoning. He would force the *majo* to reverse this magic and return everything to the way it had been before.

And then Eela would send *him* into the future, if the *majo* could still accomplish such an impossible feat. There, Omori would be safe from the One Child and away from such incompetents! There, he would build his power base again and return with an army of followers and weapons, more powerful than ever.

One of his personal guard—it was Fujiwara—nervously awaited him at the front of the house. "Lord," he said. "Thank the *kami* you were not harmed. A runner has arrived with a message."

A runner? Now what?

A peasant knelt at Omori's feet, head bowed. He wore dirty pants and a cotton shirt and his head was wrapped in a bloody rag.

"Well?" Omori asked. "What is it?"

"Lord Omori," the peasant began. "Your commander of forces at the southern gates urges me to tell you that they are under attack."

"Huh! What kind of monster is this then? More *nue*? A four-headed dragon perhaps? A flock of flying turds?"

"No, Lord. An army. An uprising. The attacking force comes from the people of Odawara itself."

Omori seethed. He held the torch only a nose-length from the face of the runner, barely able to control the trembling in his arm. Yes, he could see in the peasant's eyes that the man told the truth. He forced himself to keep quiet, to not scream aloud at the heavens, to not kill another of his men in the familiar murderous rage that was building inside him. An uprising? Yet one more of the *majo's* failures! The warlord could fight the monsters or he could fight the revolt. But he couldn't fight both. "You," he said, pointing at one of the monks who had joined him in the alley. "You and Fujiwara take reinforcements to the southern gates. One of my garrisons is nearby. Marshal as many men from there as you can and recruit any peasant that you find. I will join you later. But first I must do something."

Fujiwara bowed. "Yes, Lord."

Omori mounted his horse and wheeled back towards his stronghold, the majority of his guard in tow. *The witch. The witch will undo this or I will make him dig his own grave!*

CHAPTER 53

Kim stood a few feet away from the captured *oni*, staring at it in fascination. The huge beast had regained consciousness and had been struggling in vain to free itself from the numerous ropes and wooden stakes which several Odawaran volunteers had used to bind it face-down to the ground. Its roars had been muffled by its uncomfortable position but it remained quiet and unmoving now, casting an angry eye in Kim's direction. Its nostrils flared, its ribs heaved.

There had been a crowd earlier, eager to view this supernatural creature and those who had brought it down. They had bowed to Kim and held out their hands to touch her, muttering thanks and allegiance. They were like any person, Kim realized, past or present. In the case of the *oni*, human beings had a perverse need to view something they didn't understand, something inexplicable or grotesque, something that proved their own normalcy or superiority, that made them think their lives weren't all that bad after all. And, with regard to her—someone who could save them, who might be able to elevate them to a higher quality of life, who could verify that there was, indeed, a greater power.

I'm not a savior or a god. Just a cop who wants her baby safe.

The streets were empty now, everyone gone into hiding at her order. There may be more of these creatures, she had told them. Plus Omori and his men were on the warpath. Brewster and Hiroshi had fought against the *tengu* (*Ah, Grandmother, those old tales you told me weren't so fanciful after all!*) and giant centipedes had been sighted crawling over the fortress walls. Reports were coming in from all parts of Odawara. The danger was all too real.

So why am I standing here?

The calm before the storm, she thought. *Full circle. This is where it began and this is where it will end.* And then, sounding like a litany in her brain—*Do not be afraid to open one door; be wary of the many—Embrace the darkness; our birthing springs from the abyss—There are no differences; only perceptions—The inner self holds the true power; the outer exists only as a vessel—The end is the beginning; the beginning has no end.* She smiled and shook her head. *I've used them all up. Just like wishes from a magic lamp. I've got to follow my own way now—a sixth precept—one only I can win with, to do what is right, no matter what.*

Yamaguchi and a group of villagers rounded the corner. The young *Shuugouteki* member looked to have regained his strength and had taken a very active role in preparing to go after Omori.

"Amazing!" he cried, his initial fear replaced by a curiosity and enthusiasm that had become infectious. He had accepted the fact that he had been transported back into the past pretty well but Kim was still worried about the condition he was in when she had first found him. Regardless, Yamaguchi was turning into a good organizer and all-around rabble-rouser— no doubt, skills he had learned from the *Shuugouteki*. He had dressed himself in traditional clothes and sandals and wore a sword at his side.

"We've seen some pretty bizarre creatures running around," he said to Kim. "Although nothing like the *oni*. They've all scuttled, flown or crawled away to hide at our approach. I think they sense something's about to happen and, I'm sure, want to be around to pick up the pieces. We're over two hundred strong and have a contingent heading towards the city's southern gates. We've picked up some volunteers along the way who have swelled our ranks a little, so that helps."

He's practically beaming, marveled Kim. *It's like he's found the Grail.*

"Omori's forces are gathering," Yamaguchi continued. "And there have been a couple of skirmishes. They've been caught by surprise, to say the least, so they're a little unorganized at this point but they have us outnumbered and, given the chance, they will turn us back."

Kim's brows furrowed in thought as she noticed Yamaguchi still had his gun. "Be careful. If you have to confront Omori's men, try to protect as many of yourselves as you can and delay the samurai and *sohei* as long as possible. I've instructed Midori to have two of the Sleepers accompany you. With you and all these beasties running loose, providing we don't get caught up in that craziness, we should be able to get into Omori's stronghold fairly easily."

"Will do." Yamaguchi mock saluted and led his 'army' off down the street. "We'll keep moving and pull as many *sohei* as we can away from Odawara Castle."

Kim smiled and looked up at the ever-darkening sky. Flashes of lightning pierced the roiling cloud cover; a growling rumble of thunder sounded in the distance. She turned at Brewster's approach and smiled. *He looks like a natural for this as well,* she thought, admiring the way he walked, the determined expression on his handsome face, remembering his touch. *A newly born warrior, ready to fight the good fight, whatever that may be. I just hope we all make it out of this to fight another day.*

"Hell of a first date," he said, as he stood by her side, taking her hand.

Hiroshi stood a respectful distance away, a new staff in hand.

Yamaguchi walked to the young boy's side and began speaking to him.

Brewster smiled. "You sure know how to show a guy a good time."

"And we're not done yet." She rubbed her hand along his chest, devouring him with her eyes. He had outfitted himself in the 'borrowed' black outfit, his 'costume', as it were, and looked pretty impressive. His face was unmasked now, though the *obi* was tied around his waist. She vaguely remembered Wayne carrying her to safety after the *oni* had fallen and stayed with her until she had regained consciousness. It had taken her a little longer to get her strength back this time. The psi bolt was draining. Blood from her nose had stained the front of her kimono; her head had felt like it was splitting, her arms and legs felt weak. Could she keep this up? she wondered. There was no telling what type of 'side effects' her esper usage was causing. Plus, she hadn't been able to contact Yoshima Mitsu in the Dreamspace.

No matter. It was up to her now. She had no choice but to continue.

Yamaguchi joined them. "Mr. Brewster," he said. "Per your request, I asked Hiroshi how he learned to handle his staff. He told me a couple of the samurai he served, bastards though they were, trained him to fight. They were going to hold matches and charge admission—pitting their best slaves against each other."

"Thanks, Jackson. And call me Wayne, please."

Yamaguchi nodded and walked off.

"I'm glad he's with us," Kim said. "We can use all the help we can get."

Brewster smiled. "So, about this outfit of yours?"

With young Midori's help, Kim had clothed herself in a similar type of 'ninja' style. "I had a mental image of Yoshima Mitsu at the end," she replied. "This kind of clothing was what she was wearing when she died. If I look like her, and Omori sees me clothed like her when he had her killed, then the shock might be even more profound and could work to our advantage. Besides, the clothing's actually pretty comfortable and easy to maneuver in."

"Kim, listen—" Brewster began.

"Not now, Wayne. Please. When this is all over."

"You said you can't see the future. There may not be one for us. I have to tell you—"

"I am sorry, Mitsu-san. But we are ready."

Kim jerked in surprise at Midori's interruption. "Why did you call me that?" Kim asked. "Why did you call me Mitsu?"

Midori bowed, dressed in worker's pants and shirt and carrying a long, wooden staff of her own. A short sword was belted at her side. "Yoshima Mitsu is who you are," she replied softly. "The Luminous One. Yes? That's who history will remember today."

Kim nodded, surprised at the wisdom of one so young. "Yes," she said with a reluctant nod. "I guess you're right."

She glanced slyly at Brewster and told him what Midori had said. "And I'd say you, my friend, will be remembered as the Ebon Warrior, yes?"

Brewster grinned and shook his head. "It looks like we're all doing our best to get into the history books one way or the other!"

"All right, everyone," Kim said, addressing her eclectic

entourage. She spoke in English for Wayne's sake, letting Jackson translate for the others. "Let's go over this one more time. It's not an elaborate plan but one we'll have to implement as fast as we can. According to Midori, there are two ways into Odawara Castle.

"The main entrance is the one Wayne was led to by the monks. But there's another opening on the back side of the castle, a rear entrance to the interior of the lower level which has been bricked up."

Kim gestured to the Sleepers. "Honorable Samurai, you will go through the main entrance and try to work your way up the castle to the pavilion situated at the top of the main keep. You'll serve as a major distraction while Wayne, Hiroshi and I go around the back and attempt to sneak in that way. The interior of the castle's lower level, we've been informed, is riddled with a series of passageways and tunnels. We're hoping they won't be as well guarded since they're rarely used. Our objective is to break through the brick wall and confront Omori and this other associate of his that Wayne described, who, I feel, may also have a link to our time.

"We must get to this Pavilion of Black Dragons, as it's called, find Omori, and end this. Just getting to him right now is going to be a hard enough task. I don't want to kill him if we can avoid it. I don't want to be in the assassination business. If we can capture him, imprison him, then that's fine. If not..." Kim sighed. The Plan B that Parker had alluded to still nagged at her. What did he mean? Did Omori have some kind of back-door escape planned out? Did he have a secret weapon? Brewster had told her about the 'associate' who had been in charge when he had been taken by the monks. This one had spoken perfect English, using idioms not employed in this time and place. And by Brewster's description, he was surely the one she had seen on the mountaintop when she had first slipped back in time—the one who had overseen the burning of her ancestor.

Another time-traveler? *Interesting.* Was that what Parker had alluded to? Were Omori and this other man planning on escaping via the timelines? She wondered again if this one could be the shadow-tracker's future handler, in the flesh? If so, how?

"Kim." Brewster gently broke in on her thoughts. "How are we sure Omori is even there now? He might be out with his men."

Kim nodded. "No, he's at the castle, all right. I can feel his mental presence there, the same one I followed earlier—it's as clear in my mind as smoke from a fire. But we have to hurry—that's where our final showdown is going to be." She looked at Brewster, grinning. "Don't you read your history?" Before Brewster could reply, Kim kissed him. "For luck," she said. "Don't get yourself killed, yes? We have a conversation to finish."

"Agreed," Brewster said with a smile. "Let's *all* of us get out of this alive."

"Midori," she said, turning towards the young girl. "There might be people who'll need shelter and medical care if all hell breaks loose here. You can stay here or—"

Midori bowed again. "We have people here who can assist," she said. "I wish to go with you. My father and his father anticipated this moment all of their lives and trained me for the same purpose. It would be difficult for me to wait here but I will do as you command."

Kim nodded. Indeed, how could she make this brave, young girl sit here and wait? And Kim would need her if her plan was to work. "Very well," she said. "You can lead the Sleepers and coordinate their assault on the main part of the castle." *And I have no doubt you can do it.*

Midori's eyes lit up. "*Domo arigatu, Kim-san,*" barely suppressing a smile.

"And what about Hiroshi?" Kim asked softly with a smile. Despite the young woman's reserve and strict adherence to custom, she saw Midori's eyes dart ever-so-quickly in Hiroshi's direction.

Midori blushed. "Yes. I will worry for him. He wants to fight by Master Brewster-san's side. There was nothing I could say to change his mind." She looked into Kim's eyes. "Is that strange, Mistress? I hardly know Hiroshi-chan."

Not Hiroshi-san but Hiroshi-*chan*—a more endearing suffix. Kim threw a quick glance at Brewster. "No," she said softly. "Not strange at all." Facing Midori again, she said, "I promise to watch out for him." Wayne had vouched for the boy although it had been plain to see he hadn't been happy about putting him in danger either. But, it seemed, nothing short of mind-control would dissuade Hiroshi from accompanying them and she was reluctant to do that. She squeezed Midori's hand. "We'll get through this."

Midori nodded.

She turned and faced her friends. The Five Precepts of Yira. Well, Kim Yoshima could play the philosophy game too. The Sixth Precept—"To win the day, you have to follow your own path." *Corny and simplistic,* she thought. *But it'll have to do.* "OK, everyone." She donned her black face wrap. "Ready? Let's go!"

CHAPTER 54

Brewster, Kim, Hiroshi, Midori and the ten Sleepers walked through a virtual ghost town. Half of the Sleepers had taken point, emulating some ancient military maneuver, while the rest brought up the rear. The two young people held hands as if drawing strength from one another. Gently, Brewster grasped Kim's fingertips with his own. He felt a spark at contact and his heart leapt.

The streets of Odawara were deserted as was the sky above them—not a bird or insect flew its cloud-enshrouded breadth. The only signs of life on the ground were the occasional group of *sohei* and nervous samurai who patrolled the streets or the odd cat or dog wandering aimlessly. Each barely acknowledged Brewster and his friends' presence. It was as if the very air had been sucked out of the city itself, to be replaced by a blanket of fear and helplessness.

Periodically, Brewster would see the shapes of creatures unknown sidle back into the shadows at their passing. Once he saw a 'flock' of *tengu* circle overhead and felt a chill at the memory of his encounter with them.

The Odawarans had fled indoors or, in some cases, escaped the city entirely before Omori had ordered the gates barred. It was a type of martial law Brewster couldn't understand. Why lock your people inside with the very danger you're supposed to protect them from?

Insane, he thought. *Power mad megalomaniac.*

They waited across the street from the wall's main gated entrance to Odawara Castle. Was it only a few hours ago that he had stood there himself, a prisoner of Omori's men? So much had happened even in that short time. He looked at Kim Yoshima, barely able to suppress a smile. He'd see this strange adventure through with her to the end. Nothing would keep him from this amazing woman's side now. Nothing.

A larger contingent of samurai milled about the main entrance leading through the wall and up the paved causeway to the castle, uncertainty and fear flickering across their faces.

Omori went past this checkpoint just a little while ago, Kim psi-cast to her companions. The words invading Brewster's mind were less uncomfortable now as Kim got better at 'transmitting'. *I can track his mental footsteps up to the castle itself. He must be somewhere inside his stronghold or his control center—the Pavilion of Black Dragons. So, let's take care of these samurai first.*

She took a deep breath and closed her eyes. Brewster watched the samurai suddenly stop and put their hands to their heads. Slowly, they started to wander off in various directions, eyes unfocused, some unsheathing and dropping their weapons. The entrance to the gate in the wall now stood unguarded.

Amazing, Brewster thought. *How does she do that?*

As they rushed up to the gate, Brewster stopped and retrieved one of the swords the samurai had dropped while under Kim's mental influence. He held it up, seeing his reflection in the shiny blade, admiring the weapon's artistry. *This might come in handy,* he thought and sheathed the weapon through his *obi*.

At the wall gate, Kim undid the latches on the other side of the wall, employing her telekinetic power as a kind of psychic lock-picker. Brewster and Hiroshi pushed the gate open.

All right, everyone, Kim mind-sent, as they all walked through. There were no guards on this side of the wall. *This is where we split up. I'll keep in touch. Good luck.*

It was then that Brewster noticed Kim wipe some blood away from her nose.

CHAPTER 55

Kim, Brewster and Hiroshi clambered down a back path, riddled with switchbacks cut into the side of the hill. *Grandmother Mitsu*, Kim thought with a touch of irony. *Did you ever think your Kimmy-chan would become a ninja long before you were even born? What a comic book adventure this would make for Bobby!*

She thought then of her nephew and her friends Lazo, Jenny and Joe, hoping they were all right, regretting leaving them in such an abrupt, unreal fashion. If she and Brewster and the others could pull this off, if they could fulfill their unbelievable roles in history-past, then everyone and everything would be all right. As crazy as it sounded, she was sure of that. But most of all, she thought of Shioko and her connection to Ko the Little. Once again, she wondered, how was that to come about? What metaphysical or cosmological quirks would allow that historical anecdote to come true?

That was the biggie, she knew. According to the old texts, Yoshima Mitsu was the victor here. But it was the unspoken role of Ko who had to really win the battle. If that didn't happen…

She wouldn't think about that now. She scanned ahead through the milieu, pinpointing the rear entranceway with two samurai guarding it.

She and her companions came to a bend in the path, which

overlooked the back of the castle where the scene in her mind's eye crystallized into reality. There, ahead a couple of hundred yards, a rear entrance, simply a cave or tunnel at one time, yawned partially open in the castle's lower casement. Workmen, covered in sweat and dirt, were dismantling a brick wall that blocked the tunnel opening.

Great, Kim thought. *Saves us the trouble.*

The two samurai guards stood on a small ledge in front of the tunnel which branched off the downhill path on the far side. They kept careful watch, standing rigid and alert on opposite ends of the ledge.

The Kanto Plain lay spread out beneath Kim and her comrades, the view of it from this height vast and daunting despite the overcast day. In the distance, a hawk circled in the darkening sky, its whistling cry echoing off the distant hills. And then, like a deadly missile, a larger flying figure suddenly dove out of the cloud cover, its bat-winged, alligator-shaped body slamming into the hawk and ripping it apart in mid-air with its snapping jaws.

The workers looked upward, uneasy, their body language tense with apprehension. One of the samurai turned and shouted at them to keep working.

Another creature from the inter-dimensional overflow. Omori must want this entrance opened up for some reason. I wonder what the previous warlord used it for? Kim readied her powers to use on the guards. *A simple psychic 'stun' should do it.*

Both samurai fell to the ledge like rag dolls. The workers, afraid they might be the next victims of this invisible force or just taking their chances to escape, took off running down the opposite side of the slope.

Making sure no one else was around, Kim led the way into the tunnel, squeezing through the partially dismantled wall. A few feet past the rubble stood a huge wooden door built into the casement itself.

Kim worked her mental lock-picking skills again. This time she had to exert more psi energy to move the giant dead bolt from its rocky cradle. Brewster and Hiroshi pushed on the door.

They entered a work of art. The cave-like aspect vanished completely once they crossed the door's threshold. The underground passageway hadn't just been dug—it had been crafted. The length of the walls and ceiling were adorned with elaborate carvings, embossments and triptychs. Stylized stone dragons, birds, embattled warriors and haughty princesses loomed over the passageway like frozen sentinels. Flickering torches set in wall sconces lit the way, shedding dancing, skeletal shadows on the walls and supporting columns. The floor was smooth, some parts actually having been tiled with abstract, mosaic designs. Pottery, jewelry, gold and silver-encrusted art lay in abundance. The interior didn't smell musty or enclosed, as if fresh air was coming in from somewhere.

"Quite a sight," Brewster murmured.

"It is said Soun Ujitsuna had this built to house the treasures and wealth he had taken from the Omori clan," Hiroshi said. Kim realized with a start that this was the first time she had heard the young boy say anything more than two or three words at a time. "The entrance had been blocked to keep thieves and bandits out and all of this was to be distributed to the people of Odawara."

"And now," Kim guessed, "Omori was going to take all this booty out, to use it for god knows what."

Abruptly, once again, Kim sensed danger.

(*above them, part of the wall*)

"Get back!" she cried. A rumbling, tearing sound emanated

from the roof of the cavern. A large statue of a fantastic two-headed creature, three times the size of Kim and carved in a ship's figurehead style, had broken loose from the wall near the ceiling where it had been anchored. It came crashing down towards them.

Kim mentally deflected most of the falling debris just in time but the huge bulk of the statue wasn't stopped completely. It crashed onto the floor, its splintering bulk separating Kim from Brewster and Hiroshi. But the mental deflection had allowed them to get out of the statue's deadly downward plunge.

"Kim!" Brewster called out from the other side of the broken statue. "Are you all right?"

"Yes," she answered, coughing in the raised dust. "But who knocked that thing down?"

A loud screeching cry answered Kim's question. There, above her, hanging from a broken piece of ceiling rock was a large animal that looked like, of all things, a weasel. It hissed at Kim, holding onto the cracked stone with long, very wicked-looking claws.

"A *kamaitachi*!" Hiroshi cried from the other side of the downed statue. "Its demon talons can cut through rock itself! Hyaaa, demon! Begone!"

Kim smiled as a rock flung by Hiroshi struck the wall near the strange beast. With another hiss, the *kamaitachi* slithered up into a hole in the ceiling and disappeared.

But they weren't free of the inter-dimensional refugees yet. Immediately, Kim's prescience flared up again. She detected something else.

Someone approached from Brewster's and Hiroshi's direction.

CHAPTER 56

The shadow-tracker's acute hearing picked out the sounds of the pack. Somewhere in the tunnel complex, her brothers and sisters (the pups she had birthed, her mature litters) were on the move.

She had picked up other information too. At her last feeding only moments ago, there had been two samurai who brought her food. They had talked of an attack from outside; of how their comrades were trying to defend the Eminent Lord's stronghold against mysterious infiltrators; of how an uprising of the people was occurring within Odawara; of rampaging monsters on the loose; of how the Eminent Lord, despite his power and planning, had let the defense of the city slip from within. Overconfident, they had said. Too full of himself and his glory.

And then there was the matter of her handler—the young master. The so-called *majo* had been holed up in some adjacent tunnels with some of the newly bred shadow-trackers. Eela had been worried and afraid—she had actually smelled his fear. He had run past her prison and shrieked that the world was ending. The *tengu*, he had cried, the *tengu* were killing everyone.

Something had changed. Fear, tension and confusion permeated the dank, underground air.

Now is the time, she thought. *If I am to escape this fate, I can't remain a prisoner any longer.* She looked down at her shackled leg.

There was a way to free herself but it belied everything the young master had hinted at once upon a time so long ago, in a time yet to come—that she and her huntmate were unique among shadow-trackers; that they had been instilled with more human elements than the others in their breeding.

But to gain her freedom, she would have to act the Beast.

She bent down, her supple upper body allowing herself to easily place her jaws just above her broken, useless, captive ankle.

Quickly, but with deliberation, she began to chew.

CHAPTER 57

Brewster ran over to the fallen statue. "Kim!" he shouted. "Kim, there's an opening, a crack, at the head of the statue. We can get through. " A warning cry from Hiroshi, "Brewster-san!," caused him to grudgingly turn back, clinging to the base of the broken rock that he had begun to climb.

Brewster squinted into the gloom ahead. A dark figure stood in the shadows of the cavern in front of them. Hiroshi had taken a defensive stance. Brewster peered into the dusty murk.

A woman of indeterminate age emerged into the checkered light. Dressed in a shabby robe, her long, gray hair undone and hanging down past her waist, she stared at Brewster and Hiroshi with cold, feral eyes. Fingernails, abnormally long and curling, extended like claws from her wrinkled hands.

"Hiroshi," Brewster called, a bad feeling inching up his spine. He motioned to the young man to back off as he stepped back down onto the floor. "Kim!" he called over his shoulder. "Kim, are you all right? I think we may have a problem."

The woman smiled a ghastly grin and opened her mouth. Brewster was never sure afterwards, but he swore the woman's jaws widened like a shark's, completely blotting out her face.

Her chest seemed to swell with raw power as she bent forward and screamed.

No, Kim thought, as she shot a quick scan at the screaming woman. She had been uninjured by the fallen statue and had quickly climbed to its top. *It can't be!* She darted through the break in the statue and formed the strongest psi-shield she could muster around her, Brewster and Hiroshi, as a deadly barrage of sound erupted from the woman's mouth. Even with the esper energy field surrounding them, Kim felt the power of the killing sound wave spreading throughout the tunnel.

Hiroshi knelt with his head on the ground and his hands covering his ears. Kim and Brewster cringed together against the aural shockwave that raged outside the shield. Kim forced herself to watch as the structure surrounding them became blasted and seared by the ancient power unleashed by the woman.

Overhead, rippling cracks developed in the ceiling as some of the ornate statuary shook loose from their bases. Rocks and detritus spun in a swirling vortex of sound. The very mountain itself seemed to tremble in the dangerous energy's wake.

And then it was over. Like in the aftermath of a great storm, dirt and small debris whirled through the air. An eerie silence now lay heavily throughout the tunnel. Cautiously, Kim dropped the psi-shield.

The woman lay on her back, arching her body in pain, her eyes rolled back into her head. Her mouth lay open, drooling and gasping.

"Kim," Brewster breathed softly. "What the hell was that? Who is this woman?"

The screamer had stopped convulsing and lay still, her breath slow and ragged. Kim knelt at her side. "Another inhabitant of the mythological world, I think," she said.

THE SIXTH PRECEPT

"This one possessed a power called the *kiai* or Spirit Cry," Hiroshi said. He looked up, eyes wide.

Kim rose, suddenly shaken. "It's all so impossible!" she suddenly cried, running her hands through her hair. "Insane!" She backed away from Brewster's approach. "I never wanted this...this power. I never asked for it. My god, I've killed with it! And all because of some damn preordained...destiny. Why is this happening? It's not fair. It's not fair!"

"Kim, listen," Brewster pulled her to him, holding her tightly at arms' length. "You can't be afraid of these abilities anymore. Now, more than ever, you need this gift. We're all here for the same reason. We have to face Omori together or else he *will* win! We've got to continue! You're the Yomitsu!"

Kim laughed at the earnestness in his voice, the tension in his manner and the absurdness of her hesitation—they were in ancient Japan, after all. What else could she do?

She turned her gaze from Brewster and was greeted by the startling sight of Hiroshi prostrating himself before her and the man-in-black. He knelt on the ground with head and hands touching the surface of the tunnel floor. He was murmuring something and looked to be trembling.

Hiroshi risked a glance at Kim with an expression of awe and a little fear. His eyes darted back and forth between Brewster and Kim.

"Hey, Hiroshi," Brewster said, releasing Kim and walking toward the young boy. "It's OK. It's just us. Nothing to be afraid of." He stopped and turned to Kim. "Tell him, will you? What? Kim, what's wrong?"

"He's terrified of us," Kim said, shaking her head. "This is what my power has caused. Fear and some kind of misplaced hero worship. He's seen me stop the Spirit Cry and defeat the *oni*. He thinks now that I'm certainly a *kami* or a god and not a real person at all. I'm the Luminous One *and* the Yomitsu, for god's sake!" She reached out a thin spark of mental reassurance and soothed Hiroshi's fear. It was quicker that way.

"Forgive me, Mistress," Hiroshi whispered, as he rose to his knees, head still down.

"Nothing to forgive, Hiroshi," Kim answered in Japanese. "Please, stand. We're all equal here."

The young staff-wielder raised himself up, grasped his weapon and moved to Brewster's side. He bowed deeply. "Thank you, Yomitsu-san," the boy said, his eyes reflecting respect and wonder. "I...I was afraid."

Kim smiled wearily. "We all are, Hiroshi. But you have been a courageous comrade and I thank you for it. I couldn't do this without you." She turned to Brewster and, in English, said, "Without all of you."

Hiroshi bowed again. "Too long have I been a slave of evil men. I will continue to fight with you and Brewster-san if you will have me."

Kim nodded and turned to Brewster's questioning face. The young boy's courage was contagious. "You're right, Wayne. We have to go on. I'm sorry. It's tough being a super hero. I guess that's what I am." She laughed again, a sudden weight lifted from her. "Just like you, Ebon Warrior."

And then to Hiroshi, in Japanese, "Are you ready, Hiroshi-san?"

"*Hai*! Yoshima-san!" he cried.

Kim let her gaze linger on Hiroshi a moment. *This one,* she thought. *And Midori. I have a sense their story isn't going to end here. This is just the beginning for them. Princess Midori and Chancellor Hiroshi.* She kissed Brewster on the lips, turned and led him and Hiroshi through the crack in the statue to the other side of the tunnel.

THE SIXTH PRECEPT

It wasn't long before they came to a fork in the passageway. "Which way, Kim?" Brewster asked. "Can you sense anything?"

"Not yet. I think so far into the interior of the mountain, the rock structure here is interfering with my psi abilities to a degree." She looked down both tunnels and made her decision. "We should split up."

"I don't think that's wise."

"We can cover more ground this way."

"But—"

A sudden clamor from back the way they had come reached their ears. "A big crowd of people," Kim said, trying to mentally pick up some finer details of what she sensed, "coming this way."

"All right," Brewster said. "That decides it. Hiroshi and I will see what's going on and try to delay them, whoever they may be. I—"

But Kim was gone, running up the left passageway. She moved quickly. The tunnel curved to the right. There seemed to be a light shining up ahead. *Go!* she thought-sent back to Brewster. *I don't sense any danger from that crowd. Be safe!*

CHAPTER 58

The samurai who came to feed her never saw her coming. His chest burst open as easily as tearing paper, the leather armor ripping apart just like his shattered ribs. The shadow-tracker laughed as she knelt over his lifeless, bleeding body, her bloody talons dripping. Even as a prisoner, as wounded as she was, her strength and determination hadn't failed her. She bent down and ravaged the man's entrails, gorging herself on his lifeblood.

Resisting the urge to howl in triumph, she pulled the *obi* from around the samurai's waist and tied it tightly above where her foot used to be to staunch the flow of her own blood. She then ripped a strip from his bloody under-vest to wrap her stump in.

Yes, that was much better.

With her hands and one good foot, she hopped up the steps leading to the level above. The pain where her missing foot had once been was excruciating. But she compartmentalized those feelings, placing them in the back of her mind. Only one thing mattered now—to find and kill the young master. To make him pay for the lies he had fed her, her huntmate, and all of her kind. To reject what she had become—the mother of all shadow-trackers.

This time she would succeed.

She reached the upper level and looked down through the netting and poisoned spikes of her former prison. She would never go back there. She would kill the so-called *majo*, Eela, or die trying. Either way, there would never be any more of her litters for her handler to breed and subjugate!

She moved again, a wounded animal yet with an animal's instinct and power. She gave in completely to the Beast. The Beast would help her to survive; the Beast would assist in completing the task she had started.

She rounded a turn in the hallway, the walls and floor here man-made, like those of the pit. Wood and mortar shaped themselves to the curves of the passageway, mold and mildew crosshatching their dirty surfaces. Cockroaches and other vermin scuttled in the torchlight. The shadow-tracker stopped, cocking her head to listen.

Voices. Up ahead. They were ones she recognized. Her sharpened hearing picked up pieces of a conversation, an argument—

"Where is your magic now, witch?"

"How was I to know?"

"Lying piece of dung! Make things as they were or I swear I'll gut you here and now!"

"There are monsters out there, you fucking maniac! Real monsters! I never counted on this! I...I thought the entries describing these creatures in the *Totou's* history were just fables or metaphors! I never thought—"

"You have power, Eela. Even so, are you that afraid?"

"Aren't you? Jesus, God, man. And you're asking the freaking impossible! First you want weapons from the future and now you want me to snap my fingers and make everything go away?"

There—a samurai stood guard in front of an open doorway.

She raced forward, even as a cripple, silent and deadly. She leaped up and tore the guard's throat out with one vicious swing of her claws.

She didn't stop but flung herself into the room, the Beast turning her into a demon avenger. Another samurai went down before her. The young master and the Eminent Lord himself stood facing each other, looks of shock and confusion painted on both of their faces.

The shadow-tracker slammed into the Eminent Lord, knocking him across the room. She turned on her handler, her jaws slavering, her bloody claws reaching for him.

She took him down, sinking her teeth into his shoulder. Eela screamed, trying to fight her off. She raked her claws across his face, shredding his ear and jaw. He shrieked in pain and terror. "I will take you slowly," she whispered into the bloody hole where his ear had been. "You will suffer as I have."

She stood up on both legs, ignoring the burning pain in her stump. She howled as she held the despised enemy above her head. Voicing a triumphant roar and using a strength brought up from deep within, she threw him against the wall.

A noise behind her…

Too late she turned. Something sharp ran through her, piercing her stomach to exit out her back. She stood there, dumbfounded, holding onto the blade of the Eminent Lord. The blood running from her sliced hands joined that of her body as it flowed onto the floor.

The Eminent Lord twisted his weapon, gouging the wound and then yanked his sword free. The shadow-tracker crumpled to the floor. She lay there, her blood pumping from her body as the Eminent Lord walked over to the fallen *majo*, grabbed the young master by his hair and dragged him out of the room.

Didn't even check to see if his men were still alive, she thought dizzily, the pain in her stomach throbbing through the rest of her body. The room spun and grew dark. Her eyes fought to stay open. *Eminent Lord, I used to pray to you, to call your name for guidance, for help. Now who do I pray to? Who…?*

CHAPTER 59

A cry of pain within the ambient-milieu; a recognizable but surprising mental presence. *The shadow-tracker. The one from the book haven!* She hesitated before the stairway ascending to the castle keep and then darted down a side hallway.

She entered a large circular room lit by torches. Below was a pit, what looked to be a small, bowl-shaped amphitheater. Rope netting and bamboo spikes covered the top opening like some giant, obscene spider web; a man lay in the sand, cruelly disemboweled.

Kim raced past the pit and entered another hallway. Mortar, wooden supports and paper *shoji* screens lined the walls of the tunnel. Another mutilated body lay outside an open doorway. Kim turned and entered.

"Yomitsu," a familiar high-pitched voice whispered weakly and edged with pain. "Somehow I knew you would come."

Stepping over a third corpse, Kim approached the dying shadow-tracker. The she-beast lay on her back, her head propped up against the wall. Blood flowed from a gaping wound in her stomach, her hands and what was left of one leg. Kim knelt at her side and tried to ease her pain. But it was too late. There was nothing she could do.

"I'm…I'm sorry," she said softly, feeling genuine sympathy for the one who had tried to kill her.

The shadow-tracker attempted to smile, her eyes slowly dimming. "We were enemies once," she croaked. "I would have killed you. But now I know you are the only one who can stop this…" Her clawed, bloody hand encircled Kim's wrist. "I have failed my huntmate, the rest of my kind and myself." A rattling cough. "My handler. Eela, he calls himself here. I never knew his real name; he who was from our time and now rules at the Eminent Lord's side. We traveled here to this time and place together. You must stop him. He…he…" The shadow-tracker shuddered once and let out a long breath as she died.

So, Kim thought, as she pried the she-beast's hand from her wrist. *It* was *her handler all along, after all.*

She turned to run back the way she had come but Omori's mental trail directed her to continue down the hallway. Another entrance to the top, perhaps to the main keep and the pavilion itself — *Yes! He's gone this way!*

She started up a set of stairs cut into the rock.

CHAPTER 60

Omori spat in anger. What was happening? Where were the rest of his men? Had the uprising been put down? Who were the two strangely armored samurai who had invaded his pavilion? How many more creatures of the Left Hand Path had crossed over? Would this filthy *majo* stop babbling and answer his questions? HOW COULD ANY OF THIS HAVE COME TO PASS IN THE FIRST PLACE?!!

With a snarl, Omori kicked the wounded *majo* in the side. Eela groaned and rolled over, his head and shoulder a mass of blood and torn flesh. Omori bent down, shouting, "I should have let the dog-bitch kill you! *I* will if you don't work your vaunted magic."

He left the injured *majo* and walked over to where his two surviving *sohei* stood over the fallen samurai. The first one killed lay on his back, his head almost severed from his body. The other, a woman it seemed, lay fallen over the first's body as if trying to protect him. The *sohei* had stabbed her in the back as, already wounded, she had crawled over to her companion.

But not before both intruders had killed several of his monks whose blood-soaked bodies lay strewn over the ravaged Pavilion of Black Dragons. Silent and methodical, the strangely-armored samurai had fought bloodily and efficiently.

Almost supernaturally. It was only because of so many wounds sustained that they finally succumbed.

Omori shivered. Enough of this then. It was time he rejoined his men. There was much to do. Suddenly, the two *sohei* looked behind him, their eyes widening. "Lord," one said, pointing a shaking hand. "Lord, look!"

"Eh?" Omori turned and gasped. With the dark sky and flashing lightning as a surreal backdrop, an apparition walked out from the *donjon* and up the steps of the pavilion facing towards him. It stood proud and haughty, arms outstretched at its sides, black *obi* flapping in the wind. Its eyes seemed to bore a hole right through Omori, full of anger and determination.

It was her! The shirabyoshi *ninja!*

"No!" Omori cried, shakily drawing his sword. His knees felt weak. His heart pounded. He had seen monsters aplenty today, a day unlike any he had ever experienced. But this…"It can't be. You're dead! You're dead! The shadow-trackers killed you. I saw your corpse. My men burned you, Ghost!"

The ghost walked to within a few feet in front of him, a grim smile upon its lips. "So you're Omori Kadonomaro," it said softly with a strange accent. "After all this time we finally meet in the flesh. And now I know where this 'ghost' thing comes from." It shot a glance at the two dead samurai as its lips twisted into a snarl. "Well, now, you murdering bastard," it said. "It's time to say goodbye." The Ghost's eyes widened as a sudden, invisible force gripped Omori and hurled him backwards. He crashed into his two *sohei*, all three falling to their backs.

The warlord arose, trembling, holding his sword, his body bent into a crouch. The two monks moved behind him, fear emanating from them in waves. "You cannot hurt me!" Omori cried, exhibiting a bravado he didn't really feel. "I defy you, black *kami*! Only the One Child can defeat me. Not you! Not a spirit from the darkness! The Prophecy states it!"

THE SIXTH PRECEPT

"You fool, Omori! !" Eela had gotten to his feet and was holding on to one of the pillars supporting the tented roof of the pavilion. His head lolled to one side, his legs shuffled for purchase. Blood smeared his torn face. "She's not a ghost!" he cried hoarsely, breathing hard. "She's from the future as I am. She's the freaking cop! I…I knew her before, in my own time, before I came here. She has powers but can still be killed." He pointed a palsied finger at the ghost. "The bitch can be killed!"

Omori grunted. His own anger flared within him, overpowering his fear. Was the *majo* finally helping him? Did anything make sense today? He had killed a demon corpse-eater earlier. Why not a ghost who wasn't a ghost? "Release the shadow-trackers, witch!" he shouted, and raising his voice in a high-pitched war cry, charged the apparition.

CHAPTER 61

As Brewster and Hiroshi approached the fallen statuary blocking the tunnel, the sounds of oncoming footsteps drifted from the rear entrance. A cacophony of voices, a choir of pitched cries, shouts and curses echoed off the walls, heralding the approach of a large group of people.

"OK!" Brewster exclaimed. "Kim said there's no danger here but let's take up positions out of sight until we can determine what we're up against." At that moment, a crowd of men and women, from all walks of this era's life, all bearing weapons of one type or another, appeared from behind the fallen rubble. Climbing over the debris caused by the spirit cry, a smartly armored soldier led the way—one of the Sleepers. And behind him, walking calmly through the break in the fallen statue, was—

"Jackson!" Brewster breathed a sigh of relief. "What's happened?"

"We beat back Omori's men." Yamaguchi was beaming. "Can you believe it? The element of surprise, you know. Power to the people!" Yamaguchi walked out from among the crowd, a huge grin on his face despite the fact his clothes were torn and bloody. He glowed like a proud father. He held his Glock up in one hand. "This helped. I merely fired it in the air, which scared the hell out of most of the samurai. But we need to move quickly before they regroup."

Brewster shook his head, a smile on his lips. At least one of them had managed to hang on to their modern weapons. "You've really gotten into this, haven't you?"

"My god, yes! If the other members of the *Shuugouteki* could see me now. Although I do miss my smart phone. But never in my wildest dreams did I ever imagine this!"

Wildest dreams? Brewster thought with a chuckle. *You don't know the half of it!*

"Midori?" Hiroshi interrupted. He looked back towards where they had come, concern and confusion written on his face.

"I'm not sure," Yamaguchi said, alternating his replies in Japanese and English. "She led the rest of the Sleepers to the front of the castle per Kim's orders."

A chorus of screams burst from the rear of the column of Yamaguchi's 'army'. Brewster heard the word '*tatsu*' being repeated over and over. The crowd of people directly behind Yamaguchi began to mutter and whisper among themselves, their eyes and faces displaying surprise and sudden fear. Hiroshi looked toward Brewster, another questioning look on his own face.

"Go!" Brewster said, pointing, and then to Yamaguchi, "Jackson, you speak the language. Tell him—" But Hiroshi had apparently understood and was running back to where they had last seen Kim to try and locate Midori.

"*Tatsu?*" Brewster asked. "What—?"

But Yamaguchi had already started running back toward the rear entrance of the tunnel, his people stepping aside for him to pass.

Brewster followed, reluctantly drawing the samurai's sword from his *obi*. Kim's welfare was still uppermost in his mind but instinct took over. Despite Yamaguchi's followers, he still might need help with whatever danger threatened them now.

Yamaguchi's followers formed two lines on each side of the tunnel, a passive gauntlet more than willing to let their impromptu leader take on this new danger. They all eyed Brewster curiously, pointing and whispering at this man in black.

The screaming and general sounds of confusion became louder as they got closer to the entrance. Some members of Yamaguchi's 'army' ran towards them from the outside, obviously terrified, some hysterical with fear. A burning smell assailed Brewster's nostrils, a high-pitched shriek of some large animal split the air.

He and Yamaguchi ran out onto the ledge of the rear entrance of the castle. The rear guard of Yamaguchi's fighting force was retreating back down the stairway, screaming. Most of the brush underlying the base of Odawara Castle was on fire; some of the rock looked to be melted. The smells of ozone and burning flesh were overpowering as smoke filled the air.

Brewster looked up. He heard Yamaguchi say something in Japanese.

The *tengu* had been one thing—fantastic and impossible. The *oni* had been even more fearsome and incredible. Even the shadow-trackers were like something out of someone's twisted imagination—real yet unreal. But what Brewster saw now (flying, though it had no wings, its angled, pointed head crowned with long horns and its face sporting long whiskers, its silver-scaled body long and serpent-like) was a creature more awe-inspiring, more unbelievable, more elemental than anything Brewster could have ever imagined.

And it wasn't the first time he had seen one. *Tatsu*. Dragon.

It was indeed a dragon, lean and supple, much like the one

he and Kim had encountered in the *Box Factory*, that rode the wind above them, despite having no wings, but much bigger. Arcing and twisting, spiraling and tumbling, the great beast trumpeted like a rogue elephant, a pillar of fire erupting from its mouth. It dove toward the ledge. Long, taloned paws reached out as the dragon dropped downward.

The giant serpent unleashed a column of flame right at the ledge. Tongues of fire enveloped the rocky outcropping, causing parts of it to explode and rocket straight at Brewster and Yamaguchi.

Brewster turned and grabbed Yamaguchi by the arm, pulling him against his body. They both hunched together behind an outstanding boulder. A wall of fire enshrouded them; a roaring inferno of heat and flame wreathed the rock like emblazoned serpents.

The fiery cascade melted away, revealing that the rocky outcropping on the outside of the boulder had been melted and glazed.

The *tatsu* turned for another pass. The very air of his passing was like a flaming windstorm; a hint of brimstone, musk and death floated on the wind.

"I don't have any suggestions, Mr. Brewster," Yamaguchi said helplessly, his newfound confidence evaporating. "We have no way to fight it. If we could only get everyone into the tunnel!"

"You do that," Brewster said quickly. "I'll divert it, try to keep it occupied while you get everyone under cover. Give me your gun."

Some of the crowd let out a cry, pointing upwards. Brewster followed their surprised gaze. Another creature, another dragon, had appeared in the darkening sky. Smaller than the *tatsu*, it moved more quickly on outspread wings, breathing its own deadly fire. It appeared to be heading on a collision course with the *tatsu*.

"Yes!" Brewster said. "Maybe this one can be our diversion."

The second dragon spiraled around the bigger beast, attacking it. It shot darts of fire at the great creature's flanks and nipped at its tail. The *tatsu* roared and snapped back at its smaller tormentor, its body twisting and curling up on itself. But like a gnat irritating a much larger foe, the second dragon flew in circles, harassing its larger opponent.

Those in the crowd shouted, "*hairyu*," over and over again. Yamaguchi turned toward Brewster, smiling. "They're saying it's *Hairyu* the Dragon-Bird come to save us! He's the only Japanese dragon that has wings and is a good guy."

"We need more of those 'good guys'," Brewster replied. "Let's get everyone into the cave now while they're occupied! We've got to find Kim and the others!"

CHAPTER 62

Jackson Yamaguchi stood at the rear entrance to Odawara-jo, supervising the last of his followers. Traces of burning brush wafted around him like smoky serpents. Odawara Castle loomed above. They had done it. Elation shot through him like the *tatsu*'s still smoldering fire. They had reached Omori's stronghold.

Wayne Brewster led the way inside the rear entrance of the castle,. Brewster said he was fairly certain he could figure out how to get into the castle proper, having already walked some distance into the lower level passage.

Yamaguchi was grateful for the man's help. And happy at his own chance to participate in the unbelievable series of events that had brought him here. He had literally fallen into this time and place afraid and injured. But a renewed strength coursed through him now. His *Shuugouteki* training had asserted itself and he had been able to organize this group of people as a fighting force and gather valuable information. Even more so, he found he had actually inspired them.

And, in the process, himself as well.

Yamaguchi watched the dark sky where the two reptilian leviathans were still battling. The dragons had taken their airborne duel away toward the distant horizon but their shrieks and roars still reverberated throughout the Kanto Plain. The whoofing of their great lungs as they breathed fire sounded like hot air balloons in flight.

Dragons, Yamaguchi thought in awe. *Hot damn!* The young man's body tingled with nervous anticipation. But more than that, he felt a door opening within him, a deepening of purpose and conviction, a truer belief in a higher power than he had ever felt before.

All the years he had gone through the rigorous training and education by the *Shuugouteki,* the things he had given up, the places he had never been able to travel to, the relationships he had never been allowed to forge—there had been times when he wanted nothing more than to live a normal life.

But now…

He had been chosen! Of all the *Shuugouteki* agents throughout history, he, Jackson Yamaguchi, had been picked as the one to travel into this past era, to this moment in time. He had been the one to accompany the legendary Yomitsu to help fight the warlord, Omori.

If his friends and colleagues could see him now! He hoped he didn't wake up from this dream; this incredible, awesome, fantastic—

He tore himself away from the astonishing sight overhead and walked to the rear of the line, where the last of his recruits were entering the tunnel. A young girl, perhaps close to his own age and carrying a wooden rake as her weapon, turned and gazed at him with her brightly smoldering eyes—eyes filled with admiration and respect. She was dressed in simple peasant garb, a scarf tied around her head, yet Yamaguchi found her dazzling.

"Jackson-san," she said softly, holding out her hand as she bowed her head and lowered her eyes. "I am Aimi. Please come. We need your strength to lead us."

Aimi. He remembered her now. As he and his followers had fought their way to the castle, as they had ambushed several small contingents of disorganized samurai, she had used her rake to fight against the enemy. She had been as tough and determined as any soldier. *Brave,* he thought. *And beautiful.* Without thinking, Yamaguchi took the girl's hand, feeling a spark jump between them. He suddenly found himself lost in those eyes, which were raised once more to his. "Yes," he said with a smile. "I'm here."

"Ugh!" Midori landed hard on her backside. Despite the jarring pain, she brought her staff up instinctively in a defensive counter-move. The samurai who had knocked her down stood over her, his longsword poised for the kill strike, his features ravaged with hatred and crazed uncertainty.

The blade slashed downward, cutting Midori's staff in two. Midori rolled to one side, barely avoiding the *kitana*'s blade again as it whisked over her head. She rolled to her knees, pulling her wakizashi and swinging it around in a desperate swipe at her attacker's shins.

She struck the leg of her attacker, her shortsword's blade ripping just between where the samurai's shin-guard ended and the chainmail on his upper leg began. He stumbled backwards, his surprise at the wound just long enough for one of the Sleepers to reach up behind him and cut his throat. The samurai fell face down on the cobblestoned causeway, gurgling and coughing in his own blood.

"*Arigatu*, Sleeping One!" Midori rose to her feet and whirled back towards the battle. She and the ten Sleepers had broken through the outer perimeter of Odawara-jo, using the element of surprise. The fact that the Sleepers fought like demons, unnerving Omori's defenders, had also been a big advantage. Two of their number had managed to forge ahead to try and reach the Pavillion of Black Dragons before the keep's defenders had mustered.

She used her own martial skills to parry and distract, to disarm and even kill the enemy. Here, in the main ground-level bailey, amidst gardens and fountains and sculpture, blood flowed and men screamed in terror and agony. In the face of what was considered more invaders from the supernatural world, Omori's defenses crumbled.

As the remaining defending samurai fled back into the castle, leaving their dead and dying comrades, Midori saw one of the Sleepers had been lost as well. *Seven left with me,* she thought, out-of-breath. *Plus the two who had managed to breach the castle's defenses to get to the Pavilion of Black Dragons and the two who accompanied Jackson-san.*

Without warning, the closest Sleeper pulled Midori to him. Both crouched behind his shield as a storm of arrows rained down on them from above. Some of Omori's warrior monks stood behind the castle's second level balustrade, shooting and notching their bows to shoot again and again with uncanny rapid-fire speed.

As the arrows fell around her and bounced off the Sleeper's shield, Midori glanced warily at her unlikely comrade. *Can they feel?* she wondered. *Do they care what they're doing? What were their lives before this? After all this time of guarding their resting place and preparing, it is still so strange.*

Her arms shook, both with the effort of battle and with the fear and disgust that ran through her. She had never killed before but the training and skills taught her by her father had forced her to become a reluctant warrior. She had always been a poet and artist. Both art forms were necessary to her in order for her life to have some balance, some other reason for being other than the Sleepers' guardian. To destroy something, someone, even though it was necessary, was anathema to her.

I must focus! she scolded herself, as she and the Sleepers rose and, huddled together against the storm of arrows still being unleashed, marched toward the castle. *This is what I was raised to do and Kim-san has allowed me to do it. I must follow the Luminous One no matter what. It is written! Or else everything my family has believed in will be for nothing.*

What had not been written, however, were her feelings for Hiroshi. Those had been a completely unexpected surprise and now, as the Sleepers battered at the castle door, she realized the young staff-wielder was the one she thought of first.

Hiroshi zig-zagged his way up the rough-hewn staircase beneath the great castle. Unerringly, he had dashed through the lower tunnel beneath Odawara-jo, taking the opposite path Mistress Kim-san had taken. Somehow this seemed right; somehow he knew this was where Midori would be.

Midori-chan. He had been drawn to her from the first. He, a poor boy from the Gettoo; a slave to the samurai. Never did he dream that someone as beautiful and privileged as she would feel the same for him.

And now she might need help. Nothing would stop him from finding her! Brewster-san had been his savior; the man-in-black had rescued him and given him purpose. He would now use that newfound strength to help Midori.

I will never be a slave again! He threw his weight against the door at the top of the stairs, not even bothering to slow down.

The door gave way, opening onto a gilded, carpeted hallway within the castle.

Hiroshi had no time to admire the hanging tapestries, the tiled floor and ornate ceiling, as an axe-like blade sliced through the air at his head. He barely dodged the *naginata* blow and swung his staff laterally.

He caught the *sohei* in the thigh with the staff, throwing the monk off balance. Hiroshi pivoted and brought his weapon up toward the *sohei's* jaw. The monk, his bare head and face bleeding, his clothes torn from some earlier battle, blocked the staff easily and kicked out at Hiroshi's midsection. Hiroshi fell backwards and hit the floor, doubled over and gasping for breath.

The *sohei* limped toward him slowly, a mad glint to his eyes. He raised his *naginata*.

A door at the end of the hallway crashed inward. The *sohei* whirled as Hiroshi shakily scrambled to his feet. *The Sleepers!* he thought giddily. *And Midori!*

Sure enough, the young Guardian and the Sleepers raced into the hallway. Two of the strangely armored samurai raced up a side staircase while the rest marched toward Hiroshi and his attacker. A bellowing war cry from behind Hiroshi signaled more *sohei* coming from the opposite end of the hall.

Hiroshi entangled the distracted monk's ankles with his staff and tripped him, throwing the startled *sohei* to his back. Hiroshi ran toward Midori, his feet barely touching the floor.

"Hiroshi!" Midori cried, her face alighted upon seeing him. "Come! We must follow the two Sleepers upward."

And there we will find the warlord. Hiroshi nodded as he took Midori's hand. Together they began bounding up the tiled steps. Hiroshi paused for a moment to look back over his shoulder.

THE SIXTH PRECEPT

Below them, covering Midori's and his escape, the Sleepers met the *sohei* in the middle of the wide hallway in an explosion of flashing metal and blood.

CHAPTER 63

Kim ducked under Omori's charge, hitting the warlord with another psi-stun. The esper-beam knocked the warlord off-balance, sending him tumbling to the floor.

Kim turned toward the two remaining warrior monks, her muscles aching, her breath fluttering in her chest. She was beginning to weaken. *Have to keep going. I'm the only one left.*

The *sohei* approached her warily, detecting her weakness and circling like sharks. Kim narrowed a psi-scan at the one closest to her. *Attack your master,* she commanded, exerting mental control as she penetrated his neural pathways. *Attack Omori!*

The monk shook his head, looked at the *daimyo,* who was getting back to his feet, and leaped toward him. He swung his *naginata* as the baffled second monk reacted instantly and parried it, herding his crazed companion away from their master.

Kim created a psi-shield around herself just as Omori recovered and attacked again. His sword bounced off the shield. He stepped back, surprised, and then resumed his assault, determined and relentless. "I will send you back to your future, Ghost!" he cried, as he slashed at the shield over and over. "With your head in your hands!"

Kim pushed outward. The psi-shield expanded and caught

the warlord hard, shoving him backwards. Dropping the shield and concentrating her strength, she leaped and whirled in mid-air, cracking the warlord of Odawara across the face with a well-aimed kick. Omori spun around and crashed to the floor.

Kim tried to maintain her balance as she landed but stumbled and fell on her back. *Got to end this now*, she thought dizzily. She attempted to reach Omori's mind as she had the monk's, trying to encase him in a binding psi-shield, but the very power that was giving her the advantage was now weakening her. She sensed only dark emotions, hatred and bloodlust. They were like a wall, blocking her.

On one end of the pavilion, the two warrior monks continued to fight but not with each other. Midori and Hiroshi, followed by two Sleepers, had appeared from nowhere. Each Sleeper leaped forward and fended off one of the *sohei* as the soldiers strove to protect their lord from these two new adversaries.

Kim sensed movement at the entrance to the *donjon*—Omori had ordered his 'witch' to release the two chained shadow-trackers. This was the young master—Eela, the dying, female shadow-tracker had called her handler. The shadow-trackers had been released but Eela was retreating—trying to escape with his monstrous charges rather than help his master.

So much for loyalty, she thought, struggling to get to her feet. *Let's get this over with.*

Omori recovered first, rolling over and pushing himself up on his elbows. He yelled at his two embattled *sohei*. "Kill them, you fools!" he shouted The Sleepers stood back-to-back, parrying the sword thrusts of the adversaries as Midori and Hiroshi ran toward her.

Midori! Hiroshi! Stop! Let the Sleepers drive them my way!

Kim looked upward and formed a beam of reverse-telekinetic force. She directed it at the black tenting above, parts of it already torn and flapping from the high wind. The beam pushed and sliced into a large, ripped section of silk like a knife and rent if free from the ragged shreds still holding it. The flap of tenting dropped directly onto the back-pedaling *sohei*. They fell, tripped up and tangled in the silk.

Pain lanced through Kim's head. Blood began flowing from her nose. She got to one knee. Too late, she sensed Omori on his feet and charging. His boot caught her in the temple, once again knocking her to her back.

"I can kick too, Ghost," he sneered, standing over her, blood trickling from his own nose and mouth. "So much for your magic. You will make the second servant of the Left Hand Path I will kill today. And then I will take back my city! And no one, not even the One Child, will stop me!"

Suddenly, everything seemed to be running in slow motion as if time had wound down. Kim tried to form another psi-shield, a stun, anything, but her body and mind were like sludge, refusing to move any faster. Omori raised his weapon, lightning flashing behind him, but slowly, so very slowly. Midori and Hiroshi ran towards her.

Like attacking Parker in Shioko's room, Kim did the only thing she could think of—her mind screamed into the ambient-milieu.

At the same time, the wind kicked up, tearing loose more of the pavilion's canopy, knocking over some of the sculpture and potted plants. Thunder rumbled like cannon. Omori put his hands to his head, squinting and grimacing in pain as Kim's cry encased him.

Kim picked herself up, staggering to her feet. She tried to reenergize herself as she had done before. Yes, yes, that worked a little. She faced Omori as the clouds finally burst. Rain poured from the darkened heavens.

But there was something else…

A tremor, a vibration, the beginnings of a tremulous, flashing light—just out of reach of the physical but there, on another level of reality. Kim felt it as, once again, Omori rushed at her, his face contorted in rage and hate.

No, she thought, recognizing what was happening. *Not now.*

The sky exploded.

The white light of a temporal displacement tremor cascaded around her, blinding her, the force knocking her to her knees. She struggled for breath as she raised her arm to shield herself from the rapidly dissipating light.

A small child stood in the middle of the floor of the Pavilion of Black Dragons. Dressed in 21st century children's clothing and wearing sunglasses, she looked as strange yet as wonderful to Kim as anything she had ever seen.

"Shioko?" she whispered. "My god, Shioko!"

Shioko smiled. *"Oneesan!"* she cried. "You told me you'd be here."

"What?"

A strangled cry brought Kim's attention back to Omori. He stood shakily, staring at Shioko, his eyes bulging as he held his sword out in front of him with two trembling hands. "The One Child," he said softly. "What sorcery is this? How?"

The rain still fell, though not as heavily now as if the elements themselves needed to have a clear view of what transpired below in the Pavilion of Black Dragons. A child thrown into an adult chaos not of her making, Shioko pursed her lips. A great decision made, she strode right up to the warlord. "Shioko, no!" Kim exerted what power she could to muster a thin psi-shield between the child and the *daimyo.*

Shioko stood with both hands on her skinny hips, looking up at Omori. "You're a bad man!" she said in Japanese, pointing at the warlord. "An evil man." She reached out for the warlord's sword. *This is it,* Kim thought, reluctantly lowering the filter. *I have to let her do it. This is her destiny—Ko the Little. This is what we've all been fighting for. This is how it all happens.* Shioko placed four small fingers on the flat of the warlord's blade and pushed it aside.

"You had Mitsu-san killed," Shioko said, tears running down her cheeks from behind her dark glasses. "And you've hurt *Oneesan*. And you made me hide from you and your monsters. I hate you. I hate you!" Shioko rushed forward, beating her small fists against the warlord's stomach.

Oh, my brave little girl. Kim rose unsteadily to her feet, ready to hit Omori with as much psi force as she could to protect Shioko, prophecy or not. Midori and Hiroshi stood watching, their faces wrought with incredulity; the Sleepers stood silently as stone, their swords at the ready. But the warlord backed off, holding his sword at his side, his manner suddenly full of confusion, his eyes flicking back and forth. "No," he said. "This is madness! You are but a child!"

He raised his sword.

At that moment, several figures appeared at the front of the pavilion—Brewster, Yamaguchi, a couple of the Sleepers and a group of what Kim guessed to be Yamaguchi's followers. Brewster began running in her direction.

"Kim!" he shouted. "We have other trouble. Dragons!"

Shioko had backed Omori up almost to the stone railing surrounding the back of the pavilion, the little girl still crying and lashing out. The warlord's worried gaze darted from Shioko to Kim and then to the gathering crowd, his sword hand frozen. The two *sohei* had freed themselves from the entangling silk and were placing their weapons on the floor, kneeling down and bowing in surrender to Yamaguchi and his people.

Omori flung a final fierce look at Kim. "I swear by my ancestors," he shouted. "If there is a way, I will come back and I will surely kill you!"

The warlord of Odawara turned and stepped on top of the railing casement. He stood on the wide stone and raised his arms and sword in the air. Throwing his head back, he bellowed out to the sky above, a cry of pain and defeat...

...and jumped.

No! Kim shouted into the ambient-milieu, stumbling over to Shioko. *I won't let you take the easy way out, you bastard!*

But Kim never got the chance to telekinetically snag Omori out of the air, as a rushing of hot, musky breath intermixed with the rain and lighting. A roaring of another kind rumbled through the diminishing sounds of thunder, shaking the foundations of the pavilion. A dragon out of legend reared up from the below the castle's summit.

And dangling from its serpent jaws was Omori Kadonomaro.

Screaming and covered in blood, the warlord thrashed within the great beast's half-open mouth, struggling to escape. The dragon clamped down on the hapless *daimyo* with its enormous jaws, shook its head back and forth and spat out the shredded remains of the Warlord of Odawara, as if the dragon, too, could not stomach its victim's vileness. At the last, Kim picked up the dreaded daimyo's final impressions--Omori Kadonomaro, who had dreaded the menace of the Left Hand Path for so long, splattered against the side of Odawara castle and fell spiraling to earth, a bloody victim of his greatest fear at last.

The dragon hovered, eyeing more potential prey. Shioko screamed as the great beast reared back and expanded its chest. Its mouth opened.

"Kim!" Brewster shouted, lunging toward her as he flung his sword to the floor. "Get Shioko down!"

THE SIXTH PRECEPT

Kim reached Shioko at the same time as Brewster. She pulled the young girl to her body as Brewster enfolded both in his strong arms. The fiery breath of the dragon shot toward them. As if striking an invisible wall, the flames curved around the huddled threesome, deflected by an invisible protective barrier.

"Way to go, Kim," Brewster said breathlessly. "We ran up against this beastie before."

"I...I think I've got everyone in the pavilion covered but the problem is I'm spread too thin." The strain of her fight with the warlord, and now maintaining the shield, were taking their toll. "I can't use a psi-stun or anything else against that monster unless I lower the shield. And that will leave us exposed."

"*Oneesan*!" Shioko cried. "What are we going to do?"

I don't know. Kim looked at Brewster, panic starting to set in.

"*Oneesan.*" Shioko looked into Kim's eyes. "I'm not afraid. I know you and Mr. Brewster will save us."

"Oh, my baby." Kim hugged the girl to her, rocking back and forth.

"The heat," Brewster said, sweat starting to bead on his face. "Kim, if there's something you can do—do it now."

The dragon roared, a hideous shriek that split the very air itself. Rearing back again, the creature opened its great maw.

Not this time. Pushing Shioko into Brewster's arms, Kim dropped the psi-shield and stood in front of the giant beast. She concentrated her energy like she had done against the *oni* and, once again, felt the power build within her. She held her hands out in front of her and unleashed those same bolts of mental energy, shooting them from her trembling body like sunbursts.

At the same moment, the dragon unleashed its fiery breath.

The two opposing primal forces collided head-on—Kim's esper energy and the dragon's fire met in a violent cataclysm of fire and heat.

The space in front of Kim erupted into white light.

A driving hot wind picked her up and flung her to her back. She reached out frantically for Shioko as unconsciousness once more tried to overtake her. Instead, Brewster's strong grip anchored her to the floor.

And then it was over.

(*A flash of light, a thin beam of radiant energy diminishing in the distance, a shifting and rearrangement of metaphysical planes.*)

The air crackled around her. She looked up—the fire and heat were gone. And so was the dragon.

The rain, now a light drizzle, felt good on her skin, cool and comforting and rejuvenating. She raised her head and opened her mouth, letting the water trickle over her. A murmur, a collective sigh arose from the crowd at the far end of the pavilion.

"Is it over, *Oneesan*?" a small voice asked, a voice with a very big heart. "Is the monster gone?"

"Yes, honey," Kim answered. She embraced Brewster hard. "Thank you," she whispered.

Brewster smiled. "Anytime."

Slowly, Kim got to her feet and walked to Shioko's side. "I do think it's over, Shioko. I really do." She hugged Shioko. "You were so brave," she murmured in the girl's ear. "Thank you." She nuzzled Shioko on the cheek and then turned towards Brewster. They both smiled at each other as warm laughter began to bubble up in their throats. Kim kissed Brewster and laid her head on his shoulder, giggling like a schoolgirl.

"The Yomitsu and Ko," Brewster whispered. "I'm glad you two are on my side."

THE SIXTH PRECEPT

Kim turned to see Yamaguchi and his followers gathering around them. Looks of awe and reverence graced the faces of the fighting force. "Magnificent," Yamaguchi said. "Absolutely awesome."

Kim wiped the blood from her nose and looked to her right. The bodies of the two dead Sleepers and their live companions were still there. *They're different somehow,* she reasoned. *But the others—the dragon and possibly all the other wayward creatures—they've all been returned to wherever they came from.* Kim turned to Shioko. "Honey, how did you get here?"

Shioko smiled. "You sent me, *Oneesan.*"

"I did?" *So, somehow, we get back to our time and place and I...* "How can I send you back? I don't have that kind of power."

Brewster snorted. "No? Look what you've done! You've got power, Kim. It's just a matter of knowing how to use it."

And then it happened again—Kim's mental alarms went off. "Another tremor, an aftershock, something," she said, grabbing both Brewster's and Shioko's hands. "One's coming and let's pray it slingshots us back to Pittsburgh. Hang on, you two, we might be going home!"

"No, *Oneesan!*" Shioko broke free of Kim's grip and ran to Yamaguchi. "I'm staying."

Kim's mouth dropped. "What? Shioko?"

The little girl smiled, her lips trembling. "I want to, *Oneesan.* I'll miss you but this is my destiny. The motorcycle-lady explained it all to me. I want to help. And I'll see you again. I know it!"

The motorcycle-lady? The roaring got louder. The light began to strobe. "No! Shioko!"

"She's right, Ms. Yoshima," Yamaguchi interjected, his voice breaking up in the dimensional static. "Remember the texts? Ko the Little helped rebuild Odawara along with its new ruling council. I'll bet that will be me and Midori and Hiroshi. Yes. I'm staying too. I always wanted to get into politics."

"But…she's just a little girl! And Eela is still on the loose!"

"I've got her. And I'll take care of her. And bring Eela to justice. I promise."

With one hand holding onto Brewster and the other desperately reaching out for Shioko, Kim felt herself slip into the time stream.

CHAPTER 64

Pittsburgh, Pennsylvania, 2010 C.E.

The temporal displacement tremor that sent Kim to Odawara was much smoother this time—not like the mistakenly created unnatural process which had been rough, unpredictable and dangerous. This was a kinder and gentler transport, more focused, more balanced. Kim found herself standing in a room, oddly familiar and filled with equipment and computers, some of it gutted or damaged.

"Kim, are you all right?"

She turned to fall into Brewster's arms, her legs weak.

"Hey, hey, Kim," Brewster said.

"I'm OK," Kim said, gently pushing away. "I'm just tired."

Brewster nodded. "So am I. And beat up. It's all starting to catch up with us. It's hard to believe all that happened in just one day."

"One day several hundred years ago."

Brewster looked around. "Is this—?"

"I think the *Totou* may have used this room to try and harness the power of the timelines. I remember seeing it when I scanned the factory."

"Brilliant! But how could they have done that? What kind of science and technology would they have employed?"

"Don't know. And we may never know, seeing the condition they left this stuff in."

"Yeah. Looks like they beat it out of here in a hurry, plus a lot of this stuff is pretty banged up. I wonder if our dragon friend had anything to do with that. It's too bad. With such technology…it's just fantastic!"

"O…*Oneesan*? Is that you?"

Kim whirled. Her heart leaped. "Shioko!"

The young girl ran to Kim's outstretched arms. Kim hugged Shioko to her, squeezing her tight. "How did you get back?" Kim said, choking up. "I thought I'd lost you!"

"The motorcycle-lady came and got me," Shioko said, her little face beaming. "She told me everything. Well, almost everything."

The motorcycle-lady again. "Shioko, what are you talking ab—?" Kim started and looked at Brewster.

Brewster nodded, understanding slowly dawning on his face. "She hasn't gone back yet, Kim."

"No," Kim realized. "No, she hasn't."

"You have to send me back, *Oneesan*," Shioko said, confirming their guess. "The motorcycle-lady told me you can do it. I want to go back and help. She said it's my…my destiny."

Destiny again. Kim thought with a frown. *Karma. God, I'm so sick of those concepts!* "It's dangerous, honey. Yes, I'll be there too but—"

A firm hand grasped her shoulder. "Kim, it's already happened," Brewster said. "I don't think you have a choice, not if the outcome is to be the same, not if you and Shioko and I are to be here, in this moment, right now."

"And how do I do that?" Kim asked, her voice breaking as she looked into Brewster's eyes. "Just wave my magic time-travel wand? And if I can, why don't I just go back to before Omori becomes a *daimyo* and stop him then? Why do we have to go through all this?"

Brewster shook his head. "I don't know. But you must. On some level, the knowledge is there because you already did it. Shioko came back. You just have to dig deep to access the how-of-it. Somehow, this is the way things are supposed to happen. We had to experience all of this."

Kim knelt in front of Shioko. "Shioko, who is this motorcycle-lady?"

Shioko smiled again, sadly this time. "You'll see, *Oneesan*. She's waiting for you outside. And she's told me everything. She told me Mitsu-san is dead, that Omori had her killed. She told me Omori hurt you and Mr. Brewster. But...but..." Shioko paused, tears rolling down her cheeks. "But not how it all turns out. I don't know really what happens after I get back. She wouldn't tell me that. She said I had to do what needed to be done without any...any—"

"Foreknowledge," Kim whispered.

"Oh, *Oneesan*."

"Baby, baby." Kim hugged her again, feeling the little body jerk with gasping sobs. Kim looked down as something caught her own tear-stained eye. There in Shioko's hand was clasped a pair of sunglasses. *To keep her from being blinded by the explosive light the displacement causes.*

"Damn it!" Kim held the girl at arm's length. "You're too young for such a responsibility. It's not right. You're just—"

Shioko shook her head. "I want to help! I want to make everything right. That evil man made me afraid all this time. He made me hide and, while I was hiding, he hurt my friends and did bad, bad things. Please, *Oneesan*, let me help."

"All right," Kim whispered, her heart heavy, knowing she had no choice. "I'll try."

Brewster took Shioko's free hand. "You're going to be brave and strong back there, Shioko. Believe me. You're going to make your *Oneesan* proud."

"I'm already proud." Kim bent her head, closing her eyes. "But I need help." *Ancestor,* she thought. *Mitsu-san, I couldn't reach you before. But now, if you're there, I beg you—help me.*

A flickering in the…the Dreamspace. A face from out of time appeared to Kim in her mind's eye. *I am here,* Yoshima Mitsu said, her eyes full of compassion and power, of knowledge beyond normal understanding. She floated in front of Kim, shimmering, a spirit caught between worlds. *Now, at this juncture, I have been allowed to intervene,* she said. *I will show you the way and add my power to yours. To ours. One final time.*

Thank you. Yes. Kim could see it now. Feel it. There was more here than just a room full of broken equipment. This was the Nexus Point. The energy was all around them. This was where the time anomaly was the most prevalent. Like a vertical cold spot in a haunted house, this was where everything originated.

She stood up, moving like one empowered. "Move back, Wayne. Please." She leaned down and kissed Shioko on the top of the head. "Be careful, kiddo, and good luck." She ran her hand through the young girl's hair. "Remember me, yes? I love you."

Shioko smiled that heartbreaking smile. "Yes, *Oneesan.* I will never forget. And I love you too."

Kim Yoshima held her arms out at her sides and closed her eyes. Now that the decision had been made, now that she had allowed herself to accept what had to be…*Yes,* she thought, seeing the way as Yoshima Mitsu had directed, as plain as the nose on her face. *That's how you do it.*

When it was over, she awoke, groggy and groaning in Brewster's arms. Every bone in her body, every hair on her head, every tooth in her mouth hurt. She lay on the floor, the man-in-black cradling her head and shoulders in his lap.

"What…what happened?" she stammered, looking around wildly. "Shioko!"

"Easy, Kim. You did it. You sent Shioko back into the past. You were like a great light, glowing and blazing like the sun. Huge arcs of some kind of energy seemed to be channeling through your body. It was amazing. You were absolutely… luminous! Although I was pretty worried there for a moment. I didn't know what to do or expect."

Kim laughed weakly. "Me neither." With Brewster's help, she got to her feet, panting, spots dancing before her eyes. She paused, head down, as a startling realization hit her. "They're gone," she said, looking at Brewster. "My psi powers. They're gone!"

"What? What do you mean?"

Kim shook her head, holding onto Brewster's arm. Her eyes widened. "I mean I can't feel them anymore. It's like a big hole inside me, as if that last psychic act just drained everything out of me." She looked at him again. "They're just…gone."

That's when she saw the young woman.

She pulled away from Brewster and walked slowly toward the short-haired, black-clad figure standing in the doorway. There was something familiar about her.

"I take it you're Shioko's motorcycle-lady," she said, stopping a few feet from the doorway.

The woman nodded, her face a sea of emotions. "Yes," she said softly, her eyes welling with sudden tears.

Kim felt as if she was falling off of a cliff. "Shioko?" she asked, her stomach clenching. It wasn't a revelation due to any lingering psi ability, or even a physical recognition. Kim just knew. "Shioko, is it you?"

"Yes…*Oneesan*."

Kim stood rigid, her mouth open, and then flew toward the adult Shioko, throwing her arms around her. Shioko hugged her back, both women giving way to a flood of tears. "You've grown up into such a beautiful woman," Kim said, standing back. "But how did you get here?"

Shioko smiled, that simple action just as brilliant and offsetting as when she had been a child. "Jackson helped me," she said, wiping her face with her hand. "He's here with me now."

"Jackson?"

"Yes. He came forward with me, leaving his life in Odawara behind just like I did in order to fulfill what was to be. He'll be along shortly."

"How?" Kim asked. "How did you travel into the future?"

"Jackson figured out a method of predicting the tremors and where they would end up. Some kind of *Shuugouteki* trick. We didn't arrive exactly on target but—"

"Close enough." Kim realized she was holding Shioko's hand. "Now what?" she asked the young girl who wasn't a girl anymore. "What are you, we, going to do?"

Shioko let out a nervous laugh. "I want to stay here. My work back in Odawara is done."

"You have so much to tell me."

"I want to tell you everything—how I was treated like a princess and a hero; how we tried and failed to find Eela and his shadow-trackers; how we started the *Shuugouteki*; how I helped to create a new Odawara; how, later on, I became lonely and depressed and hated you for leaving me in the past even though that's where I was from and wanted to stay; how I missed the life I had here with you and how much I wanted to be a part of this future once I had had a taste of it; how I missed being a little girl."

"Shioko. Shioko…"

"I don't hate you, *Oneesan*. I never did. It's just that I haven't had the most normal of upbringings."

THE SIXTH PRECEPT

Kim smiled sadly. "No, that you haven't. But, of course, you can stay with me. There's no question. We can…we can try it again, if you want. We can make it work this time. You're room's just the way you left it, of course."

Shioko smiled and nodded, her eyes alight.

"Midori?" Kim asked. "And Hiroshi?"

Shioko smiled again. "Long story but when I left they were together and happy. It's been twelve years for me but so many lifetimes ago."

Brewster approached the two women. "Hello, Shioko. It's good to see you again."

"Hello, Mr. Brewster." Shioko held out a trembling hand.

Brewster gently took it. "Call me Wayne, please."

So much loss, Kim thought, a great sadness enveloping her. *All those we met in Odawara. Midori and Hiroshi—dead all these centuries.* "Shioko," she said, trying to concentrate on the living. "You remembered me sending you back to Odawara when you were a little girl and returned to fulfill that part of your life, here and now?"

Shioko nodded. "I was afraid to come even though I wanted to more than anything. I…I don't know exactly why."

"It's OK. We have a lot to talk about."

A voice calling Kim's name sounded in the corridor outside the room. Kim looked at Brewster in surprise. "It's Lazo. Over here, Laz!"

Shioko smiled. "Yes. He couldn't wait anymore when he saw me and Jackson. But after we convinced him that we were really who we said we were, he agreed not to call the police. Jackson has contacted the *Shuugouteki* on Lazo's phone. Members of his group should be here shortly to clean up this place."

Lazo's presence triggered a memory. "Bobby and Joe and

Jenny," Kim said urgently. "We've got to see if they're all right!"

"Yes. Jenny and Bobby are," Shioko said. "Lazo told us. Plus Joe had called from the hospital to let him know that Bill was doing fine."

"So," Kim said, laughing despite herself. Everything had worked out. Thank God or whatever ancient powers had guided them on this journey. "Let's go greet them then. Plus I'd like to meet some of the *Shuugouteki*. Say, what time is it?"

Brewster grinned. "That's a loaded question, don't you think?"

Kim laughed. "You can say that again!"

"I wouldn't wait around to meet any of the *Shuugouteki* right now, *Oneesan*," Midori said. "You'll be mobbed like a celebrity. You are the Yomitsu, after all."

Brewster nodded. "Might be a good idea to wait a couple of days. I'm sure they'll be in touch. Plus, you should rest. Sleeping is what we all need right now."

"Nah," Kim said with a wink. "I say we go celebrate and get something to eat. I could certainly use a drink, yes?" Hooking a hand each around both Brewster's and Shioko's arms, Kim steered the three of them out into the hallway.

"Kim!" shouted a relieved Lazo at the end of the corridor. "Thank God!" The big man, holding a gun in his hand, began to run toward them. A slightly older and much shorter-haired Jackson Yamaguchi waved from behind him.

Kim sighed and closed her eyes for a moment, thinking of the future.

(*Not the past, never the past anymore except to remember those they had lost*)

And, right now, at this moment, the future looked pretty good. It would be a challenge—a lot of explaining to do to her superiors, no more extraordinary psi powers, an all grown-up

THE SIXTH PRECEPT

Shioko and, of course, Wayne Brewster in her life. But she had always relished a challenge and figured the potential rewards were worth it. It was going to be a brand new day tomorrow and her life was never going to be the same.

Kim Yoshima didn't think she needed to be a psychic to foresee *that*.

EPILOGUE

Ise Jingu, the Grand Shrine of Ise—Ise, Japan—1910, C.E.

Yoshima Ayako Mitsu stood up from her kneeling position on the ground outside the inner shrine of the Ise Jingu. She turned and clapped her hands as Shinto tradition dictated upon entering and leaving a holy site. Basking in the comfort that always surrounded this place, she gazed at the small, simple wooden building with reverence.

Ritually deconstructed and rebuilt from the strongest Japanese cypress every twenty years, the shrines, both inner and outer, never looked old yet radiated a wisdom and power that transcended time and mere physicality. Ayako felt at ease within the wooded park that made up this part of the grounds, coming every month to pay her respects to the sun goddess, Amaterasu, as her mother had done for so long before her.

A sadness gripped her at the thought of her mother, dead now these past two years. It had fallen on Ayako, only fourteen years old when her mother had died, to take care of her family—her two brothers and her sick father. She was lucky to find the time to get away each month to make the offering to Amaterasu. Luckily she and her family lived near Ise so it wasn't a long journey.

Reluctantly she turned to go. It was so peaceful here but she had responsibilities, she knew. She walked through the tree-lined pathway to the entrance *torii* or gateway, that straddled the walk, and began crossing the Uji Bridge. Below, the Isuzu-gawa river flowed clear and quiet. The sky above shone a brilliant blue, the clouds mere wisps of feathery whiteness. The sounds of twittering birds and running water were like music to her, soothing and comforting.

Dressed in one of her mother's *kimonos* and clogs, her hair done up in an older, more mature style, Ayako had tried to appear respectful and adult. But she and her family were poor and didn't have much. Her brothers brought in some money but they had to scrape to get by, every day a struggle. Sometimes Ayako felt ashamed of the old clothes she had to wear, of the jobs she herself had to take just to put a little more food on the table.

"Hello, little sister."

Ayako jerked in surprise. She had crossed the bridge but had been so preoccupied with her own thoughts she hadn't noticed the man until she almost walked into him. She bowed, apologizing. "So sorry, Exalted Sir," she said, using the formal address mode for one so old and, no doubt, wise. "I didn't see you."

The man was of African lineage, his skin the color of approaching dusk. He wore a European suit and hat and leaned forward on a cane, which appeared to be damaged. He looked very, very old yet the eyes below his wrinkled, white-haired brow sparkled with youthful wit and intelligence.

He smiled, a pleasant and generous nature emanating from him. He spoke perfect Japanese. "No need to apologize, my dear. Actually, I was hoping to see you here."

"Me, Exalted Sir?"

"Yes. Will you sit with me, child? I won't take up too much

of your time, I promise. There is something I must talk to you about."

A warm feeling washed over Ayako. Despite the fact he was a stranger, she felt drawn to the old man and, against her better judgment, agreed.

They sat side-by-side on a nearby wooden bench. The old man sighed as he rubbed his shoulder, flinching as if in pain. "Ah, that's better," he said, taking out a handkerchief and wiping his brow. "This old body has seen better days, I must say, although it's served me well."

Ayako stirred, noticing for the first time that one of the old man's wrists seemed bent in an unnatural way. Parts of his clothes were dirty as if he had fallen. Small pinpricks of blood dotted his face.

"Exalted Sir," she said, concerned. "Are you injured?"

"Be at peace, child," the old man said. "I am the best I have ever been."

Ayako felt reassured then as if a soothing balm had been laid across her forehead.

"I have something for you to give to your granddaughter."

Ayako's brow furrowed. "My granddaughter? I have none. I am only sixteen years and unmarried. Perhaps you have mistaken me for someone else?"

"No. It is you I wish to speak to." The old man held up one finger. "And you will have these things, little sister. I guarantee it—a husband, children, grandchildren. One of whom, your granddaughter, will be an extremely important person." He leaned closer. "Extremely important! The teachings of the group I belong to know it to be so. And I know now that you are the one. I can see it now. It is most gratifying." He reached his hand into the inside of his jacket and pulled out a small book. He looked at the cover and handed it to her.

She took hold of the book tentatively, seeing the lettering on the beautifully bound frontispiece was scripted in gilded Japanese. Ayako was fortunate enough to know how to read but had never held a book so grand and expensive-looking.

"Give this copy of the *Sacred Artifact* to your granddaughter, my dear, when the time comes. You will know when. That's all I ask."

Ayako looked up at him, puzzlement written on her face. She shook her head and looked back down at the cover of the book—*The Teachings of Yira*—*The Five Precepts to Enlightenment*. She knew then, that, no matter what, she would do as she had been told.

"But Exalted Sir," she said. "How will this happen? What will my granddaughter do that will be so important and why will your book matter to her?"

The old man stood up, slowly and carefully. "Don't worry about that," he said. "Just have a good life and teach your granddaughter the wisdom of the old ways." He started to walk away and then stopped and turned back. "I'm going away now. It's been a long journey. Now that I've given you the book, I'm going to visit some old friends of mine whom I haven't seen in a while." He smiled and waved.

Ayako stood up and bowed. When she looked again, the old man was gone. She sat back down, staring around her. *Was I dreaming?* she wondered and then smiled, a blush creeping up her neck. *A husband. And children. A very special granddaughter. Will this really happen to me? How strange. How wonderful.*

She looked at the book again. Her brothers were home today and their neighbor, Master Sakai, was helping to watch her father. She had a little time, surely.

Yoshima Ayako Mitsu opened the book and began to read.